Praise for P. T. Deutermann's

SPIDER MOUNTAIN

"Fast-paced… imaginative plotting." —*Publishers Weekly*

"Another pulse-pounding thrill ride…An unnerving, tightly woven thriller." —*Cincinnati Library*

"The stuff of series heroes...a battle royal." —*Kirkus Reviews*

"Non-stop action." —Mysterylovers.com

"One of the crime genre's more original and memorable creations…a welcome change from the usual sort of thriller villain." —*Booklist*

Praise for

THE CAT DANCERS

"Gripping. . .original and intense." —*BookPage*

"Full of surprises. . .keeps you reading past your bedtime." —*Charlotte Observer*

"A spellbinding novel of suspense…quite possibly his best." —Nelson DeMille

THE FIREFLY

"Complex...fascinating." —*Washington Post*

"A first- *ournal Constitution*

"A deft —*Library Journal*

MORE…

"A top-notch thriller from a top-notch writer."

—Nelson DeMille

"Addictively enthralling...(wait till you get to the jaw-dropping ending!)." —*Entertainment Weekly*

HUNTING SEASON

"Explosive tour de force....The author exceeds his near-perfect *Train Man* with this ripped-from-the-headlines plot pitting a middle-aged Rambo with a small but deadly arsenal of spy gadgets against spine-chilling villains, corrupt agency brass, and powerful political forces. Deutermann never sounds a wrong note in this nonstop page-turner."

—*Publishers Weekly* (starred review)

"You think you have read this before. Trust me. You haven't. And you should...a great read." —*Tribune* (Greensburg, PA)

"One of the lasting conventions in thriller writing involves putting the hero in a situation where the reader is forced to ask, 'How can he possibly get out of that?'...Deutermann...exploits that convention to the hilt in *Hunting Season*."

—*Houston Chronicle*

"Enough techno and black ops to satisfy Clancy fans, enough double-dealing, back-pedaling internecine treachery to keep Carre fans reading, and enough plot turns and suspense to keep Crichton and Higgins Clark devotees guessing." —*Florida Times-Union*

"Deutermann's previous novel, *Train Man,* was a marvelous, bang-up action novel...in *Hunting Season* he equals the thrills...Deutermann writes with authority and inventiveness. Add in top-secret gizmos, heroes meaner than villains...and you've got one of the best by one of the best at what he does." —*Telegraph* (Macon, GA)

"The tale is loaded with political and bureaucratic skullduggery, and there are plenty of well-banked curves and clever twists. A solid read from an author whose own tradecraft is every bit as good as that of his characters." —*Booklist*

"Deutermann has sold three novels to Hollywood already. They're blind if they pass on this one." —*Kirkus Reviews*

DARKSIDE

"Gripping...thoroughly absorbing." —*Publishers Weekly*

"Deutermann...writes page-turners. And this one has a surprise ending—one that comes as a bombshell."
—*Houston Chronicle*

"A dead-on sense of place and appealing characters in tight corners...satisfying." —*Kirkus Reviews*

"Deutermann has now published seven pounding-pulsers. For this book, he was back at Dahlgren and Mahan, updating his reef points." —*Baltimore Sun*

TRAIN MAN

"Deutermann delivers his most accomplished thriller yet. Intelligent, expertly detailed, and highly suspenseful."
—*Publishers Weekly* (starred review)

"Another solid performance from Deutermann, this time about a train-hating, vengeance-hungry madman and the FBI agents seeking to derail him. Quality entertainment: the details convince, the people are real, the plot twists legitimate." —*Kirkus Reviews*

Books by

P. T. DEUTERMANN

The Cam Richter Novels

The Cat Dancers

Spider Mountain

The Moonpool

Thrillers

The Firefly

Darkside

Hunting Season

Train Man

Zero Option

Sweepers

Official Privilege

Navy Adventure Novels

The Edge of Honor

Scorpion in the Sea

THE MOONPOOL

P. T. DEUTERMANN

St. Martin's Paperbacks

This is a work of fiction. All of the characters, organizations, and events portrayed in this novel are either products of the author's imagination or are used fictitiously.

THE MOONPOOL

For information address St. Martin's Press, 175 Fifth Avenue, New York, NY 10010.

Library of Congress Catalog Card Number: 2008009458

ISBN: 0-312-94412-8
EAN: 978-0-312-94412-4

Printed in the United States of America

St. Martin's Press hardcover edition / June 2008
St. Martin's Paperbacks edition / May 2009

St. Martin's Paperbacks are published by St. Martin's Press, 175 Fifth Avenue, New York, NY 10010.

10 9 8 7 6 5 4 3 2 1

This book is for all the dedicated folks who operate and maintain the nation's nuclear power plants. They do a dangerous and often thankless job that requires constant vigilance and a zero tolerance for error. They do so with the daily knowledge that if anything does go wrong, they will be the first to meet the Dragon.

ACKNOWLEDGMENTS

I've taken some technical as well as geographical liberties in telling this story; that said, I appreciate all the generous help I received from several people in the Wilmington area, both in local law enforcement and the nuclear power industry.

WILMINGTON, NORTH CAROLINA

Allie Gardner was desperate to find a place to pull over. Her throat felt like it was on fire all the way down to her stomach, and she was having real trouble with her breathing. The interior of her car felt hot even though she had the A/C on max and it was only in the mid-fifties outside. The traffic out on College Road was crawling, and she was trapped in the wrong lane. She'd had her clicker on for two minutes and no one, but no one, would let her over. For a moment she thought she saw spots floating across her eyes, but then she blinked rapidly and her vision cleared. Then she spotted the convenience store on the corner.

Screw it, she thought, and began pulling to the right, provoking a long blast from the horn of the SUV on her right quarter. Her car was much smaller, but she made it clear she was coming over, come hell or high water, and the angry SUV driver finally had to put on the brakes. Guy's an asshole, she thought, just like my thieving brother.

Eighty thousand dollars and he just took it. Bastard. But she was going to fix that, and him, just as soon as she got back to Triboro.

Traffic stopped entirely for the red light, and she stopped along with it, mostly in the right lane. She took another long pull on the bottle of water. It didn't help. How in the hell had she caught strep throat that fast, she wondered. It hurt to swallow, and it was beginning to hurt when she tried to take a deep breath.

Strep. Had to be something like that. Throat on fire. Maybe they'd have something in the store. C'mon, light.

The light finally changed, and she was able to pull all the way over and up into the gas-pump island at the convenience store. The SUV honked at her again, and she halfheartedly flipped him off. It was dusk, and the sudden blaze of sodium vapor lighting startled her when the fueling-area lights buzzed on. She pulled the car up alongside a pump and shut it down. Without the air-conditioning, she immediately felt even hotter, and her eyes were throwing a perfect storm of black spots now. She opened the driver's side door and took one final hit on the water bottle. Still no help, and her stomach felt like there was a mass of warm lead in it. She capped the bottle and then dropped it without knowing it and got out of the car. She had to hang on to the door to stay upright. She was surprised to see the water bottle rolling across the concrete, where a tractor-trailer was pulling in to the diesel line. The truck ran over the bottle with a loud pop. It sounded like a gunshot, but her reactions were off, way off. Everything was taking a long time to penetrate.

She focused on the front door of the store. Has to be a ladies' room in there, she thought. Pray to God it's empty. She tried not to stagger as she went across the oil-stained concrete and through the door, but the clerks were busy with other customers, and no one so much as looked at her. She tried for another decent breath of air, but it wasn't coming. Her lungs felt like they were shutting down, like she was trying to inhale an entire steam bath. Holding on to the edges of shelves, she managed to make it back to the rest rooms. The door to the ladies' was cracked open, and she practically fell into the tiny bathroom. It reeked of pine oil disinfectant, but it was cleaner than most. She remembered to close the door and lock it, and then she sat down on the john, only she missed it. She felt a jolt as she landed alongside the toilet bowl, banging her elbow on the cold porcelain.

Hug the bowl, girl, she thought, as her brain started to wander. Just like college, only she wasn't beer sick this time. Her head was getting very heavy, and she felt her chin digging into her front. Try as she might, she couldn't close her mouth. *This is serious,* a part of her brain told her, and another part answered back with a cynical *No shit, Allie.*

Panicking now, she fumbled in her purse for her cell phone, gonna call 911, gonna get some help here. This was terrible. It wasn't a heart attack, and she didn't feel nauseous, just hot. Hot all over, especially in her throat, mouth, and now her entire upper chest. Each breath became harder than the last. She tried to call out for help but could only manage a raspy croak, and even that hurt like hell. She stared at the door, the spots getting bigger in her field of vision. She willed someone to open the door, to see her on the floor with her mouth on fire, and most of all, to call 911.

But the door didn't open. Then she remembered she'd locked it. She tried for another croak, but it didn't come. Her heart was thumping in her fiery chest and there was a roaring sound in her ears.

Then she felt her heart just stop.

Just like that, she thought, as the room became very bright and everything finally stopped hurting.

TRIBORO, NORTH CAROLINA

I was wrapping up my day as president, CEO, and chief coffee wrangler at Hide and Seek Investigations when my phone rang. Being a retired bureaucrat, I automatically glanced at my watch, ever mindful of the enduring office rule: Anyone who answers his office phone in the late afternoon deserves to be stuck with the inevitable hairball. Then I saw the caller ID, which displayed the words HOMICIDE BUREAU and a 910 area code. I picked up and identified myself.

"Hey, Lieutenant Richter," a man said. "This is Bernie Price. Used to work in Triboro. I was city po-lice when you were still with the Manceford County Sheriff's Office."

"Yeah, Bernie, I remember," I said. "D-One, right? How've you been? Nine-one-zero—that's Wilmington?"

"Yes, sir," Price said. "I'm number two in the homicide bureau now. And we got us a little situation down here."

"And this involves our snoop posse how exactly?"

Price didn't laugh. "Y'all got a lady named Gardner, Allison E., working for you?"

I felt a pang of alarm. Had Allie somehow intruded into a homicide investigation? "Yes, we do, and yes, she's on assignment in Wilmington. She works wayward spouse cases. She's retired from the Job, too. What's going on?"

Typical of a homicide detective, Detective Price answered my question with a question. Another alarm bell. "Can you tell me what she was working on here in Wilmington?"

Oh, shit, I thought, leaning forward in my office chair. "Did you say 'was'?"

Price sighed. "Well, yeah. Was. Sorry to have to tell you this, Lieutenant, but she turned up dead last evening, in a gas station ladies' room."

I swore, and my two German shepherds appeared in the doorway to my office, ears up.

"What happened?" I asked.

"Don't know yet. No smoking guns at the scene. Medical examiner has the remains at County right now. No signs of foul play. She have ticker trouble, maybe?"

"Not that I knew about," I said. *Allie's dead?*

"What was the gig down here?"

"Some Triboro shyster's wife thought he was stepping out on her. She hired Allie to get corroboration. Nothing dramatic—the wife told Allie where they'd be staying and who the brand-X woman was. She's apparently got a divorce gunfighter cocked and ready. I think she just wanted pictures."

"This wife or her husband violent types?"

"Beats me, Bernie," I said. "But I don't think so. Like I said, this was beyond routine. The subjects were staying at that riverfront Hilton, as was Allie. She called in yesterday afternoon, said she had the goods. She said she had to take care of some personal business, but then she'd be back today, late."

"So she wasn't working any kind of whodunnit?"

"Nope. The lawyer and his girlfriend—I think she's a lawyer, too—apparently were regulars. Allie said they arrived on schedule, shacked up, and stayed shacked."

"So this didn't require Ms. Gardner to go creeping in bad neighborhoods or anything like that?"

"Negative. She sounded mostly bored."

"And she doesn't do drugs or bet the ponies, anything like that?"

"Allie? Hell, no. Good cop, solid citizen. No way. Definitely not the substance-abuse type. One glass of wine, she got silly. Two and she went night-night. Drugs would have rendered her comatose."

"You understand I have to ask, right?" he said apologetically.

"Absolutely. Shit. This is awful. But she never worked anything really dangerous for us. Her own ex ran off with some biker bimbo while she was riding patrol in the sheriff's office, so when she came to work for me, she specialized in helping women who were facing the same problem. She liked her cases interesting, but this one definitely wasn't."

"Is now," Price observed. "Can you help us with next of kin?"

I had to think for a moment. "Lemme see," I said. "I think she said she had one old-maid sister who works in the Defense Department overseas school system. She's in Turkey or Greece, don't remember which. I can look her up for you."

"In that case, could you possibly come down here, make the formal ID for us?"

"Well, yeah, sure," I said, the full enormity of the news finally hitting me. Wilmington was about a four-, four-and-a-half-hour drive from Triboro. "Tomorrow okay?"

"Tomorrow's fine, Lieutenant," Price said. "We're downtown, 115 Red Cross Street, five streets west of Market Street, which you'll come in on. I'll position a parking pass at the front desk." He gave me his phone extension, voiced the pro forma regrets again, and hung up.

Well, fuck me, I thought. I told the dogs to stand down and tried to get my mental arms around the news that Allie was gone. She had been one of the original members of our merry little band of snoops when I first started H&S. I wondered why homicide had it, and then remembered: It was an unexplained death.

Running a private investigations firm hadn't originally been my idea. I'd come off of two decades with the Manceford County Sheriff's Office under something of a cloud following the cat dancers vigilante case. Sergeant Horace Stackpole, one of the guys who'd worked for me in the Major Criminal Apprehension Team, or MCAT for short, had taken retirement a few months after I had. He and I had gotten together one night to have a drink, and then I had to listen to him bitch about the boring nature of the work he was doing at the time, which was running small-scale investigations for the district court in Triboro.

The honorable Robes and their swarm of courthouse lawyers had a seemingly unending requirement for people who could retrieve information and documents, develop reluctant witnesses, and execute other odd jobs quickly. Ex-cops knew how to do all of that, and they also had the networks to get at people and information even quicker than the active police bureaucracy could, or would, depending on which judge was asking. Anyway, a third guy joined us and suggested that I form a company, hire only ex-cops, and then we could work as much or as little as we wanted to. I'd suggested that Horace start the company, but, as he pointed out, I was the one who no longer really had to work.

So I did, and Hide and Seek Investigations, LLC, stood up a month later, with a condition of employment being that you had to be an ex-cop who had retired in good standing with your department. We'd started with six, with the other five doing most of the work while I dealt with really significant management issues, such as sorting the mail. Our first office had been on the second floor of a bail bondsman company in downtown Triboro. It was pretty Spartan, but it had the advantage of being near Washington Street, so the guys could still hit the sheriff's office and the metro cops' watering holes for lunch and afterward. Besides Horace Stackpole, Tony Martinelli and Pardee Bell had joined us from the wreckage of the MCAT. None of us worked full-time, and the money from the contracts went proportionally to the people who put in the most hours. Most of them were filling up 401(k)s, while I took a dollar a year and the biggest office, a massive corner suite some twelve feet square and overlooking a culturally interesting back alley.

The other two of the original "guys" had been women, Allie Gardner and Mel Lindsay. They'd both gone through the trauma of having husbands slide way off the marital reservation, Allie twice, and now did a flourishing business of pre-divorce-court reconnaissance work for outraged spouses. They *loved* their work, and the rest of us enjoyed their after-action reports, although with sometimes nervous laughter. Of the two, Allie had been the sweetheart. Pretty in a plain way, she arrived every morning with a sunny smile and a positive attitude, which inevitably brightened when she had some stone-hearted, sneak-cheating, low-down, good-for-nothing sumbitch husband in her evidentiary gun sights. She was an expert with photographic evidence and sported a collection of her best pictures in a rogues' gallery on one wall of her office. She'd bring the prospective client, inevitably an angry woman, into her office and ask: This what you need? It worked every time. She wasn't a man-hater, per se, but simply one of those women who'd been kicked in the heart enough times by careless men that she no longer cared for their social company. I think the guys in the office were the only men she talked to, and we, of course, didn't count on her life's scorecard.

But not anymore, I realized. I looked out the window at the streetlights coming on in the business park we'd moved to from our Washington Street hovel. I wondered now if I should call some of the original six—five now, wasn't it—and give them the bad news. I decided not to: no point in spoiling everyone's evening. I'd call a meeting tomorrow morning before leaving for Wilmington.

Allie Gardner was dead? Maybe it *had* been a heart attack, or one of those artery-bombing embolisms I'd been reading about. She'd been an unrepentant smoker, as were about half the people working at H&S. So maybe the cancer sticks had done their evil work. But surely not a homicide. I couldn't think of a single soul who would want her dead, except maybe one of her two ex-husbands. The truth was that we'd never had any indications of an ex coming back at the PI. They were usually too embarrassed at having been caught in the first place. If they were mad at anybody, it was the ex-spouse for hiring a snoop in the first place.

I'd have to get into her personnel records to find out what family she had left. I vaguely knew about the sister, but Allie had been closemouthed about the rest of her family. I'd gotten the impression that they hadn't approved of her forgoing college to become a cop in the first place, and that she was estranged from them.

"C'mon, mutts," I said to my shepherds, Frick and Frack. "I need a drink. Let's go home."

WILMINGTON

I met with Sergeant Price the next day right at lunchtime. We went down the street to get a sandwich, and then Price drove us east to New Hanover Regional Hospital, where the Wilmington city morgue was collocated. We checked in at the security desk and then began the inevitable wait.

"Face up or TV?" Price asked.

"Has there been an autopsy?"

"No. If there's gonna be an autopsy they go to Jacksonville or Chapel Hill. This here is just stage one. Our ME takes a look and signs a toe tag. If cause of death is obvious, say, an MVA injury, or a gunshot to the head, then that's usually it. Otherwise, off they go to the state pathology guys."

"Okay, face-to-face, then." I've seen a cop's share of dead people, but since it was Allie, I felt obligated to do this in person, so to speak. Price seemed to understand. He went back to the desk and asked for the viewing room, and then we waited some more until the morgue attendant came to get us.

I made the identification, trying to ignore the stark fact that one of my colleagues was gone. Allie Gardner had never been a beautiful woman, but hers was a familiar and trusted face, and I was grateful not to have to look at the butchery of a pathology examination. She had died with a surprised look on her face, which wasn't that unusual in my experience, although her mouth looked redder than it should have. I verbalized the ID, and Price nodded to the stone-faced attendant, who rolled the gurney back to the cold storage area.

We went back out to the administrative offices to meet with one of the hospital's pathologists, who had performed a brief preliminary exam. He was a large black man, late fifties, wearing spotted scrubs and drying his hands on a huge wad of paper towels. His scrubs smelled of preservative fluids and other things best left unmentioned. He introduced himself to Bernie and acknowledged me with a brief nod.

"Based on what I saw of her throat, I think she was poisoned," he announced. "We're definitely going to want an autopsy on this one."

I stared at him in disbelief, and even Price seemed to be surprised. *Poison?*

The doctor pitched the sodden wad of paper towels into a biohazard trash can. "Only thing I've seen like it was a case where a really angry woman poured a can of drain cleaner down her boyfriend's throat while he was sleeping. Sodium hydroxide. I didn't scope her, but they won't have to. I'm guessing there's severe esophageal burning as well as damage to the stomach lining. I'm talking chemical burns here, not fire."

"You mean, like acid?" Price asked.

"I don't have a clue right now as to what it was. I didn't smell what I smelled with the Drano case, for what that's worth."

"Any signs that she was *forced* to drink poison?" I asked.

"And you are, again?" the doctor said, looking for some kind of ID badge on my shirt besides the visitor's tag.

"He's with me," Price said, leaving it at that.

"O-o-kay," the pathologist said with a shrug. "No, there was no bruising of the face or lips, and no evident indication of restraint. But an autopsy may contradict that. My job is to see if I can determine an obvious cause of death. If not, she goes upstate. We'll transport tonight, get results back in a couple of days if they're not overloaded up there."

Price took me back downtown, where I retrieved my Suburban and went to check in at the riverside Hilton. Allie's car had been towed away from the gas station, and I didn't think it would be worth my while to go see a convenience store bathroom. I decided to call an old friend who had moved to Wilmington, former park ranger and current college professor Mary Ellen Goode. First I had to find her number, so I called the University of North Carolina at Wilmington, known locally as the U, and tried to get her office number. I'd forgotten how much academics, for all their fervently professed individualism, love their bureaucracy. I think I could have driven out there and asked any passing student quicker than it took for a succession of politically correct office persons to finally, grudgingly, part with a phone number and an extension. Which got me voice mail, naturally, but it was Mary Ellen's lovely voice and it was good to hear. She called back a half hour later.

"Cam," she said. "What a nice surprise. Are we in danger?"

I chuckled at that. We had met in the Great Smokies National Park during the cat dancers case, and again when I'd helped her sort out an especially nasty assault on one of the park's ranger probationers. We'd clicked, and pretty hard, but my penchant for attracting violent encounters with violent people had finally overwhelmed her natural sensitivity. Her question was not entirely frivolous.

"Not this time," I said. "I'm in town on business, but there shouldn't be any major explosions, leaping panthers, or gunfire for at least, oh, hell, a couple hours or so. How about a drink?"

"I'd love to," she said. "I've got one more seminar. Where are you staying?"

I told her the Hilton, and she said she'd meet me at seven in the riverfront lounge.

Even closing in on the big four-oh, Mary Ellen Goode could still light up a room when she arrived. That's how I'd remembered her—the lady who lit up the room. Big bright smile, softly pretty face, and an aura of vulnerable femininity that made every male in range want to protect her, or at least lay on hands. But then I took a second look as she crossed to my table. Maybe it was the tight white skirt enclosing shimmering legs good enough to dent the low buzz of conversation in the lounge. Or that direct, lips-parted smile as she arrived at my table and gave me a second to take in the glorious package before I got a big hug. I tried hard not to grin like a schoolboy who's just scored the head cheerleader's prom ticket. I think I failed. I assumed she'd gone home to attend to powder and paintwork, because if this was how she looked in the classroom, none of the boys there were going to remember anything at all about environmental science.

Drinks ordered and appreciated, my biggest apprehension was that, once I told her what I was really doing in Wilmington, her enthusiasm at seeing me again would drain right out of those bright blue eyes and the evening would be a bust.

So I lied.

I told her I was in town meeting with the local authorities to make sure our company had all the proper licenses to work in this part of the state should we ever have to. Then I quickly asked her how she liked academia in comparison to being the chief environmental scientist up in the Great Smoky Mountains. She got a wistful look in her eye.

"I can't deny that I miss it—the mountains, the park, I mean. And most of the rangers."

"Most of the rangers. Ever hear from Ranger Bob?"

It was an inside joke, and she smiled shyly. "I do believe Ranger Bob got in over his head," she said, and I laughed out loud. "But at least he made a run," she continued. "Most of the men I've met in academia are—different."

"Those who can, do . . ." I began—and then realized I was slinging that nasty little adage at her, too, now that she had gone back to the ivory tower. Except she'd already proved herself more than once on the "doing" side of that equation, and she knew that I knew that. Had she said "most" of the men?

"Well, sort of, at least for the men who went off to college and basically never left. One encounters the occasional ego who equates a big intellect with genuine manliness. You can tell because they talk too much."

That's my girl, I thought. Of course, I had the advantage of never having been encumbered with an oversized intellect, myself.

"No hits at all?"

She smiled again. "There's one guy I've been seeing. He's an oceanic engineer." She saw my confusion. "That's a mix of environmental science and undersea engineering," she said. "He keeps construction companies from running afoul of the various EPAs. How about you—anyone?"

I shook my head. My last really enjoyable time with a woman had been with a seriously go-ahead lady SBI agent whom I'd hoped to entice out of the state womb and into our investigative crew. We'd ended up working the Spider Mountain case, in which Mary Ellen had also been involved. "You remember Carrie, of the SBI?"

She gave me an impudent grin. "Unh-hunh," she said. She was leaning back in her chair now, squaring her shoulders, sipping some wine, and doing something with her legs that made a guy at the next table slop beer down his front.

"Stop that," I said.

"You were telling me about Carrie of the SBI?" she said, ignoring me but allowing that sexy smile to stay on her face.

"Well," I said, clearing my throat, "I offered her a job with H&S, but she got a better offer from the SBI. I think they were afraid that she'd sue them or something after that mess on Spider Mountain."

"So she did the smart thing."

"She did. And now I'm all alone, sad, depressed, picked on, and I don't know what-all I'm ever gonna do."

"And Frick and Frack?" she asked, still looking right at me. I began to feel a little bit like that proverbial deer in the headlights. They were lovely headlights, but she appeared to be a woman with some loving in mind. I was hugely flattered, while having a tiny little problem concentrating on the conversation.

"Fuzzy, smelly, barking too much, shedding, lazy. The usual. Frack's getting older, slowing down a bit. Frick is Frick."

"They're not with you this trip?"

She knew I normally never went anywhere without my two shepherds. Keeping up the legend, I told her this wasn't an operational outing, so I'd left them home this time.

"Now I feel much safer," she said. "No shepherds, no bad guys." More body language, with lots of independent movement. I realized I'd finished my wine. I don't even much like wine.

"You need to refresh that?" She indicated my empty wineglass. Then she cocked her head. "Or is there somewhere more private? Where we could . . . talk?"

I caught my breath. She was doing what nice girls are never supposed to do: looking straight into my eyes and communicating on the limbic channel. I couldn't really find my voice, so I just nodded, slowly, and pushed back my chair. She drained her glass, stood up, and smoothed out her skirt, looking away at nothing while she did it but once again creating a cone of bumbled male conversations in the immediate vicinity. The girl was on fire, and every hetero man within range was hoping I'd just fall over and die so he might come to her rescue. What little female talent there was in the lounge was shooting daggers.

I was so entranced I forgot to pay my tab, but, hell, they knew where I was staying.

I'd come down to Wilmington on short notice, so the only thing available had been one of the expensive top-floor suites. We sat out on the river balcony and enjoyed some more wine. It was actually a bit cold to be sitting out there, but neither of us had seemed to notice. What I had noticed was that Mary Ellen Goode was a genuine damsel in distress. Physical distress. Horns so long she was having to go through doors sideways. I was in pretty good shape for a man of my advancing years, with daily workouts at the Triboro police gym, ten-mile runs every other evening with the shepherds, and a diet that emphasized red meat for protein and Scotch for carbs.

She, on the other hand, led a semi-sedentary life as an

assistant professor of environmental science, whose only concession to physical exercise was a three-mile walk down city sidewalks to and from her apartment. And still she wore my delighted ass right out, coming at our lovemaking with an urgency and desperate need that damned near flattened me in the worst possible context of that expression. We'd approached intimacy in our previous connections, but we'd never actually gone to bed. I should have tried a whole lot harder and a whole lot sooner. I did have the sense not to talk.

Afterward I ordered up a room service dinner for two and we went back out onto the balcony. We were wearing those terrycloth bathrobes the Hilton puts in their suites, but she had neglected to close things up. I'd been relieved when our room service waiter turned out to be a sweet young thing who was either oblivious to the layer of lust-scented ozone in the suite or else a really good actor. He hadn't even looked twice at Mary Ellen in that loose robe. Maybe it was because he was concerned about my respiration rate.

I'd switched to Scotch and was trying not to think about anything while Mary Ellen excused herself and went into the bathroom. Then she was back.

"Ready?" she asked brightly, interrupting my mental drift.

I cowered behind my napkin and tried not to squeak. "Ready?"

"I am *so* glad you called," she said, that bright stare back in play. "But it's been a *long* dry spell, and, well, you know. Night's young, yes?"

"Oh, yes," I said. Not exactly a squeak, but not entirely authoritative, either. Bad guys would not have been impressed.

She gave me a mock look of impatience. "This is a Hilton—the bathtub in there is a hot tub."

I hadn't noticed. I'd been distracted. Now she was slipping out of that useless robe, and I was even more distracted. The cold air did amazing things to her superstructure. I waited for sounds of ships colliding out there on the Cape Fear River.

"Tub will take five more minutes," she announced. "Why don't you get us some champagne."

With that she pranced across the balcony and into the living room, heading in the direction of the bathroom. I sat back in my chair and wondered if I could get oxygen with that.

The new and much improved Mary Ellen decamped the next morning at eight, still smiling. I thought about getting up and going for a walk around the tourist district. Getting up I could manage. Walking was out of the question. I went back to sleep instead. A phone call from Bernie Price woke me up around ten.

"We have developments," he said.

"Developments are good," I said, wiggling my toes to make sure they'd still work.

"Not always," he said mysteriously. "I'll be down to get you in twenty minutes."

"Make it thirty," I said.

"What—you hungover?"

"No, just a long night."

"Lucky you." He laughed.

"You have no idea," I said.

This time he drove us to the New Hanover County medical examiner's offices. The ME himself was not available, and since he hadn't been willing to tell Price what the developments were over the telephone, we remained in the mushroom mode while they rustled up a substitute.

Price had given me a long once-over when I got into his unmarked Crown Vic. "Mmm-hnnh" was all he said.

"Jealousy doesn't become you," I replied.

"Good thing we're not walking to the lab," he said.

"I can walk just fine," I said.

"You squeak pretty good, too."

We finally met with one of the assistant medical examiners, a visibly agitated, middle-aged black woman wearing a doctor's white coat and radiating a disapproving attitude. She swept us into a tiny conference room and asked Price to close the door.

"Who's this?" she asked him, pointing at me with her chin.

"Closest thing to next of kin and also the DOA's employer," Price said. "He's a retired police lieutenant. What's the big deal here?"

The doctor thought about it for a moment, looked me over belligerently, but then apparently consented to my remaining in the room.

"The big deal," she said, "is that your College Road DOA turned out to be highly radioactive."

I saw Price frown, as if he were confused. "Radioactive" is a term cops sometimes use to describe another cop who has sufficiently pissed off the brass that all the other cops begin keeping their distance. Then I realized she meant literally radioactive.

It turned out that they'd sent Allie's remains to the state autopsy facilities in Jacksonville, where the requisite cutting and gutting had been duly conducted. When the remains were rolled by the nuclear medicine office on their way to cold storage, three separate radiation monitors had gone off simultaneously. The people in the nuclear meds office had started tearing the place up looking for the problem when the monitors suddenly went silent again—which implied that the highly radioactive something had gone by and was no longer in range.

They caught up with the morgue attendant in the hallway and had him roll his draped gurney back down the corridor. All the alarms went off again. When they explained what that meant to the attendant, the attendant went off. He'd abandoned said gurney and beat feet down the hall, at which point the entire facility had gone to general quarters. The feds had been summoned, and there were lots of questions flying around and apparently lots more inbound.

"You said they did the autopsy," Price said calmly. Being the good bureaucrat that he was, Jacksonville being in a state of pandemonium wasn't necessarily his problem. "Do they have an opinion?"

"An *opinion*?" she repeated, almost shouting. "Yeah, they have an opinion, Detective. Severe radiation poisoning. She apparently drank something that was highly radioactive."

"Literally radioactive?" I asked.

"There's a damn echo in here," she snorted. "Whatever it was, it was hot enough to burn the bejesus out of her innards. Mouth, esophagus, trachea, heart, lungs, stomach—the works. First-class case of radiation poisoning. The lab people up there are beside themselves, and, of course, the whole damn world wants to know where it came from."

"Beats me," Price said equably. "But I guess we do have ourselves a homicide."

I thought she was going to brain him, so I intervened. I explained what Allie had been doing in Wilmington, and that there was no plausible link between a pending divorce case and radiation poisoning.

"That all makes sense to me," she said, "but inquiring federal minds are going to explore that notion in some detail. So I'd recommend you stick around here in Wilmington, Mr. Ex-police-lieutenant. And now I need to speak to the detective sergeant here in private, if you please."

Price came out a few minutes later and shook his head. He put his finger to his lips until we were in the elevator. "Full-scale Lebanese goat-grab spooling up in the ME circles," he said as we rode down. "Jacksonville is yelling at New Hanover for sending up a radioactive DOA, and New Hanover is yelling back that they had no way of knowing, et cetera, et cetera. You sure you've told me everything you know about this?"

"All I know is that Allie is dead. How she came in contact with radiation is beyond me. So now what?"

"The state chief medical examiner's called in the Nuclear Regulatory Commission. The NRC has called the Bureau. The federal host is inbound, as we speak."

We went out to his car and climbed in. He sighed and looked around the peaceful parking lot, which we both knew wasn't going to stay that way much longer.

"She give you *any* details?" I asked. "Like radioactive what?"

Price said no. She had told him they wouldn't know the "what" until a lab very different from the state facility reviewed the case and the corpse. "She mostly wanted to vent, and I was the nearest cop. We're the ones who sent the body to New Hanover, so somehow, this is all our fault."

"That sounds familiar," I said. *What the fuck, Allie,* I thought again. I'd felt like washing my own hands on the way out.

"So where do they sell radioactive fluids in beautiful downtown Wilmington, North Carolina?" I asked as we drove out of the lot and headed back to the city police building.

"We've got the Helios nuclear power plant over next door in Brunswick County," Price said. "Did your legal lovebirds have any connection to the nuke industry?"

"Hell, I don't know," I said. "All lawyers look alike to me, and, besides, Allie wasn't taking pictures of them at work."

Price's cell phone rang as we stopped for a red light. He picked up, listened for a minute, grunted an okay, and hung up. "They're he-e-e-re," he chanted. "Boss wants me back downtown ASAP. You really want to dance in this cow pie?"

"No way," I said. "Gave that shit up when I retired."

"Retirement's starting to look *real* good." Price sighed longingly.

Ten minutes later, he pulled into the parking lot. "I'll let you out here, if that's okay. You stayin' overnight?"

I grinned at him. "As in, don't leave town, there, stranger?"

Price shrugged. "Naw, not really. The federal suits will want to talk to you at some point, but otherwise . . ."

"Yeah, sure," I said, immediately thinking of Mary Ellen Goode. "I'll stay over another night. Anything I can do to help, you holler. They going to be able to keep this out of the media?"

Price shook his head. "Probably not," he predicted. "Specially if somebody ties that radiation shit to the power plant over in Brunswick County. Which would be a real surprise—those folks have *damned* good security, and the guy who runs it is downright scary. What's your cell number?"

I gave it to him, and he promised to stay in touch.

Two hours later, the phone at my bedside rang. I picked up. It was Bernie Price again.

"Lieutenant Richter?" Price said, speaking formally, which told me immediately he was probably calling from a room full of feds and other undesirables.

"Having fun yet, Bernie?" I asked.

"Not at all, sir," Price said, without an audible hint of humor. "Would you be available to meet with two special agents from the FBI this afternoon?"

I looked at my watch. There wasn't all that much left of the afternoon. "I'll be in the hotel lounge in an hour," I said. "Got names?"

"Special Agents Caswell and Myers," Bernie said.

I smiled. Creeps Caswell and Missed-it Mary Myers. This could be interesting.

"I can't wait," I said. "I'll fill you in after I see them."

"Probably not, sir," Bernie said, and then paused. I got the message.

"You've been told to sever all connections with itinerant ex-cops meddling in city business, have you?"

"That's absolutely correct, sir," he said.

"Gosh, Bernie, this really hurts my feelings. But maybe when all the dust settles, I can buy you a beer, hunh?"

"Count on it, sir," he said. He sounded relieved that he hadn't had to spell it out for me.

I thanked him, hung up, and went out onto the balcony to do some stretch exercises and try to wake up. For some reason I suddenly missed my shepherds. Then, looking at the other chair, I realized I also missed Allie. Had she been the victim of some random act of God, or had someone done this to her? The angry pathologist had used the word "ingested." So she drank radioactive . . . what?

The Hilton's lounge was spacious, modernistic, and relatively empty. There was a nice view of the Cape Fear River as the sun started down. The dark gray bulk of the battleship USS *North Carolina,* parked now as a World War II museum across the river, filled up the downstream windows. I got myself a beer and took a corner booth away from the main bar. The two FBI agents showed up fifteen minutes later, and I smiled when I caught the bartender staring at them.

I had encountered Special Agent Caswell and his partner only once during my active-duty career, and he had provoked the same reaction from me. He was a supervisory special agent, now in his late forties, with a spare, six-foot-six, permanently stooped frame. He had long, intensely black hair plastered straight back from his forehead, hooded eyes, an elongated, bony nose, large teeth, the original lantern jaw, and undertaker's white hands and fingers, which seemed to protrude unnaturally from his suit jacket. He was a man who moved silently, and he tended to rub those porcelain hands together a lot. He had a soft, whispery, almost unctuous voice, reinforcing the funeral director impression. I didn't know who'd given him his unofficial nickname, but I suspect it was one of the female agents over in the Bureau's Raleigh field office. He was reputed to be a challenging interrogator, who, as I recalled, specialized in science and technology crimes.

Special Agent Mary Myers had apparently come to the Bureau with a high creep threshold if she was still partnered up with Brother Caswell. She was a well-fed, late-thirty-something blonde, five-seven or -eight, with watery blue eyes, a bunny rabbit nose, and round, horned-rim Wall Street eyeglasses, which framed a permanently puzzled and near-sighted expression on her otherwise unremarkable face. I figured she probably had an accounting degree and was one of those tenacious detail miners the Bureau used in complex white-collar financial crimes. Her Missed-it Mary nickname had arisen in the course of a stakeout incident during her first and only assignment as a street agent. Mary thought she'd been fired upon from a parked car and had emptied her service weapon in return, hitting three other parked cars and managing to set two of them on fire, while leaving the suspect vehicle untouched and her fellow agents watching in awe from beneath their own vehicle.

"Special Agents," I said as they approached my corner table. I had not actually worked with either of them before, so they introduced themselves, flashed the appropriate picture-plastic, and sat down.

"So, how can I help you?" I asked, addressing myself to Caswell. Even sitting, he seemed to tower over me and the table, and I'm six-foot-plus. He began rubbing those undertaker hands together.

"We understand," he began, "that Ms. Gardner was an employee of your company and that she was pursuing evidence of marital infidelity, involving one or more officers of the court?"

"I think just two philandering lawyers, actually," I said. I saw Special Agent Myers discreetly opening her notebook. "I've gathered up the details of Allie's investigation for you right here," I continued, and handed a written summary to Myers so she wouldn't have to take so many notes. She looked at it warily and then handed it to Caswell, who fished out some Silas Marner glasses and scanned it for a moment.

"Thank you very much, Mr. Richter," he said, folding the two fax pages lengthwise and sliding them into his suit jacket pocket. "It is 'mister' these days, am I correct?"

"Absolutely," I said, knowing full well that Caswell was telling me I'd been vetted before they came to see me. I had some history with the Raleigh Field Office, not all of it pleasant. "I haven't been in law enforcement since I declined to testify in the cat dancers case."

"Yes-s-s." Caswell nodded, a bit startled that I would bring that up. "I do remember that case, but not *why,* exactly, you declined to testify."

"Because I couldn't tell the good guys from the bad guys anymore," I said. "And I had a civilian to protect as well. So: Where'd the hot stuff come from?"

Myers rolled superior eyes and looked away. Caswell gave me a patient if somewhat disappointed smile. "You know how this works, Mr. Richter. *We* ask the questions. You do your civic duty and help your Bureau. Or perhaps not, I suppose, in your case."

It was my turn to smile. "It's not my Bureau, Special Agent," I said. "But nothing's ever forgotten, is it."

"Almost never, Mr. Richter. You're quite right there. Quite right. Now, back to Ms. Gardner: Did she report anything at all which might have a bearing on how she died?"

I decided to quit sparring. "Nothing at all. As I told Detective Price, the case was entirely routine, to the point where Allie said she was coming back early. She had the goods, and that was it."

"May we have access to 'the goods,' as you put it?"

"If our client is willing, we certainly won't get in your way. But I should warn you, the client's a Georgia redhead, and she's really pissed off. In Georgia, that's usually a legitimate pretext for gunfire."

"Thank you for the advice, Mr. Richter," Creeps said, peering at me over those antique specs. "As you may remember, we're always extremely grateful for advice. And even if the client is not willing, may we please have her name and address?"

"Sure," I said. I knew perfectly well that they could get that information, one way or another.

Caswell turned formally to his partner. "Special Agent Myers?"

"Do you have any idea why Ms. Gardner was at that particular gas station?" Mary asked.

"Getting gas?" I said. Her eyes narrowed. "Or do you mean her being over in the university district?"

"The latter, Mr. Richter," she said patiently, pen and notebook poised.

I'd wondered about that, too. "Two possibilities, I think. She was just out for a drive, saw that she'd need to get gas before coming back the next morning, and hit the first station she came to. Or."

"Or?"

"Or, all of the above and then whatever she drank got to her before she could get back to the hotel. She felt ill and found the nearest bathroom. I never did hear a time of death."

"Where would you have heard a time of death?" Myers asked.

"At the county morgue?" I said.

"You were at the morgue?"

"I was. I was asked to make the ID for Detective Price. Talked to an assistant ME. Or rather, listened to one."

Myers looked at Caswell. It was obvious she thought my talking to the assistant ME represented a grave breach of some federal procedure or another. Caswell nodded, rubbed his hands, and changed the subject.

"Do you know of anyone who might have wanted to harm Ms. Gardner?" he asked. Myers, back in her box, subsided and resumed taking notes.

"Her ex would be a long shot," I said. "He left her for another woman, but that was eight, maybe nine years ago. She divorced him and then whacked him financially, at least as she tells it. Told it. But Allie was a pretty tough lady, so that's not really likely after all this time."

"And at work? At your, um, company? Everything okay there?"

I grinned at him. "It's a real company, Special Agent. Licensed, bonded, the whole nine yards. We can even carry guns if we want to. And, yes, indeed, Allie was fine at work. Lots of boys and girls having trouble keeping their pants on, apparently."

Myers sniffed, as if the notion of people without their pants on disagreed with her. I got the impression that lots of things probably disagreed with Special Agent Mary Myers, and that she *always* kept her pants on. I wondered if she even knew what her unofficial handle was.

"Was she personally involved with anyone that you know of?" Caswell asked.

I shook my head and had a sip of beer. I hadn't bothered to offer the agents a drink. Bureau people are always on duty. Always. It's one of the things that makes them formidable. "I think the both of them—Allie and Mel Lindsay, her partner in the firm—were tired of men and their bullshit."

Myers blinked. Actually, she almost smiled at that. The lounge was starting to fill up.

"A relationship there?" Caswell asked.

"No, just work. They often traveled together. They were lethally thorough and enjoyed their specialty. Mel was seeing some guy for a while, but then discovered that he was married, so that ended abruptly. But, no, they were not a pair in that sense."

Caswell almost looked disappointed. Creeps indeed, I thought. He looked at Myers and raised his eyebrows. She closed her notebook. We were done. I exchanged cards with Caswell. He asked me to call or e-mail him if I thought of anything else, and reminded me he needed Allie's client's name and address. He started to push back his chair and then stopped.

"You're an investigator by trade, Mr. Richter," he said. "Please tell me you are going to stay out of this one, correct?"

I looked at him. That was a question and a warning. "Sure, Special Agent," I said, perhaps sounding more casual than I felt. "With you guys on the case, who needs me, right?"

"Precisely the right answer, Mr. Richter," he said with a charming if patronizing smile. "Don't disappoint your Bureau. We'll be in touch."

I signaled the college-student waiter for another beer. He brought it and asked me who the weird-looking dude was. I told him that the weird-looking dude was from the Darkside, and he nodded knowingly. Awesome, he said. Totally, I replied. We had communicated, and life was, like, good. So was the beer.

I put Allie's death out of my mind for a few minutes and just enjoyed my drink and the sight of the sun going down on the battleship's dimpled gray hull. The setting sun turned the river into a sheet of bronze, which made everything out there pretty much invisible. My inner self was still somewhat aglow from the previous evening with Mary Ellen. We had come so close to physical intimacy in our previous acquaintance that I'd half-expected to be disappointed. Instead, she had been almost intimidating in her need. Naturally, I felt used. Used, abused, and hoping like hell she'd want to do it all again.

Then I remembered something. Allie had said she'd be back the next day after taking care of some personal business. What might that have been? I should have said something to the special agents, but then again, maybe I could tease out a few more facts before I closed that loop.

"Mr. Cameron Richter?" a deep baritone voice inquired over my left shoulder. I looked up. A stocky black man stood next to my table. He was immaculately dressed in a stylish suit, and he was holding a leather-covered notebook across his middle.

"Yes?" I said. I would have stood, but I couldn't get up without running into him, and he didn't look like he'd move a whole lot.

"Forgive the intrusion," he said. "I'm Aristotle Quartermain. May I have a word, please? This concerns the recent misfortune of Ms. Allison Gardner."

He proffered his hand, and I automatically shook it. He was in his late fifties, and his skin was not just black but *blue*-black. He had a glistening, oversized bald head and intense owl-like eyes. He was built like a fire hydrant under that six-hundred-dollar suit, not tall as much as broad, and his hand felt like a silk-covered vise. He sat down carefully opposite me and put his notebook on the table.

"You have the advantage of me, Mr. Quartermain," I said. "A drink?"

"That would be very nice, Mr. Richter. I believe I have one coming."

"That sure of yourself?"

"It's a fault, Mr. Richter. I'm the chief of technical security at the Helios nuclear power station. I'm afraid it's gone to my head."

The same waiter brought Quartermain his drink and gave me a conspiratorial look over my guest's shoulder. The Darkside was everywhere tonight. Then I realized what Quartermain had just announced.

"Ah," I said.

"Yes," Quartermain replied, sampling his Scotch. He unzipped the fine-grained leather binder, extracted a neck chain containing his credentials, and slid it across the table. I examined the three plastic badges, each with his picture and the logo of the power company, PrimEnergy, which apparently owned and operated the Helios atomic power station.

"I'm technical security. Another gentleman is physical security. I'm in charge of keeping the nuclear process safe. The other guy is watching for bad guys coming over the moat. Technically, he works for me."

"Why?"

"Because if our side of the security equation goes south, physical security becomes moot. Nobody will be trying to get *in* to the power plant under those circumstances, if you get my drift."

"Got it," I said. I studied the badges and handed them back. "Those look good, for the moment, anyway."

"I've been at the bar," he said, retrieving the badges. His fingers were large and impeccably manicured. "I did not want to intrude until the FBI people left. Special Agent Caswell is a sight to behold, is he not."

"True enough," I said. I'd decided to let him lead. He knew who I was and why I was in Wilmington, and he knew the Bureau people by name. The pleasant, isn't-this-a-nice-evening expression melted off his face, and suddenly I was looking at a no-shit security officer. The transformation was dramatic.

"Your associate," he said, lowering his voice, "was killed by ingesting about a pint of highly radioactive water."

"How high is high?" I asked.

"High enough to permanently expose twenty-seven plates of X-ray film." He paused, looking around to make sure no one was eavesdropping. "Twenty-seven plates that were stored fifty feet away from the main analysis room in that lab. She might as well have crawled into an industrial-sized microwave oven, set it on high, and spent the night in there."

"All this from one bottle of water?"

He leaned back in his chair and it creaked. "We don't know that, of course. What the container was, I mean. We're assuming that she drank it thinking it was just water, since there were no indications of coercion. Right now the situation up at the state forensic lab is somewhat—chaotic."

"I can just imagine," I said. "And they *know* this stuff came from the power plant?"

"No, no, they don't know that. The NRC—that's the Nuclear Regulatory Commission—is involved, as is, of course, the Bureau. Needless to say, they're both looking hard at Helios as a possible source."

"And let me guess, the plant and the company are circling the wagons at warp speed just now."

He smiled and shook his head. "The company understands their concerns, of course, but the NRC technical people, at least, know that there's no way radioactive water can come out of that plant and into the community absent a major, and I mean major, accident. Even then, it would appear in the form of water vapor. Not something you could drink. No. Technically, this isn't possible."

"And yet . . ."

"Yes. And yet. The isotopic fingerprints would normally tell the tale, except for the fact that any credible analysis of residual isotopes is going to be obscured by their having gone through human tissue."

I just looked at him. Isotopic fingerprints? He saw my confusion. "When I was in nuke school," he said, "the professor would sometimes say something in Greek and we'd all get blank expressions on our faces. Every classroom had a whiteboard or six. In the corner of one of the whiteboards there was always a rectangle with a circle drawn inside it. Inside the circle were the words 'I believe.' That was the I-believe button. If the instructor realized that he'd just baffled the entire class, he'd invite us to press the I-believe button and then he'd proceed with the rest of the lecture. Sometimes the problem cleared up, sometimes it didn't. So: Say, 'I believe.' "

I did. He grinned.

"What's funny?"

"I was thinking about Special Agent Caswell's reaction to isotopic fingerprinting. He tried to pretend he knew what it was. So I asked if the Bureau's laboratory could do some for us. Special Agent Myers made a note to call them. That will be an amusing, if short, discussion."

"Back to the problem at hand, Mr. Quartermain," I said. "My associate, as you called her, is in an autopsy drawer. The technical impossibilities aside, I want to know how this happened and why."

"I apologize," he said at once. "I didn't mean to trivialize what's happened. In fact, that's why I've come to see you. I'm here to offer you a job of work."

"Me?"

"You and your company. That's what you people do, correct? Investigations?"

I shifted in my chair. This was going just a bit too fast. "Mr. Quartermain," I began.

"Please, call me Ari," he said. His voice was genial enough, but those zero-parallax eyes never left mine.

"Okay, Ari. You saw me talking to the FBI people. If you know anything about the Bureau, you'll know that the last thing they will either want or permit is my involvement in this mess. Double-oh-jay is the term of art they prefer when civilians get in their way."

It was his turn to blink. "Double-oh-jay," I repeated. "Obstruction of Justice, with a capital *J* in their case. Say: 'I believe.'"

He laughed then, a great big gut-trouncing bellow of a laugh that had people in the lounge looking over at us.

"I believe," he said, still chuckling. Then his face sobered up again. "Look," he continued. "The feds are cranking up a circus and a half over this incident. A joint NRC-FBI team is going to be arriving at the plant first thing tomorrow morning. We, and by 'we' I mean reps from the company, the plant operators, various contractors, and nuclear safety engineers, are going to demonstrate that there's no way hot water got out of that plant in a form that could be consumed. It'll take a day or so, maybe longer, but then they're going to go away and look for some other explanation."

"So what is it you would want me and my people to do?"

"You want to find out what happened to Ms. Gardner?" he asked. "As opposed to, say, finding grounds for some kind of lawsuit?"

That pissed me off. It must have shown in my face because he sat back in his chair and raised his hand defensively.

"Okay," he said. "That was out of line." He hesitated. "Look, I came to you because of some things the FBI people said about you. That you were known to them and that you played by your own rules. That you were an outsider, and the fact that Allison Gardner was from *your* organization was ringing bells for them." Another pause. "I think I need someone like you, but not until the feds back out."

"Because there *is* a way that hot water could escape from your plant? Is that it?"

He took a deep breath. He looked like a man who was about to take a significant risk. "Possibly," he said, "but not from the reactors, per se. The energy side, I mean. And it would require some inside help."

"Okay, then where?"

"From the moonpool," he said.

I leaned back in my chair, looked around for the waiter, and signaled for another round and a switch to Scotch for me. I had no idea what a moonpool was, but his other implication was clear. He was wondering if he might not have himself a bad guy in his favorite nuclear power station. I knew nothing about the technical side of a nuclear power plant, but I was aware that the entire industry lived life on a political and environmental knife-edge, where the least mistake could cost a power company tens of millions. Which is probably why he was talking to me: He wanted to scope out any such problem *before* the feds came to the same conclusion and swarmed back to shut the place down.

"Let's get two things straight right away," I said. "*If* I agree to help you, and I haven't decided that yet, and we uncover some felonious shit, said shit gets handed over to the appropriate federal authorities at once."

"Of course," he said. "Especially if there's a terrorist angle to this."

That hadn't occurred to me, although now that I thought of it, it should have.

"And second?" he asked.

"And second, my concern is not for your power station. Allie Gardner was a close friend and associate. She was good troops and a stand-up cop in her day. She got a raw deal from two serial-asshole husbands, and this was not what should have happened to her. Okay?"

"Got it," he said.

I theorized that since Allie hadn't been doing anything remotely related to the Helios power station, what had happened to her had probably been a random event. He nodded, but didn't actually say anything.

"So: What's a moonpool?"

"It's an old engineer's slang term for the spent fuel storage pool in a nuclear power plant. A power reactor doesn't consume all of its fuel before the uranium bundles become inefficient, so we regularly remove spent fuel elements and transfer them to a deep pool within a containment structure for storage. Right after a refueling event, the rods are really hot, physically and radiation-wise, and they make the water glow this incredible, otherworldly blue color. Moonpool."

"And this water is radioactive?"

"You wouldn't want to swim in it," he said. "It's not so much that the water is radioactive as that the spent fuel assemblies are. Now, if one or more of those assemblies is a leaker, and particles of radioactive material get loose in the water, then the water is, for all practical purposes, radioactive."

"But they're not supposed to be leaking, right?"

He shrugged. "Metallurgy mutates in the presence of an ongoing, long-term fission reaction. The actual uranium fuel is cladded, but the fission reaction can sometimes burn holes or weak spots in the cladding. That's why the moonpool is forty-five feet deep."

"And if they do leak, the water could be hot enough to do the kind of damage the ME was talking about?"

"Not if you're just standing next to the moonpool. But if you ingested it? Oh, yes, easily."

"Look, Ari," I said. "You don't know me or my people. None of us is qualified to snoop around a nuclear power plant, and with the feds in it, we'd inevitably bump up against each other. In my experience, they don't play well with others. I think we're gonna pass."

He nodded. He was visibly disappointed, but perhaps not surprised. "Okay," he said. "It was worth a shot. I can tell you that you may never find out what happened to your associate, though."

"Meaning the feds'll clamp a lid on this and weld it shut?"

"Yes," he said. "You'll know that's what's happening when a special agent brings you some security forms to sign, where you promise not to divulge any piece of this in the interests of national security, homeland defense, and apple pie."

"What if I decide to just decline to sign?"

He smiled at me. "You're licensed by the state government, right?" he said. "Who do you think they check with before issuing those kinds of licenses?"

Point taken, I thought. "What exactly would you want us to do?"

"Let's wait for the current shitstorm to settle down," he said. "Then let's talk again."

I walked Ari out to his car, said good night, had dinner, and then went for a stroll down the riverwalk toward the center of town. The evening was cool and clear, and the boardwalk was empty. The Cape Fear River was running strong as the tide went out, tugging audibly at pilings and coiling up clumps of trash in small whirlpools along the banks. The buoys out in the channel leaned toward the Atlantic Ocean as if they wanted to escape. The few tourist joints down at the base of Market Street still operating during the off-season were doing a desultory business, with overdressed seating hostesses standing by their patio rostrums, smiling longingly at me as I ambled past all those empty al fresco tables.

I became aware of the three guys who had started following me. They'd appeared in my wake about the time I passed the Cape Fear Serpentarium. Since I couldn't be sure they were following me and not just out for an after-dinner walk of their own, I turned left into the next street and walked uphill, away from the river. At the next corner I turned left again onto Front Street and headed back toward the center of the tourist district. They kept going along the riverwalk and went out of sight when I made that left on Front. I went four or five blocks, made one more left, and walked back down toward the river, where, lo and behold, there they were again, this time standing on the boardwalk, patently admiring the battleship across the river. They were fit men, dressed in khaki trousers, ball caps, sneakers, and dark windbreakers. They looked like a security detail whose protectee had dismissed them for the night. Or maybe not.

I was on the diagonal corner from them when I got to Water Street. I thought about going over to them and commenting on the weather, but then decided to go on back to the hotel, which was only three blocks away. I'd have to cross one relatively dark parking lot and then walk up the flood ramp in front of the lobby, but there were people up there, and it didn't look like a promising place for a mugging. When I went through the hotel doors and glanced back, I didn't see anyone following me. Okay, too many late-night TV movies. I stopped at the lobby PC to check my e-mail, then went upstairs.

The corridor on my floor was empty and quiet. There was a room service tray with dirty dishes in front of the suite diagonally across from mine, but no other signs that there were humans about. I keyed open my door, flipped on the light.

And there they were.

One was standing by the window with his back to me, looking out at the river. A second was sitting at the desk chair, facing me, and holding a large black semiautomatic out at arm's length, pointed at my stomach. The third, older than the other two, was sitting in the other chair, hands behind his head, and grinning at the expression on my face. I stopped short, keeping the door open, mentally kicking myself for not having the shepherds with me.

"Oh, shut the damn door, Lieutenant," the older one said. "This is just a social call."

I thought about shutting it and running, but had not yet looked at the fire escape card to see where the stairs were. There was also the wee matter of that .45 looking right at me.

Some social call. The young guy with the big black gun was not smiling. Plus, the older one had called me lieutenant.

"C'mon," he insisted. "We've all had dinner, and none of us wants to chase your ass around the hotel. Come in and close the door. Please?"

"Well, since you said please," I said, putting on the best front I could muster. The guy looking out the window hadn't turned around, but I knew he was watching me in the reflection of the room lights.

"Thank you very much," the older guy said. "You're wondering how we got in here."

"Question crossed my mind," I said.

I felt increasingly stupid standing in the little entrance alcove next to the bathroom door. I wondered if there was anyone in the bathroom, or if they'd found my own weapon in the hidden compartment of my toiletries bag. The rest of my stuff didn't look as if anyone had been through it. "So what're we here to talk about?"

"Actually, I'm here to talk, and you're here to listen, if you don't mind," the man said. He was about fifty-five, with a hard face, a hatchet nose, and reddish gray hair planed into a flattop haircut. Like the others, he was wearing a windbreaker, khaki trousers, and military boots. There was a small black knife in a pouch on his right boot.

The other guy whose face I could see looked Italian. He was much younger, maybe in his late twenties. He was obviously trying to look like some kind of unblinking, lizard-eyed, hardboiled young *soldato* in a crime family. He was succeeding. All three of them were in shape, with flat bellies, big chests, and heavy shoulders under those oversized windbreakers. I wondered how long the young guy could hold that heavy .45 out at arm's length like that. My arm was getting tired just watching him do it.

"A lot of that going around tonight," I said, trying to look more relaxed than I felt. I could not possibly get to my gun before the guy in the chair could do some damage. "First the FBI, then—"

"We know," the man said, waving his hand dismissively. He had a large gold university ring on his left hand. "Especially, we know Dr. Quartermain. That's kinda why we're here, Lieutenant. Dr. Quartermain's operating way off his patch, talking to a civilian like you."

"So, what, he's operating on your patch, perhaps? And who is 'we'—you got a mouse in your pocket?"

The man gave me a patient, mildly annoyed look that said, *I'm not done talking and you're not done listening.* The hoodlum wannabe shifted in his chair, as if waiting for the command to jump up and bite me or something, but that .45 never wavered. The third man continued to take in the sights out on the river, but he had one hand hanging casually in the folds of his jacket.

"We are the other half of security at the Helios power plant," he said. "The so-called physical security half. We're the guys who deal with the Navy SEALs when they run federally sponsored intrusion drills on the plant."

I guess I was supposed to be impressed, but I was getting tired of standing at the door. I waved my right hand to include everyone in the room. "This is a little extreme for a bunch of rent-a-cops, isn't it?"

"Ow," Hatchet-Nose said. "Now you've hurt my feelings. But let me make sure the message gets through. You need to do two things: go away, and stop talking to your new best friend, Dr. Aristotle Quartermain."

"According to Dr. Quartermain, you work for him."

"Yes, he would probably say that. But security in an atomic

power plant is a complex business. Multi-layered, if it's done right. Lots of need-to-know barriers. The administrative wiring diagram doesn't always tell the whole tale."

"Let me get this straight—you're security contractors at a commercial power plant who've followed me, broken into my room, with at least one gun visible, and the reason I shouldn't break out my cell phone and dial 911 is . . . ?"

"First of all, your cell phone is over there on the desk, and we have the battery. And young Billy here isn't going to let you go over there and get it or anything else."

I looked at young Billy, whose arm remained straight out with nary a tremor. That really was impressive.

"Secondly, your 'going away' is the operative part. It's really good advice. We're sorry for your loss and all that. We don't know what happened, either, but what we do know is that the bad shit, whatever it was, didn't come through my perimeter."

My Bureau, and now my perimeter. "It came through somebody's perimeter," I said. "You got a name? Cops'll want to know."

He laughed softly. "You're not going to call the cops, Mr. Richter. Unless you startle young Billy here, nothing's going to happen. We're going to leave, and you're going to pack. Feel free to spend the night, but tomorrow, you're going back to your fascinating private-eye work in beautiful downtown Triboro, North Carolina."

"And if I don't?" I said.

"There will be unpleasant consequences. The array of federal agencies involved in keeping nuclear power plants safe is, let's see, how shall I put this—legion?"

"Oh," I said. "Legion. Dozens of inept bureaucracies, tripping over each other while fucking up by the numbers? *That* legion? When you said unpleasant, I thought you meant Billy the Kid here."

His semijocular, we're-all-buddies-in-this-together expression slipped a little. "That can be arranged, too," he said. "He's young, but he's impressive."

"Holding that .45 straight out like that for all this time—that's impressive," I said. "But I'd guess he needs two other guys for anything personal."

Billy's eyes narrowed. I'd hurt some more feelings.

The third man turned around at last. He, too, was lean from top to bottom, in his early forties, with close-cropped blond hair and the face of a Nazi death camp commandant, complete with disturbing pale blue eyes. "You can try me if you'd like," he said.

"Actually, I prefer girls," I said. I stepped to one side and held open the door. I saw Billy's trigger finger, which had been resting alongside the trigger guard, slip into firing position. For some reason, though, I didn't think he'd shoot. They hadn't come here to shoot people. This time, anyway.

"Why don't you clowns just leave?" I said. "And now'd be nice. You're rent-a-cops, and you have zero authority outside of your contract area. The fact that you're even here means you probably *do* have a hole in your so-called perimeter, so why don't you go work on that instead of bothering Mr. Hilton's paying guests?"

The older guy sniffed and then got up, zipping up his windbreaker. "Okay, Mr. Richter. We'll leave. But trust me, you will, too. C'mon, people."

He walked past me without a second glance, as did the SS officer look-alike. Billy sat in his chair for one second longer than necessary, and then pocketed the .45 as he got up.

"That must be a relief," I said. "My arm was getting tired just watching you."

Billy sauntered by, never taking his eyes off my face. "Later," he muttered.

"Earlier is better than later," I said to his back. "That is, if you're man enough without your ace buddies there. Nighty-night. *Kid*."

I closed the door and slid the bolt and chain. I went into the bathroom and checked for my weapon. It was there, but the magazine was gone. So they *had* found it. I picked up my cell phone, and yes, it felt lighter than before. I picked up each of the two house phones, but neither of them worked, either. Thorough contractors, I'd give them that. If I wanted to squawk, I'd have to leave the room, and I really didn't want to venture too far from my room just now. The best I could hope for was that Billy would come back to prove he was a man. I decided to prepare for that possibility.

Fifteen minutes later, there was a quiet knock on the door. I knew better than to peek through the little plastic optic. Our homicide crew had once found a drug dealer pinned to his hotel door by an ice pick that had been hammered into his eye through that little piece of plastic.

"Who is it?" I said in a singsong voice.

"It's later," a voice replied, and I recognized young Billy. Oh, good.

"Well, Billy," I said, "you surprise me again. Why don't you come on in and get your ass kicked."

I stepped across the alcove, staying underneath the eyehole, removing the chain as I went. Then I crouched in the closet on the other side of the room door and wedged my shoulder against the wall. I unsnapped the dead bolt, and then, putting one foot about in the middle of the door, I reached over and pushed the door handle down.

He did exactly what I expected him to do, which was to kick the door as hard as he could the moment he heard that handle unlatch. If I'd been standing where someone normally stands when he opens a hotel room door, I'd have been hit in the face with the edge of said door and probably knocked unconscious. As it was, I was able to let the door swing halfway in against my cocked leg, and then I sent it back in *his* direction with the full force of *my* right leg. The edge caught him in the forehead and knocked him all the way across the hall, blood spurting from his nose and forehead as he slumped, cross-eyed and barely conscious, into a sitting position against the opposite wall, his scrawny ass on the room service tray. I reached up to the closet shelf, picked up the hallway fire extinguisher I'd lifted ten minutes earlier, and flooded his face with dry powder. He hadn't let go of his .45, but dropped it now to protect his eyes.

It was a peppy little fire extinguisher. He was still sufficiently stunned that he failed to tuck and roll, and I flat covered his eyes, nose, mouth, and chest with that noxious powder until the spray petered out. Then I threw the empty extinguisher as hard as I could at his right knee, achieving an entirely satisfactory crack and a loud grunt from young Billy. A small cloud of white powder puffed out from his lips when he cried out.

I stepped out into the hallway and retrieved his .45. It looked a lot like mine, a SIG-Sauer model 220. Better than mine, it had a full magazine. I stepped back into my open doorway and then checked the hall. At the far end, to my left, near the elevator bank, stood the older man, leaning against the wall with his hands in his jacket pockets. He was looking at Billy and shaking his head. If ghosts could get nosebleeds, that's what Billy looked like.

"Good help is hard to find," I called down to him.

"Ain't that the truth," he said. I closed the door so he could retrieve his semi-wrecked, extremely white bad boy. I kept Billy's gun.

I sighed as I washed some white powder off my own hands. I was pretty sure I'd get to see Billy again one day, and next time he probably would bring his friends. Then again, so would I.

Right now, however, I thought it best to leave town. Billy had been all noise and testosterone, but those other two guys looked like the real deal. Until I knew more about what the hell was really going on here in Wilmington, I'd probably be safer back home. I decided to take a shower, hit the sack, and go back to Triboro in the morning. Or I could call Mary Ellen Goode. I did that and got an answering machine. I told the machine I'd be back in a week and hoped to get together again.

A week later I surveyed my new digs in the village of Southport, a small but pleasant tourist town situated southeast of Wilmington on the estuary where the Cape Fear River pushes a gazillion gallons of fresh water a day into the Atlantic Ocean. The house itself was a two-story, multi-bedroom affair that rented for obscene sums of money for the five months or so of the summer tourist season and then usually sat empty for the rest of the year. It had spacious wraparound screened porches on both levels and overlooked the river beach and the barrier islands across the Cape Fear estuary. I could see the ferryboat that went over to Fort Fisher ploughing dutifully through a light chop as it approached the landing north of the town. The air smelled of seashore and there was a fine layer of white sand on everything.

I was no longer flying solo, having brought two of my original MCAT team members, Tony Martinelli and Pardee Bell, down from Triboro. Pardee had been one of two black detectives in the MCAT. He was a big guy, two inches taller than I was, who had really enjoyed getting in criminals' faces, especially black criminals, so he could punk 'em out, as he was fond of saying. Everyone thought Pardee had been brought onto the team to provide some in-house muscle, but he happened to have a degree in computer science from NC State and could do some real damage with a desktop. He was married to a whip-smart trial attorney in Triboro, and he'd lasted for about one week in "retirement" from the sheriff's office before said lady lawyer told him to go find something useful to do besides cleaning the house twice a day and generally driving her nuts. He'd been a level-headed, highly focused, and very professional deputy sheriff, and we were delighted when he'd called in to join the old crew at H&S.

Tony Martinelli, on the other hand, was half-crazy, in the southern sense of that term, which connotes wary respect for the truly eccentric. He was a little guy, maybe five-seven or -eight with the right boots on, but an effective cop because no one, bad guys or good guys, knew quite what he would do next. His specialty on the MCAT had been finding and then following persons of interest. We'd learned early on to intervene if Tony had been on someone's tail for more than, say, a day or so, because he would get bored with it and then things were likely to go sideways. With jet-black hair, emotive brown eyes, and a puckish grin on his face, he looked like an altar boy who'd been caught trying out the sacramental wine. Women usually fell all over themselves to take him under their wings when he went out to party.

And, of course, now that I was in a house instead of a hotel, my trusty German shepherds were along for the ride. Frick was an American-bred sable bitch who would happily amputate the extremities of any intruder. I was her human, and she declined to share. Frack, the larger and older of the two, was an all-black East German border-guard model. He had a disconcerting habit of sitting down and staring at strangers instead of running around and barking like too many shepherds did. He had amber, lupine eyes, and lots of people were more than willing to believe me when I told them that Frack was really a wolf. As any dog owner knows, deterrence is ninety percent of the battle.

I watched Aristotle Quartermain coming down the oceanfront street in an elderly but shiny black Mercedes, holding a piece of paper on the steering wheel and counting house numbers. He finally looked up and saw me waving. The beachfront road was guarded by parking meters on the beach side of the street, and he found one with some time left on it. We gathered in the kitchen, where the coffeepot was happily making a fresh batch of Tony tar.

I'd briefed the whole H&S crew back in Triboro about my visit to Wilmington, cautioning them that the information about radiation poisoning was close-hold, at least for the moment. After a collective expression of shock, none of them knew what to make of it, or what to do with Ari Quartermain's offer of employment. There was general agreement that I should go back, with help, and see what we could find out about what had really happened to Allie independent of whatever the feds were up to. I had asked Mel Lindsay to see if she could figure out what Allie's personal business might have been about.

Mel and the office manager had finally managed to unearth a phone number for Allie's sister, who was indeed a Department of Defense schoolteacher at a joint Turkish-American air base. Mel knew from conversations that Allie's sister's first name was Meredith, but she didn't know her last name. They tried Meredith Gardner, but the DOD school system drew a blank on that. They did have a Meredith Thomason at the base in Turkey, so we gave that a try. I'd made the actual call and got a surprise.

The phone connection wasn't great, but it quickly became clear that Ms. Thomason wanted nothing to do with the aftermath of Allie's death. Allie's decision to become a cop in the first place had never met with the family's approval, and the fact that she'd come to a bad end came as no surprise. She'd said this with more than a hint of comeuppance in her voice. She was neither interested in nor capable of making final arrangements. Basically, Allie was estranged from her family. She was as on her own in death as apparently she'd been in life.

I wasn't sure how to respond to that, and I surely didn't understand this woman's total lack of sympathy. I hadn't told her precisely what had happened, and was tempted to when she gave me the brush-off. Then she asked me, as Allie's employers, could we please just "take care of it"? Somewhat appalled, I'd said I would do that and simply hung up on her.

I brought Ari back to the kitchen and introduced him to my crew, both two- and four-legged. There was a big table in the kitchen, so Pardee, Ari, and I plopped there. Tony went upstairs to get something. I offered coffee, but Ari declined when he saw Pardee's spoon freestanding in his cup.

"So," he asked, "what changed your mind?"

I told him about the visit from the Helios physical security posse. He frowned when I told him about Billy the Kid.

"Those guys are mostly ex-military," he said. "Their boss is a retired Army colonel, name of Carl Trask. Nicknamed Snake. He was one of those beret guys—Ranger or Delta Force, something of that ilk. Has been hiring only former military men, and takes himself and his job very seriously."

"As well he should," I said. "Talk about a good terrorist target."

"Not as good as the movies make out, Mr. Richter," he said. "Still, yes, there is a threat, and when we hear submachine-gun fire in the swamps, Colonel Trask provides a measure of comfort."

"Say what?" Pardee asked.

"The government runs intrusion drills on the protected area of the station. They're called force-on-force exercises. The director's office knows when one's coming, but, supposedly, they don't tell Trask. The NRC uses Navy SEALs, or people from the FBI's hostage rescue team. The rule is, once physical security detects a possible intrusion, Trask alerts the station director, who gives him a code word that tells Trask it's a drill. Then they hand out the blank ammo and go play cowboys and Indians with their buddies in the tall weeds."

"What if real bad guys ever penetrated this intrusion exercise schedule?" Tony asked, coming into the kitchen. "Or had some help from the inside?"

I hadn't realized he'd come back downstairs. Being quiet was one of Tony's useful skills. He displayed other traits that were not useful but were always exciting.

"That could be very interesting, I suppose," Ari said.

Tony put a finger to his lips and then spoke very softly. "As interesting as the fact that you were followed here? And that two guys in a PrimEnergy van are pretending to work on a telephone pole while they listen to what's going on in here?"

There was a moment of silence around the table, and then we all got up to take a peek through the front window curtains. A white utility van was parked half a block away, with the PrimEnergy logo conspicuous on its side. The rear doors were open, and two men in coveralls were busy doing something at the base of a telephone pole. Their equipment and uniforms looked convincing, except for the cone of a distant sound concentrator propped inside the van and aimed at our front windows.

Tony stood next to one window, turned his back on the outside world, and pulled out a Glock. He nodded to Pardee and me, and we produced our own weapons. Then he racked his weapon right next to the glass and announced in a loud voice that none of us should shoot until he started it. We each racked our weapons and then watched the "utility" men scamper for cover behind their van. The concentrator seemed to be working very well.

"Okay, I'll take care of this bullshit," Ari said and went out the front door. We all followed him out onto the porch and stood there in plain view of the van, guns in hand just in case this wasn't what it looked like. Ari went to his car, got something out of the glove compartment, and then hustled over to the van, where the two men were starting to stand up now that they realized they'd been had. I wondered if Ari had stopped off to get a weapon, but instead he walked up to them and began firing one of those disposable flash cameras in their faces. They tried to block their faces with their hands, then slammed the van's back doors shut, hopped in, and drove off at a respectable clip.

"Goddamn Trask," he muttered as he came back up the front steps, pocketing the camera.

"You sure?" I asked.

"Yeah, I think I recognized the one guy. We have a recording scanner at the Pass and ID Office that'll confirm it."

"Well, you're obviously consorting with suspicious characters," I said as we put away our weapons and went back into the kitchen. I was relieved that none of the neighbors, if indeed there were any, had been out on their porches.

"Did you tell this young man to check for someone following me?" he asked.

"Nope. He's suspicious by nature and just chock-full of initiative."

Ari grinned at Tony and thanked him for catching the tail. Tony said you're welcome and then excused himself to go check for "smooth," now that we had just chased "rough" away.

Ari blinked at that and then grinned again. "You guys are good," he said.

Tony slipped out the back door while we resumed our conversation at the kitchen table. Quartermain explained what he wanted from us.

"Just as the federal government runs what we call force-on-force drills on the fences," he began, "I have some budget money to run technical intrusion drills on my side of the perimeter."

"Define your side of the perimeter," I said.

"There are three security circles around a nuclear plant: the so-called corporate area, the protected area, and the vital area. Corporate means the public can be there—hunting, fishing, et cetera—if they abide by the company's rules for the use of the land."

"No fences?"

"Nope—the first fence defines the protected area. That takes pass and ID access to get in. That's the area around the industrial plant and its buildings."

"And the vital area?"

"That's where the dragon lives—defined as the area where access makes the release of radiological materials possible."

"That's a little fuzzy, isn't it?"

"By design—the vital area is what we nukes say it is. Think layers. Snake Trask and his people *patrol* the corporate area. They'll *protect* the fenced perimeter; they'll *defend* the vital area, with deadly force if necessary. The system works in reverse, too."

"You mean protecting the rest of us from the reactor?"

"Exactly. The nuclear reaction happens inside a stainless steel reactor vessel. That vessel lives in a concrete, lead, and steel containment dome. The dome lives in a steel building. Trask keeps bad guys out; my people and I keep the dragon in."

"Which puts you in charge."

Ari smiled. "Like I said before, if *my* dragon gets loose, the security of the physical perimeter is no longer the issue."

"Can it get loose?" Pardee asked.

"Yes, most likely through human error, compounded by an instrumentation failure," Ari said. "The Russians hold the world records, plural. The Chernobyl melt was a classic example of unsafe design compounded by human error. The low-order detonation in the Chelyabinsk district back in 1957 was simple Communist stupidity."

He went on to describe how the Russians had kept filling a radioactive waste tank until it overpressurized, started a partial reaction, and then literally exploded, contaminating a six-hundred-square-mile area. They then took to dumping their waste into a nearby lake. When the lake dried up in a drought and the radioactive sediments blew away in the wind, it created a no-man's land the size of Maryland, which exists to this day.

"How about our own Three Mile Island?" I asked.

"The RCS, that's the reactor control system, detected a problem and shut itself down. Should have been end of story. But then a valve opened and stayed open, while reporting to the control room that it was closed. That drained out all the cooling water."

"If the reactor was shut down, why was that a problem?"

"Because even after the fission reaction shuts down, the residual heat of decay is still very high. Without cooling water, it can melt the core assembly. That's what happened at TMI before they realized the instruments were lying. What's forgotten is that it all stayed inside the containment structure, that movie not withstanding."

"We're not exactly qualified in nuclear engineering," I pointed out.

"I know," he said, "but I'm talking about helping me with a different problem."

"Somebody who *is* technically qualified, and who might be screwing around?" I said.

"Exactly." He sipped some coffee and made a face. "Like what happened to Ms. Gardner."

"So you *do* think that came from your plant?"

"Officially? That would be an unequivocal no. And I'll defend that position for as long as I want to keep my job."

"But."

"Yeah. But. Fortunately for PrimEnergy and Helios, the

feds are focusing elsewhere. There's apparently been intel that the Islamists have given up the idea of smuggling in a nuclear bomb in favor of trying something with nuclear waste."

"A dirty bomb instead of a Hiroshima bomb."

"Yeah. A plutonium or a highly enriched uranium bomb has a very distinctive signature, and the ports—airports, seaports—are pretty much wired for that. Nuclear waste products, by definition, come in radiation-tight containers. No signature."

"And Wilmington has a big container port," Pardee said.

"Big enough. Not as big as Long Beach or L.A., but big enough, and about to double in size. A radioactive DOA in Wilmington set off all sorts of alarms. They're going through the motions at Helios, but officially no one really believes that's where this stuff came from. It would, simply stated, be much too hard."

"But not impossible?" I asked.

He stood with his back to the sink and shrugged. "Actually, as an engineer, I'd think it would be very difficult, but, no, not impossible. And as the security officer it's my job to exercise a little paranoia here."

"You have somebody in mind?" I asked.

"It's not so much one individual," he said. "Look—technical security depends on three things in our industry: rigid adherence to approved engineering practices, a personnel reliability program, and the power industry's version of what the military calls the two-man rule."

"I believe," I said, and he smiled.

"Okay. Briefly, here's the idea. The two-man rule means no one individual is ever left in a situation where he could put the atomic reaction process at risk. Personnel reliability, or what we call fitness to serve, means that a guy who gets a DUI or gropes an undercover cop in a public men's room gets looked at to see if he should keep his ticket as a plant or reactor operator. And procedure means just that: line-by-line read-back procedures for everything that happens in the control room or in the plant itself. One guy reads the operating procedure, say, for lining up the steam system, and a second guy reads it back to him before actually doing it."

"That must be really slow."

"It's tedious, but reliable. It also requires a certain degree of technical openness. Nothing happens behind closed doors."

"So?"

"So, if somebody tapped a source of radioactive water in the Helios plant, he would have to have violated all three wedges of technical security."

I thought about the appearance of a tail on Quartermain's visit out here today. "Would he need some help from the physical security department?"

He nodded. "Yes, I'd think so, and that's the one division at Helios which is comparatively opaque. There's a cast of dozens involved in bringing a reactor online and feeding the grid. But most of the time, nobody knows what the hell Trask's people are doing."

"Except following you around and breaking into my hotel room, presumably just because you and I met."

"Well, there is that."

"But I thought Trask worked for you—why not just fire his ass?"

"Truth?"

"Please."

"My theory is that he's got something on the director, because every time I've voiced my 'concerns' up the line, I get shut down. Can't prove that, of course, but that's what I'm beginning to think."

"So you want us to take a look at them? Trask, his people, and any possible ties to the director?"

"Yeah."

Before Quartermain could elaborate, Tony Martinelli came back into the kitchen from outside. He looked pleased with himself, which worried me a little bit. He saw the expression on my face and waved me off.

"It's cool," he said. "But not what I expected."

"Ree-port."

He looked at Quartermain and raised his eyebrows, as if to ask, *Okay for him to hear this?* I motioned for him to continue.

"Okay, so I go around the block, walk towards downtown for five minutes, turn around, and come back towards the house on the beachfront street. Just another tourist, out for some fresh salt air and a cigarette. And one block away, parked on the beach side of the street, I come upon a Bureau ride, complete with two specials sitting in the front seat trying to look inconspicuous."

"In their suits and ties. At the beach."

"But they were such inconspicuous suits."

"Can you describe the agents—a man and a woman, perhaps?"

"Negative. Just the usual Buroids with the usual sunglasses and happy faces. They looked bored."

"So lemme guess: You stopped, stared, waved, said hi-there, peed on their tires, and then took their pictures?"

Tony feigned profound disappointment. "Absolutely not, boss," he said. "I never said hi-there. However, I did notice their parking meter was expired, so I sicced a meter maid on them."

I had to grin. "And then watched them flash some creds."

"Aren't you proud of me?" As in, lots of other options had come to mind.

"I am, Tony, I am," I said, counting myself lucky that he hadn't crawled under some cars and attached a towing chain from their rear axle to a tree. He'd seen that in a movie and often said he'd like to try it.

"So, the question is: Who're they watching?" Pardee asked, sticking as always to business.

"Great question," I said, turning to Ari. "You, us, Trask's snoops, or all of the above?"

"I have no idea," he said.

"Well, let's find out," I said. "Why don't you leave, and we'll see if they follow you out of here. If they stay put, we're the target. If not . . . But before you go, Pardee here is going to help us create a way we can communicate securely. In the meantime, Tony and I will step out for some more of that salt air."

I left Pardee and Ari in the kitchen to sort out secure comms. I asked Tony to get us into a position from which we could watch both the house and the watchers when Ari drove off. Tony had parked his car behind the house, so we used that to get set up behind the Bureau vehicle in one of the metered spots on the beach.

After about five minutes, we watched Ari come down the front steps of our rental unit and go to his car. *Don't turn around and wave, Ari,* I thought. *Just get in and drive away.* The mental telepathy must have worked because that's what he did. We waited. The two agents were just silhouettes in the car parked ahead of us, but we could see one of them talking on a cell phone. Then they cranked up their Bucar and surprised us by executing a U-turn.

"Down 'scope," I said, and we both slid down in the front seat of Tony's car. When they had passed us, we drove back to the house.

Pardee had brought some electronics gear, including two laptops, which were running in parallel in his version of a baby supercomputer. Using these, he had created a Web site on which Ari and I could post and retrieve messages using a secure password system. He hosted the site on our office server back in Triboro, so there'd be a cutout.

He also reported that our office manager had closed out Allie's affairs by notifying her ex-husbands of her demise and sending her personal office effects to the sister in Turkey, no matter what she'd said. Fortunately, there were no remains to deal with, as the federal government still had that problem bagged up in a lead-lined vault somewhere. It was personally disturbing to think about Allie being stored in a locker like a side of meat, but, as Pardee gently reminded me, that wasn't Allie. I knew he was right, but still.

It was noon, so we went out to find a place for lunch. Southport had a decent selection of lunch places, and we found something suitable on the main drag. The beauty of a small tourist town was that no one paid the three of us the slightest bit of attention. You were either born there or you were "from away," like the Yankees say.

After a quick bite, we left the café and walked back to the car. I heard Tony swear and saw the parking ticket under the wiper blade. Then I saw that the meter was green. He lifted a folded piece of paper, read it, and handed it to me. There was a single line that read: *ET come home. Now would be nice.* It was signed with a large letter *C*.

"Sneaky futher-muckers," I said, looking around. Tony grunted and pointed, and there, across the street, was the Bureau car we'd watched drive away. Apparently, not very far away. The agents waggled fingers at us. Tony rubbed his nose with his middle finger in response. The agent driving the car put his hands up to his face in mock horror.

"Okay, let's go back and face the music," I said.

"Who's C.?" Tony asked.

C., as I'd suspected, turned out to be Creeps himself, minus his ditzy assistant this time. The other agents had followed us back to the house and were now waiting outside, reading magazines. Creeps was standing on the front porch when we got there, so I was pretty sure he hadn't been inside. The shepherds were in there, staring out the front windows and definitely not looking like Welcome Wagon material.

I introduced my two helper-bees, and then we all went in. Since Pardee had set up his computers in the kitchen, I invited Creeps to sit in the living room, which meant that he had to fit that gangly, Lincolnesque frame of his into one of the sandy wicker rocking chairs. Wicker apparently is the furniture of choice for a beach house; everything in the living room was made of it.

"Welcome to our humble rental unit," I said. Pardee and Tony leaned on opposite sides of the living room entryway. "Have we been bad?"

Creeps rubbed his hands together while he thought about what he was going to say. "I certainly hope not, Mr. Richter," he said, "but, given the nature of our last conversation in Wilmington, your Bureau just wanted to make sure you hadn't returned to investigate Ms. Gardner's, um, unfortunate demise."

"You were quite clear, I thought," I said. "Back out, stay out, and assist my Bureau in any way I can and should as a good citizen. Right?"

"Yes, indeed," he said warmly, smiling his best undertaker smile. Given that he'd signed his little love note "C.," he had to be putting at least some of that bullshit on. "So: What, may I ask, *are* you doing down here with or for the technical security director of the Helios power station?"

"A job of work," I replied, recalling Ari's quaint phrase.

Creeps raised his eyebrows in a go-on expression.

"The details of which have not yet been made entirely clear," I continued, fudging just a little. "Something to do with overlapping jurisdiction within the plant's security apparatus. He's the technical guy, and there's a separate department that handles physical security. We'll probably know more tomorrow."

Creeps frowned. It took the frown a couple of seconds to spread across that huge, lachrymose face. "How does this bear on the Gardner case?"

Clever Creeps. You never knew where he was going with his questions, but he probably did, and all the time. "It doesn't," I said. "At least as far as we know. Besides, we're not supposed to get involved in the Gardner case, remember? I guess you could talk to Mr. Quartermain."

The frown vanished. "Oh, yes, indeed," he said. "We'll be talking to Mr. Quartermain, at some length, I suspect."

"Well, while we're on the subject of Allie Gardner, do you guys think that evil shit came from the plant or some other source?" I saw Tony and Pardee, who were standing out of Creeps's line of sight, trying to suppress grins.

Creeps did a tsk-tsk number. "Mr. Richter, really," he said disapprovingly. "I do hope you're not intending to mess around with your Bureau. You know how we hate that. Although I can tell you this much: Right now, the NRC people don't think the radioactive substance did come from Helios.

There's simply no way to do that without exposing the taker to the same radiation that would ultimately kill the takee, if you follow me."

"Yeah, that occurred to me, too," I lied. "But, honestly, I think Quartermain wants us for something totally unrelated. As I understand the politics of the situation, PrimEnergy wants to put some distance between what happened to Allie and the Helios station."

Creeps nodded, but then changed the subject. "Under what modalities is Mr. Quartermain engaging H&S Investigations?" he asked.

I explained the contract money Ari said he had for security intrusion exercises. Creeps nodded again, as if he knew all about that program.

"You understand, Mr. Richter," he said, "that those are federal dollars? And that any such intrusion exercises, whether force-on-force, tabletop war games, or otherwise, are supervised by the NRC? Which is itself a federal organization?"

"Makes sense," I said. "But for us contractor weenies, a dollar is a dollar. We agree on a statement of work, a price, and the client's boundary conditions. Then we do our thing, write a report, and send in the bill. As long as he can write the check, we don't much care which budget line item governs the money."

"Perhaps you should," he said. "Because federal money brings federal oversight, and your Bureau is reasonably competent in the oversight department."

"Oh, for God's sake," I said, tiring of the games. "We know the rules, Special Agent. I told Quartermain that if we stumble onto anything that faintly resembles evidence of a real security problem, we're obligated to take it to you guys. Why don't you ask him?"

"We certainly shall do just that," he declared. "Allow me to be frank: What happened to Ms. Gardner might be a one-off, or it might be the first indication of a much more serious problem, one we've actually been anticipating, and with no little trepidation, I might add."

I recalled what Ari had said. "You think someone's finally managed to get something nasty through that big-ass container port upriver?"

That surprised him, and people didn't surprise Brother Creeps that often. He wagged a long, bony finger at me. "You be very careful talking about that little theory," he said. "You people intrude into anything along those lines, and you might find yourself languishing on a certain Caribbean island."

I put up my hands in mock surrender. "Got it, okay? As I've said, we're not quite sure what Mr. Quartermain has in mind for us."

"For what it's worth, Mr. Richter, we think he wants to use you, as a genuine outsider, to demonstrate that his technical security system is intact, and that, ipso facto, no radiological release ever occurred at Helios."

"I thought the NRC was going to do some kind of isotope analysis. What happened to that?"

He thought about that for a moment, obviously trying to decide if it was prudent to tell us anything at all. Then he nodded. "Yes. Well. The initial analysis was inconclusive. The residual radiation in Ms. Gardner's tissue has decayed along with the tissue."

"Was that the only way they could *prove* the stuff came out of Helios?"

"The only technically conclusive proof, yes."

It was my turn to think. It seemed to me that Quartermain was basically going on the offensive by bringing us in; the NRC wouldn't be able to tag Helios with a radiological release. If we couldn't find a hole in their security, then he'd done what the company wanted him to do—cover their corporate asses.

"What would be the consequences if someone were to discover, inadvertently, of course, that it *did* come out of there?" I asked.

"The NRC would shut them down, and then the real fun would begin, Mr. Richter. So take some care, and remember whose side you're on when it comes to national security versus corporate liability. If there's a dangerous hole in the plant's security, and you spot it, I'd better know about it before Mr. Quartermain does, understood?"

I told him it was, and he levered himself out of the creaking wicker chair. He stared down at the floor for a moment, as if making sure it was going to hold him. Then he looked back at me. "We're operating under different rules these days, Mr. Richter. The war against terror has seen federal law enforcement crossing some lines which we used to hold fairly sacred."

"Meaning?"

"Meaning, these days, if you interfere, you can disappear."

Then he left us.

I breathed a sigh of relief after letting him out the front door.

"Now that's a weird m-f," Tony said. "Does he always speak in code like that?"

I went back into the kitchen and sat down. "That wasn't code, guys. There's something seriously amiss down here, and this time, I think we're going to have to play by their rules. If it weren't for Allie's involvement, I'd back us out of this right now."

"Allie's beyond caring, boss," Pardee pointed out, "and we don't know squat about a nuclear power plant. What exactly is it this guy wants us to do?"

I still wasn't quite sure myself, so I went sideways. "Why don't you bring up the site and see if we've got mail?"

He did and we did. One message from Ari. He told us to report to the Helios administration building to begin processing for vehicle passes and ID cards.

We took two vehicles. The shepherds and I went in my Suburban; Tony and Pardee went in Pardee's black Crown Vic. My Suburban was a plain vanilla 2500 series with the rear seats flattened to accommodate the mutts. Pardee's ride was every inch the cop car—tinted windows, souped-up mill, several antennas, and those all-rubber semi-slick tires engineered for extreme road-handling. I think he missed being in

Major Crimes. Also he liked to speed, and that getup plus a few other secret signs and totems pretty much guaranteed a pass from the state police.

We took Highway 133 up to the plant's main entrance and turned in. It was a beautifully landscaped entrance that gave onto a four-lane, undivided parkway. As we turned in we heard a low siren wail in the distance. It sounded like the shift-change whistle at a manufacturing plant. The road made a broad S-turn once we got past the main entrance, and then a second one lined us up with the main gates. Somewhat to our surprise, we found a squad of armed and flak-jacketed men arrayed across the gate area as we approached. I slowed the Suburban and lowered my driver's side window. Tony pulled in right behind me. One of the guards stepped forward, while the others spread out their line, keeping what looked like Colt M4s at a loose port arms.

"Yes, sir, can we help you?" the guard asked, eyeing the two big dogs behind me. He was courteous, but warily so. I realized then that the siren had gone off when some invisible sensor detected unauthorized vehicles approaching the main gates. I explained that we were guests of Dr. Quartermain and that we were supposed to meet him at the pass office. The guard nodded and told us that this was the plant entrance and that the admin office was another half mile down the road. We'd apparently driven right by it. He showed us where we could U-turn and wished us a nice day. The line of armed guards had relaxed fractionally, but they were still in position to shoot the two vehicles to pieces if that need were to arise.

The admin building looked like every other admin building I'd been in. I told the guys to leave their weapons in their vehicle. I unstrapped my own .45 and jammed it down between the seat and the center console. I set Frick up in a harness and leash rig and took her into the building with me. I lowered the windows and instructed Frack to guard the Suburban with his life. He promptly lay down for a nap.

Once inside, we were taken to Quartermain's office, where we were met by a thirty-something brunette hottie who'd obviously been told to expect us. If she was impressed by the sight of two large and one medium-sized, very fit men, one of them being attached to an equally fit German shepherd, she gave no sign of it. She eyed Frick and said that the dog might present a problem. I told her that the dog was a service dog and that federal law required admission of such dogs if they were harnessed, leashed, and suitably trained.

She bent forward to address Frick. "Are you suitably trained?" she asked. Tony made a small noise in his throat when she bent forward, but Frick merely looked at her for a second and then just barely wrinkled her lip.

"Why yes you are," the young woman said, straightening up. "We won't mess with your dog."

I had to admit that it had been fun watching her straighten up, and she also was no dummy. "The dog is just part of the act," I said. "But: There is another one out front."

"Then we'll need two dog passes, won't we," she said and went to get the paperwork. Watching her walk away continued to be fun. I asked her where Mr. Quartermain was. "In a meeting," she called over her shoulder. I asked if Mr. Trask was in the building.

"You mean *Colonel* Trask?" she asked, just to make sure we knew how to address His Lordship.

"Older guy, reddish gray hair, face like a hatchet? Really pleased with himself?"

She turned her face away for a moment, trying to control a smile. The nameplate on her desk read SAMANTHA YOUNG, ADMINISTRATIVE ASSISTANT. Tony was still standing in the doorway, the veritable picture of a man fallen deeply in lust. Tony did that often.

"Did you really want to see the colonel?" she asked.

"Actually? No. You see one colonel, you've kind of seen them all."

She nodded. "I asked," she said, "because he's supposed to sign your security passes. Is that possibly going to be a problem?"

"Why don't you get Dr. Quartermain to handle that," I suggested. "Probably save everybody a lot of time."

At that moment, Aristotle Quartermain came into the office through a second door. "Handle what, Sam?" he asked. She explained the problem, and he waved it off. "I'll sign these passes," he said. "Give all your info to Sam here, and then let's talk. I need them to have vehicle passes and smart-tags, too, Sam, okay?"

We did the paper drill, took mug shots and thumbprints, and then sat down with Quartermain in his inner office while young Samantha went down the hall to emboss and laminate our ID cards. I parked Frick over in one corner, where she decided to stare at our host. He thought that was pretty cool. Pardee had to snatch Tony by the collar to keep him from following Samantha. Quartermain had noticed.

"Ain't she something?" he said admiringly. "Hired her about a year ago when my original assistant up and moved to Florida for some strange reason. She goes for her noonday run in this little gold spandex outfit? Now half the guys at the station are out exercising. *And* she can shoot, too. That's a great dog you got there. He'll need a pass, too, though."

"It's a she, and Samantha is getting the passes."

Tony had closed his eyes, probably trying to visualize the spandex outfit. Tony's idea of exercise was to stow two cases of beer in his fridge, not just one, but that might change. Pardee helpfully told him to stop drooling.

I told Quartermain about Special Agent Caswell's visit, noting that that was the second time we'd had an "exchange of views," and that between Trask and the FBI, the hospitality angle for H&S Investigations was disappointing.

"Yeah," he said. "I'm not too surprised. Let me bring you up to speed."

He told us that the first attempt to retrieve radioactive particles from Allie's body had been a bust, which corroborated what Creeps had told us. The docs were pretty sure that whatever it was, water had been the medium and alpha particles the radiation vector. Then he took us all over to the visitors' center, which had been closed to the public in the wake of the 9/11 disaster. There he showed us a diorama of the power station, a mockup of the control room, and some animated flowcharts that showed how the reactor system worked.

"As you can see, the nuclear reaction provides the heat. Some of the water that cools that reaction boils into steam and goes over here to the power plant, where the steam spins a turbine, which spins a generator, which makes big-time juice. The spent steam goes down here to a condenser, where cooling water from the river turns it from vapor to liquid water, and then it's pumped back into the reactor vessel, where the whole cycle is repeated."

"And that water is radioactive?" Pardee asked.

"The whole reactor vessel and everything in it is highly radioactive, but only because it's an integral part of an ongoing nuclear fission reaction. It's also pressurized—it's a boiler, after all. So between the heat, the radiation, and the steam, it's not something you can just reach into and get yourself a container of water. You'd be dead in about an hour if you tried."

"So where's this moonpool you talked about?" I asked.

He took us to another wall chart diagram, which was titled THE REFUELING SYSTEM. "The technical name is the spent fuel storage pool. As fuel elements outlive their usefulness, they're taken down from the reactor core and transferred underneath the reactor building to an adjacent building, which contains the storage pool. There they stay until the government gets a permanent storage site up and running."

"And that area's radioactive?" I asked.

"Sure," he said. "It's a lot like the reactor vessel itself, except the fuel elements aren't bundled close together because we no longer want them to create a fission reaction. But the more recently they've been put into the moonpool, the hotter they are."

"So what killed Allie could have come from there, as opposed to the main reactor itself?"

He paused for a moment. "*If* the stuff came from a power plant, it is much more likely to have come out of a moonpool than the reactor vessel, for the basic reason that the moonpool is not pressurized. As I said, the reactor vessel is a closed, very hot, radioactive, and pressurized system. The pool's a pool—atmospheric pressure, forty-five, fifty feet deep, a little scary-looking, but it's just a pool."

"Can we see it?" I asked.

"Gonna show you the whole shebang, Mr. Investigator, soon as those ID cards are ready."

Three hours later, we returned to the admin building, following an extensive tour of the power plant. Quartermain himself conducted the tour, and it was obvious he knew his stuff as a nuclear engineer. We'd hit that I-believe button several times in the course of the tour. The shepherd attracted lots of stares, but most people in the plant seemed to be paying close attention to business, which was comforting.

We hadn't actually seen either reactor—there were two at Helios, Unit One and Unit Two—and, as Ari pointed out, one never did want to actually see the reactor, because that would mean that its containment had been breached. The last persons to have seen an operating reactor had been at Chernobyl, and they were all very dead.

"You see one when it's being built and installed, and you see it again when the plant gets decommissioned. Otherwise, you don't want to see it."

"Why do power plants get decommissioned?" I'd asked.

"Metallurgy," he'd responded. "After twenty, twenty-five years of living in the energy flux of a uranium fission reaction, metal alloys can change state. The piping, the valves, the pumps, the fuel control mechanisms, even the instrumentation sensors become embrittled or otherwise metallurgically altered, sometimes to the point where the materials they were made out of no longer have the strength characteristics they had when they were brand-new."

"So they shut 'em down, permanently? As opposed to replacing all that stuff?"

"Cheapest option," he said. "The military does the same thing—they refuel their ship plants once, maybe twice, but when a warship's reactor systems wear out, they scrap the whole boat. I've seen satellite shots of the Soviet naval bases with entire submarines rusting in the mudflats because the reactors gave out. Two, three billion dollars a copy. Talk about nuclear waste. Incredible."

The moonpool had looked just the way Ari had described it: a large, deep concrete structure filled with ethereal blue-green water. There were detachable glass partition walls along the sides, and steel railings at the base of those walls. The dim shapes glimmering down at the bottom were the spent fuel, encased in gleaming metal tubes and arranged in a geometric shape that prevented fission from restarting in the pool.

"This is the area that worries Snake Trask," Ari had told us. "In the other type of power plant, the pools are below-ground. As you can see, this one is mostly aboveground. A commercial airplane crash here could theoretically split the walls and dump the water."

"And that would be bad?"

"Yes, because we'd probably get a fire or a hydrogen explosion and a big radiation release. There are systems in place to refill the pool; that's one of the reasons these BWR plants are positioned near big bodies of water. But still, the moonpool is probably the most fragile part of a boiling water reactor plant."

It was Colonel Trask himself who was waiting for us, or rather Ari, when we got back to Ari's office following our atomic walkabout. He did not appear to be a happy camper. He demanded to speak to Dr. Quartermain in private, but the closed door didn't afford them much privacy. As we stood around in the reception area trying not to stare at the lovely Samantha, we could hear Trask detonating on the subject of issuing clearance and physical access to people like us. I couldn't hear what Ari was saying in reply, but, whatever it was, it wasn't mollifying Trask very much. It was also clear from all the racket that the security chief and his people intended to make our stay on the plant grounds difficult.

I quietly told Pardee and Tony to go on back to the beach house and wait for me there, and meanwhile to see what they could do about getting us a boat.

"What kind of boat?" Tony asked.

"Twenty-footer or thereabouts, shallow draft, inboard engine, with a radar set if possible. Not for the open ocean. Strictly for river work. Try the marinas around Southport, or maybe Oak Island."

"We drive, or they drive?" Pardee asked.

"We drive," I said.

It sounded like the choleric colonel was winding down in there, so I asked Samantha if she could escort my people to the egress. I sat down in one corner of the reception area with Frick parked next to me on her leash. Trask glared at the two of us as he stalked out of Quartermain's office. He was wearing green Army utilities this time and a large sidearm. A moment later, Ari appeared in his doorway and motioned for me to come in.

"Was that fun?" I asked, shutting his door behind me. If he was perturbed, he didn't show it. He waved me to a chair.

"It's all he knows how to do," he said. "Shout and bluster. You know, asses will be kicked, hides flayed, things will be turned every which way but loose—all the standard Army bullshit."

"He works for you—why don't you indulge in some of the standard bullshit right back at him?"

"Because he's useful," he said. "He's got a perpetual red-ass, and he is completely unpredictable. Since nobody knows where he's going to turn up next, he tends to keep his *and* my people on their toes."

"I can't imagine nuclear engineers putting up with verbal abuse like that," I said.

"Yeah, the hoo-ah stuff doesn't play in technical security, because the assumption there is that we're all focused on the same thing: keeping the dragon in its cave. Physical security assumes the good guys are in here, while everyone out there is a bad guy until proven otherwise."

"Why the perpetual red-ass?"

Ari ran a hand over his gleaming scalp. "He's convinced the country's gone soft, especially on this war on terrorism. America has lost its manhood, is embracing appeasement, throwing away good soldiers' lives in shitholes like Iraq and Afghanistan, paying court to billionaire Hollywood marshmallows, stuff like that."

"He may have a point there," I said.

"Yeah, well, it's a democracy, isn't it. Personally, I think it's more of a classic case of a man confusing the deterioration of his own aging faculties with the rest of the nation. You know, grumpy old men. Old guys are always saying everything's going to hell. Not like it used to be in my day, by God, when I had to walk three miles to school through ten feet of snow, et cetera."

"How old is Trask?"

"Mid-sixties, actually." He saw my surprise. "I know—he doesn't look it."

"Where'd he get the nickname?"

"He apparently likes snakes. You know, some kind of offbeat hobby."

We talked contract and agreed on the broad provisions of a statement of work. "I have a request," I said when we were done with that.

"Shoot."

"I've sent my people home, but right now I'd like to take a little outside tour with my vehicle. Drive around the plant perimeter. Outside the protected area, but inside the corporate zone. Get the lay of the public land."

"A lot of it's swamp," he said. "About twelve hundred acres in all, including farmland and designated wetlands. Stay on the roads, and don't mess with any protected area fences—they're wired six ways from Sunday. If you do run into the security people, show those badges. The worst they can do is escort you back to the main gate. You work for me, not them."

"Gosh, you think I'll run into Trask?"

"Isn't that why you want to go out there?" he asked with a grin.

By sundown I was parked along the banks of the inlet canal, a man-made baby river that branched off the much larger

Cape Fear River. It had been built to provide cooling water for the turbine steam condensers in the generator hall. I'd driven around the fields and ponds and swamps for about forty minutes before finding the spot I wanted. It was getting dark when Trask's people finally showed themselves. I picked up a distant tail about halfway through my excursion. It looked like a Bronco or similarly boxy SUV, but they kept far enough back that I couldn't tell how many people were in the vehicle. Ari had given me a road map of the so-called corporate area, and I'd meandered over most of it.

I was out of my vehicle, taking pictures of the power plant in the distance, when they finally made their move. The complex was now blurring into a twinkling cluster of sodium vapor lights silhouetting the big buildings in the center when the Bronco came in, skidding to a stop from an unnecessarily high-speed approach. Three doors popped open, and three security guys piled out, all decked out in partial SWAT costumes and brandishing stubby assault rifles of some kind. I waited for the *Freeze, motherfucker!* but instead two of them spread out into covering positions behind the headlights while the third approached me. His clear plastic faceplate revealed white bandages on his nose and forehead, and I recognized Billy the Kid. I didn't see Trask, and I didn't recognize the other two guys.

"Let's see some identification," he said, keeping his rifle at port arms and pretending we'd never met.

I wanted to point out that I was in the public domain area of the complex, but instead I just lifted the chain with my plant ID cards over my head and handed them over. He pocketed them with one hand while keeping his weapon ready.

"Those are not valid," he announced. He hadn't even so much as glanced at them.

"How would you know?" I asked. "Or can't you read?"

"Because our office didn't issue them," he said with a hint of triumph in his voice. "You'll have to come with us."

"Where we going, Billy?" I asked, just so the other two guys would know I'd recognized him. "And by the way, isn't this the public area?"

"You were seen conducting surveillance of the power plant," he said, coming closer to get right in my face. "We have you on camera. Turn around."

"No," I said, putting my hands on my hips. I was about an inch taller than he was and a whole lot bigger. "I'm authorized to be here and, for that matter, inside the protected area if I want, by the director of *technical* security. Your boss's boss, as I understand it. He told me you had no authority over me unless I showed up in an unauthorized place, such as within the vital area."

Billy was visibly angry now, so I slowly positioned myself to deflect any sudden moves. I could see that his forearms were trembling, meaning that he wanted to club me with that weapon. The other two remained in position, but they didn't seem to be getting excited just because Billy was.

"I said turn around; *do* it!" he yelled.

"Make me, Billy," I replied, and then I whistled. The shepherds came out of their hides in the underbrush from behind the other two guards. Each one grabbed a mouthful of a guard's wrist before the men were even aware the dogs were there. They both yelled in surprise, but they also both had the sense to make no sudden moves. Billy reacted by taking one step backward and swinging his weapon around, but then he, too, froze when he saw that he couldn't shoot the dogs without hitting his two buddies. I itched to just clock him right there and then, but there really wasn't any need.

"This is a great time to be very still," I announced to the other two guys. "You twitch, those two will each amputate a hand. You guys understand me?"

Both of them nodded quickly, trying not to look down into those intent canine eyes. Their faces were red in the Bronco's taillights. Even with semi-SWAT gear on, they had to be feeling close to fifty pounds per square inch of jaw pressure, and that was just the I-got-you squeeze.

At that moment, the fourth door on the Bronco opened. Colonel Trask stepped out into the headlights and walked over to where Billy and I were standing.

"Billy?" he said.

"Yes, sir?"

"You are so fucking fired," Trask said. "Gimme that."

Before Billy could respond, Trask took his weapon away from him, retrieved my IDs, and told him to get into the backseat of the Bronco. Then he looked at me and bobbed his head in the direction of the shepherds. I called them off and they trotted over to me, taking up positions on either side of me and locking on to Trask. He looked down, flashed an admiring grin, and then told the other guards to take the Bronco back to the plant and wait there for him. He handed over Billy's weapon to one of them as they left.

Once the Bronco had driven away, Trask and I strolled over to the bank of the inlet canal and stared out over the swamps at the cluster of lights around the plant. The inlet canal was a good hundred yards across, and the water was deceptively still. On the other side of the plant, where the hot water came out of the main condensers, two huge nozzles from the plant blew steaming water five hundred feet down a concrete exit channel. There had to be a big current under the surface on the inlet side.

"It's pretty out here," he said, handing me back my IDs. "But don't try this in the summertime."

"Mosquitoes?"

He fished out some cigarettes, offered me one, which I declined, and lit up. "Yeah, buddy," he said. "They arrive in formation, take your vehicle first, eat that, and then they come back for you."

"This a truce?" I asked.

He gave me a sideways look that was half glare, half frustration. "I've got the NRC, the FBI, PrimEnergy's head of security, federal, state, and county environmental engineers, local law, and now you wandering around in my perimeter. How would you feel?"

"I guess I'd have issues with all that," I said.

He made a disgusted noise. "Issues? *Issues?* I hate that fucking word. You sound like some goddamned liberal. *Issues,* my ass. There is no way somebody took a cesium cocktail out of this plant, I don't care what anybody says. We would have had any number of gamma detectors screaming bloody murder before they ever got to the first fence. Not to mention the fact that the guy's hand bones would be glowing through his skin by now. They're looking in the wrong place."

"Maybe it wasn't cesium," I said.

"Whatever—same rules apply. They're searching the wrong place."

"What's the right place, then?" I asked.

He pointed across the mile or so of swamps and inlets to the cluster of lights flooding the container port upriver. "Right over there," he said. "That's where it came from, and there's probably more of it there right now. That place is a fucking turnstile for terrorists. Ten zillion pounds of stuff comes through there every day from all over the world, and they physically inspect—are you ready for this?—*none* of it."

"From what little I know about it, I'd tend to agree with you," I said, thinking back to my last conversation with Creeps. "I think the federal crowd here has to rule Helios out before the main focus returns across the river."

He took a deep breath and then let it out. "Maybe," he said. "But then I can't figure out why Quartermain has brought someone like you into it."

"Someone like me?"

"Oh, c'mon, you have zero expertise in the field of nuclear energy or industrial security."

"Let me ask you something—do you get advance warning when there's going to be one of those force-on-force intrusion drills?"

He looked sideways at me again. "Yeah, we do. Otherwise, someone might get shot."

"What's your record, then?" I asked. "The bad guys ever get through?"

"That's nobody's business but ours."

I smiled. "Let me put it another way," I said. "Your force-on-force drills ever assume the other side has inside help?"

He thought about that before answering me. "Possibly."

"So how do you do that—someone role-plays, right? Someone's designated to unlock a door or look the other way, and then you guys have to run that scenario to ground."

"What's your point?"

"Hypothetically, you use one of the Helios nukes to do that, or does one of your own security force people act the part of a bad nuke?"

"One of ours," he said. "Hypothetically."

"Hypothetically, right. But suppose there's a real one in there somewhere, some engineer who might actually let a bad guy in if the bribe money was good enough, or the blackmail dangerous enough—you drill for that, do you?"

"That's Quartermain's—" he began, then stopped.

"Unh-hunh," I said. "That's Quartermain's bailiwick. Look, my people and I are not going to fuck around, cutting fences or trying to plant a fake bomb in the reactor building. What we work on out there in the world is mainly people-hunting. I've brought a surveillance expert and a computer hacker with me. We're going to look hard at Quartermain's program, not yours. And for the record, I'd just as soon do that without having to deal with guys in SWAT gear jumping out of the bushes all the time. That shit irritates my dogs."

He stared out over the canal for a half minute. "Maybe we can work something out," he said finally.

"Were those your people we ran off in Southport? The two guys pretending to be PrimEnergy utility workers while they pointed an acoustic cone at our windows?"

He frowned and shook his head. "Negative," he said. "We don't work off-site."

I gave him a spare-me look.

"The Hilton?" he said. "That was unofficial. How'd you run 'em off?"

I told him, and he grinned.

"How'd you get your nickname?" I asked.

"My degree was in biology," he said. "Herpetology, to be exact. I find snakes to be more predictable animals than most humans."

Then his phone began to chirp. He stepped away from me, listened, swore, and snapped it shut.

"What now?" I asked.

"There's been another one," he said. "They got a radiation hit on a container." He pointed with his chin at the forest of lighted gantry cranes upriver. "Over there, in the port." He gave me a triumphant look. "See?" he said. "Told you that shit didn't come from here."

Then my phone rang.

"That'll be Quartermain," Trask said.

It was.

Tony, Pardee, and I met him at the Hilton, since none of us really knew our way around Wilmington yet. He was in the lounge having some coffee. He signaled the waitress to bring us some when he saw us.

"So," I said, sitting down. "You and Helios off the hook?"

"Temporarily," he said. "They got a radiation hit down in the container port. They have monitors all over the place, and each truck leaving the docks goes through two radiation scanners, one they know about, one they don't."

"What constitutes a hit?"

"They're looking for gamma, primarily," he said. "Gamma radiation indicates enriched uranium or plutonium, the bomb stuff. But any radionuclide will do it, and if a detector goes off, they lock down the entire port."

"Bet that's popular."

"Oh, yeah. A colossal backup of cargo, containers hanging in midair. Ships that were supposed to sail at midnight missing their departure windows. Instant financial impact. *Big* deal."

"Tough shit," I said. "There is a war on, or so I hear."

"Yeah, but that's why they called us, among others. They wanted an instrument decon team from the Helios nuclear safety office. They've got radiation on or in a container but can't find a source object."

"How do we fit in?"

"I want you to see how an actual radiation incident is handled."

He reached down and brought up a briefcase, opened it, and gave each of us a radiation dose monitor called a thermo-luminescent dosimeter, or TLD. It looked like a Dick Tracy wrist radio. I'd seen everyone in the plant wearing one, or more, and we'd been given temporary TLDs for our tour.

"These are your permanent TLDs," he said. "They've been logged out to you by name and badge number, and you'll turn them in weekly for readings. It's your responsibility to look at them daily to make sure you have not received a dose you didn't know about."

"Good deal," Tony muttered, examining the TLD suspiciously. It was bigger than the ones we'd worn for the tour. "I can remember when 'receiving a dose' meant something altogether different."

"Same basic equipment tends to fall off your body," Quartermain said without even a hint of a smile. "My team is already down there. Let's boogie."

We followed him in his official PrimEnergy car up to Third Street and then east through Wilmington to the container port. We went through some surprisingly elaborate security at the main gate, where we were given yet more, if temporary, ID badges, vehicle passes, and plastic hard hats. All this happened after they'd searched both vehicles, inside, out, and under. None of the people doing the searching seemed to care about the shepherds. There was already a double line of semis, each with a seagoing container strapped to its back, parked along both sides of the exit lanes. Some of the drivers were out along the road, smoking cigarettes and waiting for the flap to subside.

A container port requires vast amounts of horizontal space; Ari told us that the one in Wilmington consists of four hundred acres, most of it paved. There were none of the conventional warehouses one would associate with a seaport. The beauty of containers is that they're weatherproof, so they just stack the outgoing containers ten high all over the place until it's time to go to sea. Most of the incoming containers get dropped directly onto flat-frame trailers and go down the highway within minutes, literally, of being offloaded.

Unless there's a problem. A twinkling cluster of red and

blue lights down on the pier indicated that there was indeed a problem.

The gate people had told us not to drive onto the handling piers near the gantry cranes, so we parked next to a ten-pack stack and walked in. As we approached on foot, we could see several emergency vehicles parked at odd angles out on the pier but not too many people; apparently the nature of the problem was no longer a secret, and savvy humans were keeping their distance. I could see two guys in white spacesuits working around a single truck-and-trailer rig in the glare of both portable floods and the overhanging spotlights of an enormous gantry crane overhead. There was a cluster of mostly Asian faces peering curiously down from the high bows of a sixty-thousand-ton container ship.

I left the dogs in the vehicle. Quartermain took us over to a command center van bearing the markings of the Customs and Border Protection Agency, where a small crowd of Border Patrol cops, Coast Guard officers, and port authority officials stood around watching the moonwalkers inside the perimeter do their thing with instruments and sample kits. I noticed that the van was positioned upwind and that the bystanders were keeping a respectful distance. I half-expected to see the gangly figure of Creeps in the crowd, but none of these people looked like Bureau types. Tony popped a cigarette out of a pack, but one of the port authority guys immediately shook his head at him. Quartermain explained that some radiation came in the form of tiny airborne particles, so a spill scene was no place to be taking deep drags of air.

"Spill scene?"

"Procedurally, we're treating this as a radiation spill, even though we know that's not what it is," he explained. "That's a spill team, and they're trained to find and decontaminate radioactive materials that shouldn't be there."

The back doors of the container had been opened, and we could see a stack of cardboard boxes filling the opening, packed right up to the container's ceiling. One spacesuit man was incongruously on his back on a mechanic's creeper, taking readings underneath the rig, while the other was on his knees holding a floodlight for him. A worried-looking middle-aged man in a suit and white hard hat came over when he spotted Quartermain, who introduced him to us as Hank Carter, security director for the Wilmington Port Authority.

"This isn't making any sense, Dr. Quartermain," he said. "We've got alarms, your guys are getting a lot of noise on the detectors, but we can't find a single frigging point source on that can."

"You got gamma?" Quartermain asked.

"No, alpha. It's not high intensity—the levels are too low. It's also spread out, like somebody painted the container with something radioactive."

"Like water, maybe?" I said in a quiet aside to Ari.

He nodded. "Tell them to look for any accumulations of water, and test those," he said.

"Water?" Carter said. "This is a container port; there's water everywhere."

"Tell them to look along the edges of that container or on the bottom of the trailer itself, in the cracks. All the places where water might linger after coming down off a ship. And check the truck."

Carter gave Ari a sharp look, as if wondering whether the Helios security director knew something he didn't and, if so, how. Then he went over to the command van and climbed in. Moments later we saw one of the spacesuited guys stop, listen to his radio, and give a thumbs-up sign that he understood. There was a rough-looking white man dressed in jeans and a sweatshirt sitting inside the van looking very uncomfortable, and I guessed that he must be the truck driver. I sent Tony and Pardee to go for an inconspicuous stroll around the temporary perimeter, just looking. I told them to fan out and see who or what might be watching the circus with more than casual interest.

A few minutes later, there was a commotion in the command van, and Carter beckoned Ari over. I went with him.

"You were right," Carter said. "It's water. Or some kind of radioactive fluids pooled on the trailer frame, underneath. Not the container. Which brings up my next question."

"Just an educated guess," Ari said. "Based on the recent incident downtown. We're assuming that was water, too, because the victim drank it."

"Damn. Can your people help us decontaminate?"

"Yep. I'll send for a foam generator. They'll spray the entire underside of the trailer and then wait for the foam to harden. Then it can be broken off as a solid, bagged, and taken back to our low-level waste holding area."

Carter looked vastly relieved. "Should we sweep the entire pier?" he asked.

"Have you searched inside the container itself?"

Carter shook his head. "That was next," he said.

"Okay, do that and let my guys sweep whatever comes out," Ari said. "Then I'd sweep the ship that container came off of, and I'd suggest you talk to and sweep all those guys watching us right now up there, if that's the ship." He pointed at the row of oriental faces sixty feet above us. To a man, they all vanished.

"No problem," Carter said, opening his flip-radio and barking out some orders. Moments later, the huge gantry crane rumbled into life and rolled down the pier to where the ship's gangway was positioned. A crew of hard hats emerged out of the darkness and attached cables to the gangway, and then the crane just lifted it off the ship. Whoever was onboard was going to stay there or go for a night swim in the Cape Fear River.

One of the customs agents in the van stuck his head out and told Carter that the FBI was at the main gate and inbound.

I looked sideways at Ari, and he understood. He said that he would stay there to coordinate the decontamination team's efforts, and that we outlanders should make our creep. I saw Tony and Pardee standing under a light tower a hundred yards or so down the pier. I went back to the car and let the shepherds out, and then we walked down to join them, giving the spill scene a wide berth.

"What'd they find?" Tony asked.

"It sounds like it's the truck and trailer, not the container, but of course it could have dripped down from the container. It's a mystery right now. You guys see anything of interest?"

"Lots of ladders," Pardee said. He pointed to the edge of the concrete handling pier, which itself was a hundred yards wide and constructed as a bulkhead pier along the riverbank. I could just see the round tops of ladder railings leading down over the edge of the pier.

"They're every hundred feet or so," Tony said.

"Meaning, if this hot stuff didn't come from overseas, it could have come by boat? From the river?"

"Isn't that what you wanted a boat for?" Pardee asked.

"Don't be a smart-ass," I said. Up near all the strobe lights, we could see a trio of Bureau cars pulling in to join the evolving radiation incident. "Let's move right along, shall we?"

We strolled casually down the entire length of the container pier, which was easily a mile long. I let the shepherds range out to the edges of the lighted area. The dark river and the even darker wetlands stretched off to our right. I thought I could make out the lights of Helios downriver. To our left were the container stacks, whose rows seemed to go on forever into the terminal yards. There was one other ship tied up alongside the pier, and two gantries were busy snatching containers from the pier and lifting them up into the massive ship, which had developed a slight starboard list as the cans, as they were called, came aboard. The gantries with their projecting booms reminded me of medieval siege towers, only with lights.

We walked down to the very end of the pier area, checking for security cameras and fences where the industrial area ended. There appeared to be a railroad switchyard inboard of the container work and storage area. Large forklifts were hoisting containers onto flatbed railcars in the glare of sodium vapor lights. On the far, landward side of the yard we could see what looked like a container junkyard outside the security fence, filled with damaged or badly rusted steel boxes dropped haphazardly on a low hillside.

A white pickup truck with a police light bar mounted

over the cab drove by, stopped, and backed up. We walked over. The security guard inside, who had to be at least sixty years old, wanted to know who we were and what were we doing down there. I told him we were with Dr. Quartermain, and we all flashed our temporary gate IDs. He gave the shepherds a wary look, rolled the window up, and then made a call on his radio. We couldn't hear the response, but apparently it satisfied him that we were not saboteurs. He nodded and drove off.

"That's not much of a deterrent," Tony observed.

"The bad guys wouldn't know that until they got close to the truck, and I'd guess he has a panic button in there. This place is huge."

We'd come to the very end of the container pier. The Cape Fear River was nearly a half mile wide at this point, and looked wider because of the total darkness on the other side. Channel buoys winked at us all the way down the river. We could hear that muscular current swirling through the dolphin pilings at the end of the pier. The water smelled of salt marsh and diesel oil; some seagulls overhead on night patrol screamed at us. The visible debris in the water was streaming by at a good five knots.

"Something's not computing here," I said. "I mean, look: If some bad guys are trying to smuggle in radioactive material, why in the hell would they, first, plant some in town, and then, second, splash it on the *outside* of a container here in the port?"

"How do we know it got downtown?" Pardee asked.

"We don't," I admitted. Pardee had a point. If Allie ingested the hot stuff, she could have done that anywhere. The fact that she was downtown when it got to her didn't mean anything.

Pardee nodded.

Tony finally lit up his cigarette. "Yeah," he said, exhaling a cloud. "You'd think, if the jihadis were trying to get a dirty bomb or something in, they sure as hell wouldn't want to alert that crew back there."

"And not once, but *twice*? Radiation getting loose in the Wilmington area? Maybe from the Helios plant, maybe not. Now this. Maybe it's some whack-job stealing shit from a hospital radiology lab, spreading it around town just for grins."

"The fact that it was outside may be important," Pardee said. A seagull appeared out of the darkness and landed boldly twenty feet away. Frick went for it, resulting in a lot of squawking and feathers. Frack, showing his age, just watched.

"Yeah, I agree. I wonder if it's maybe a—"

At that moment, we saw a commotion up at the tractor-trailer. They had unloaded about half the boxes from inside the container. From our vantage point, it looked like they'd gone all the way to the front wall of the container, but then I realized there weren't enough boxes out on the pier. They'd hit a fake wall.

The Helios team was backed out, and a bunch of border cops jumped into the container and went to work on the wall. We started walking back to get a closer look, but stayed close to the first row of stacked containers as we went up the pier. The cops appeared to be getting nowhere fast, so they filed out and let a couple of longshoremen climb into the container with axes in hand. I saw Ari walk over to the edge of the pier, obviously searching for a cell phone signal.

Then there was a shout from inside the container as the fake wall burst open and a dozen or so men bolted out, piled right over the startled longshoremen, and ran flat-out into the container stacking area, fanning out in all directions, before the cops could comprehend what was going on. Everyone at the scene was caught completely flat-footed. A couple of cops pulled their weapons, but then realized they couldn't shoot the stowaways just for running. One security truck peeled out in pursuit and instantly collided with the corner of a container in a true Keystone Kops moment. Tony started laughing.

Then we heard a shout from our left. It sounded like it had come from down below the edge of the pier. We ran to the edge in time to see Ari Quartermain floating past in the current about twenty feet off the pier, waving frantically. The lights from one of the gantry cranes shone down into the water, or we would never have been able to see him.

"Get it," I yelled at Frack, who went over the side in one big jump and splashed down into the water. He surfaced a moment later and began paddling in the direction of the struggling Quartermain. Tony found a life ring with a rope attached, and we started walking to keep up with the current as Frack dragged the man closer to one of those ladders we'd spotted. The dog had Ari by his jacket collar, and, fortunately, Quartermain wasn't fighting the dog, but swimming with him instead. When they got close enough, Tony made sure Ari could see the life ring and then tossed it to him. Once he had it, Tony belayed the rope on the pier and let the current bring both man and dog alongside, close enough for Quartermain to grab one rung on the next ladder. Up the pier I could hear sirens approaching.

Frack still had a mouthful of Quartermain's jacket, but Ari, thinking faster than I might have managed under the same circumstances, held on to the ladder with one hand while he poked the life ring over the dog's front end. I called Frack off, and the three of us hoisted him back up to the pier while Quartermain clung to the bottom of the ladder. I'd swear Frack was grinning as we hauled his fuzzy wet butt over the edge of the pier. That mutt loves an adventure.

Tony went down the ladder and helped Quartermain climb up. Once they were topside, Ari flopped down on the concrete, gasping from his exertions in the icy water.

"What happened?" I asked him.

"One of those runners knocked me into the river," he said, still puffing. "I think he went in, too, but I didn't see him again."

Frack stuck his nose into Ari's face and gave him a big lick. Ari patted the dog's head and thanked him formally for saving his ass. Up the pier there were more cops arriving, and several vehicles were starting to prowl the virtual canyons between all the stacked containers. We flagged down a passing security truck and asked the rent-a-cop to take a badly shivering Ari up to the scene to see if they could get a blanket for him.

Tony and Pardee automatically had started to walk up the pier, but I called them back.

"Bad idea," I said. "Bunch of embarrassed cops and feds up there. Time for us interested parties to dee-part."

As we drove back into Southport, I asked Tony if he'd found any decent gin mills in town. Tony, being Tony, knew of four; he was nothing if not attentive to important logistical details. We stopped at one a block in from the municipal beachfront. I left the shepherds in the vehicle. The place was about as dead as an off-season beer joint could be, which suited us just fine. The bartender was down at one end of the bar, eyes glued to the evolving story of a mass escape of stowaways down at the container port.

"Well," Tony said, "Quartermain wanted the attention off Helios; that mess should do it."

The television was now showing aerial views of the container pier.

"Anybody ever say if the radiation they got over there was similar to what they found inside Allie?" Pardee asked.

"They think they had alpha at the truck scene," I said, "and that's the best candidate for what got Allie."

"Yeah, that's kinda my point," Pardee said.

"As in, these could be two related incidents?"

"Three incidents—Allie, the hot trailer, and now a bunch of illegals in a container."

Tony finished his drink and put the glass down with an audible clink. "I don't know, boss," he said. "Maybe we should just do what Creeps suggests. Radiation poisoning? Gamma fucking rays? Human smuggling? That's all federal shit. This is no place for us local gumshoes."

"Granted, but I still want to know what happened to Allie."

"We *know* what happened to Allie," he replied. "We just

don't know why." He paused to deliver a mild burp. "Although I have a theory."

"Which is?"

"She ran into a 'thing' in the night," he said. "A national security 'thing.' It went bump and then ate her up from the inside out. I'm sorry for her, don't get me wrong. But shit happens, you know? As in, wrong time, wrong place?"

This wasn't what I wanted to hear. "Pardee?" I asked.

He shrugged. "I'll stay if you want," he said. "But whatever the hell's going on here is gonna go major league after tonight, and I, for one, don't want to disappear into one of those overseas rendition centers."

I sighed and studied my glass for a moment. I could understand where they were coming from. When we set up H&S Investigations, we agreed that it would be mostly part-time work—basically, guys would put in as much time as any of them wanted or needed to make some money. None of us had to take on a case if we didn't want to, and, after a life of chasing vicious street criminals, additional excitement was typically not the objective.

"All right," I said. "I copy all that. Lemme talk to Quartermain tomorrow, see if we're still in the picture. Although . . ."

"Although what?" Tony asked.

"You guys are probably right—we should back out of this hairball. On the other hand, working some bullshit for Quartermain likely gives us our best chance to find out what happened to Allie—and why."

"Isn't that what the Bureau's gonna do?"

"They might, but if this is part of a larger national security picture, they just might bury the part that involved Allie."

I looked over at the television, where the bartender was switching through the local Wilmington channels with the mute button on now. The same picture kept coming up—an overhead of the container port from a helicopter and the world's supply of flashing blue and red lights dispersed along the pier, trying to surround the gazillion containers stacked out there. The runners were definitely not in evidence. I suggested it was time to call it a day.

* * *

The next morning, I left a message for Quartermain with the delectable Ms. Samantha Young. Then the three of us went down to the marina below Southport and picked out a boat. We settled on an Everglades 290, which was twenty-nine feet long, with a supposedly unsinkable fiberglass hull and twin 225-horsepower Honda engines. It was designed primarily for daytime sport fishing and was rated to carry up to fourteen people. It had an enclosed cockpit structure amidships, a GPS navigation system, two radios, a fathometer, and a Decca short-range radar set. I booked it for two weeks, with the understanding that it would be berthed each night back at the marina. I paid in advance for the first week's rent, full-replacement insurance, and a damage deposit. Tony was a boat enthusiast; I had owned a lake boat at one time, but he would be the designated driver.

Quartermain called my cell as we were finishing up at the marina. He wanted me to come to the plant. I told the guys to find some charts of the area and to lay out a track to get up to the plant from Southport. Then I drove over to the power plant. I left Frack in the Suburban and took Frick in with me. I didn't really need a dog with me, but I wanted everyone I encountered to know that when they saw me, they'd better look out for at least one German shepherd.

Samantha escorted us over to the main reactor complex this time, and then into the spent fuel storage building security office. There I was surprised to run into Colonel Trask, who said he'd take me to the upper-level control room himself. One of the security people checked me into the building, duly noting the presence of the dog in the facility log. A plant technician took me into an adjoining room, where I dressed out in a lightweight spacesuit and registered my current TLD reading. Then Trask and I proceeded into the moonpool access area.

The building was constructed of heavy, steel-reinforced concrete and presented three layers of security checks before we could access the moonpool itself. Because the spent fuel pool was mostly aboveground, we stepped out of an airlock chamber through a heavy steel door and faced a solid wall of heavily studded concrete. I noted surveillance cameras trained on us through each step of the security points. We had to climb eight sets of steel ladder-stairs to get to the top, passing a mezzanine level on the way. Trask didn't say much beyond directions on when to step through doors. Interestingly, it took swiping both his badge and mine to get through the doors. Trask explained that this had to do with the two-man rule: No one was allowed to go anywhere in the vital area by himself. Just before going inside the main pool enclosure, he positioned both of us in front of a wall-mounted video camera and verbally identified us to the camera lens. After a moment, the door in front of us was remotely unlocked, and Trask pointed me through it.

Quartermain was waiting for me in what looked like a monitoring anteroom along with some technicians. His eyes looked a bit puffy, and he was moving awkwardly, although that may just have been because he, too, was already suited up in a white whole-body coverall. There were no windows in the building, and the air was humid and surprisingly warm.

The moonpool itself was still spooky-looking. The water was incredibly clear and suffused with that ethereal blue-green light down toward the bottom, caused apparently by the residual radiation. And whereas the reactors were caged in huge hemispherical reinforced concrete domes, the spent fuel storage pool was open to view from catwalks on all four sides. It looked like the water was actually moving a little bit. Quartermain said it was and again explained the mechanics of the pool, the water cooling and the emergency backup refill system.

"So why'd they build them aboveground?"

"Pre-9/11 reactor design considerations," he answered. "Robotic machines defuel and refuel the reactors, since humans can't go anywhere near that stuff. There's a whole tunnel complex underneath this building. The robots pull the fuel elements down out of the core, turn them sideways, cart them through a tunnel to the moonpool, stand them back up again, and then set them up for long-term storage. Takes months to do it, and after a while the pools get full. Then any other elements have to go into cask storage. Basically, it's easier to transfer the stuff from an aboveground pool to the dry casks."

"Casks, as in big lead-lined tanks?"

"Yup. Exactly. Steel and lead. We have some here, but they're empty. So far, anyway. But if they don't open Yucca Mountain pretty soon, we'll be using them."

"Is spent fuel a valid terrorist target?" I asked.

"Yes, there's some bad shit down there at the bottom. That's one of the main reasons we have people like Trask and his ex-Rangers here. Now: about last night."

"Other than your unplanned swim, you got what you wanted, right?"

"I think we did. My spill team still has to write up their report, and we'll be doing some more analysis on the foam once we get it back here."

"Anyone tying the material to the stowaways?"

"Internally, Homeland Security and the Bureau are treating it as an attempted RDD attack, although the official cover story is only talking about the runners."

"RDD?" All the acronyms were beginning to overwhelm me.

"Radiological dispersion device—dirty bomb, in English."

"Except there was no bomb, right?"

"We had hot stuff *and* illegal males hidden in the same box. All sorts of conjecture about that. For all we know, there's a bomb still over there, in another container."

"They catch any of the runners?"

"Two," he said. "South American, not Middle East. The ICE guys are baffled."

More acronyms. "ICE?"

"Immigration and Customs Enforcement. More feds. You need to brush up on your alphabets."

"I'm trying not to. So now what?"

"They'll determine the destination for that container, and then screen the entire system for any other containers going to the same destination. If they find one, that's where they'd expect bomb components to be."

I thought his reasoning was a little tenuous. "You didn't exactly find a thermos of bad stuff in that container, Ari," I said.

"Yet," he shot back.

"Okay, so let the big dogs run with it. You no longer need me or my people, right?"

He didn't answer right away. He glanced sideways at three fully masked technicians who were taking readings from some instruments suspended in the pool. We turned our backs to them and the glowing pool before he replied. Frick, who seemed nervous, stayed close by my side. I wondered if the dog could sense the presence of something dangerous down there in that shimmering water.

"Actually," Ari said, "I'd like you to stay. Remember my telling you that we might be able to trace marker isotopes when Ms. Gardner was killed?"

I nodded, although that hadn't worked out with Allie's postmortem.

"We have been able to recover the isotopic markers from our spill team's monitors."

"And?"

"The markers aren't unequivocal," he said grimly, indicating the moonpool with a sideways nod of his head, "but one could make the case that they point right here."

"Who knows that?" I asked, wanting suddenly to get out of this foreboding building.

"At this moment, nobody but me and my lab people. They'd just brought me the report when I called you. But I will have to notify the company and, more importantly, the NRC. And then we're probably going to experience some more interesting times, in the Chinese sense."

I remembered Creeps saying they'd shut the plant down if they could prove the water came from the moonpool. "You're saying you now think somebody *did* take radioactive water or materials, or both, out of this facility?"

"Seems impossible, doesn't it," he said. "You've seen the security. And, of course, it could have come from another

BWR plant. But we're the closest. Plus, you can't and you wouldn't get near an operating power reactor, so . . ."

I looked around as I digested this bit of news. The pool was contained in a sealed concrete building, swarming with radiation-monitoring instruments, accessible only through three layers of security checks, one manned, two electronic, and under constant television surveillance from a control room. So it wasn't likely that someone just wandered up here with a rope and a bucket.

"Who's the guy in charge of this area?" I asked.

"Not a guy," he said. "Her name is Anna P. Martin. Doctor Anna Petrowska Martin, to be specific."

"Judas Priest!" I said. "You've got a damned *Russian* on your management team?"

"Now, now, don't rush to judgment. We also have Indians, Pakistanis, Chinese, Japanese, Koreans, and, yes, one Russian, and even some native-born Americans."

"You *do*?"

"Consider the state of public education in this country these days, Mr. Richter. You think America's producing bumper crops of nuclear engineers? If it weren't for technically educated foreigners, there'd be no nuclear power or any other high-tech industry in this country. What we can't rape and pillage from the Navy's nuclear power program, we make up with foreigners. All of whom are fully vetted American citizens, by the way, as is Dr. Martin."

I shook my head. I had strong views on Russians even being in this country, having dealt with my share of them in the Manceford County major crimes office. The Russian gangs made the Mafia look like pasta-bellied pussies. They were vicious beyond belief, and I firmly believed we should deport every damned one of them back to their beloved *rodina* tomorrow.

I was about to expand on these sentiments when I realized that one of the white-suited techs was standing behind me. He took off his headgear. *Her* headgear. I'd formed a mental image of a fullback-shouldered Madame Khrushchev when

Ari had told me about Comrade Dr. Martin, but this was most definitely not the case.

"Did I hear my homeland being mentioned?" she said, shaking out a wave of platinum-blond hair. She was one of those chiseled Slavic beauties, with pronounced cheekbones, bright ice-blue eyes, and a challenging mouth. I could hear the Eastern European accent, but she'd obviously been in the States for some time. I'd paid no attention to the "guys" in the baggy white suits, or I would have noticed that one suit wouldn't necessarily be called baggy.

Ari introduced us, explaining that I was a professional investigator, and that I'd been contracted to help him with an internal problem. She gave him a quizzical look, and me a condescending smile. Then recognition dawned in those polar eyes.

"Ah, yes, the policeman with the Alsatian dogs," she said, extending a gloved hand.

We shook hands clumsily through all the protective gear. Her grip was firm, and, based on the mildly amused look on her face, she'd overheard my sentiments regarding the presence of a Russian on the staff in the vital area of the plant. I mumbled something polite, which she ignored. She turned back to Ari to ask what more he had heard about the incident last night. He demurred and said he hadn't any further data at the moment. She smoothed her hair one more time and then looked back at me.

"Are you a technical person, Mr. Richter?" she asked. "An engineer, perhaps?"

"Afraid not," I said. "Just run-of-the-mill police."

"Oh," she said with a distinctly dismissive smile. "And you don't care much for Russians, do you?"

"That's right," I said. "I think they belong in Russia."

"But America is the land of opportunity, yes?"

"As a policeman, all the Russians I've ever met were savages, whose idea of opportunity in America was to rape, maim, steal, and kill. Seeing as you're a Ph.D. and working here, I guess I'm willing to give you the benefit of the doubt."

"Well, my goodness," she exclaimed, stepping back away from me. "You are beginning to remind me of the police back in my birth country. I thought your job as a policeman was to protect and defend."

"To protect and defend Americans," I said.

"I'm an American citizen, you ignorant oaf!"

"Anna," Ari said.

She glared at me again, relayed some technical information in nuke-speak to Ari, and then stomped off to rejoin her team. Or tried to—it's hard to stomp in paper boots.

Ari was grinning at me. "Sorry," he said quietly. "She has a temper, and you did step on her toes just a wee bit."

"Do I look sad?" I asked.

"You look like every other normal male who meets her for the first time," he said, still smiling. "She's hardcore about her job and her science, though. She just fired one of her senior techs for breaking protocol on an emergency procedure exercise. When it comes to the moonpool, she's serious as a heart attack."

"Then how did some of this evil shit get loose?" I asked, pointing with my chin at the glowing pool.

"Good question, Mr. Investigator," he replied evenly.

In other words, *There's your mission impossible, Mr. Phelps, should you choose to accept it.* I told him about my guys' reservations after last night's circus on the pier, and that I'd told them they could back out if they wanted to. He actually thought that might simplify things. One stranger wandering around the complex ought to attract less attention than three.

"I'll need their badges back," he reminded me.

"Does Comrade Martin know that the stuff on the truck might have come from here?" I asked.

"She will as soon as I file the NRC report," he said. "She will feature prominently in the resulting internal investigation."

"Is that control room over there manned 24/7?"

"No," he said. "Just when they're running tests or some other evolution. Otherwise, there's no one up here."

I hesitated before asking the next question, but there was no way around it. "If the NRC is going to investigate this from the outside, and the company's going to be turning over rocks from the inside, and the Bureau is going to be watching both, tell me again what you want *me* to do?"

He glanced around the steel deck once more. Dr. Martin and her techs had disappeared, and we were alone with the moonpool and its unearthly glow. It looked like some Northern Lights had drowned down there.

"Do you know what a Red Team is?" he asked.

I did not.

"It's a government expression, normally used in war gaming. When the government conducts a war game, it postulates a hypothetical crisis scenario, and then pits a group of actual government officials against the crisis. These are real officials, but they're role-playing. Someone from the White House staff will play the president. Another person, say from the Defense Department, will play the role of secretary of defense."

"Yeah, I've read about those."

"Right. The game directors gather them into a room and throw a tabletop crisis situation at them. They work the problem until they either solve it or it beats them. The good guys are called the Blue Team."

"I believe."

"Good. The Red Team sits in another room and reacts to what the Blue Team does, typically by throwing complications into the game. The idea is to make the war game truly dynamic, and to test how well the Blue Team can handle an *evolving* crisis situation when all their nicely preplanned contingency plans go off the tracks. Plus, the Red Team is privy to the Blue Team's assumptions and contingency plans before the game starts. They hit those assumptions, and the Blue Team now has to deal with a changing crisis situation."

"So the Red Team people are the bad guys."

"Exactly. The Blue Team assumes their simulated Katrina relief convoys can get to New Orleans on the interstates. The Red Team knocks out all the bridges."

"So you want me to act like a bad guy? See if I can get

through the perimeter, break in here and swipe some radioactive water or some spent fuel rods, then go package it and, what? Sell it?"

"Not exactly," he said patiently. "Unless you have a death wish. But here's the problem: The NRC's going to come in here this time and try to prove that radioactive water got loose from Helios, either from the moonpool or somewhere else in the reactor system."

"Reasonable reaction," I said.

"PrimEnergy has to defend itself, and the company is going to take the position that it not only didn't happen but couldn't happen. Now: Unless some unhappy camper stands up and confesses to a crime that would jail him for about ten successive life sentences, it's going to end in a Mexican standoff."

"Which would suit the company, right?"

"Frankly, I think that would suit the government, as well. They don't *even* want to hear that there's been a clandestine radiological release from an operating plant, because that would probably lead to an industry-wide shutdown of this type of nuclear power plant."

"Why all of them?"

"Because the security system here is common to all of them. It would be a very big deal. Nobody at the NRC or in the industry wants to do that."

"You're telling me the NRC would cover it up?"

"No, no, not if they find something concrete, some glowing gun, so to speak. But if it turns into a stone-cold mystery, they'll 'study' it. They might keep probing, but, basically, they'll keep all the BWR plants turning and burning."

"And you want me to do what, specifically?"

"I want you to Red-Team it. Not actually do it, mind you, but see if you can figure out a way to get radioactive water out of this plant and into Wilmington. I want you to do this independently, without the official, approved assistance of *anybody* at this plant, including me."

"But if the experts can't prove it, how can I?"

"You weren't listening—the experts on both sides of this

equation don't *want* to prove it. So, absent some glaring, oh-shit technical hole in the system, the books are probably going to close on the demise of Ms. Gardner and the hot truck chassis across the river."

"You're serious, aren't you," I said.

"It's got to be a people problem, not a technical problem. The NRC's going to send in nukes. PrimEnergy is going to defend with the likes of Anna P. They're literally going to be looking at piping systems for leaks. There aren't any. I need someone to probe the people side. Again, without inside help."

"Ah."

He smiled grimly. "Yeah. Operative words: inside help. Everybody else has a stake in this. You wouldn't. If I've got a sleeper, I think it'll take an outsider to find him."

This could be a very dangerous game, I thought, given those stakes he was talking about. "What about Trask and his people—you going to cut them in?"

"No, but I'll let you develop a working relationship with them as you want to. Your current access extends only to the protected area, not the vital area. You're in this building only because Trask let you in and I'm escorting you."

"I wouldn't have access here?"

"Would you know what do to in here? How it even works? I don't need a technical investigator—I need someone who can uncover a *human* weakness here, not an engineering defect. I believe that's what you guys do."

His argument made sense. Unless, of course, *he* was the bad guy. "How would we communicate?"

"Can we keep that computer link we have now?" he asked.

"Yes, until the feds tumble to it. I mean, they'll look at everyone's computer once your investigation starts, especially the Bureau people. Yours included."

"The NRC won't bring the Bureau in immediately, not until they find that smoking gun or a suspect."

"The Bureau may have its own thoughts about that," I said. "Listening to Special Agent Caswell, they're already in."

"The NRC will be in charge of this investigation," he said impatiently. "They find a person of interest, they'll turn the Bureau on. Look: You said you wanted to find out how *and* why Ms. Gardner got killed. I need a neutral outsider to test my system. And, what the hell, this beats watching lawyers fornicate, doesn't it? You said you were bored."

"It was Allie Gardner who was bored," I said. I felt like I'd been talking to a car salesman. But Ari was walking over to the control room to talk to Dr. Anna Petrowska Martin, Ph.D. Frick was sitting against the main steel wall of the moonpool room, giving me one of those shepherd looks that says, *Don't do it, dummy.*

"What are you looking at, dog?" I said. "Aren't you up for a little adventure? I mean, what could possibly go wrong, hunh?"

That afternoon, I carefully nosed my new water toy into the entrance of the plant's inlet canal. I'd owned my lake boat for about four years, and, while this one was longer and heavier, driving a boat is like riding a bicycle—once you learn, you've pretty much got it. River navigation was quite different from lake driving, but Tony had laid out a perfectly clear track, and if the sixty-thousand-tonners could manage it, so could I. The 290 handled nicely and had plenty of power, and the raised cockpit provided excellent visibility. The shepherds seemed comfortable enough, especially since we were driving around in perfectly still waters. I'd stayed out in the ship channel coming up the Cape Fear River, which was serious overkill in terms of water depth for my little craft—the Corps of Engineers kept the channel dredged to forty-two feet to accommodate the huge container ships, and the 290 drew twenty inches. Between the GPS and the river buoys, even I could find my way to the inlet canal.

There were a couple of fishermen in smaller boats hanging around at the entrance to the inlet canal, and they waved as I turned in. I cut the big Hondas down to idle so as not to throw up too big a wake. As I approached the power plant,

I saw a small tug and cargo barge parked at a bulkhead pier. There didn't seem to be anyone working or guarding the barge, so I had to assume it was carrying routine, non-nuclear supplies for the plant. From a security standpoint, a barge probably presented less of a threat than a truck, but it, too, was nowhere near close to the main buildings.

I'd reluctantly sent Pardee and Tony back to Triboro, after they confirmed that they'd just as soon not get involved in this one. Pardee reiterated his willingness to stay and help, but I'd finally decided I'd work this one myself. I asked him to continue to manage the comms support for our supposedly secure channel to Quartermain's computer. Tony wanted to make sure I didn't think he was leaving me in the lurch, and I reassured him that was not the case since what I needed down here was *competent* help. That got the usual snort out of him. I received one e-mail message from Ari just after noon, which said simply that the fun and games had begun. I decided that it would be a great afternoon for a boat ride.

The marina people had briefed me on the rules concerning both the container port and the power plant canals. While the access to both was nominally public, Notices to Mariners had been published that security considerations could and would take immediate precedence if circumstances so dictated, meaning they could run your ass out of those so-called public access areas whenever they chose to do so. If you argued, they could confiscate your boat. If you really argued, they could sink your boat. They also explained that most of the real fishermen liked to go into the discharge canal over on the other side, because the heated water attracted more fish.

The container port was approachable, but there, too, the Coast Guard had some hard-and-fast rules. You had to stay at least a hundred yards away from any ships at the pier, and that no-go line expanded to two hundred yards at night. Any boat operating in the main channel or the approaches to the pier had to give way to any ship maneuvering in that area. That was kind of a no-brainer, with the informal but implacable law of gross tonnage being the enforcement mechanism. Sixty thousand tons versus four thousand pounds was how boats, even unsinkable boats, became debris. The bottom line was clear: The port authorities were nervous, and this was probably a good time to avoid the container port and all its works.

My objective in making this trip was to do it once in daylight before I tried it again at night. The inlet canal provided river water for the steam turbines' condensers. It ended at a huge grated concrete blockhouse assembly where the cold water was drawn into the maws of the big steam condensers under the power house, some four hundred yards distant. A line of buoys prevented boats from getting close to the actual inlet, more for their own safety than the plant's. There was visible turbulence around the inlet grates and a baby logjam of river debris plastered against the screens. I saw tinted hemispherical television camera pods on telephone poles around the inlet.

I was wearing jeans, sneakers, a baggy sweatshirt under a light windbreaker, a floppy hat, and oversized sunglasses. The shepherds should have been out of sight of the cameras unless there were some I hadn't seen yet, and there probably were. But as I made a slow turn at the business end of the canal and headed back toward the river, there didn't seem to be any reaction from plant security. Nighttime might be a different story. I was careful not to spend too much time staring at the two big green buildings of Helios, where the atomic dragons soaked in their elemental fires. And then my cell phone chirped.

"Richter," I answered.

"Yes, we know," a voice replied. It was my new best friend, Colonel Trask.

"So where are you, Colonel?" I asked, as I nudged the boat's throttle up one notch, heading for the egress.

"I'm in central control," he said. "My eyes are in that little green fishing boat on your starboard bow."

I looked, and there was the "fisherman" who'd waved. He was holding binoculars on me, and behind him I saw the TV camera, mounted backward on his windscreen, pointed in my direction as I approached the river.

"I feel safer already," I said.

"There you go, making assumptions again, Mr. Richter," he said. "What were you doing at the moonpool this morning?"

"Dr. Quartermain wanted to show me something," I said, "and I got to meet one of your Russians. Gotta admit, that was a surprise."

"I'm with you on that one," he said. *"Omnia Russians delenda sunt."*

"How's the visitation going with the NRC?"

"The way it always goes when they get their black hats on, Mr. Richter. Lots of noise and motion, but not much movement. Everyone's really serious, of course, and very important. I understand you got to watch the wetback marathon last night over across the way."

"Sure did," I said. "Lots of noise and all kinds of movement. Including Dr. Quartermain. In fact, one of my mutts helped fish him out of the river."

"So we heard," he said. "A good German shepherd is hard to beat. Look—you take a drink of whiskey from time to time?"

"No more than once a day," I said. I was abeam of the "fisherman," who was no longer covering me with his binocs. His TV camera, on the other hand, was swiveling just fine, probably under the control of whatever room Trask was in. Only then did I notice that the boat was anchored at both ends.

"There's a pleasant little watering hole down in Southport, called Harry's," he said.

"How original," I said. I felt the main river current grab the boat's bow and begin to slide us toward the south bank of the canal. I kicked up the power and veered out toward the main channel.

"Yeah, well, it's kind of a hangout for various stripes of Helios people. How's about I buy you a drink, say, around eight thirty or so?"

"I never say no to a free drink," I said. "Do I have to be on the lookout for Billy the Kid anymore?"

"I don't think so, Mr. Richter," he said. "But bring your shepherds."

"Count on it, Colonel."

I put a call in to Mary Ellen Goode when I got back to the beach house. This time she answered. She sounded as warm and friendly as ever, but at the same time, a bit reserved.

"Cam," she said. "I got your message. You're back?"

"I am indeed," I said. "Can we get together?"

"Um," she began. Surprised, I let a small band of silence build.

"The thing is," she said, "I don't think that'd be, what's the word I'm looking for—appropriate?"

"Seemed pretty appropriate the other night at the Hilton," I said. "Don't tell me you're embarrassed about that, are you?"

"A little," she said. "I have to confess to using you, in a manner of speaking."

"Well, damn, woman," I said, trying to keep it light while hiding my confusion. "If that was using me, you can use me and even abuse me any time you want. C'mon, Mary Ellen, what's going on?"

"The thing is, I'm getting married in a month."

"Oh," I said.

"Yeah," she said.

"And, lemme see: You were getting married in a month and a week when you came out to see your old buddy from upstate."

A slight hesitation. "Yes."

"So what was all that—your bachelorette party?"

"In a way. Well, no, that's not fair. I just, well, I just wanted to know what it would be like. Edward is a nice guy, but he's nothing like you. I had to know."

I couldn't decide if I should be mad or disappointed. "Know exactly what, Mary Ellen?"

"Cam, that night was incredibly exciting and eminently satisfying. What I had to know was whether or not I was in love with you, and you with me, or just turned on by the fact that you are so very different from all the men I work with and see every day."

That sounded a bit lame to me. "As in, get it on with the pool boy one last time?"

"No, no, no. Please, don't be angry, even though you have every right to be. But let me ask *you* something: Are you in love with me?"

"I hold you in great affection, Mary Ellen," I said, suddenly the weasel. "You know that."

"Yes, I do, but do you want to marry me? You want a family? A house in the academic suburbs and some kind of normal, nine-to-five life, one that doesn't involve gunfights in the dark?"

I sighed. We both knew the answer to that question.

"Right," she said, and I felt my heart sink, even though I knew she was absolutely right. I'd been married, and I was way past my sell-by date to go there again, even with this lovely woman.

"We smoked some mirrors that night, Mary Ellen," I said. "You gotta admit, when we were good, we were very good."

"Stop reminding me, Cam. But the truth is, I want all of those things, and it's kind of now or never as I see it."

"I guess I wasn't really calling about having a drink, was I," I admitted.

She giggled. "And I appreciate the sentiment," she said. "Shit. This is hard. I thought all I'd have to do is send you a Dear John and go on with my life. Tell me one more thing."

"What's that?" I asked. I thought I knew what she'd want to know, and she did not disappoint.

"Are the shepherds with you?"

Bingo, I thought. "They are. And, yes, I am. You didn't buy the admin story, did you?"

"Wanted to," she said. "*Really* wanted to. But . . ."

"This mean I can't call from time to time? Just to see how you're doing?"

"You might get Edward."

"Aaarrgh," I said.

"Cam: It's been more than great. But now . . ."

"Got it, babe. All the very best in the next chapter, and I mean that most sincerely. I do have to say, just for the record, mind you, that I'm sorely disappointed in missing out on some more use and abuse."

I could almost see the smile I could hear in her voice. "Good-bye, Cam."

Okay, I thought. *A clean shoot-down if there ever was one. Let's go see what kind of a date Carl Trask is.*

Harry's Bar was located in the second-to-last block before the Southport municipal beach and fishing pier. It was a traditional layout—a long, dimly lit, and smoky rectangular room, mirrored bar and stools on one side, a single row of tables on the other. At the back was a jukebox, a worn-looking dance floor, and a stairway with a sign that said POOL, with an arrow pointing up the stairs. I didn't think they meant swimming. There was a neon Budweiser sign in the window, along with a dusty and somewhat tattered liquor license taped to the glass near the door. A dozen-plus metal stools decorated the bar, all occupied by what looked like workers from the plant, based on all the badges and TLDs. Not a particularly rough-looking crowd, but it was definitely hard hat country. Some of the tables near the dance floor were occupied by small groups of women who were making a giggling reconnaissance of the bar until I showed up with a large German shepherd in tow.

The tables up front were empty, so I chose one in the front corner near the door and sat down with my back to the wall. I had Frick on a harness with me, and I put her under the table with her back to the wall. Some of the guys at the bar noted the shepherd, but most were busy drinking and talking, in that order, and paid us no mind. The women started giggling again. The bartender tried to protest about the dog, but Frick showed her teeth and he elected to retire with his dignity and his ankles intact.

I ordered Scotch and was enjoying my drink as much as I could having just been dumped by the prettiest woman I knew. A polite, even complimentary dumping, but still. Then Ari's assistant, the lovely Samantha Young, came through the door. This time the giggling really stopped, and was replaced by some frustrated stares from the Southport debutante conga line huddled over their exotic drinks along the back wall. Samantha was wearing what I think are called designer jeans, a light jacket over a heartbreaker sweater, and slightly more war paint than I'd noticed at the office. She carried a small, businesslike leather purse under her left arm.

She closed the door, shucked the jacket, and inhaled. I think most of the guys at the bar inhaled, too. Some of them even whimpered. She gave them a casual once-over, ignored all the daggers coming down the line from the back tables, and then chose the table next to mine. I tipped my glass at her when she sat down, and she gave me a friendly nod, scoring many points for me at the bar. The tables were close enough that we could talk without moving into each other's space. I asked her how things were going in the head shed at Helios.

"Lots of new faces and interesting questions," she said. "Which one is that under your table?"

I told her, and then had to explain the genesis of their names. A couple of the more lubricated members of the stool staff were starting to cast lustful if bleary eyes at Samantha while making the usual delicate anatomical observations. She ignored the boozy chatter and accepted a glass of white wine from the bartender. He raised an eyebrow at me, and I nodded.

"Ari said one of your shepherds pulled him out of the river?"

"Yeah, that was Frack—he's out in the Suburban. Frick here doesn't much like water. They get everything cleaned up over there in the port?"

She shrugged, indicating she didn't know. Then she looked over my shoulder at the front door. "*Achtung*," she said quietly.

Colonel Trask stood in the doorway, examining the crowd

at the bar like a cop about to make a general roust. There was a tightening of shoulders and turning of faces among the regulars. Then he saw me sitting next to Samantha and walked over. He, too, had changed out of work clothes and was wearing khakis, running shoes, a red and black lumberjack shirt, and an ancient Marine utility cap, complete with a faded eagle embossed above the brim. I was a bit surprised to see what looked like a holstered .357 Mag strapped onto his right hip. He saw me looking.

"Never leave home without it," he said, ignoring Samantha. Then he noticed Frick. "May I sit down?" he asked the dog politely.

Frick looked at him as if he were crazy, and I said it was okay, that she'd been fed. He grinned and sat down, but he kept his feet well under his chair. Frick, too, had noticed the hand cannon, and the sight of guns in the open made her alert.

"You're ahead of me," he observed and motioned for the bartender to bring him a Bud by pointing at the neon sign. The bartender nodded.

"You're a single-malt man?" Trask asked. He sat with his back to Samantha, and was probably the only man in the bar who hadn't looked at her twice.

"It's Scotch weather," I said. "The NRC found any smoking neutrons yet?'

"Early days, Lieutenant," he said. "Most of them are scientists, and they take a while to organize a proper clusterfuck."

So now I was a lieutenant again. Coming up in the world? But then I realized he was calling me lieutenant because he expected me to call him colonel. Well, hell, I could do that.

"They'll be looking at your operation, too?" I asked.

"Oh, shit, yes. But I have a standard answer for that line of questioning—I offer to give any or all of them a can of chicken soup, and then challenge them to get it through my perimeter."

"Chicken soup."

"Yup."

"Radioactive chicken soup?"

"Nope. But it does come in a metal can, as would any radionuclides that decided to go walkabout with human assistance."

"Are there other ways for radionuclides to get loose?"

"Surely you jest," he replied.

"Actually, I don't."

"Then go online sometime and Google for a site called RADNET plus the word 'an-thro-po-genic.' Familiarize yourself with the term Accident in Progress. See what our government's been co-facilitating in the field of nuclear safety. Have your lunch first, though."

"You biting the hand that feeds you?"

"You bet. But back to the chicken soup: I'm talking about someone trying to smuggle radioactive water out of Helios. They wouldn't put it in a Ziploc bag, no matter what the TV ads say."

"Unless, of course, you're dealing with a prospective Muslim martyr," I said. I thought Samantha might be listening to everything we were saying, but the jukebox started up, and then she had to fend off some prospective dance partners. She looked a tad annoyed; maybe she was put off by all the drooling.

Trask nodded. "But then we should have had a second incandescent DOA," he said, "and that didn't happen."

"Or they haven't found him in the Dumpster behind the mosque," I said. "Those guys are fucking serious."

"You're right as rain about that," he said. "Problem is, we Americans aren't. Islam has declared a religious war and we've declared democracy back at them. Imagine, democracy in the twelfth century!"

"Probably seemed like a good idea at the time," I said, but he wasn't listening. I sensed a rant coming, and sat back to let him vent.

"I don't know why I give a shit anymore," he said. "This country is finished. Washed up. Weak in the knees and damp in the panties. Genetically diluted by millions of illegal aliens, all squalling for their 'rights,' for God's sake. Distracted by video games, talk shows, and prancing heiresses' crotch shots. Half of the population looks like it just graduated from a Chicago feedlot. America deserves what's coming."

"There are men and women fighting overseas right now who'd argue with you," I said.

"Those are the legions on the frontiers of the empire," he said, warming to what had to be his favorite subject. "Most of them choose to stay out there among the barbarians because they're disgusted by what's going on back at the ripening core. A do-nothing, tax-and-spend government, sweaty, sticky-fingered politicians, usurping judges, thoroughly corrupt political parties, elected pedophiles prowling the United States Capitol—shee-it! The new pope got it right: Islam is a religion of blood and iron, but most Americans are happily focused on money, food, sex, and the latest Xbox video game."

Yee-haw, I thought. Ari had warned me, too. I wanted to argue with him, but I recognized a zealot when I saw one. Besides, I thought he had a point: For a country at war, life in America sure looked like business as usual. I let him babble on, nodding and going along, because I still didn't know why we were meeting. Finally he began to run down.

"You really a herpetologist?" I asked, trying to steer us out of all the political foaming at the mouth.

"Not in the practicing sense," he replied. "I studied snakes because I admire them. Elemental creatures with an unusually perfect predation design."

"Keep them as pets?"

He laughed. "No. Snakes can't really be pets. They're reptiles. Primitive animals. A pet implies an emotional quotient, like your shepherd there. Snakes hunt, eat, digest, doze off, sometimes for weeks, and then they hunt again. Kind of like the falcons in days of yore—they were never hunting for their so-called falconer. They were hunting because they were starving. That's how you train a falcon to hunt, by the way. You capture it, and then you starve it. When it's just about ready to fall off its perch, you take it hunting."

"I've been reading about people turning pythons loose in the Everglades," I said. "That's kind of a scary thought."

"That will be interesting, over time," he said. "Depending on the species, they never stop growing."

"A threat to a human?"

"Not in the sense that a python can eat a fully grown human. But a big one can surely kill you if you happen to encounter him in or near the water. They prey on monkeys a lot. Catch one drinking from a pond or a stream, grab its face and pull its nose underwater. Then they wait."

"How big is big?"

"A Burmese can be six to seven meters," he said. "A hundred fifty kilos, maybe more. They have prehensile tails—always attached to something. Their teeth are an inch long and they slant backwards, so if they achieve a solid bite, you're not going anywhere. With both ends secured, they throw coils around you. That much weight, you can't stand up. Once down, they just lie there. When you inhale, they do nothing. Every time you exhale, though, they squeeze. Pretty soon you can't inhale. Like one of those goddamned seat belts in the backseat—the ones made for baby seats? Every time you lean back, it tightens and locks? Just like that."

"Lovely thought."

"Yeah, well, a primitive being can be scary. You know, it's an artifact from the Pleistocene. And then it moves. You're wondering why I called you."

"Yup," I said, glad to get off the subject of snakes. I don't much care for snakes.

"Ms. Luscious behind me turned in the badges and TLDs for your two sidekicks, which tells me two things: They're smarter than you are, and they've probably gone back to West Bumfuck, North Carolina."

"That's Triboro to the inhabitants," I said.

"But you're still here."

"So I am."

"Which means Quartermain's got you doing some shit."

I didn't respond. He seemed to have all the answers so far. He leaned back in his chair. Samantha was looking bored, but I noticed she'd changed chairs, which put her one foot closer to us, either for some protection against all the barroom cowboys or to hear better over the jukebox. Trask was obviously waiting for me to say something.

"He does," I said. "But I have to do it solo, without any help from anyone at Helios. If it's any comfort, I do not intend to come creeping around the perimeter at night with fence cutters and a bag of grenades."

"So you said," he replied. "Too bad—we do grenades." Then he was serious again. "Okay, here it is," he said. "You're on my radar. I'm pretty sure you're not a bad guy, so I'm not here to tell you how bad things could go for you or any of my usual horseshit. But know this: There may be other players in whatever game Quartermain has going. I'm guessing he wants to use you as a Red Team. Private PI as agent provocateur. If that's the case, you would do well to have me as an ally."

"Unless you're the subject," I replied, just to throw some shit of my own into the discussion.

He was startled. "The subject?" he asked.

"As in, subject of interest. The target of an investigation. The objective of some kind of play. The individual under surveillance. It's a law enforcement term."

He blinked at that. He'd supposedly done tours with the military police. He had to know the usage of that word, so his question had been a stall for time. I decided to press him a little.

"As to other players in the game," I continued, "I have to assume the feds have at least one agent under, if only because Quartermain would want to cover all his bets *and* his ass. You know, the Roman emperor's wistful question: Who guards the guards?"

I waited, but he just sat there, staring at me.

"Actually, though," I continued, "that's not my real problem."

"What is your real problem, then?"

"I think some evil fuck killed one of my people," I said.

"That was probably a coincidence."

"There are no coincidences," I said. "First rule of homicide."

He looked away, ostensibly taking in the dance floor scene, but thinking now. He still hadn't even so much as said hello to Samantha, a woman he knew and probably the most attractive female in the town that night. Suddenly I thought I understood—Samantha's being there was no coincidence, either. I heard noises out there in the woods.

"There's one more thing," he said finally. "Billy."

"Oh, dear. Billy."

"Yeah, well, he was a holdover from the previous security director. Cousin of somebody's mama, I think. Local Southport boy. Once I started bringing my people in, he sort of stood out, and not in a good way. I told you he wouldn't be a problem, but I may have been wrong about that."

"Okay," I said. "Thanks for the heads-up."

He smiled. "I guess I expected you to say, *Bring it on. I can handle that young punk,* et cetera, et cetera."

"I can handle Billy if I see him coming," I said. "I can't handle Billy if he's a long-gun kinda guy."

He nodded. "That is very good thinking," he said. "The good news is that he's not a shoot-from-the-weeds kinda guy, in my opinion. The bad news is that he's been running his mouth, and he said if he couldn't get to you, he'd get to your furry friends. So be careful out there, okay?"

My new best friend, I thought. "Thanks again for the warning."

"Warnings," he said. "As in plural."

"I'll give you this much, Colonel. If I detect a clear and present danger to your vital area, I will most definitely let you know."

He nodded. "Fair enough," he said. "Back at you."

He finished his drink, dropped some cash on the table, gathered his jacket, and got up. This time he did acknowledge Samantha, and she waved back at him over the shoulder of a large man who was sporting a half-dozen dangling Helios badges and trying to score a dance. I decided this was a great time to make my creep before one of the hefties at the back of the bar asked me to dance. I rehooked Frick, went over to the bar, and settled up. Then we left.

I let Frick run around for a minute in the parking lot and then jumped her into the back of the Suburban, fired it up, and drove out of the lot. I went slowly around the block, drove back into the lot, and parked in a dark corner where I could watch Harry's front door. I dropped the windows and settled in to wait. Sure enough, about two minutes later, out came Samantha. She was still clutching that purse in her left hand like a football and talking on a cell phone. She looked around the parking lot, as if checking for lurking muggers or rapists.

I didn't move, and I didn't think she'd seen me. She then walked over to a plain vanilla Ford and got in. The phone conversation went on for a few minutes, and then she signed off. She pulled the rearview mirror over, checked her makeup, then lit the car off, backed out of her parking space, and drove directly over to where I was parked and pulled in, nose to tail. She smiled at me as she rolled down her window.

"It was the purse, wasn't it," she said.

I nodded. I'd seen too many just like it under the arm of just about every female FBI agent I'd ever met. Compact, hard leather, big, easily accessible snap, and perfect for a concealed weapon. Some of them even had springloaded pouches, so all she had to do was unsnap the purse, hit the butt of the weapon with her open hand, and go to town.

"You think Trask knows?" she asked.

"I don't think so," I said. "He's too busy trying to pretend he doesn't notice that glorious bod of yours. It's a military thing, I think—if the troops are all salivating and acting like teenagers, the colonel should remain aloof."

She rolled her eyes, but at least had the grace not to protest about sexist comments and such. She was a genuine beauty, and it was tough not to just look at her. Which is why, when Frick suddenly barked, I realized I'd been well and truly had. Three large men in dark clothes and sporting what looked like H&K MP5s were standing on the other side of my Suburban. One of them presented his FBI credentials through the passenger side window. As I took the situation onboard, a black Suburban rolled up behind us and stopped. I looked back over at Samantha.

She gave me a wistful smile. "Sorry about this," she said. "Nothing personal." Then she rolled up her window, backed out, and drove away.

They were actually polite. No cuffs, no perp walk, no reading of rights in the headlights or anything like that. They let me take the dogs back to the house and put them inside. They told me to leave my cell phone and any weapons I might be carrying, which I did. Then I was escorted to the black Suburban and settled into the backseat with one of the agents. Two more got in the front seat, and a fourth took my car keys and followed us in *my* Suburban. We were a regular parade.

They were acting like this was just a normal office call among professionals, but still, I didn't even think about resisting or giving them any lip. I sat there in the backseat with my seat belt fastened and both hands clearly visible in my lap as we drove north toward the lights of Wilmington, up over the Cape Fear Memorial Bridge, down into town, and then east toward the container port, which is where I thought we were going.

Wrong. We turned north onto Shipyard Drive, away from the port, and went several blocks north before turning right into a cluster of two-story brick buildings. We drove around to the back of one of them, which was right next to a fitness center, and parked. They took me through a cipher-locked back door and into what I assumed was the FBI's resident agent's office in Wilmington. I was escorted down a hallway to a conference room. There was a cardboard box on the conference table. The agent who seemed to be in charge told me that it would be just a few minutes.

"What will be just a few minutes?" I asked.

"Your ride."

An hour later my "ride" drove through the gates of what looked like a state hospital for the mentally challenged.

There were grim, twenty-foot-high brick walls along the front, an ornate if presently unguarded wrought-iron gateway, and a central paved road pointing toward a large, five-story brick building in the distance. Alongside the road were low, boarded-up white structures that looked like vintage World War II Tempo buildings.

I was now wearing a set of bright orange nylon overalls, courtesy of the cardboard box in the conference room. My ankles were connected by eighteen inches of thin stainless steel wire, and my wrists were similarly constrained. When we pulled up in front of the Victorian-looking main building, one of my escorts in the front seat asked me to lean forward so he could drop the hood over my head. Throughout the entire process, I hadn't said a word, and I didn't say anything when the cotton hood was draped over my head and neck. There were no eyeholes, so I was now totally dependent on the two escorts to shuffle me out of the car and into the building, with quiet instructions about steps, the door, turn right, turn left, turn around, okay, sit down. I was physically larger than either of them, but the restraints and now the hood reduced me to something very small indeed. I could see light and blurred shapes through the hood, but nothing else. Every time I inhaled, the hood flattened against my face. It smelled of industrial-strength laundry soap.

I sat on what felt like a park bench in what I assumed was a hallway. I could hear voices coming from another room nearby, but there was no alarm or excitement, just the casual conversation I remembered when doing a routine booking. Some low laughter, a phone ringing and being answered, someone stirring a coffee mug, football talk, and the shuffle of papers. The hallway smelled of institutional disinfectant and stale coffee in equal proportions.

There'd been no drama at the RA's office, either. A walk down the hall to the bathroom, where I was asked to strip down to my underwear, given a cursory examination for weapons, and then handed my new costume. Then back to the conference room to wait. Being an ex-cop, I knew that my best move at this point was to keep my mouth shut, which I did. I didn't know what charges, if any, were being filed, or if I was really even under formal arrest, although the orange jumpsuit had not been an encouraging development. No one came in to ask questions, and the people who were handling me had obviously not been interested in idle chitchat.

Hands appeared at my elbows, and I stood up. Turn left, the sounds of an electronically controlled door, walk straight ahead, turn right, stop. Elevator sounds. Step in, turn around, stop. Doors closing. Elevator movement, with four dings indicating that we were going to the fifth floor. Doors opening. Step out, turn right, walk straight ahead. A firm hand on each elbow, but no antagonistic pressure holds. I'd seen pictures of the Al Qaeda detainees at Guantanamo, and wondered why their heads always hung down. Now I knew: The only things I could see were the tops of my feet.

Finally, stop here. The sounds of another electronic door. Turn right, step through the door, that's good, now three more steps, turn around, sit down. Elbows free. Good. The hood came off. And there was Creeps, stretching out his long, awkward frame in a too-small metal chair across the room. My two hallway helpers stood by the door, within reach. They were dressed in Marine combat fatigues and had distinctive military haircuts. One of them crumpled up my hood in his large hands.

The room was about twelve by fifteen feet square. I'd been expecting a cell, but it wasn't like that. There were two windows, dark now, of course, a normal single bed with a night table and a reading lamp, a small desk and chair, and two other armchairs. There was a door that I hoped led to a bathroom. The walls were painted a muted green, and the floors were polished linoleum. The only thing that indicated I was in a cell was the fact that there was no doorknob on the inside, just a card reader.

Creeps watched me take it all in before speaking. "Mr. Richter," he said.

"Special Agent," I replied. If they'd expected me to protest or otherwise spout off, I meant to disappoint them. For the moment.

"I apologize for the hood," he said, "but it's become standard procedure for military detention facilities these days. Tends to take the piss and vinegar out of prospective rebels, you understand. That said, there is a plus side: Nobody sees who's being admitted to the facility, either."

He waited for a response; I remained silent. I knew full well that every interaction between a prisoner and his guards of whatever stripe was part and parcel of an interrogation record. I hadn't been Mirandized, but then again, he had just mentioned the term "*military* detention facility." When he realized there wasn't going to be a reaction, he leaned forward.

"Right," he said. "Let me explain why you're here. Were you and your associates present at the scene of a radioactive material spill at the container port yesterday?"

I nodded. I'd looked for a video camera, but hadn't seen one.

"Were you present when the trailer in question disgorged several illegal aliens into the container stack area?"

I said yes.

"Were you warned by me, personally, not to get involved in the matter of a previous radioactive material incident involving one of your associates?"

"Sort of," I said.

He looked down that long bony nose. "Sort of?"

"I'm an investigator for hire, Special Agent. Until I spoke in detail with Dr. Quartermain, I could not know that what he wanted me to do involved either incident."

"Do you remember what I said as I was leaving your rented house?"

"Interfere and disappear."

"Yes, indeed. Guess what?"

"I give up."

"You will be detained at this facility until further notice. You will be allowed no contact with the outside world until further notice. If you cooperate with the established regimen of detention, you will be given certain privileges, such as an operating television, this room instead of a rubber room in the psychotic isolation cells down in the basement, access to library materials, unfettered exercise outdoors within the confines of the grounds and the rules, and even some choices of meals. The converse to all that is also true."

"What about my dogs?"

"Your shepherds. Right. We have contacted your associates and asked them to come retrieve your dogs. One—" He fished out a notebook and read his notes. "One Anthony Martinelli is coming down tonight to retrieve them and return them to your home in Triboro."

All of that left the obvious question unspoken.

"We told him that we had received a call from you asking for one of them to come retrieve the dogs. That you did not sound as if you were under duress but that you would be out of pocket for some time on your new assignment and, for reasons known only to you, could not take the dogs."

I wanted to ask him if he thought Tony really believed that bullshit, but thought better of it. The two guys in military fatigues were standing at parade rest, looking bored. The one guy had reduced the hood to a compact orange wad.

"Do you understand what I was telling you about privileges, Mr. Richter?"

"What I don't understand is how you think you can abduct me, transport me to some American version of the Lubyanka, and hold me incommunicado 'until further notice,' without a hint of a criminal charge or even a Miranda. Since when has the Bureau been doing this kind of shit to American citizens?"

"Since the passage of the Patriot Act, Mr. Richter."

"That's for baby-burning Islamic terrorists."

He stood up. "I'll get you a copy of the act, Mr. Richter. You might be surprised when you read the whole thing, and even more surprised if you read some of the action memoranda flowing from said act. Few people have actually read it, I'm told, including an embarrassing number of congresspersons." He looked around my new home. "In the meantime, please behave. This is as good as it gets. The alternative accommodations are reportedly unpleasant."

"Reportedly? This isn't *your* fun house?"

"Oh, no, Mr. Richter. You're now in the hands of the Department of Homeland Security. Your Bureau does not indulge in detention facilities. Gentlemen, would one of you please swipe your magic card?"

There was a pamphlet on the bed, along with a green magstripe card. The pamphlet spelled out the rules in straightforward, military language. The bathroom was shared with the room next door. Swipe the card—if the bathroom was available, the door would unlock. Take the card with you, because if you didn't, you'd be in there until the cleaning crews showed up. Detainees would be served three meals a day. Breakfast would be at 0730. Lunch would be brought in at 1130. Dinner at 1730. Exercise periods would be scheduled by the guard force.

The second page had more rules. My official status was detainee. In case I was wondering. Each detainee was restricted to his or her room for twenty-two hours a day. There would be a two-hour exercise period within the grounds. There were rules for the time one spent outdoors: Detainees had to stay thirty feet away from any perimeter fence. There was a white chalk line on the grass indicating the thirty feet. Detainees could not speak to any other detainees while out on the grounds. Detainees would wear a hood the entire time they were outside of their rooms, including during exercise periods. The fence around the grounds was under continuous surveillance. There were guard dogs involved in that surveillance. Detainees would obey the instructions of any and all guards, but would not speak to guards unless the guard spoke first. Deadly force was authorized throughout the facility. Enjoy your stay with us.

I tried the card on the bathroom door and got lucky. Then I came back to my new room and tried the bed. It was a bed. There were no clocks on the wall, and the television, mounted high on one wall, was silent. I got up and turned out the overhead lights. The windows revealed that the building was near a river, but I didn't know which river. The trip from downtown

Wilmington had taken at least an hour. There were lights on the building shining down onto the grounds. I could actually make out those chalk lines against the perimeter fence, but there was a jumper barrier ledge under my window, so I couldn't see directly down into the exercise yard.

Terrific, I thought. Then I was startled by two loud raps on the door. I waited to see what would happen. Two more raps.

"Well, come right in," I called, turning on the bedside lamp.

"There's a hood in the closet," a voice said. "Put it on."

I looked and found it. Same haute couture orange, much lighter, and this one had eyeholes. I put it on, turned on a reading lamp, and told my caller to come in again, wondering how much I looked like a Klansman.

The card lock beeped and a major of Marines stepped through the door, along with two new escorts. The major turned on the overhead lights. He was an extremely fit white male, dressed in pressed and stiffly creased cammies, highly polished boots, and a Marine-green utility cap. He had either gone completely bald or had shaved his head. He wore a large gold ring on his left hand, which I presumed was the source of the raps. His two escorts looked just like him, only much younger. They wore black leather gloves, which made them more menacing than the previous two escorts. I wondered if things were finally going to get physical.

The major looked at me and then consulted a clipboard. "Mr. Doe," he said. "I'm Major Carter. I'm the OIC of this facility."

"My name isn't Doe," I said. "It's—"

"It's Doe. Actually, J. Doe Five-Seven. That's what it says here on your entry paperwork, and that's all we need to know. I'm here to explain a few things to you."

I perched on the edge of the bed, feeling more than a little ridiculous in my orange jumpsuit and KKK headgear. "Go right ahead, Major."

"Thank you, Mr. Doe. As you can see, we are United States Marines. Temporarily, this facility is a military reservation, so military law applies."

"I thought this place was a state loony bin."

"And you would be correct about that, Mr. Doe. It has been used for that purpose, but it was decommissioned sometime after 9/11. Now it is a federal loony bin. *My* federal loony bin, to be specific."

"I guess I'm a little surprised to see Marines."

"Marines go where they're told to go and do what they're told to do, Mr. Doe. Now, speaking for myself, and probably for my two escorts here, we'd all rather be back in the Happy Valley participating in Uncle George's Assholes for Allah program. That's like our Toys for Tots only lots more fun. But, sadly, we're here instead. And so are you."

"Who put me here? Can you tell me that?"

He sniffed and glanced at his clipboard. "The Octopus put you here, Mr. Doe. That's what we call the Department of Homeland Security. Tentacles every fucking where. Black ink billowing out in noxious clouds if anyone gets too close or pokes sticks at it. Big, round, intelligent eyes. And an even bigger beak in the middle." He looked back up at me. "This would be the beak, Mr. Doe."

I shook my head in wonder. This couldn't be happening. He'd apparently seen that look before.

"The good news, Mr. Doe: there's neither a *C* nor a *T* after your number five-seven. That means you are neither a criminal nor a terrorist detainee. That would require different accommodations."

"Oh, like the basement?"

He seemed surprised. "The basement? There's nothing in the basement but rats, wires, boxes of records, and rusty pipes. My Marines use the basement to hone their hunting skills against the day they go back to real Marine work. No, sir, any *C*-code detainees at this facility are held on another floor, and the *T*-codes go see a little bit of Fidel's Communist paradise. Let me get through my brief, please. It's late and I need my beauty sleep."

One of the escorts twitched with what may have been a smile. I sat back on the bed and let Herr Kommandant read me some more rules. The basic premise was as Creeps had described it: Be good, don't give the guard force any shit, and this would be like any other motel, only with one-way doorknobs and perpetual room service.

"Isolation is the rule here, Mr. Doe. Hood's on when outside the rooms. You don't talk to guards, other detainees, the housekeeping people, and especially anyone outside the fence. When you use that card to access the bathroom, the other person's card won't work until you've used yours to exit. If you tarry overlong in the bathroom, your card will stop working. You want to live in there instead of in here, be our guest."

"Do I get my one phone call?"

He shook his head. "Isolation means just that, within and without. Octopus rules."

"And for how long does this go on?" I asked.

He shrugged. "That's up to the Octopus, Mr. Doe. Did you perchance ignore a warning from someone in authority to stay away from something or someone?"

I nodded. "It's possible."

"Well, that's it, then. Whoever that authority is, they'll make the decision, and then the Octopus will wave one of its many arms and you'll return to main pop out there in civvieland. Or not."

I stood up, and the escorts made subtle adjustments in their stance. They weren't armed, but they both looked like men who didn't need a gun to get things done.

"The government can't hold me forever, Major," I said. "Even military prisoners have rights."

"The housekeeping people will deliver a menu each morning through this slot in the door, Mr. Doe," he said, ignoring my declaration of human rights. "You can indicate the items you *don't* want each day. Your tray will be delivered through that drawer. When you're finished, put the tray and all utensils back in the drawer."

"Okay."

"Your mommy doesn't work here, Mr. Doe. You will be responsible for keeping your room clean. Housekeeping will clean the bathroom daily, and sanitize the room once a week while you're out in the exercise yard. Lights go out at 2200, and the door card readers lock down at the same time. See that red button?"

He pointed at a red button next to the hallway door. I nodded.

"That's the panic button. If you have a genuine emergency, you push that button. If we feel it's not a genuine emergency after we've responded, you'll get yelled at. If you get yelled at twice, the panic button is disabled, and then when you do have a genuine emergency, you'll just have to die. Clear?"

"Crystal," I said. "Don't fuck with the panic button. How about television? Books?"

"Let's see how the first few days go, Mr. Doe," the major said. He looked me up and down. "You look like a guy who works out. Maybe even a tough guy? There's a weight set in the yard; not many of our detainees use it. Feel free. If you get the urge to rumble, we can set up a smoker with some of my Marines. Do a little boxing instruction, maybe some hand to gland. Fun stuff like that."

His Marines looked mildly interested. There's a brand of soap products called Arm and Hammer. Their logo is a muscular arm raising a small maul. These guys looked like the maul. "What time is it now?" I asked.

He almost looked at his watch, but checked himself. "It's late, and it's dark, Mr. John Doe Fifty-Seven. From now on, please just play by my rules, and pray that the Octopus doesn't forget you're here. They do that, you know."

I lay back on the bed when they were gone, wondering what the fuck I'd gotten myself into this time. I heard the card reader on my side of the bathroom door click and saw the little light go red. A noisy bathroom fan went on. Someone, my neighbor, I supposed, had come into the bathroom. Thirty minutes or so later, the fan went off and my bathroom door LED went green. I fell asleep, wondering how long before Tony and the guys came looking. Soon, I fervently hoped.

Two days later, I was moved to another room on the same floor. No change in amenities, and I figured it was a housekeeping issue. Life in the detention center went pretty much as briefed. The food was mess-hall chow. Mass-produced, acceptable, if not exactly cholesterol conscious. I began drawing lines through some menu items on the second day, concerned about my girlish figure and the fact that I had nothing to do but sit or sleep. The two-hour exercise window was precisely measured, with one surprise: There were fenced lanes in the grounds, running from the building to the perimeter fence, beyond which I assumed was the river. The lanes were fifty feet wide and nearly five hundred feet long. I know. I paced mine.

Other detainees were out in their own lanes, and no one seemed interested in making eye contact, which, admittedly, would have been difficult as we were all wearing hoods. With eyeholes, we could see straight ahead. If anyone was curious about his lane neighbor, he would have to turn his head, and my guess was that this movement would be visible to the guards or on whatever surveillance system was covering the grounds.

If there was a weight set out there, I didn't find it. I concentrated on doing stretching exercises, a brisk walk, a jog, and then a real run, up and back, for about forty minutes. It got hot under the damned hood. After that, I reversed the order to cool off. I saw only one other detainee doing something similar; the rest just walked, back and forth, inside their fences. It was surreal, this procession of baggy orange jumpsuits, humping dutifully back and forth between the perimeter and the hulking, concrete building. I'd expected guard towers and spotlights, but there was just a fence, and not a new one at that. Beyond the fence was a field of dormant grass, and then some dense woods. I'd caught a glimpse of the river from my fifth-floor window, but it wasn't visible from the yard.

At the end of two hours, a police whistle would sound, and the Orangemen all trudged back to the steel double doors. We were required to sound off and identify our numbers, and then we were admitted to the interior and walked in groups of five detainees with a Marine at each end of the line to the freight elevators. The elevator was as close as we got to another human being, but there was no contact. We were marched to our respective rooms and told to stand in front of our doors. The doors all clicked at once, up and down the hallway, and we went through. My neighbor apparently was let out for a different exercise period, and the yard was busy all day with orange jumpsuits walking the line.

On the fifth day it rained, and a voice came by my closed door and asked if I wanted to stay inside or go out. I chose to go out; many others did not. The Marines issued me a full-length plastic slicker that had a rain hood. I spent the whole two hours outside, getting damp in the process but determined not to miss a chance for fresh air and exercise. During the time I was out there, a group of Marines humping full battle packs came jogging around the perimeter fence on the outside, soaking wet but keeping perfect time to the subdued chanting of their sergeant, who ran, similarly encumbered, right alongside. I noticed the major was also running, with *two* packs on, one rank in front of the rest of the group. Gotta hand it to Marine officers—they know how to lead from the front.

When I got back to my room, I found a stack of books and my watch on the desk. It was all nonfiction and not very recent, but I was delighted to have books at last. The television remained dark, but I didn't care very much. I'm not much of a vidiot under the best of circumstances. I worried about my mutts, and wondered for the umpteenth time if my guys were looking for me. I couldn't see Tony believing anything the G-men told him, but, on the other hand, he'd had doubts from the git-go about what I was doing down there at Helios. If Quartermain happened to back up what the agents told him, he'd probably go into the watch-and-wait mode.

My secret surprise came late that night, when I was awakened by a sound I couldn't place. The rain was still coming down outside, so the room was dark except for the light coming in under the door from the hallway. Instinctively I reached for my trusty .45 and then remembered I was fresh out of heat.

I heard it again: The hinges on the bathroom door made a

faint squeaking noise. I tensed in the bed, not knowing what to expect, and then a human figure loomed out of the darkness and sat down on my bed.

"Hi, there," a female voice said. "I'm Mad Moira Maxwell, and I'm your neighbor. What's your name?"

Coming from a relatively sound sleep, it took me a few seconds to gather my wits, sparse as they were.

"Cam Richter," I said. I could just make out her face, but the rest of her was wrapped up in a lumpy bathrobe. Her eyes were wide and, I realized, just a little crazy-looking. Had she said *Mad* Moira?

"So what'd you do?" she asked, making herself more comfortable on the edge of my bed. She didn't weigh much, and her hair was disheveled. Red hair, I realized. There might be something to that Mad business after all.

"Failed to heed a nose-out warning from appropriate authority. Twice, I think. And you?"

"Sedition with a computer or three," she said brightly.

"I haven't heard that word since high school civics. *Sedition*?"

"It's come back into vogue these days," she said. "The government is taking itself a lot more seriously than it used to, and here we are."

"How'd you fiddle the bathroom door locks?" I asked, mindful of the major's warnings about being good *and* not talking to other detainees. I sat up in the bed to give her more room. That didn't work. She slid closer. She smelled of soap and healthy young female.

"When you can do sedition with a massively parallel computer system, door locks are a piece of cake," she said. "I am—I was, I suppose—a professor of computer science at the U in Wilmington. How about you?"

"I was a lieutenant in the Manceford County Sheriff's Office, back in Triboro, for far too long. Now I'm a freelance investigator. Or maybe just lance, now that I think about it. Free I am not."

"Know that feeling," she said.

"How long have you been in here?" I asked.

"One year, one month, ten days, and a wake-up, as the Marines like to say."

She laughed when she saw the surprise registering on my face. "Oh, yes, lieutenant, this can go on for a long, long time. Especially for sedition in time of war, even if it is an undeclared war."

"Fuck me," I said, without thinking.

"Right now?" she asked, and then she laughed again. It was an appealing laugh, but those eyes still had that penumbra of lunacy around the edges. I figured her for about thirty-five, maybe thirty-eight or so. It was hard to tell in the gloom, and I wasn't about to turn on a light.

"I'm sorry," I sputtered. "I mean—aw, shit . . ."

She waved a hand. "No offense taken. In fact, I kind of like the direct approach. Especially after being locked up in here. The last guy in this room was a Muslim of some stripe, and he was scared to death of women. He threatened to report me when I visited. I told him I'd throw menstrual fluids on him in his sleep if he opened his yap. That seemed to do it."

"Ri-i-ght," I said. Mad Moira indeed.

"Yeah, well, I tend toward direct action. They don't call me Mad Moira for nothing. You have anyone on the outside who's going to be wondering where you went?"

"Actually, I think so. Or maybe it's more like hope so. And you?"

"The Arts and Sciences faculty was probably relieved all to hell when I went 'on sabbatical,' as I suspect they've been told. If anyone has inquired, they've probably been damned tentative about it."

A legend in her own mind, I thought. "You one of those feminazis I keep reading about?" I asked.

"You bet," she said proudly. "Although I'm not anti-male. I am definitely anti-government, especially this government, which I believe to be illegal, unconstitutionally elected, and guilty of all sorts of perversions of the Bill of Rights. You going to escape?"

Oh, great, I thought. Another fanatic. She ought to meet

Carl Trask. They could rant together. As to escape, the thought had occurred to me, but so had the nature of the guard force. These guys weren't your typical paunchy, chain-smoking, union-card-carrying, fifty-year-old penitentiary screws. That little group jogging around the perimeter fence in eighty pounds of full battle regalia hadn't been out there for a picnic, and none of them, not one, had been even breathing hard. If I did try to escape, I'd better succeed on the first try. Plus, I didn't exactly know my newest best friend all that well.

"Thought about it," I said finally. "But it looks really hard. Besides, I don't fancy living in a real cell. I'm hoping my friends get some really nasty lawyers to start looking." Even as I said that, I wondered if it was likely, at least in the near term, especially if Quartermain was part of the cover. I realized that he was increasingly the unknown element here.

"I've thought about nothing else," she said, shifting on the bed. In profile her face was quite pretty, and, yes, that was red hair. "If I could get my hands on the computers that run this place, we could walk out of here in five minutes."

"Then what?" I asked. The same government agency that rounded her up in the first place would more than likely round her up again, and this time she might have to learn Spanish or some other foreign tongue. "Are you familiar with the term 'rendition'?" I asked.

"Oh, yes. In fact, that's what attracted their attention. I was getting a pretty good handle on the size and scope of that program. Of course, I had to break through some federal firewalls to do it."

"Yeah, they hate that," I said. "Frankly, I used to hate it when hackers went after our sheriff's office computers. If they were local assholes, we'd drop by and do something physical about it."

"Oh, so I'm an asshole now?"

"Look, Moira, I don't know you. I do know that I have not been fucking around with the federal government's war on terrorism. I ignored a warning from an FBI agent to stay out of a case that got one of my people killed, so here I am. If you went hacking into the feds' computer networks, they have to assume you're part of the problem, just like the president said."

"So it's okay for the government to kidnap citizens in the night and lock them up for the duration?"

I shrugged. "Personally, I favor prosecution in open court. I'd certainly be willing to take my chances in that venue. But: Did you do the crime?"

She didn't answer.

"You know the saying. And I have to tell you, as an ex-cop, this is pretty cushy time."

"Yet here *you* are," she said. "You don't think what you did was a crime, but you're doing the time, just like me."

She had me there. "I guess I think someone's eventually gonna try to get me out," I said. "Maybe not right away, but soon enough. My people are going to see through the smoke screen and, being all ex-cops themselves, they'll push it. Someone 'in authority' will come in here one day and ask me if I've gotten the message, I'll play nice, and then I'll be out."

"I used to think that, too," she said. "See how you feel a year from now. Or two."

"Why do you say that?"

"You're not thinking it through," she said. "Why would they let you out? To have you on the outside, running your mouth about what happened to you just because you pissed off the FBI? They've done the hard part—they've swept you off the streets and covered their tracks. Your people can push as hard as they want, but the United States Government, and that's spelled with a capital *G* these days, doesn't have to say one fucking word. They have zero motivation to let you out. And you know what else?"

"I give up."

"I've talked to six other people in this place. And given the rules, that's been harder than you might think. No one knows of *anyone* who's ever been let go. Moved, yes, but not just let go. I'm not saying it hasn't ever happened, what with the lovely headgear and all, but, best I can tell, we're all in here for life."

"Don't you have family? A husband? Or at least one good friend?"

"Nope," she said. I waited, but she didn't elaborate. When I thought about it, though, neither did I. If the guys at H&S bounced off the Octopus shield and then gave up, I had nobody who would keep trying, except maybe my shepherds. She was watching my face.

"That's why I asked if you'll try to escape, because if you do, I want to go with you. And I can help."

It was my turn to study her. "How do I know you're not from the Octopus, as the major calls it. That you're not in my room because they're *letting* you into my room, to find out if I'm going to be a good boy or if I've been sitting up here, lo, these few nights, plotting and scheming."

"You don't," she said immediately. "I'm able to fiddle these doors because one of the nice señoras dropped her hall pass card. It only works on the bathroom doors, not the room doors. But I can get us out into that hallway, and there are fire stairs at each end of that hallway. The elevators are computer controlled. The fire stairs are not."

"How do you know this?"

She stood up and shucked her jumpsuit. Underneath she was wearing a long white football shirt that reached down to just below her knees. She put her hands behind her head, stretched, and turned around slowly to show off. Even in the dim light, I could see her body. She was lovely in all respects. "This is what I work out in when it's warm outside," she said. "The Marines are all horny young American males. The major does not go down into the basement, ever, no matter what he says."

She picked up the jumpsuit and wiggled back into it, all the time watching me watching her doing it. "Girls and boys have their needs, and Marines are nothing if not direct. I'm telling you, I can get us out of this building. What I can't do is get over that final fence."

"Or what's probably on the other side of it," I said. "And there's still the problem of afterward."

"I'll take my chances. And if I can get to my computers, they'll wish they'd never *ever* tangled with likes of me."

Her computers had probably been reduced to burned blobs of plastic in a landfill, but I didn't tell her that. I was busy rearranging my covers to hide my reaction to her little tease. "Where does the 'Mad Moira' business come from?" I asked.

"Because I'll do absolutely anything once," she said with that sly, half-crazy look. "Even you, big guy."

Then she was gone, and the light on my bathroom door was green again. I got up to look out the window, just to make sure I hadn't been dreaming. On my way back to the bed my bare feet discovered a filmy little unmentionable.

Okay, I thought. I hadn't been dreaming.

Time to think. A redhead with a radical left political agenda who admitted to being part crazy wanted to light off an escape attempt from a prison run by Marines. What could possibly be wrong with that proposition?

The next morning, I heard the familiar sounds of guards in the hallway escorting prisoners, excuse me, detainees, to exercise. My turn came two hours later, and I shuffled down to the elevator with six other people, all indistinguishable in their jumpsuits and hoods. If my newfound ally was among the group, I had no way of telling, but it seemed as if they didn't let adjacent rooms out together.

Once outside, I went through my regular routine. There were guards here and there, but they seemed almost uninterested in what the detainees were doing, or not doing—some just sat on the benches against the side fence and smoked. There was no smoking permitted in the building, but cigarettes were provided to the real addicts when they came out for their fresh air.

I covertly watched the other people, trying to see if I could make out Mad Moira in the group, but it was impossible. The jumpsuits were identically baggy, and the hoods revealed nothing that would indicate the gender of any detainee. I did glance up at the top floor to see if I could see a face at her window, but the glass appeared reflective. No luck there, either.

Then a detainee tried to escape.

It was almost ordinary. I was doing some stretching to relieve incipient cramps in my legs from the sprints when I saw a detainee who was three lanes away walk calmly over the end chalk line to the final fence and begin to climb. He didn't bolt or yell or do anything dramatic. He simply crossed the line, grabbed a handful of chain-link, and began to clamber up the wire. I looked around to see what the guards would do, and was surprised to see them do absolutely nothing. One guard who had stopped to watch when the man started up the fence lit a cigarette and then sat back down on a bench. That gave me a bad feeling: If the guards weren't concerned, the escapee had better be. They were expecting a show.

The orange figure climbed steadily until he reached the top. He looked back as if expecting machine-gun fire from within the exercise yard, but the guards were all just watching and still acting unconcerned. There were no guard towers or other weapons stations around the building—just that fence. There were three strands of barbed wire at the top of the fence, tilted inward, but the detainee pulled a couple of bath towels out of his jumpsuit, doubled them over the barbed wire, wobbled for a moment at the top of the fence, and then tumbled over.

The other detainees had all stopped doing whatever they'd been doing and stood there, watching, just like I was. I expected sirens, a prison escape alarm—some kind of institutional reaction to the escape attempt, but there was only silence and the watching guards. Who had to know what was about to happen.

As the orange-clad figure began climbing down the other side of the fence, I heard a bang from over my left shoulder. I first thought it was a gunshot, but then realized it was a large wooden trapdoor opening and closing in the building's wall. I saw something come through that door, something black and moving fast. It was a large rottweiler. Full grown, ugly as a stump, and rounding the far corner of the fence at the speed of heat in that bearlike gait they have. It made not a sound, but ran as hard as it could to the point just below the detainee, who'd by now seen the dog coming. He stopped his descent about halfway down the fence and stared. I could see the dog's spittle flying as he came, head down, ugly pig eyes locked on to his prey, and those massive black haunches driving him forward. The escapee was still a good eight feet in the air, and he'd frozen in midclimb, his arms stretched one over the other, and his feet in a similar disposition, one up, one down.

He started back up as the thick black dog arrived, but he might as well not have bothered. The rottie screeched to a stop, took one measuring look, barked once, a nasty, wet sound, and then jumped up onto the fence, all four legs driving. To my amazement, the damned dog began scrambling *up* the fence, using his enormous teeth to help him climb. He overtook the man's lower leg at probably ten feet off the ground and clamped down on his ankle. Then he let go of the fence. The man screamed in pain as the dog's clamped-on, dead weight took effect. I almost thought I could hear the bones crunching, and I could absolutely see bright red blood spurting out of those clenched jaws. The man screamed again, and clung to the chain-link with white knuckles, his free leg swinging in the air now while the dog just hung from the other leg, growling and biting down harder, the froth in his mouth running red from the terrible damage he was doing to the man's lower leg and ankle.

It was no contest. The dog must have weighed over a hundred pounds, and between the dead weight, the horrible slaughterhouse noises, and the dog's own squirming, the man simply could not hold on. They both fell to the ground, and I held my breath. I thought surely the rottie would let go and then go for the man's throat, but he didn't let go. He began pulling the screaming man along the fence, back toward the corner from which he had appeared, matching each scream with a growl of his own and a sharklike shake of his massive head, as if determined to drown out the human's piteous cries and simultaneously rip off his prize. He dragged that poor bastard all the way down the fence line, jerking backward around the corner, and then backed into the trapdoor, where they both disappeared into sudden silence.

I remembered to breathe. I looked over at the guards, who had gone back to their routine of walking back and forth along the interior walkway, as if nothing out of the ordinary had happened. The rest of the detainees in the exercise area were still frozen in their tracks, as was I. I'm sure we were all wondering what would happen next, inside that door, but the show was definitely over and that was that. It had taken all of maybe ninety seconds. I glanced back up at the top floor, and this time I thought I saw a blurred white face in Moira's window.

Okay, neighbor, I thought. *Still want to make a run for it?* I looked back out at the fields and woods beyond the perimeter fence. The trees were perhaps two hundred yards across the open field from the fence. I assumed the river was just beyond that tangle of willows, scrub oaks, and haphazardly piled flood debris.

But then I saw a welcome sight.

Frick and Frack were looking back at me. They were sitting just inside the tree line, clear as day, if you were looking.

When I recovered from my surprise, I began walking casually toward the perimeter fence, conscious of the fact that absolutely no one else was getting anywhere near it. I was sure the guards were watching and wondering if the madness was contagious, but then I turned around at the chalk line and did a light jog back to the other end of my pen. I did this twice more, and each time confirmed that I could see my shepherds' heads sticking up through the weeds just inside the tree line, watching me.

Okay, I thought, *if* they're *watching me, then there's a human out there, too, hopefully with binocs.* On the third trip back to the perimeter, the whistle blew. I scoped the guards out of the corner of my eye. They were gathering to assemble the detainees to go back into the building. I got to the white line, stopped, stretched, got down on one knee with my hands on the ground, and pushed the other leg out behind me. Then, keeping my body between the guards and my hands, I made an imaginary pair of scissors out of my two hands and mimed cutting through the fence. I got back up and walked casually to the other end, where a guard was waiting for me. I heard another Marine bark out a command, reminding the small line of prisoners that there was no talking allowed.

"Nice pet you-all got there, Marine," I said. "What's his name?"

"Kibble and Bits," he said. "Step out. Fall in. No talking. Clear?"

Clear as a bell, I thought. I stepped out, fell into line on the sidewalk, and shut my yap. If the dog hadn't already done it, they were going to have to amputate that poor bastard's foot.

That evening after supper I went in to use the bathroom. There was a message soaped on the mirror: *Well?* It was signed *MM* and followed by the words *erase this*. I erased the message with a wet cloth, picked up my soap bar to reply, but then put it back down and went about my business. On balance, I still didn't know if I could trust Moira to be who and what she said she was. First of all, what were the chances they'd put a man and an attractive woman in conjoined rooms? Even with all the elaborate key card security, she'd still managed to get into my room. And how had she done that? With a conveniently dropped key card, which was never reported missing? Third, she was a wild-eyed redheaded female. I'd tangled with one of those in my younger days, and tangled was the operative word. In my view, red in the head meant Celt in the blood, and that tribe had always and only been about mortal combat.

I wedged my door open with a towel, retrieved her skivvies,

and put them on the edge of the sink. Then I retreated to the relative safety of my room. Whatever I was going to do about escaping, I wasn't going to complicate it with Mad Moira.

Unless, of course, I wanted use of that magic key card.

I sat down at the little desk and thought about it some more. Obviously, there was no going over the fence in broad daylight with that *thing* on ready-alert. So: first things first. See if my guys out there got the message about cutting the fence. I got up and looked out the window. It was raining again, and now there were tendrils of fog creeping up from the river through that band of trees where I'd seen Frick and Frack. Maybe tonight, they'd make their move.

The next day was gray and overcast, but without the rain. I took my usual exercise period, this time around midafternoon. Which exercise pen you got depended on the whim of the guard, but I'd noticed that the first guy in the lineup after coming out of the building went to the first pen to our left, and so on. I set myself up so that I was shut into the same pen as yesterday.

I did my standard exercise package, but ended up near the perimeter fence instead of the base of the pen, where I faked a leg cramp. I sat down on the grass and did a little kabuki, pretending to suffer through the act of straightening out my "cramped" thigh muscles. In between grunts and twitches, I examined the fence. I was looking for signs that it had been cut, but it hadn't.

Well, shit. So much for that.

Then I scanned the grass and weeds outside of the pen. Immediately beyond the fence was the perimeter running track the Marines used. Beyond that, it was just wet weeds and foot-high grass all the way to the edge of the woods. And, yes, there were signs something had come across that field to the fence. Subtle signs, but to anyone who'd done any tracking, they were there.

I examined the fence again. I had to be very careful here. I had to assume there was a video camera focused right on me because I was lingering near the forbidden fence and the white line of death-by-rottweiler inside the pen.

I stood up, and then sat right back down again with a grunt of simulated pain. Two feet closer to the fence. I stared hard, but the fence was intact. What wasn't intact was all the clips along the bottom of the panel of chain-link wire in this pen. They were all there, but they had all been severed. Assuming there was enough slack in this fence, I should be able to push my way out under the bottom of the chain-link.

Okay. The guys had been watching.

I got back up again and hopped around on my good leg while trying to make the other one work properly. In the process I turned out toward the woods, pointed at my watch, and then stretched three fingers against my stomach. Then I began limping back toward the other end of the exercise pen. I saw one guard watching me, but he looked more sympathetic than alarmed. I hobbled back to the end of the pen and sat down on the ground again, continuing to massage my thigh muscle.

"You okay?" the Marine asked quietly through the fence.

"Yeah," I muttered. "Fucking cramp."

"Heard that," he said, one workout guy to another.

I kept up the gimp act all the way back to my room. I heard the last cohort of exercise-bound people being mustered out in the hallway, and it sounded as if my next-door neighbor's door had opened and closed. I waited fifteen minutes, and then went into the bathroom, where I took a long, hot shower to soothe my "cramped" limbs. When I was finished in the bathroom, I soaped a single word onto the mirror: *talk.*

The lights went out throughout the facility at ten o'clock. Mad Moira was in my room ten minutes later. This time she was wearing her jumpsuit, and I could confirm what I needed to know—she was slim. I was the one who was going to have a problem getting under that fence, assuming we could even get out to it. I told her I was going out tonight.

"Wow," she said. "That was quick. You have someone waiting?"

I ducked her question. "Can you get us to the exercise pen that's the third from the left?" I asked.

She thought about that for a moment.

"I can get us to a door that goes outside; after that, it'll depend."

"On?"

"On the alarm system—the hallway room door card readers are locked down after ten o'clock. I don't think the bathroom doors are. I think it's a fire safety thing—they want one door that can be operated by a housekeeping card in case the main system goes down."

"You *think*?"

She shrugged. "Well, I can hear the room card readers click off at 10:00 P.M.; I've listened to the bathroom hallway door reader, and it doesn't."

"So it's still possible there'll be an alert the moment you key that door?"

"Sure."

She must have seen the look on my face.

"Look: The difference is, that door will open. These room doors won't. There aren't any readers on the stairwell doors—again, think fire safety. My plan was to key the door, open it, and run like hell for the fire stairway. After that . . ."

"Yeah," I said. "After that, it could get really interesting."

She shrugged again. "I'm ready to give it a shot. I've seen loading dock ramps that go down to the basement on the back of the building. The first floor is where the security station probably lives. I'd say try for the basement, then out."

"That's where that damned rottweiler came from," I said. "If he's loose in the basement, we're hosed."

"The dogs aren't loose down there," she said.

"And you know this how?"

"The Marines hang out down there at night. They use pistols, .22s, to hunt rats. They do it with rat-shot, so's to avoid ricochets. They drop garbage in the basement corridors, turn off all the lights, wait for a while, and then go out with night vision goggles. They wouldn't do that if there were dogs loose."

"And if they're down there tonight? Maybe the basement is the wrong objective."

"If they are, they'll be drinking beer right now. They like to get a buzz on before they go killing things in the dark. But they're usually done by midnight—the major gets them all up at five thirty for PT."

It was my turn to think. I'd mimed the number three and pointed at my watch. Hopefully, this had been observed by my pals with binoculars hiding in the woods. Assuming they'd known it was me under that hood, and assuming they were even there. Lots of assuming. *If* they'd understood what I meant, we had to roll out of here a little after 2:00 A.M. to make it to the trees by three. One minute to get from the door to the stairs. Two to get down into the basement. And then?

"Do you know if those stairs go to the basement or just to the first floor?"

"Basement," she said.

"You really party with these guys?"

"Nothing else to do," she said. "Why the hell not? They're physically fit. Besides, they're just doing a job, so the guard thing isn't personal. They didn't put me in here."

"I wonder what the major would say if he knew his guards were sexually abusing the female prisoners."

"It's not abuse, big guy," she said with a grin. "And the major most certainly knows about it. Besides, from what I hear, he's not too crazy about holding American citizens. Iraqi insurgents? That's different."

"You suppose you could sweet-talk one of your guard buddies to look the other way if he caught us trying to get out?"

"Nope," she said promptly. "These are Marines. They have a duty, and they'll do it, no matter what they think about it."

"Even if they think it's wrong for American military people to be holding American citizens?"

"The major tells them that higher authority knows what it's doing, and points out that nobody here's being tortured, interrogated, or otherwise mistreated."

"Unless, of course, you try to go over that fence."

She winced and nodded. "Yeah, I saw that. But even then, it wasn't a Marine gunning down a detainee. The major keeps reminding them that, mostly, we're being kept out of circulation for the convenience of something they call higher headquarters."

"Right. The only thing we have to do is submit. That's the attitude that made the Gestapo possible."

She snorted. "If you knew anything about the real Gestapo, you wouldn't use that word," she said.

"Ge-sta-po," I replied. "*Geheime Staatspolizei.* Secret state police. Heinrich Himmler's flower children. Started as brownshirts, keeping order at meetings of the Nazi faithful. Graduated to *much* bigger things, didn't they. If this place is any indication, just give it time."

But the fact was, I didn't want to get into a human rights discussion with Mad Moira. I wanted to get out of here. She sensed my uncertainty.

"So what's it gonna be?" she asked. "You want to try it, or not?"

"My brain says there's too much we don't know. My gut says now or never."

"Right on," she said. "When?"

"Tonight at 2:00 A.M. Pray for fog."

Our prayers were answered. At a few minutes before 2:00 A.M. I took one final look out the windows and saw a solid wall of fog. I'd thought about flashing a signal out into the woods with the room lights, but not with this pea-souper outside. All I could see out the windows was the glow of lights down in the exercise yard.

I was dressed in my exercise jumpsuit and shoes, minus the KKK headgear. There was nothing I needed to bring from the room. Moira had told me the sequence for fiddling the bathroom doors. She'd tap three times on her door with her bathroom card. I'd tap three times on mine. Then we'd position our respective cards, and next she'd tap four times slowly but in a definite rhythm with something hard. On the fourth tap, we'd simultaneously swipe our cards. According to Moira, either both doors would open, or alarm bells would go off downstairs. Or both, she'd said, sweetly.

In the event, both doors yielded and we met in the bathroom. We each rolled up two bath towels in case we ended up having to go over the fence. We listened for a few minutes to see if anyone was coming down the hallway in response to our simultaneous card swiping. I could hear Moira breathing fast, and realized that, for all her bravado, she was as scared as I was. If the guards came now, we could claim that we'd been getting together for some boy-girl fun. But once we left the rooms and got out into the building, there'd only be one explanation for what we were doing out there.

Even if we got to the fence, there was still that tiny little problem of the hellhound. And if my people were not there, we'd be making our stand with our backs to a river. It put me briefly in mind of the old bear joke: I didn't have to outrun the rottie; I only had to outrun Moira. I decided not to share that thought with her just now. She saw me smile.

"What?" she asked.

"This is about the worst-planned escape attempt I've ever considered," I said.

"Yeah, but think of it the way the jihadis do: They never set a date and time for doing anything. They plan the operation, and then they wait. They see an opportunity to strike and they do. There's no way for military intelligence to know in advance because the jihadis don't know in advance."

"And you know this how?"

"I believe the whole Iraq war was based on a lie," she declared. "I'm always on the side of the freedom fighters. In the case of Iraq, that ain't us."

"You say shit like that in public a lot?" I asked.

"All the time," she said. "I'm one of those people who believe we brought 9/11 on ourselves, and that they hit precisely the right people when they did it."

I had to take a deep breath. The air in the bathroom was getting warm, and I was suddenly not so sure I wanted this left-wing nutcase along. I thought about cold-cocking her and taking the damned card. But she knew the building and I did not. Plus, she wasn't trying to con me: That's how she felt, and there it was.

"We make it out of here," I said, "you're on your own. If my people are out there in the woods, we'll get away from here. But after that . . ."

"My sentiments exactly," she said, her eyes defiant.

"Okay," I said. "Swipe that sucker."

She did, and we both heard the door lock click. She opened it and we stepped out into the hallway. We closed the door and stopped to listen, but the only thing we heard was the click as the bathroom door card reader LED reset itself to red.

Our rooms were on one corner of the building. The elevator and the fire stairs were at the other end. On the outside wall were the room doors. On the inside wall were some cleaning-gear closets and one marked as a linen closet. There were red dry-chemical fire extinguishers mounted on the wall every fifty feet. The floor was more of the polished linoleum that decorated the rooms. Half the overhead fluorescent lights were off. My government saving electricity.

We hurried down toward the other end of the hallway. I didn't see any surveillance domes in the ceiling or along the walls, but that didn't mean there wasn't anyone watching. On the other hand, it was an old building, with concrete interior walls and ceilings, so back-fitting built-in cameras and wiring would have been difficult. When we got to the fire stairs, though, we discovered that Moira had been wrong about card readers. There was one, and its LED glowed bright red.

"Oops," she said.

I felt a pit in my stomach. Trust a liberal to fuck it up. Then we heard the elevator machinery start up, and saw the green numbers over the elevator doors begin to light up in sequence as the elderly machine ground its way toward our floor, probably filled with a Marine reaction force.

To our right was another hallway, identical to ours. Rooms on the outside, closets and storage on the inside wall. The building was probably a hollow square, with an air shaft in the middle. There was a set of fire stairs down at the far end, but even from where we stood, we could see another little red light laughing at us. That pit in my stomach was growing. I looked at Moira, whose face was tight with fear. The green light marked 2 went off, and the green light marked 3 lit up.

Then I remembered what I'd done to Billy the Kid. There was a fire extinguisher mounted right next to the elevator door. I grabbed it and told Moira to grab another one and get back here. She understood immediately and ran to our right, so that she'd be out of the sight line when the elevator doors opened. The green light on 3 went out, and the light for 4 came on. Here they came. Thank you, Moira: wrong about damned near everything. Or part of the detention program.

She was back, and I showed her how to remove the seal without firing it. I positioned her on one side of the door, and myself on the other.

"That door opens, step in front of them and pull the trigger. It shoots low, so aim just above their heads. We want to blind them, pull them out, get in the 'vator, push *B* for basement, and then hit the door-close button."

Assuming it went to the basement, I thought. And that it didn't require a card reader to operate. My pit was becoming a bowling ball.

I readied my extinguisher and hoped like hell it was charged. The green light for 4 emitted a tiny ping. If the reaction force was properly constituted, there'd be no guns. Prisons had learned a long time ago never to arm the guards if they were going into the population. The elevator thumped to a stop behind the sliding doors. The doors opened in a blaze of yellow light. I nodded to Moira, and we stepped out.

We faced two very startled Marines. Fortunately, they were neither armed nor dressed out in any particular kind of SWAT gear. They wore the usual cammies and black gloves, and each carried a police baton under one armpit like a swagger stick and what looked like a black mace canister in his hand.

I fired first, but Moira was right there with me. In an instant the Marines' faces were covered in white powder and they had dropped the sticks and canisters in an attempt to protect their faces. I stopped shooting for a second, and they instinctively went into defensive crouches, and then I resumed, coating their hands and spraying more white stuff in their faces. Moira's extinguisher piled on with equal fervor. Then I dropped mine and grabbed the first Marine by his right sleeve and flung him out of the elevator, where Moira turned and continued to spray stuff into his face. The second guy tried to resist, so I kicked him hard in the shin and then flung him on top of the other guy.

"In," I said to Moira, and in she jumped as I hit door-close and then *B* for basement. The doors shut with agonizing slowness, but Moira had kept her extinguisher and continued to shoot it fiercely at the two white figures on the floor until the doors closed. I let out a big sigh of relief when the elevator began to head down.

Now it would be a matter of how fast the two disabled guards could make contact with their control center and get someone to intercept the elevator before we got to the basement. I hadn't seen any shoulder mikes or radios, but that didn't mean there wasn't a security phone they could get to. Once they could see.

Moira bent down and collected the Mace cans and the batons. We were leaving 4 and headed for 3. "These might be useful," she said.

"Forget the batons, but we'll keep the Mace cans," I said, and I showed her how to fire the Mace. We passed 3 and headed for 2.

"Why not the sticks?" she asked.

"You ever fought a man with a stick?" I asked. "There's an art to it."

We passed 2 and headed on down to 1. That's where we'd find out if we were going to make it to the basement or have to fight our way out the front door, which, of course, wasn't ever going to happen.

As we came up on the first floor, I heard voices shouting in the hallway outside, but the elevator, bless it, kept going. A few moments later, the door dinged and opened into the basement vestibule. I had my Mace can ready and pointed at the doors in case there was a welcoming committee, but the vestibule was empty. I jammed Moira's fire extinguisher in the elevator door to disable it. The fire stairs did make it down to the basement, and I tipped a fifty-five-gallon drum of floor wax under the handle just to slow things down a little. Now we had to find those loading docks.

The basement layout matched the floors above in the hollow square configuration, except all the interior walls were steel mesh interspersed with concrete structural columns. The lights down here were single bulbs in metal frames, and instead of rooms there were storage cages, holding tools, boxes of old files, and supplies. The ceiling was crisscrossed with pipes and electrical cables, and the whole area smelled of old pipe lagging, dust, and heating oil.

"Which way?" I asked.

"Down this way," she said, pointing straight ahead, and then indicating we'd need to go left to the other corner. "That's where the loading docks should terminate."

We took off, running this time and making no effort to be quiet. From here we could see that the building was built in the shape of a capital *B,* with two air shafts, not just one. There was heating and air-conditioning machinery at the base of the air shafts, and we were running from the lower left corner of the *B,* across the base, and up to the middle area where I remembered the loading area ramps ought to be.

Then all the lights went out.

We stopped running but kept moving, using the light from the heating and air-conditioning machinery control panels. I visualized some Marines coming around the corner with their rat pistols and night vision gear, but hopefully they'd secured by now. I glanced at my watch—two ten. At least we were on my timeline.

We pushed forward in the darkened passageway, and I couldn't shake the feeling that we were not alone. I wondered where they kept that rottweiler at night if not in the basement—outside the fence? I gripped the canister of Mace even harder.

Feeling our way along the wire mesh walls, we got to the

corner of the first passageway and turned left. All the storage cages on our right appeared to be stuffed to the gills with cardboard boxes marked MEDICAL RECORDS. To our immediate left was a boxy, oil-fired boiler, whose orange flame was visible through the boiler front inspection port. The boiler room wasn't really a room, but more of an area enclosed in wire mesh walls with chain-link fence doors. The area stank of heating oil, and wisps of low-pressure steam were visible in the nest of pipes leading up into the main building. Two ancient water pumps ground away in one corner of the enclosure.

I couldn't see much of anything ahead, where the loading docks should be. We desperately needed some light, because the farther away we got from the boiler room, the less ambient light there would be in the passageway. Behind us we heard banging on the door jammed by that steel drum. We weren't going to be alone much longer.

"Gotta hide," I whispered to Moira. The question was: where? If they were wearing night vision gear, there wasn't going to be anyplace to hide down here.

Except.

I grabbed her arm, and we turned around.

"What are you doing?" she whispered.

"The boiler room," I said, as I started trying doors. "That flame will interfere with their NVGs."

The banging was getting louder. It sounded like someone was using a fire axe on that door. The chain-link doors into the machinery room were padlocked.

"Climb, quickly," I said, and we scrambled up the chain-link, bent over the tops of the wobbly door, and slid back down to the floor on the other side.

Up close the boiler gave off tangible heat over the sustained low roar of the burners. Down the passageway we heard that steel drum bang down onto the concrete floor and go rolling. We scrambled around behind the boiler and crouched down between two large air ducts. The place was littered with boxes of rags, tools, and spare valve parts all stacked behind the boiler, and we made ourselves a nest out of these.

For the moment we were safe, but that wasn't going to last long. They'd spread out on NVG, search the entire basement area, and then realize that none of the doors to the outside had been opened. Since we'd jammed the elevator and the fire doors, they'd know we were still down there, somewhere in the basement area. They'd turn the lights back on and go cage to cage.

Or go get the dog.

There might be another set of fire stairs and elevators on the west side of the building, but they probably had people on those already. It was just a matter of time before they'd come in here. We needed a diversion, and quickly.

Moira tapped me on the arm and pointed. Between the two metal air ducts there was a space of about six inches, and we saw two ghostly figures slipping by in the glow of the burners. They walked by too fast for me to see if they were carrying weapons, but they were definitely wearing night vision headgear.

Just a matter of time.

A fuel pump lit off under our feet and the boiler ramped up in response to a demand from a thermostat somewhere upstairs. More air began to rattle through the combustion supply ducts.

"We need a diversion," I said softly.

"A fire would do it," she said, pointing to the glowing firebox. The machinery was making enough noise to mask our voices.

"Without a way out?"

"Fuck it," she said. "I'm not going back inside. Besides, they'll evacuate the building. They'll have to turn off the security system to do that."

That might be true, I thought. Or they might just isolate the basement, pull the handle on some kind of fire suppression system, and wait it out. Two more figures swept past the boiler room, walking slower this time. I thought I heard tactical radio voices.

Sooner, rather than later.

We had to do something.

"Okay, fire it is," I whispered. I turned around and found a large ball-peen hammer. I slithered out of our nest of boxes and crawled to the boiler front. I looked both ways out into the passageway, but couldn't see anyone. That, of course, didn't mean they couldn't see me, but that orange glow from the glass inspection port ought to show up as a bright, foggy plume on their NVGs, which would make them avoid looking in my direction.

The inspection port was a five-inch-diameter circle of heat-tempered glass. I turned over on my back, cocked an arm, and whacked it. The first whack produced a crack; the second one, harder, shattered the glass, at which point a jet of flame roared out of the hole and blew all the way out through the chain-link and into the passageway itself. It singed the sleeve of my jumpsuit, and I ducked back out of its way to the side of the boiler, which was now making noises like a jet airplane spooling up on the tarmac as the burners went unstable. Anyone on NVGs looking my way would be stone blind with all that light and flame. Then I smelled heating oil, and saw Moira whaling away on the fuel-supply line filter housing, which was already spurting thin streams of pressurized oil across the floor. Goddamned woman was a born fighter, but she might not appreciate what was going to happen next.

"Time to boogie," I said, no longer trying to keep quiet.

We slithered through all the boxes at the back of the boiler enclosure to a side wall made of expanded metal screen. Then we waited. The jet airplane effect didn't seem to be getting any bigger on the other side of the boiler, but it wasn't getting any smaller, either. There wasn't much smoke forming because that jet of flame had the entire basement's supply of oxygen to play with. Then the spreading pool of heating oil must have made its way under the boiler and out to the front, where it found a partner in crime. The ensuing fireball easily engulfed our hideout, accompanied by an ear-squeezing whumping sound. And now there was lots of smoke.

I nudged Moira, and we began scrambling over the wire

mesh wall, using the supporting studs as footholds. First one and then two fire alarm bells went off somewhere in the basement, followed by an entire chorus of smoke detectors. The fire was getting bigger by the second, and would soon discover all that paper piled up in the wire cages across the passageway.

We'd climbed from the machinery cage into the adjacent storage enclosure, which was empty. The passageway we wanted was right in front of us, but there would still be Marines out there, so we kept climbing through the row of cages, one after another, as the glare from the oil fire behind us got big enough to light up the whole basement. It was hard going, and the edges of the hardware cloth were tearing up our hands.

Then we saw the loading dock area, suddenly visible ahead and to our right—where four Marines were crouching down and talking anxiously on shoulder-mike radios. They had their NVGs pulled down, and their young, scared faces were orange in the reflected firelight.

We hung there, frozen halfway up the sidewall of the storage cage like a pair of lizards, as that light got brighter and brighter. If they'd looked up, they'd have seen us immediately, but they were all focusing on the loading ramp door. One kept trying the handle, as if they'd asked someone to unlock it remotely. The noise of the fire behind us suddenly increased, probably as a fuel line melted down and put the heating oil out onto the floor at full throttle. A modern system would have shut itself down long ago, but that boiler plant had to be 1940s vintage. I looked at Moira, who was staring at the four Marines in pure disbelief. Then a horn went off and one of the steel loading dock doors started to roll upward.

The Marines didn't hesitate. All four bolted for the widening gap between the door and the concrete ramp, hitting the floor like paratroopers and rolling under the gap as if it were concertina wire. One minute they were there, the next minute they were gone and down the road. Or at least up the ramp.

"Go! Go! Go!" I yelled at Moira, because I knew what would happen next—they'd shut that door as soon as they knew their Marines were safe. If left open, that door would create a firestorm. I could already feel the blast of cool night air headed in to help with the fire.

We scrambled the rest of the way up the wall, then went sideways along the top to the front section of the cage, heedless now of the ragged edges of hardware cloth at the top. Over the top, drop to the floor, and run like hell for that ramp, pursued now by the heavy cloud of thick black smoke that was coiling along the ceiling like an angry incubus. I took one breath of some truly noxious gases of combustion from wiring, pipe lagging, and cardboard boxes, which put me momentarily on my knees. We were forced to get down to all fours as we arrived at the ramp, just in time to hear that horn go off again.

It was harder rolling *up* the ramp than it would have been rolling down, but we had plenty of motivation coming down the passageway after us in the form of a flame front. The door slammed down onto the concrete just as Moira made it through, and the air began shrieking under it as the fire demanded more and more oxygen.

We huddled at the bottom of the ramp to get our bearings. I was almost afraid to look up the ramp, expecting to see a four-pack of smiling Marines waiting for us. But they were gone. What we could see was that every light in the building above us was on, which probably meant that there was a full-scale evacuation in progress. We'd wanted a diversion, and by God, we had one.

We crawled up the ramp on our bellies to the sidewalk from which the exercise pens extended into the foggy night. Still no guards in sight. The interior gates to the exercise pens had latches but no locks, as there were always guards out on the sidewalk when the detainees were in the pens. I quickly counted to the third gate, and we went through, closing it behind us. We could hear a commotion of voices growing on the other side of the building, but no sirens yet. The fire in the basement was invisible behind all that concrete, but we could still hear it sucking a shrieking gale of air under the steel ramp doors.

We trotted out the length of the pen through wet grass, and the building grew indistinct behind us as the fog closed in. By the time we got to the far end and the dreaded white line, all that remained was a yellow-white glow behind us and some muffled sounds of emergency personnel. We pressed up against the chain-link of the perimeter fence and stopped to listen for signs of guards. Or dogs. Moira looked back into the gloom.

"Suppose the whole place will go up?" she asked quietly.

"It's old, but it's mostly concrete and brick, so maybe not," I said. "They should have time to get everyone out."

We finally heard distant sirens in the fog, which should mean that this would be the best time to make our run for it, before the guard force was relieved by EMS people and could come looking.

I dropped down to my knees against the fence and tried to lift the bottom. It didn't move.

What the fuck! Had they found it and fixed it? Or were we in the wrong pen?

"What?" Moira asked, seeing me look up. I explained the problem. She swore and immediately began climbing the side fence. She flopped over the top and dropped to the ground, checked the perimeter fence, and hissed a "here" at me. We'd miscounted.

I went over the side fence to find her already sliding under the pushed-out skirt of the perimeter fence. I dropped to my back, pulled myself under, and got back on my feet.

"Good thing you don't have tits," Moira said with a grin, but then we heard that goddamned trapdoor bang behind us in the fog.

I don't know where they kept that dog, but, apparently, it had not been in the basement. We didn't waste time: We ran straight away from the fence and the lights, hurtling out into the fog as fast as we could go, and hoping like hell we weren't running in a big circle right back to an unpleasant canine rendezvous.

We couldn't see a thing out ahead of us, so after what seemed like the length of an entire football field, we stopped to listen. Moira was breathing really hard and went down on one knee to catch her breath. I tried to orient myself in the fog, but of course there was nothing to navigate by except our own trail through the wet grass. It looked pretty straight, but I knew we could still be way off course. The sirens were louder behind us, but the fog distorted sound direction.

The big question, besides navigation, was whether or not my rescuers were out there in the woods. There was one way to find out: I let go a short, sharp whistle. Moira made a face as if asking if I were nuts, but then I heard something coming through the grass. An animal something, not human. The new question of the moment: my dogs or theirs?

"Ready Mace," I whispered, and put us in a back-to-back stance, each with a Mace canister pointed and ready. The sirens had stopped, and now the fog had completely enveloped the building and the fire. I could feel Moira's legs trembling against mine.

We waited.

A full minute passed, then another.

Then there was a low, rumbling growl out there in the fog. I felt Moira tense up. I wanted to point the canister in the right direction, but there was no way to tell in that fog. Little beads of cold moisture were forming on my face that had nothing to do with the weather.

A second growl, seemingly closer, but from a different direction. I tried desperately to think of something we could do, but we were blind. I think it would have been better if we'd also been deaf.

If it was the rottie, he was circling us. He knew there was human prey out there, but not how many, and, once he left our scent trail, he was operating blind, too. Our scent wouldn't go anywhere in this fog.

More sounds of something moving in the grass, but not necessarily closer. The grass crunching quietly, low panting.

Another minute of aching silence, then a third growl—much closer. I leaned out, pointed my can down low, and fired a burst in that direction. I got a satisfying little whimper out of the fog and the sounds of some frantic pawing in the grass.

I reached behind me and grabbed Moira's belt, and then we advanced in the direction I'd fired until I could see a darker shape low on the ground. It saw me at about the same time, and this time the growl was more like a roar. I fired again, and the roar changed to a prolonged yipping. The rottie backed away into the fog, and I did, too, dragging Moira with me to make damned sure we didn't get separated.

We'd solved our rottweiler problem, for the moment, anyway, unless we managed to step on him out there in the fog. He shouldn't be able to smell anything for a week if I'd managed to get any of that spray onto his face.

But now we were really lost. We no longer had our own tracks away from the facility to guide on.

Screw it, I thought, and whistled again, this time louder. This time I was rewarded by a familiar woof, and we moved in that general direction. I started calling them, as quietly as I could, and pretty soon first one and then a second fuzzy friend showed up, all excited at being reunited. I told them to quiet down, and then we followed their tracks back through the dewy grass. They hadn't exactly come in a straight line, but it was better than nothing. Somewhere out there in the fog we heard a muffled, thumping explosion, and then another one. There was a brief orange glow, which quickly faded, and then the sounds of more sirens.

We literally collided with the trees, and I got a face full of pine needles. We stopped to listen for any signs of pursuit, but there was nothing out there but the fog and the sounds of my shepherds panting. I turned to start swatting through all the low-hanging pine branches when something black came out of the fog from my side and launched itself at my face.

A branch saved me. The rottie clamped hard but got a mouthful of tree limb instead of my throat, and we both crashed backward onto the ground. Moira screamed in surprise as I tried to roll out from under that monster, but then I found myself underneath the dogfight from hell, and all I could do was cover my head with my arms, get as small as possible, and practice some strenuous bladder control. It was loud and messy and scary, with three roaring, snapping, growling, slobbering, heavy dogs going at it over my inert form as I tried hard to find that fabled direct route through the earth to China.

The shepherds finally won, and I lunged out from under that writhing furball, my ears ringing and my clothes covered in spittle, among other things. Frack had a death grip on the rottweiler's windpipe from the front, while Frick had a similar grip on one of its hind legs, pulling its stumpy body taut while Frack slowly strangled it. Moira was backed up against a tree with her hands to her wide-eyed face. I sat up in the carpet of pine needles and began wiping myself off.

"Are you . . . ?"

"Yeah," I said, getting up carefully while I checked for holes. "It was mostly noisy. But, as usual, I'm awfully glad they were here."

The rottie gave up the ghost in one hard spasm, struggling to the end, and I called my guys off. I felt sorry for the dog, who'd only been doing his assigned duty, much like the Marines.

Marines. We both heard vehicle noises out there in the fog at the same time. Somewhere in the direction of the facility.

"There's no way they can track us," Moira said. "Not in this fog."

I was looking at the rottie's bloody throat, where there was a leather collar with a small metal object dangling from it.

"Oh, yes, they can," I said. I turned to my two shepherds and told them to go find it. Frack gave me his usual blank look, but Frick understood and took off through the trees, with us in hot pursuit. We ran into Tony and Pardee a minute later when we popped out of the trees and met them coming inland from the river bank to see what had happened to the shepherds.

"About damn time," I said.

They both grinned back. "We watched you out there in that yard for two days before you bothered to look up," Pardee said. He frowned when he heard the vehicles out in the fog. "We got hostiles inbound?"

"We do," I said, looking over my shoulder. "This is Mad Moira. She helped me escape. Tell me we have a boat."

I had many questions on the ride down the river toward Wilmington, with the biggest one being how they had known where to find me. It seems that I had none other than Colonel Trask to thank for that. Pardee told me they got a call back at the Triboro office from Quartermain's slinky-toy assistant one day after I'd gone off the grid, with a request to come retrieve the shepherds.

"That seemed a little strange," Pardee said. "But then, we knew there were places in that plant you might not want to take the dogs."

"How'd Trask get into it?"

"We came down and made sure the shepherds were okay. Then we waited at the beach house a couple more days, but we still couldn't raise you. So I called Samantha. She told me you and Mr. Q. had gone to an 'unspecified location' as part of your investigation. She said you'd left instructions that you'd be in touch when circumstances permitted."

I watched Tony driving the boat with his face stuck into the radar display cone. We were definitely IFR tonight; the fog out on the river was, if anything, thicker than on shore. We could hear some buoy bells ringing as our wake set them to rocking, but I never did actually see one. Moira sat in one of the two padded chairs in front of the pilothouse, trying not to look afraid.

Pardee went on to explain that, after all the radio silence on my part, he'd called Trask to see what he knew about my sudden disappearance and this so-called unspecified location.

"Trask said it was news to him, and that he'd seen Quartermain at a meeting that morning."

"Did he tell you that the lovely Samantha is an undercover FBI agent?"

Pardee looked at me in total surprise. "No-o-o, he did not. What the hell, over?"

I told him what had happened, and all about the delightful federal spa and rest camp that I hoped was going up in flames as we spoke. I also speculated about the possible reaction from the Bureau when they found out we had escaped, and how.

"Damn," Pardee said. "They're holding U.S. citizens? Right there in plain sight?"

"Not so plain sight, when you think about it," I said. "You drive by that place, it looks like a state penitentiary for the criminally insane. Not the kind of place where you'd want to go in and take a tour. It's not run by the FBI, either. Those guards were all military types."

"That would make for an interesting story in the *New York Times*," Pardee said.

"Yes, it would. But I'll bet that all the remaining detainees and their Marines will be out of there in DHS vans before dawn. They'll probably let that building burn right to the ground. How'd you actually find me?"

"Trask again. He gives us a call. Says a guy at the bar had seen someone who looked like you having a friendly discussion in the parking lot with what looked like a bunch of feds. Then everybody drove off together. Trask asked him what kind of vehicles, and figures the guy's right."

"Okay, and the asylum?"

"Trask has connections with local law, so he checks the jails and the hospitals, just to make sure. Then a guy in the New Hanover County Sheriff's Office tells him the feds have a 'research center' up on the Charing River—that's the river we're on now. It feeds into the Cape Fear. Supposedly this place had to do with AIDS research. Some big NIH grant. Old state facility for the insane; low security, really sick people, rumors of biohazards, et cetera, et cetera. Local no-go area."

"And Trask, being ex-military, would figure out that that could be a cover?"

"He got a little coy about that, but I'm guessing from what he said that he went up there, cased the place, and recognized jungle bunnies. You don't use Marines to guard AIDS victims. He calls, says he thinks he knows where you might be."

Trask the helpful herpetologist, I thought. He'd never wanted us in his plant. I should think he'd have been delighted at the possibility that I'd been swept up in some kind of Homeland Security net. "I wonder what prompted all his sudden concern?"

"Good question, boss," Pardee said, staring out into the fog. "And did Quartermain know? I mean, who told Samantha to make that call, her boss or her bosses?"

"Creeps, I suspect," I said. But, of course, Quartermain might have been in on it.

The shepherds were sleeping in the front of the boat, curled around Mad Moira's legs. She was dozing, too. Pardee went into the bow locker and got a blanket, which he wrapped around Moira's shoulders. She gave him a smile, which made him sigh as he came back to where I was perched against the steering console. Tony still hadn't taken his face out of the radarscope cone.

"I'm also wondering why Quartermain didn't come looking, too," I said.

"Well, I'd guess he was embarrassed to ask Colonel Trask where his ace investigator had wandered off to. And Special Agent Samantha was probably telling *him* all sorts of lies."

That made some sense, but the whole episode was still pretty bizarre. Except for the fact that Moira was sitting in the front of the boat, it wouldn't be that hard to doubt that I'd seen what I'd seen.

Half an hour later Tony executed a slow, sweeping turn to the left, and then the curtain of fog began to lift. His face finally emerged from the cone. We had joined the Cape Fear River, and the lights of Wilmington were visible in the distance on the port side.

"I guess I better get up with Quartermain first," I said, grateful to be able to see again. "Where *are* we going, by the way?"

Pardee grinned in the darkness. "Ask and ye shall receive," he said.

An hour later, Tony maneuvered the boat carefully alongside a floating pontoon dock that was made up alongside a boathouse. Ari Quartermain stood on the bobbing platform to take our boat's mooring lines. He was unshaven and dressed in jeans, sneakers, and a bulky sweatshirt. Behind him was a large brick house that overlooked the Cape Fear River and the distant lights of Fort Fisher Park across the water. The first faint indications of dawn were thinning out the darkness over the far Atlantic.

Tony shut it down, and I went to wake Moira and her two sleeping foot-warmers. I introduced her to Ari, leaving out the other half of her first name, for the moment, anyway, and then we all walked up to the house and went into the kitchen, my mutts included. Ari pushed the button on an ancient-looking coffee percolator.

It was a relief to sit down and stretch in a warm room. Helios must pay very well, I thought, when I saw the inside of the house. Ari plopped a box of doughnuts on the table and joined the rest of us. Frick, who loves doughnuts, sat pointedly at the edge of the table, begging hard. Moira asked if she could please spoil the doggie, and I reluctantly agreed. I made her cut it in half and share with Frack. Shepherds on a sugar high are not a pretty sight, and Moira being all cute with the dogs was scaring me a little.

"Mr. Investigator," Ari said, raising his coffee cup in a mock salute, "your guys do *really* good work. Where in the world have you been?"

"The latest incarnation of Club Fed, I think," I said. I told him the whole story, including Moira's role in our escape, and revealed his admin assistant's federal sideline. He nodded at that, as if the news solved a minor mystery for him.

"I've always wondered why Judy—she was Samantha's predecessor—up and quit like that," he said. "I guess now I know."

"Our Bureau works in mysterious ways," I said. "The larger question is why. Why do they think it operationally necessary to have someone undercover at that plant, and specifically in your office?"

"Beats the shit out of me," he said, glancing a bit nervously at Moira. "Ain't like there's a booming market for highly toxic fission by-products." Even as he said that, I think he realized that there might, in fact, be just such a market. "Oh, shit," he said quietly.

"Oh, shit, squared," I replied. "The whole world of Homeland Security is on watch for terrorists trying to smuggle a dirty bomb of some kind into the U.S. But what if the bad guys have figured out that there's no need to smuggle it *in,* if what they need is already here?"

"Then what the hell was that over at the container port a week ago?"

"A diversion?" Tony said. "Something to keep all the watchdogs focused on the port, where they actually expect to find something?"

"I've got another question," I said. "Trask. My guys would not have gotten anywhere in finding me without his intervention. Why'd he do that?"

"Why'd he meet with you at that bar?" Ari countered. "After which you got boxed and wrapped?"

"You guys are starting to frighten me," Moira piped up. "I was locked up in that place for a year plus because I poked my computers' noses into one government program. You people playing with nuclear weapons?"

I shook my head, and explained who Quartermain was and a little bit about how we'd become involved at the power plant. As Ari got up to check on the coffee, the phone rang. He glanced at his watch and picked up.

"Hey, there, Sam," he said. "You're up early." Then he listened for a minute or so. Then he looked over at me. "Uh, Sam? I'm just getting out of bed, okay? What's going on?"

He listened some more, then nodded to himself. He fished out a pen, wrote something down, and hung up.

"It seems that one Special Agent Myers called the duty officer at the plant asking for my home number. Our policy is that all such calls go to Samantha—one of the perks of her job—and then she gets in touch with me if she thinks it's a no-shitter."

"Lemme guess," I said. "Missed-it Mary is looking for one Cam Richter?"

Ari sat back down. "The Bureau wanted to know if you'd checked in with us," he said. "You heard me—I didn't exactly answer her question."

"Where was it I was supposed to be checking in from?"

The percolator behind him began making worrisome noises. "Sam had told me you'd gone exploring at the container port. That your guys had taken the shepherds and gone back to Triboro, and that you and Trask were working together on something, or so Colonel Trask had told her."

"You didn't bother to verify that with Trask?" I asked.

"Trask doesn't respond well to beepers," Ari said. "He appears when he's needed. Likes to say he'll find you, not the other way around."

"And, of course, you had no reason to doubt what Samantha was telling you."

"Exactly. I was actually encouraged that you and Trask were working together. When I finally did run into him, he told me it was all news to him. Then your guys arrived, and here we are."

I exhaled a long breath. The whole thing just sounded so damned pat. Trask supposedly tells Samantha. Samantha tells Ari. Trask reappears as Helpful Harry, then steers my guys in just the right direction. If it looks too good to be true . . .

Moira asked to use a bathroom, and were there any women's clothes in the house? Ari said she could probably wear some of his wife's stuff; she was on a business trip to New York for the week. He took her upstairs.

I looked at Tony and could see that he, too, was perplexed. Pardee had his poker face on, which meant the same thing. I hadn't been able to tell what was going through Ari's mind, but there seemed to be an awful lot of irons in this fire just now. It wasn't exactly a finger-pointing drill, but it was close. Ari came back downstairs, and then the damned phone rang again.

"Seems everybody's up early this morning," Ari said with a sigh. He looked at the caller ID, frowned, picked up, and then frowned harder. "Special Agent Caswell. How can I help you at this hour of the morning?"

He listened for a few seconds this time, pointed a finger gun at me, and then started writing something urgently on the yellow pad next to the phone. Tony got up to see what it said.

"That's very interesting. Look, that remote gate control system isn't working right now. Let me get some clothes on, and I'll be right down. Just a few minutes, okay? Thank you." He hung up before letting Creeps reply and raised his eyebrows at our merry little band.

Pardee was already gathering up the unused cups and the doughnut box from the table. I yelled to Moira that we had to run, gathered the shepherds, and headed for the back door. Tony was ahead of me, but he stopped suddenly. Through the back-door window we could see a large, official-looking patrol boat of some kind nosing in to the pier where our boat was tied up.

We backed away from the window and returned to the kitchen. I told Ari that there was probably no point in any more running.

"Why don't you go down there to that gate," I said. "See what they have to say. But look: Don't lie, and don't be confrontational. If they ask you directly, yes, we are here."

Moira came back into the room, looking surprisingly good in her borrowed clothes. I had an idea.

"Ari—you have a computer she can use?" I asked as he put a jacket on.

Ari said yes and took her to his study. I went with them and told Moira what I wanted her to do. Bright girl that she was, she sat right down, brought up a Word screen, and began typing.

Ari dutifully trudged down the front drive, which curved out of sight behind some tall evergreens. Tony kept a watch on the patrol boat down by the dock, but it had backed away from the pier and was now just sitting there, bristling with whip antennas, its running lights unusually bright in the morning twilight. I'd known they'd figure out the boat angle, but I'd been hoping the fog on the river would delay pursuit until we could land somewhere safe. I'd forgotten the old cop adage: You can outrun the cop's car, but you can't outrun his radio.

"What now, boss-man?" Pardee asked quietly, using Tony's standard line.

I explained what Moira was doing in Ari's study, and what I hoped that would accomplish if Ari came back with Creeps and some of his helpers.

"You think you guys really burned that place down?" Tony asked. Tony was thinking like an accessory to arson, among other things.

"It sounded like they were evacuating the building, not fighting the fire," I said. "On the other hand, I won't admit to starting said fire. It just sort of happened, you know, coincidentally with our efforts to get out of the basement."

"That's your story and you're sticking to it, right?"

"Yup."

"Which story won't stand up for one minute once a competent forensics tech gets into it," announced Special Agent Creeps Caswell, materializing in the kitchen doorway along with two large and extremely fit-looking special agents. They were all decked out in their spiffy blue FBI windbreakers, although I thought I spotted some black smudges on Creeps's hands. We hadn't heard them come in, and nor, apparently, had either of my two wonderful watchdogs, who had instead set the watch on the box of doughnuts. Ari Quartermain, looking somewhat sheepish, brought up the rear.

"Mr. Richter," Creeps intoned formally.

"Special Agent," I replied. No one was brandishing firearms yet, so I had high hopes for a civilized conversation around the kitchen table. We might even get some more coffee.

"Where is Ms. Maxwell?" Creeps asked.

"Otherwise engaged," I said. "Here in the house, however, if that's what you're wondering."

One of the helpers took a quick walkabout, came back, and nodded to Creeps.

"Oh, good," he said. "Your Bureau was getting tired of driving around in all that fog."

"So what happens now, Special Agent?" I asked. Tony and Pardee looked on with definite interest. Creeps's helpers looked back at them with equal interest. Ari was trying to make himself look inconspicuous. The shepherds, sensing tension, walked over and sat down next to me.

"What happens next is that your Bureau will restore the status quo ante, as that term applies to you and Ms. Maxwell," he said. He glanced at my two accomplices. "And these two gentlemen may have to join your ranks, as it were."

"On what charge, Special Agent?"

"You? Or them?"

"Me, for starters. As I recall, I never did hear a charge the first time around."

"You must have more faith in your Bureau, Mr. Richter. I'm just *so* sure there was a charge, perhaps many, and even some evidence. It may be a little hard to find in the ashes of your erstwhile detention facility, but you know us—we'll think of something. And then, of course, there's the little matter of your escape and all the excitement leading up to it. There are some Marines who would like to have a word with you."

"It's ready," called Moira from the study.

"What's ready, Mr. Richter?" Creeps asked, frowning.

"Why don't we all just go see," I said.

We trooped into Ari's study, and I invited Creeps to read what she'd written in her letter to the editor of the *New York*

Times. She'd purposefully done it in a large font, and she'd done a really good job describing her imprisonment and the facility.

Creeps read the letter carefully. I could almost see his lips moving. I watched his breathing change, and then he cleared his throat.

"You understand, Ms. Maxwell," he said, "that we have the resources to rebut everything you've said there. Furthermore, even if you transmit that, you will not be available for further comment or elaboration, which tends to diminish its chances for publication. So why don't you just move that cursor to the delete button and stop all this foolishness."

Moira looked up at him. The Mad Moira light was clearly visible in those green eyes. Red hair and green eyes—Creeps should have known better.

"So you guys don't give a shit if I send this, then?" she asked. "Is that what I'm hearing?"

"As I explained—" Creeps began.

"Well, screw it, then," Moira said brightly, reaching for the mouse and bringing up the e-mail program that had been lurking behind the Word screen. "Sounds to me like there's no harm in trying, is there? I mean, you may be right—they may not print it, but inquiring minds will want to know more, don't you think?"

She zipped the cursor to the SEND button, which was when I realized she'd already attached the document to an e-mail and was ready to spread the gospel according to Moira to lots more people than just the *New York Times*. Mad Moira showing her teeth.

"*Wait!*" Creeps said, his voice rising for the first time in our entire discussion. Moira's hand remained firmly on the mouse, and the pointer remained firmly on the SEND button. The list of addressees on the e-mail seemed to glitter on the screen. It was an impressive list.

On one hand, I almost wished she'd fired it off. On the other, I breathed a silent sigh of relief. We had him. For the moment, anyway.

Then two phones went off simultaneously—Creeps's cell phone and Ari's house phone. Creeps glared at Moira and stepped away from the computer to answer his cell. His two assistants moved into position to menace us, and then my two helpers moved in front of me to menace them. Teeth were showing everywhere. Ari, moving carefully, picked up the desk phone.

Creeps had his back turned to the rest of us, but I saw his shoulders stiffen at about the same time Ari exclaimed a startled "What?" and then said he'd be right in.

"Problem at the plant?" I asked.

"You could say that," he replied grimly. "There's a body in the moonpool."

The plant admin building was in a definite state of uproar when I got there. There was a new secretarial face at Samantha's desk—no surprise there, as her true identity had been revealed—who asked me to wait in Ari's conference room for further instructions. I had left the dogs in the Suburban because I wasn't sure what, if anything, Ari would want me to do. I was sort of hoping to be sent back home.

Ari came back into his office suite fifteen minutes later, looking like his day was fulfilling his every dismal expectation. He beckoned me into his private office and asked me to close the door.

"We're going to have to get the divers in," he said.

"Divers? In *that*?"

"Yeah, there's a firm of divers who specialize in going down into containment vessels and moonpools. Lemme show you something."

He turned on a television in his office and switched to what looked like an internal video surveillance channel. I wasn't sure what we were looking at until he did something with the remote, and then I realized we were looking down into the moonpool itself. There, way down in that cerulean glow, was the silhouette of a human body, arms and legs spread wide as if crucified on an X-beam. It was lying on top of the spent uranium fuel assemblies forty feet down. I couldn't tell if it was face up or down, but it was definitely a human form.

"How radioactive is that part of the pool?" I asked.

"Very," Ari said simply, staring at the shimmering image.

"And no idea of who it is?"

He shook his head. "And if that body stays down there long enough, any identification is going to be . . . difficult."

I had a vision of the body melting down in all that radiation. Eyes like poached eggs. Lovely images like that.

"Can't you grapple it?"

He shook his head again. "From what we can see, the body is draped across and is in physical contact with the fuel bundles. Much too hot. We'll get a diver to go partway down there, then drop a minicam, see if we can make an ID. After that, we'll have to figure out how to bring him most of the way up to the rod transfer platform, where I hope we can encase the remains. Problem's gonna be diver stay-time, as always. But it has to be done fast."

"Why?"

"You don't want to know," he said.

"Who's working the problem?" I asked.

"Anna P. is in charge. I haven't located Trask yet to deal with the physical security side. We've notified upper management and the NRC, and the company's calling for the divers as we speak. We hope to have somebody on deck by third shift tonight. In the meantime . . ." He puffed out a breath.

"This doesn't affect the plant's operation, does it?"

"Nope. This is the moonpool. What we've got down there right now is a radionuclide Crock-Pot."

"Damn," I said. "Is it likely that somebody just fell in? I mean, if you did fall in, wouldn't you just get the hell out of the water as fast as possible?"

"Yes, you would, and if you stayed at the surface, you wouldn't be too much the worse for wear. Remember, exposure to radiation is measured in terms of intensity and time. Intensity is a function of proximity."

"On the other hand," I said, "only a drowned body sinks

like that. Lungs full of water. Maybe he hit his head on the way in. Are there ladders—some way for someone to get out, assuming he could swim?"

"Oh, yeah," he said, still staring at the screen. "And railings. And surveillance cameras." He shook his head. "This shouldn't be possible. I need Trask here."

Just like the radioactive water inside Allie Gardner shouldn't have been possible, I thought. Or the hot water on that truck over at the container port. Everyone could argue that there were other, non-Helios-related explanations for those incidents, but there was no arguing with this.

"You heard from the Bureau?" I asked.

"Only that they will take over the investigation once *we* exhume the body from the moonpool."

"Exhume. That sounds like Creeps Caswell. Okay, what do you want from me?"

"You find people, right? Find Colonel Trask. Whoever that is down there should not have been able to get there by himself. Especially without a protective suit."

"There's nothing on the cameras?"

"Nada. The Bureau will have to tell us if somebody messed with them. But I really need Trask, and, as fucking usual, his people can't raise him."

His beeper went off, so he motioned for me to get going. I went outside to piddle the mutts and then decided to bring Frick back into the building with me. We went down the hallway to the physical security office, where some of Trask's shaved-head torpedoes were congregating in the shift supervisor's office.

They confirmed they didn't know where the colonel was. They seemed more concerned about all the heat they were getting from the plant's director about not being able to contact him than they were about Trask's health and welfare. One of them came forward to make friends with Frick, who obligingly lifted a lip at him, prompting a chorus of whoas from the other guys.

"The colonel does his own thing," one of them said. "Shows up at the plant at all hours, tests the perimeter patrols, the cameras, vital area doors, and that kinda shit. Doesn't exactly keep regular hours. Says schedules weaken security."

"How do you normally reach him?"

"We don't," the supervisor said. "He listens in to all our comms. If he thinks he needs to get into something, he just shows up."

"So you expect that he knows about this body?"

"Be surprised if he didn't, all the commotion."

"Sees all, hears all?"

The supervisor shrugged. If his boss wanted to play mysterious, he was cool with it.

"They check his home?" I asked.

One of the younger ones, who'd been oiling an M4, smiled. "Home? Dude lives on a boat, man. Good luck with that."

I called a buddy at the state department of natural resources and asked if he could tie Trask's name to a specific boat license. He was back in five minutes.

"Big boat," he said. "Twenty-one-year-old, forty-five-foot cabin cruiser, officially listed for Carolina Beach. License is current; insured for one twenty large. Called *Keeper.* That help?"

I told him it did indeed, and drove out to catch the ferry that crossed the Cape Fear River estuary. I got to Carolina Beach and drove down to the city marina. I left the dogs in the Suburban and went to the office, where an elderly guy, whose well-used cap read CAP'N PETE, asked if he could help me. I explained who I was and that I was looking for Colonel Trask, who I understood kept a live-aboard boat here. He pointed out the window to one of the piers, where I could see a largish cabin cruiser with the word KEEPER in white lettering across its transom.

"Right there she is," he said. "But he isn't here. Haven't seen him for a coupl'a days now."

"Any possibility we could get aboard?"

"Got a warrant?"

"Nope."

"There's your answer, then."

I asked him to wait for a moment and put a call in to Ari at the plant. He sounded harassed but understood my problem. I handed the phone to Cap'n Pete, who listened.

"Best I can do," he said, handing me back the phone. "I'll go aboard, see if he's okay or even there. That help?"

"That would help a lot," I said. "It's not like him to go off the grid for this long."

"Then you don't know him," he said. "Because that old boy does it all the time."

"Yeah, but when he does, he's usually ambushing his own security crew over there at Helios."

"Not exactly what I meant," he said, reaching for a set of keys. "I was talking about him going out at night and coming back in the midmorning. You know he collects snakes?"

"So I've heard," I said.

"He showed me one of 'em, one time. I thought it was a goddamned fire hose until it coiled. Had it right there, on board. Nobody fucks with that boat. C'mon."

I followed him out the door as we went down toward the piers. "Most of the owners here, we see 'em either once, twice a year or on every weekend. We got us maybe ten live-ons here; the rest are all just slip renters. But the colonel? He's the onliest one goes out at night. All the damn time."

Which could still be all about testing his security crew over at Helios, I thought. "Does that mean he's a fairly competent seaman?"

Cap'n Pete nodded. "Keeps his charts and safety gear up to date, handles that old dog like a pretty woman. Knows the tide tables. Can print out his met charts right on board. Refuels the moment he comes in. Runs a tight ship, he does."

"When he goes, he go into the river estuary or out to sea?"

"Ain't nobody knows," he said. "Or asks, for that matter. Here we go."

The main piers were open to pedestrians, but the finger piers where the boats actually tied up were blocked by chain-link sections and key-carded. His skeleton key opened the gate and bypassed the electronic devices.

The *Keeper* was second outboard, her bow pointed out. I'm no expert, but even I could see that she'd been well maintained. Her brightwork was polished, the hull paint clean, and the bitter ends of the mooring lines were coiled into tight white spirals. There was none of the usual recreational junk I'd seen on the other boats—bloodstained coolers, rods and lines, bait baskets, dirty clothes—anywhere in evidence. There was a small inflatable dinghy hoisted on davits above the main cabin, and even the davit sheaves were polished. The high bow had a reinforcing knife-edge on it to ward off logs and snags in the river, and this was polished, too.

Cap'n Pete asked me to wait on the pontoon pier and then walked up the short companionway to the fantail of the boat. He banged his key ring on the railing and called out for Trask. There was no reply. He went aboard through a gate in the railing, tried the aft cabin door, found it locked. He knocked on the door and called again. Silence. He looked at me and shook his head.

"If he'd had a heart attack and was inside, what would you do?"

"Call 911," he replied promptly, and then realized what I was asking. He said, "Oh," and went forward, peering into the cabin windows along the main deck. Then he went up a side ladder to the pilothouse area, found a door unlocked, and went into the interior of the boat. He was back in about a minute.

"Ain't nobody home," he said. "And that's about all I can do, legal-like."

I thanked him for looking, gave him one of my cards, and asked him to call me if Trask showed up.

He examined the card and then declared that he'd give it to Trask, when and if he showed up, and that *he* would call me, assuming he wanted to. I smiled and thanked him again. Cap'n Pete looked out for his permanent people.

I called Pardee from the car and told him I'd found the boat but no Trask. He reported that they were about a half hour north of Southport. He said Moira was a happy camper.

She had purchased not one but two computers, and apparently the university had continued to direct-deposit her salary during the time she'd been "away." The Octopus covering its bets. Interesting program.

Pardee had a question. "Seems to me," he said, "that Trask would be all over a major problem in the plant. You thinking what I'm thinking?"

I told him it had certainly crossed my mind, but until those daring divers got there, we wouldn't know anything.

I just made the Southport-bound ferry, parking on the very back of the boat. The ferry pulled out, but then slowed way down. The captain made an announcement on the topside speakers that the ferry at the other end had been delayed by a mechanical problem and that there would be a thirty-minute hold. We were all invited to enjoy the scenery while he milled about smartly in the river.

I got out of my car and walked up through the rows and lanes to the superstructure to get some fresh air. I left the shepherds in the car; the last thing I needed was for Frick to see a seagull flying by and make one of her impulsive bad judgments. Other people had also gotten out of their vehicles and were enjoying the afternoon, which was cool, clear, and breezy.

Then I saw a familiar face. It was Anna Petrowska's number two at the moonpool. I didn't remember his name, but I definitely recognized his face. He hadn't seen me, or at least I didn't think he had. I wondered what he'd been doing over in Carolina Beach when there was a dead body in his moonpool. He was talking to someone on a cell phone, so I went around to the other side of the superstructure and made a call of my own.

Ari answered on the second ring. "Anything?" he asked.

I told him about my visit to Carolina Beach, and then asked if he had the divers lined up.

"There was a crew finishing up a project up at our plant near Raleigh; they'll be here in about an hour."

"And then?"

"And then we'll have to go through all the safety checks and briefs, set the bridge up so the handlers can do their thing, and all that. Two hours or so, then the guy can actually go down. But."

"But?"

"They tell me a minicam won't be of much use for making an ID—the water's too turbulent around the stack. And they can't get that close. There are several fairly young bundles in that stack."

I thought about that. "Well, then, call the local cops and get some of their drowning-incident grappling gear. They don't have to know where you're going to put it."

He laughed, although it was the short bark of an unhappy laugh. "It's not like they'll be getting it back," he said. "Come by in an hour; maybe you'll see something interesting."

"Can't wait," I said. Having seen some floaters before, I had a pretty good idea of what was coming.

I joined the small crowd standing on the platform above the moonpool. It was, if anything, hotter and more humid in the chamber, and our paper moonsuits didn't help. A steel, gantry-like motorized bridge was positioned out over the pool. There were four handlers on the bridge, all concentrating on the stream of bubbles foaming up beneath them and a bundle of cables, tubes, and smaller wires leading down into the water to a dark, helmeted shape. A compressor was clattering away on the side of the pool. Two nervous-looking Brunswick County EMS techs were waiting by the main access door, with a body bag folded discreetly at their feet.

Dr. Anna Petrowska was sitting at a console inside the control room, wearing the same kind of headphones that one of the techs out on the bridge was wearing. Her hair shimmered in the fluorescent light, but the steel glasses she wore took all the pretty right out of her fiercely concentrating face. Three more of her people were watching assorted instruments. Ari, dressed out in a white suit, was standing at the railing with some of his people. He walked over when he saw me come in.

"Can they get to it?" I asked him.

"Don't know yet," he said. "We've had to change the cooling water circulation around the fuel bundles. That's why it's so warm in here."

"How does this work?"

"One diver on a platform that can be raised and lowered from that bridge. Another diver in contact with the diver who's down. The guy in the water is covered in TLDs. They get readings every five feet, and that portable out there computes the allowable stay-time."

"He seen anything useful?" I asked.

"Only that the body is stuck headfirst in the fuel assembly matrix." He looked at me. "That's the hottest part of the pool. Not good."

"How the hell . . . ?"

"The suction grates for the water circulation system are directly under the fuel elements."

It was bad enough the guy was dead. But sucked down into the glowing water around the fuel elements? I shivered, even in the hot air. "You get grapples?" I asked.

He pointed to the bridge, where I saw the usual drowning retrieval gear and a frightened-looking cop in a white suit trying his best not to look down into that glowing water. Then one of the bridge techs was talking to him.

They slowly began lowering the grapple hooks down into the pool while the radio tech talked them through the positioning process. Petrowska signaled for Ari to join her in the control room. I went with him.

"The diver's about three meters over the stack," she said, pointing to a television display. I could see the shape of the diver shimmering on the screen. He was hard-hatted, and the top of his head was emitting a stream of truly beautiful bubbles. "I've shut off the circ pumps, so we have some hydrogen generation and rising temps. That will be as low as he can go. He's got sixty more seconds to get that hook on, and then we'll have to extract him."

"How hot?"

"Rems," she said. Initially, that didn't mean anything to

me, but it sure got Ari's attention. Then I remembered that our personal dosimeters measured millirems. Milli, as in one thousandth of a rem.

I swallowed. There was a reason why that water was glowing down there. I wondered if the diver could see his TLDs.

The radio tech on the bridge suddenly signaled a thumbs-up. One of the others helped the cop pull on the grapple rope, while the others began to raise the suspended platform to get their buddy the hell out of his radiation bath.

The diver came up a lot faster than the body, which was understandable. He had something to lose; the corpse no longer did. But when the body broke the surface, my heart sank. The grapple had hooked the man's belt at the back, so the body was bent in half at the waist.

That wasn't the bad part, though.

From about the collarbones up, there was nothing but gleaming white bone. No skin. Just a blue-white, shining skull with no face.

And certainly no ID.

Until I saw the small, black knife pouch on the man's right boot as he dangled, dripping, on the chain. I'd seen that knife before.

"I think that's Carl Trask," I said, pointing to that boot knife.

"Oh, shit," Ari muttered. He stared at the faceless figure. The height, weight, general build made it possible. "I think it is."

One of the techs, looking a bit unwell, pointed a distant-reading radiation monitor at the sodden figure and shook his head. He signaled the bridge people, and the body was lowered back into the moonpool to a depth of about ten feet.

Anna Petrowska was staring at Ari over the upper rim of her eyeglasses from inside the control room, as if asking Tony's favorite question: Now what?

Great question, I thought. Ari Quartermain's face was a study in anxiety.

"We need the second diver to go down," he said. "That's

not a body anymore. That's highly radioactive nuclear waste. We're definitely going to have to entomb that."

A few hours later, Ari and I were sitting in the front seat of my Suburban sipping some Scotch from my emergency flask. To say that things had become complicated would be the understatement of the year.

First, they'd had to get the second, unexposed diver suited up and into the water to bag the body, which was now suspended on a chain in the moonpool, because the first diver down had come dangerously close to going over his *annual* TLD limits. Then they'd brought the bag up and called in the foam team, who'd proceeded to do the same routine on the bag that they'd done on the truck. This produced a white, oblong semisolid object some eight feet in length that was still capable of setting off radiation alarms.

The Bureau had told Ari to call them when he had a body on deck. He duly made the call, but then had to explain that there was probably not going to be a proper identification, much less an autopsy. This news did not sit well with our Bureau. They'd told him to freeze the scene and await the imminent arrival of adult supervision. I took that as a clear signal to fold my tents and steal away into the desert night.

I told Ari that I'd wait outside in my vehicle and got one of the vital area techs to escort me back out of the building. I called my guys at the beach house and brought them up to date and, once again, instructed them to be vigilant. Tony said he had one shepherd on the front porch and the other lurking in the back garage with the door open. Moira had gone to bed, but he and Pardee were planning to keep watch for a while. I reminded them that, if the G did show up in the night, they'd be after Moira and me, not them. Tony gently reminded me about the role of co-conspirators in the double-oh-jay statutes.

"Our threat to go public with their detention operation was a holding action, at best," I said. "You guys don't have to babysit her or me. You want to bail, you probably should."

"You just want to be alone with the wild woman," Tony said.

"She's as scary as the Bureau right now," I said.

"She's got some interesting shit pre-positioned on her computer, and she backed it all up on Pardee's. That girl's a hot sketch, you know that?"

"Remember her nickname, *paisan,*" I said. "Chances are, she earned it."

"What—me worry? Nice redheaded Catholic girl like that?"

Now Ari was looking longingly at the flask, but then decided against it.

"So," I said. "Who or what put Carl Trask in the moonpool?"

He shook his head slowly, as if he still didn't believe it. "He pissed people off all the time, but everybody knew he was just doing his job—as he saw it. I can't finger a single soul who'd want to kill the man."

I thought briefly about Billy the Kid, but then saw the improbability. "Well, we should be able to narrow down the suspect list pretty quick," I said. "It has to be someone with access to that building and all three levels of security."

He looked over at me in the gloom of the parking lot. "Not if it was Trask who took his killer in there," he said. "Then it could be anybody."

"But the cameras, the card readers—won't they show who went in, and when?"

"The FBI's all over that as we speak," he said. "And the short answer is—yes."

"Short answer?"

"Well, you know what can be done with video-camera data, if someone knows how."

"C'mon, Ari—you've been watching too many movies. That's harder than it looks, and it implies some detailed planning and premeditation. And I'll warn you right now: The Bureau is going to want a sit-down with you, and it won't be a casual conversation."

"Well, I am the head of technical security."

"And because this just about *has* to be an inside job. C'mon: You must have a theory about what the hell's going on here."

He stared out the window for a long moment. He opened his mouth to say something, but then his cell phone chirped. He sighed and looked at the data window. Then he answered it.

In response to a question, he said he was outside, getting some fresh air. Then he looked over at me, his eyes widening. "No way," he said. "Where'd they get that?"

He listened some more, then said he had no idea but that he'd be back inside in five minutes. He snapped his phone shut.

"That was your favorite Russian," he said. "The Bureau's apparently turned up a tape showing you and Trask going through the moonpool security tiers. She confirmed to them that you had been up there tonight. She said they wanted to know if I knew where you were."

"Yes, you do," I replied. "I'm gone."

Two hours later, Tony nosed our boat alongside Carl Trask's *Keeper* over in the Carolina Beach marina. We'd come through the narrow defile of Snow's Cut and down the city dock channel to the marina at idle and with our running lights off. The *Keeper* was tied up on one of the outboard finger piers because of her deeper draft, which kept her two piers away from most of the other live-on boats. Tony brought our boat alongside, squished some fenders, and then held her steady. I passed the shepherds up onto the *Keeper*'s deck, and then Moira and I followed. The marina office was dark, as were all the boats that we could see, and nobody seemed to be out and about on the nearby downtown streets. I was glad it was the off-season.

Tony passed up our gear and then, as agreed, backed away quietly and headed back out to the Cape Fear River. I led Moira up the slanting ladder to the bridge area, and we went through the same interior door Cap'n Pete had used to see if Trask was on board. A centerline companionway led down into the main lounge. I assumed there were cabins forward and the usual amenities aft of the lounge. Moira stretched out on a deep sofa and ran her fingers through her hair. We'd left the interior lights off, but I checked our surroundings through the portholes anyway. The shepherds went around checking out the scents and then plopped themselves down in front of the couch.

I really hadn't wanted to bring Moira along, but even she recognized that if the Bureau was going to pick me up again, they'd sure as hell pick her up as well. I'd driven to Southport as fast as I could without sucking up a speeding ticket and explained what was going on to my two guys. It was Tony who'd suggested Trask's boat as a hiding place, at least initially. Pardee had taken my Suburban over to the local Wal-Mart parking lot, parked it, and walked back to the beach house. If the FBI showed up, their story would be that Moira and I went out somewhere and they hadn't a clue as to where we'd gone after that. That would hold up for a day, at most, but by then we'd be across the river with at least some freedom of movement. Tony and I had traded cell phones just to confuse any existing eavesdropping triangulation systems.

I sat down in a recliner next to the couch and started to explain to Moira why I'd decided to run, at least until Ari Quartermain got to the bottom of this mysterious videotape.

"You don't have to convince me," she said with a wave of her hand. "Somebody parked at least one dot-exe file on my Web computer that refuses to scrub, so I figured your Gestapo still loves me."

"You've seen that before?"

She nodded. "Just before they came the last time," she said. "I had all the resources of the U's computer lab, and, short of putting the computer in a swimming pool, I still couldn't make it go away. That's a federal intrusion, and probably from a National Security Agency super."

"Can they track you physically if you go online, say, from here?"

"Yes," she said simply. "If it's wireless, say, a coffee shop or bookstore, the wi-fi network is registered to a physical place or place of business. If it's via a cell phone, they can triangulate the towers. If it's a dial-up, it's moving over a domestic or business telephone number, all of which have a physical address."

"Shit, when did all this happen?"

She smiled. "Despite Mr. Gore's claims, the Internet was created by the Defense Department. They never create anything to which they don't have supervisory access. That's not to say it can't be spoofed, and I can make it really hard. But we're talking about putting a laptop up against a Cray supercomputer or ten. Bad odds, over time."

I got up and went around to the portholes again, checking to see if anyone was coming toward or down our pier. But the marina remained asleep, so I dropped back down into the waiting arms of the recliner. Suddenly I was pretty tired and found myself trying to stifle a big yawn. That set Moira off, and then she sat up and patted the corner of the couch. I moved over as she made a pillow out of a car blanket draped across the back of the couch, lay down, and put her head in my lap.

"I just have one question, Mr. Ex-policeman."

"Shoot."

"If everybody thinks this Trask guy was murdered, won't they come here? To where he lived? Won't they want to search this boat, see if anything points to a motive or something?"

I stared down at her for a second. Of course they would. They'd rustle up a search warrant first thing in the morning and be here in force by nine or so. Shit.

"All of you ex-cops, and you didn't think of that?" she asked in mock disbelief.

"Some of us ex-cops have had a long effing day," I said grouchily, mostly because she was absolutely right. None of us had thought it through, and unless we were willing to steal this boat, we'd be seeing a herd of Buroids on deck with the morning sun. At this stage of the game, I was almost willing to just wait for them to show up. Almost.

The cell phone in my jacket pocket vibrated. It was Pardee. Tony hadn't returned yet, but the beach house had had night visitors. He'd changed the story: Tony was out on the town with Moira, and I was, to the best of his knowledge, still at the power plant. They'd asked to look around, and he'd told them to come back with a warrant, which they promised they would, and when they did, et cetera, et cetera.

"But here's the thing," he began.

"I know—we've already figured that out."

"Yeah—okay. Which is why I've turned Tony around."

Then I heard the tramp of footsteps out on the main pier. It sounded like they were coming our way.

"Turn him around again, Pardee," I said wearily. "I think we're busted."

Actually, we weren't. The footsteps turned out to be two severely inebriated yachtsmen who were trying to goose-step down the pier to their boat. I watched the two clowns make it to their gangway, where they sat down and promptly had another nip.

Too early the next morning I took the mutts down the pier to a grassy area in front of the marina office to let them make their morning insults. I left them out on deck when I got back. Thirty minutes later, I thought I heard them walking around aft as if they were interested in something back there. I went to the portholes, but it was still misty dark outside except for the lights coming from the marina parking lot. None of the nearby boats was showing any lights, and the marina office was still dark. One of the dogs scratched pitifully on the back door, so I relented and went back to bring them in from the cold.

When I opened the door, I discovered both shepherds totally immobilized in what looked like black nylon fishnets, and two space aliens dressed all in black pointing stubby assault rifles at my face. There seemed to be six more climbing over the boat's transom as I stood there like a complete idiot.

I had to admit: They were good. Really good. They'd managed to get alongside the boat without alerting the shepherds, immobilize them without a sound, and board the *Keeper* without either of us feeling or hearing anything. The leader of the squad motioned for me to back up into the narrow companionway between the galley and the vestibule leading down into the engine compartment. His face was entirely concealed by a tactical SWAT mask, but the muzzle of his weapon was in plain view and unwavering. Three of them squeezed by the leader with the muffled sounds of body armor, and then I heard a little squeak from Moira in the main lounge. A minute later, Moira and I were sitting on the couch, our hands in our laps bound by plastic handcuffs looped through our belts, and the room was filling up with men in black.

They spread out, quietly but efficiently, throughout the boat, making sure there wasn't anyone else on board. Within about a minute, the entire crew was back in the main lounge. There were none of the usual "Clear!" reports being shouted from room to room. Instead I heard a muttering sound among the group, which was when I realized they were networked on a tactical headset radio circuit. This was not your garden-variety SWAT team. They were big, and their body armor made them look huge. One of them found Moira's cell phone. He picked it up, scanned the screen, and then extracted the battery and the SIM card. Then he crunched the plastic carcass in his gloved hand and dropped the plastic bits into a trashcan by the desk.

One of the group handed his weapon to another man and stepped forward. He took his face mask off with a faint hiss of air. It was the Marine major from our erstwhile federal day-care center, and he did not look happy.

"What did you do to my dogs?" I asked.

"They're safer in the nets than running around," he said. "This way we don't have to kill them. Like they killed one of my dogs."

"I apologize for that," I said. "He was doing his job, but so were mine."

"Your 'job' was to sit tight. I want to know how you got loose in the first place."

I wasn't going to tell him anything, but then Moira spoke up. "*I* got us loose, Major Fuckface," she spat. "Your so-called electronic security was a joke."

"And I suppose you started that fire?"

"Damned straight," she said before I could deny everything. "I hope the whole goddamned place burned down."

"Got your wish, sweetheart," he said. "Now we're going to get mine. Someone wants to see you."

He snapped his fingers, and two of his masked brutes came forward. One hauled Moira to her feet by her cuffed wrists while the other pulled a black mesh body stocking over her head from the back in one smooth motion. He stretched it down to her waist, where the first man let go of her cuffs long enough for his buddy to pull the stocking all the way down to her ankles. The fabric completely encased her body. She tried to struggle, but the first guy was holding what looked like a compact hair dryer, which was already plugged into a wall receptacle. He turned it on and blew hot air all over Moira, and, to my amazement, the loose folds of fabric shrank her into a tight black nylon mummy with only her terrified eyes and nose showing. Two more men stepped forward and picked her up by her armpits and ankles and carried her toward the back of the boat and out the back door. Another one had her computers under his arms. I caught one last glimpse of her eyes. I couldn't tell if she was scared or really angry.

I was too surprised to offer any opposition, and my brain was telling me to sit very still. The major laughed.

"Surprised?" he said.

"You came for *her*?"

"You bet your interfering ass," he said. "You have no idea who you've been consorting with, Lieutenant Richter, but suffice it to say, she is most definitely part of the problem and not the solution."

This time he knew my name, and my surprise must have shown. He pulled his face mask to his mouth and said something. The room began to clear itself of black-clad soldiers. The last one to leave leaned over and slapped a black hood over my head and cinched it down around my neck with a cord.

"You gen-pop civilians don't have a clue," the major said. "You think that woman's some sort of civil libertarian, fucking around out there on the Web, making some kind of statement." I could feel him leaning closer, smell the chemical scent coming off the body armor.

"There's a war on, asshole," he snarled. "Right now it's being fought over there. People like her want to bring it over here. They *want* to see school buses blown over by IEDs. They *want* to see the jihadis get a nuke into Washington, or take down the national electric grid and put us all back to the eighteen-hundreds. Moira Maxwell is all too typical of the new and improved, college-overeducated, peace-now, anti-war, anti-male, anti-authority Movement, and that's Movement with a capital *M*. They spell America with a *k,* and for reasons nobody can fathom, they hate this country and all it stands for."

"Well, hell, then, why don't you guys just pop her?"

"Would if I could, asshole, but someone wants to see her. But here's for the pleasure of knowing you."

With that he slapped my face through the hood hard enough to make stars dance behind my eyes.

"Don't move for ten minutes," he said. "During that time, you think about who and what you're messing with. Next time you come up on *our* screens, we'll put a horse syringe through your eye and suck out your brain, assuming there's one in here. Didn't much feel like it, just now."

I heard the back door to the lounge click shut a few seconds later, but that was the only thing I heard over the ringing in my left ear. I sat back, still trying to get my mental arms around the situation. When they'd come through the back door, I'd just assumed that Creeps had sent a team over to pick us up while we slept the sleep of the innocent, trusting that we were somehow going to be able to talk our way out of this mess. Now, I didn't think those guys were part of my Bureau or anyone else's Bureau.

What. The. Fuck. Over? And who wanted to see her?

I started working on getting that hood off my head. It took several minutes of grunting and thrashing, but I finally managed. Then I looked at the cuffs. A Mickey Mouse icon was looking back at me. They were toy cuffs. I pulled my wrists apart, hard, and the cuffs popped across the room. One final note of deep and abiding respect from my good buddy, the major. I got up and went aft to the porch deck to see about the dogs.

They were still wrapped tight and unconscious. I went to the galley, got a knife, and cut them out of that webbing. Then I carried each one into the warmth of the lounge and laid them out on the carpet. Frick's hind legs began to quiver, but it was another fifteen minutes before they woke up. I found one tiny plastic dart entangled in the web on Frack, but otherwise they appeared unharmed. I wondered where Trask kept his Scotch. Coffee no longer seemed sufficient. I sat back down, called the guys at the beach house, and filled them in on what had happened.

"Who we messin' with here, boss?" Tony said.

"Bad motherfuckers," I replied. "And I still have Creeps to deal with."

"Sounds like we country boys are way out of our league," Pardee said. He left the obvious corollary to that observation unspoken.

I was getting just a little bit tired of that line. If I was going to stay with this hairball, though, I'd need their help. I still wanted to know *why* Allie had died. Pardee, attentive to the sudden silence on the line, solved it for me.

"Okay, okay, what do you need us to do?"

"Come over here around 10:00 A.M.," I said. "Come by car. I think we've been going about this all wrong."

That evening, Tony nosed our boat alongside the cargo wharf at Helios, where Ari Quartermain was waiting with two security officers and a Helios security office SUV. Tony and Pardee, along with Ari's officers, stayed behind at the wharf while Ari and I got into the SUV and went for a drive onto one of the marsh roads.

The lights of the power plant formed a blazing sodium vapor barrier behind us, while across the river we could see the tops of container ships and the towering gantry cranes that serviced them. Ari pulled up on one of the cattail points that formed a bend in the cooling water canal and shut it down.

"We going all the way tonight, or is this just gonna be more foreplay?" I asked.

He chuckled and shook his head. "Scotch in the glove box," he said. "Sorry for the paper cups. Why'd you come by boat?"

"I wanted to come in the back door," I said. "You never know what the Bureau's been telling the front gate security people."

We got settled, and then he told me all about his wonderful day at work, which had gone pretty much as I had imagined it would.

"My moonpool is acting up."

"Acting up? Do I want to hear this?"

"Some of the water from this canal goes into the cooling system for the moonpool," he said. "Heat exchangers, to be precise. Not to be confused with makeup water, which is purified and comes from the county water system. This is a circulation system: moonpool water on one side, canal water on the other."

"I believe."

"Right. Only my heat exchangers are now clogged with something nasty, courtesy of this latest incident." He looked over at me with weary eyes. "The spent fuel stack wants its cooling water, and wants it now. Left to its own devices, it tries to become a reactor again."

"And that's not good."

"Not good at all. Plus, I've got this bureaucratic war going on between something like ten different agencies and a circling swarm of PrimEnergy lawyers. I'm tempted to gather them all into that building and drain the pool. Let them see what an atomic steam explosion looks like."

I grinned in the darkness, despite the seriousness of the problem and the dizzying array of federal alphabets. "Make sure you get *all* the lawyers in there," I said. "Where's the body?"

"In a double body bag, inside a dry-storage cask parked in the moonpool building. That's become an issue, too."

"How so?"

"At least two federal entities are demanding an autopsy. I've told them the keys to the cask are available to anyone who's brave enough to open it and who's had all the children he wants to have. No takers so far."

"Still think it's Trask?"

He shrugged. "If we could figure out a way to clean the heat exchangers, we might recover some skin, but that's going to be an enormously complex operation, by which time I wouldn't think anything would be left. It's a technically unprecedented situation, so NRC-approved safety procedures would have to be drawn up, staffed in Washington, approved, blah, blah, blah."

"And in the meantime, the fuel stack is getting indigestion?"

"The worst thing that can happen in a moonpool is for *all* the cooling water to leak out and expose the fuel stack to the atmosphere. You get hydrogen and then a fire, which is not a comforting combination. So we have this system to reflood the pool if for some reason the basic containment fails. We can use that if we have to as a backup cooling system until we get the heat exchangers sorted out."

I told him about our run for the roses last night, that Moira had been picked up again, and that I thought Trask might have been behind all the problems at the plant.

"Carl Trask a terrorist?"

"*Colonel* Carl Trask creating an 'incident' in order to reawaken America to the clear and present danger," I said. "From this ex-cop's point of view, he had motive, means, and opportunities galore."

Ari let out a long sigh. "Damn," he said. "I guess it's possible. But then what happened? How'd he end up in the moonpool?"

"Apparently, we might never find that out," I said. "In the

meantime, I'm going to focus on Allie Gardner. She was either a random victim, in the wrong place at the wrong time, or somehow she's part of the mystery here. That's why I wanted to meet tonight. I'm going to need your help with this, while at the same time, I don't think I can help you anymore."

"Because you promised the Bureau guys?"

"They're right, you know. They need to run their investigation without outside interference, especially if they're squabbling with other government agencies."

He nodded. "Okay. That reads. What do you need from me?"

"I need to inspect your visitor logs—in detail—and it might be better for me to do that now, at night, with fewer people around in the admin offices."

"What are you looking for?"

"Not what—who: I'm looking for Allie Gardner. We all assumed she'd never been here, at Helios. I'd like to confirm that, before yet another assumption bites me in the ass."

An hour and a half later, we were closing in on the south end of the Wilmington container port. Tony had the boat's red and green side navigation lights on but had turned off the white lights. There were four enormous ships being worked farther up that long bulkhead pier under the glare of a forest of gantry cranes, but the downstream end was empty of activity and all the crane lights were dark. There was little moonlight, and while the container stack area was brightly lighted, the surface of the river a hundred yards out remained in darkness. Tony said we were going in on slack high water in the estuary, so the current was minimal. It would turn to ebb and increase significantly in about an hour.

Our search through the visitor records hadn't turned up anything useful. Pardee and I had slipped into coat-and-tie outfits before going with Ari to the physical security admin office. I was hoping that anyone seeing us there would assume we were just some more federal people. We'd examined the time frame when Allie had been in Wilmington and found no record of her ever visiting Helios. Then we'd done it again to see if any other names jumped out at us, but none did. There were a lot of contractors and suppliers, making it clear that Helios was heavy into outsourcing. There was one entry indicating a Thomason had visited a Thomason, but that didn't have anything to do with anything as best I could tell. I'd asked Ari if we could have a copy of those days' log pages, and he'd promised to get us one when the admin offices reopened tomorrow.

The second reason we'd come by boat was to see if it was possible to approach the container port from the river without being discovered, and, if we were discovered, what would happen next. Tony held the boat in position at idle while we waited to see if a passing security truck would notice us. Ten minutes later, one came by up on the unloading area of the pier, but passed by with no reaction to us. My guess was that either the driver's night vision was nonexistent against all those gantry crane lights farther up or he'd seen the boat and thought nothing of it.

"Okay, let's do it," I said.

Tony pointed the bow toward the end of the bulkhead pier. We crept in at idle, rounded the end of the pier about fifty feet out, and nosed up into the creek that formed the downstream boundary of the port. To our right were darkened warehouses and other semi-industrial buildings, which looked like they'd been abandoned for years along the riverbank. Stumps of long-gone pier pilings littered the bank, along with a backwater collection of listing barges, piles of rusty barrels, and dangling outflow pipes. To our left was the southern end of the container stack area, with lanes and rows of shipping containers stacked four to ten high.

"I've got five feet under the keel," Tony announced as we pushed farther up the narrowing creek.

The water stank of oil, sewage, and other things, none of them good. The bulkhead pier on our left ended in a dirt bank and some long-dead trees. Farther up the creek was that jumbled pile of damaged and discarded containers I'd seen on our first visit. The security lighting ended at the edge of the stack laydown area. The container graveyard was not lighted at all, and it was also outside the chain-link fence that defined the port perimeter. The creek ran between the fence and a small mountain of discarded containers.

"Four feet," Tony said, putting the engine in neutral and coasting forward now. He'd pointed out earlier that if we ran aground now, at high slack water, we'd be there until the next high tide came along to float us off.

"Can you put us on the bank with that container pile?" I asked.

He turned the boat toward the ribbon of oily trash bobbing along the dirt bank. Pardee went forward with a boathook to see what he could grab, while I stayed in the cockpit with Tony and the shepherds. It wouldn't have surprised me to see a body or two floating in all the mess, and, in fact, I saw at least one furry soccer ball with the head of a cat.

The boat stopped with a small bump, and Pardee hooked something on the bank to hold us there. I turned back toward the container port to see if we'd attracted any attention. The silent stacks looked back at me. The fence at the top of the opposite bank looked to be about ten feet high, but I could clearly see where the bottom of the chain-link had billowed out or been compromised by gullies washed out at low points. If we'd gone to that side of the creek, it would have been easy to climb the bank, watch for security trucks, and then slide under the chain-link. I wondered if they had a problem with pilferage in the stacks at night.

"Boss?" Pardee said.

I turned back around. He was pointing into the container junkyard, where I could see the flickering reflection of a small fire. Then I saw a human shadow on a nearby container, and then another. Frick growled quietly.

"Hobo jungle up there?" I said.

Pardee nodded. "Looks like it," he said. "I guess you could live in an empty container."

"I want to go up there, see if we can talk to somebody.

Find out how hard it is to get into the container stack yard at night."

"You taking the dogs?" Pardee asked.

"Hell, yes," I said. "Why?"

He repositioned the boathook to steady the boat, which was trying to swing around in the creek. "Because those folks up there see those dogs, ain't nobody gonna stick around to have a nice chat."

"You think they'll run?"

"I believe they will," he said. He stuck his tongue out at Frick. She lifted a lip. "I would."

I patted Frick's head. "Then they better be really good runners," I said.

In the event, they didn't run. They didn't even see us coming until Pardee surprised the shit out of a noisome collection of derelicts, drunks, and aging homeless types surrounding a small fire that was burning in a sawed-off steel drum. We'd separated in making our approach. Pardee had come in from the landward side, stepping into the firelight from between two mangled containers that had obviously been in a trucking accident several years ago. I remained in the shadows between the edge of the pile and the river, with the shepherds sitting by my side. The dozen or so denizens of the junkyard studiously ignored the large black man who was stepping carefully over two sleeping forms and into the middle of the group.

"Evening," he said.

"We ain't doin' nothin' wrong," one man said, still not looking directly at Pardee. "Just stayin' warm, is all."

"No problem," Pardee said. "This isn't a roust. I'm looking for someone."

"You a cop?" another man asked. He appeared to be younger than most of the group, with shaved hair and some piercing jewelry on his face. The vivid red splotches on his face and neck indicated active disease of some kind.

"Skip tracer," Pardee said. "I want someone who knows his way around the stacks over there, someone who can take us in through the fence and back out again without getting caught."

"Who's us?" the younger one said with a sneer. "Got a mouse in your pocket?"

"Us is me and my partner over there."

That was my cue to step out into the firelight with the dogs, the sight of which provoked some uneasy repositioning among the assembled multitude.

"Them're *po*-lice dogs," a third man said, looking around nervously to see who or what else might be lurking in the shadows. "You guys *is* cops."

"Nope," Pardee said. "And cops are definitely what we want to avoid tonight. You boys hang out here. One of you must know how to get into that stack yard over there. There's money in it for the right guy."

"If you guys are bounty hunters, who you chasin'?" sneer-face asked. I already wanted to smack him. I think Frick wanted to eat him. Pardee passed the ball to me with a quick glance.

"We're looking for a guy, late fifties, maybe even sixty," I said. "Good shape, real short haircut. Likes to give orders."

"How much money?" an older man asked. I hadn't noticed him before, but he looked like he might have been somebody once, despite the rags and the filthy beard. He was sitting in the prime spot at the fire, in the warmth but out of the smoke.

"A C-note to take us in, show us the layout, and get us out again. Twenty minutes, tops, start to finish. Then we're gone."

"You fixin' to steal some shit?" a man asked. "'Cause them cans over there? They's all locked up. They even got alarms and shit."

"I popped one, once," a seriously grubby geezer announced. He was sitting all by himself, and the crusty stains that painted the front of his clothes from chops to crotch may have accounted for his isolation. "All's was in there was a hundred-lebbenty milyun boxes of goddamn shit-paper."

"Ain't nothin' wrong with shit-paper," another observed. "Better'n usin' yer shirt, like you do."

This provoked general amusement, but I could see that the older man was interested. Pardee saw it, too, and produced the hundred-dollar bill, which got everyone's attention.

"Shee-it," the young one said. "I'll do it."

"No, I'll do it," the bearded man said, getting to his feet. Surprisingly, the young kid didn't argue. The rest of them subsided into their boozy meditations.

The bearded man was nearly my size. He was wearing jeans, boondockers, two sweatshirts, and a black knit hat. His hands were tattooed with the smudgy ink of what looked like prison art. The way he was built and the animal grace with which he moved alerted me to watch him carefully. Pardee caught it, too. The rest of the junkyard crowd were bona-fide derelicts; this one was a hard guy, probably on the run and hiding out among the human debris that seemed to be accumulating on the edges of every American city these days.

"Lead on, then," I said. Pardee stepped aside and the man went past him, giving Pardee the once-over. "You guys strapped?" he asked as we moved away from the campfire.

"What do you think?" Pardee replied, not actually answering the man's question.

"Because there's rules," he said.

"Rules?"

"Yeah," he said, stopping now that we were out of sight and sound of the others. "The security guys over there? In the yard? They know there's gonna be some shit going down, time to time. Deal is, they won't shoot at us, we don't shoot at them. They catch a guy, he's fucking caught. End of story. Don't fuck that up for us, okay?"

I nodded. We started walking again, through the piles of wrecked, burned, or simply rusted-out shipping containers. There were dozens of them, dropped onto the point of land between the stinking creek and the fenced stack yard. Pardee stayed close to our guide, while I stayed back and watched the shepherds as much as I watched the bearded man. If he was leading us into an ambush, the dogs should be able to sense it and give us warning. Then he surprised us.

"So you're looking for the colonel?" he asked over his shoulder, as we picked our way through a jumble of sheet metal and hydraulic hoses.

"Might be," I said. "How do you know him?"

He laughed. "Same way you guys do, probably. We've done some business."

"*Here?*" I asked, indicating all the accumulated junk. Even as I said that, I noticed that there was a clearly defined path through all the wreckage.

"No, mostly on that nice big boat of his," he said. Then he stopped and held up a hand. "Okay—from here on in, we don't talk. Make sure those dogs don't bark, either. See those three cans?"

There were three containers, badly dented and rusted out, that appeared to have been dropped in a line. The doors were long gone. Then I realized that they were lined up, front to back. A steel tunnel, or covered bridge, which crossed the creek and landed us on the bank below the chain-link fence up above. A perfect place for an ambush, too. There was light shining down the bank from the light standards in the yard, but that tunnel was black as the grave.

"Stay to the left-hand side, you won't fall through," he said. "I'll go first, you all come single file, and quiet-like. No lights, no talking."

I gave Frack a command, and he trotted up to join the bearded man, who looked down in momentary alarm at the big black dog that was now his new best friend. "In case there's a bad guy hiding out in all that mess," I said. "He'll let you know, and then he'll tear some shit up, if he feels like it."

Starting with you was the unspoken message, but Beard just shrugged and said okay. Pardee followed him and Frack. I went next, with Frick behind, in case the problem erupted behind us. I had my .45 out, too, rules or no rules. Pardee had his uncovered, but still holstered.

Nothing happened. We picked our way through the darkness of the three containers, our footfalls echoing quietly in the wobbly steel tube. I could sense big holes in the floor to my right, and could actually smell the creek. We used the tie-down fittings to stay upright against the slope of the tunnel. Once I heard one of the dogs scrabbling for footing on the metal floor, but the bearded man kept going, forward and up toward where the final container brought us almost to the edge of the fence. There was a well-worn track going the final ten feet from the last container to the bottom of the fence. I went forward to join our guide just inside the container.

"They have to know about this," I said quietly, pointing to the worn path with my chin.

Beard shrugged. "There's lots of scams working in this place," he said. "The people who run it expect a certain amount of wastage, as they call it. The trick is to keep it in bounds. That's what the colonel likes to say. Keep it in bounds, not too much, nobody getting too greedy, and they'll look the other way."

"For a piece of the action, you mean."

He nodded. "Up to a certain level. This seaport here is a union shop. Teamsters. Longshoremen. Merchant marine. Railroad."

"The helping-hands unions."

"Oh, yeah," he smiled. "Sweethearts, every one of them. Some guys want a piece of the action; the big bosses just want peace in the valley, you know what I'm sayin'?"

I said I did. He pulled out a small set of binoculars and began to scan the area of the stack yard along the main river. Pardee continued to watch him, while the shepherds sat down and waited for new orders.

"What was the colonel's interest in this place?" I asked, as casually as I could.

"Was?" he asked, giving me a sideways, suspicious look.

I'd screwed up, but I pretended not to notice. "Some people want a word with him, so they hired us. If he's on the run, he's not likely to be doing regular business, here or anywhere else, right now. Not our problem either way. I'm just curious."

He went back to scanning the lanes and the rows of boxes piled out in the yard.

"The colonel, he's in the import business," he said. "He's moving illegals."

Now, that was a surprise. The notion that Trask had been moving Mexican field workers across the American border wasn't much in keeping with his rant about how the country was going to hell. Then I remembered the sudden swarm of foreigners out of that one container.

"You talking wetbacks in seagoing containers?"

"Oh, hell, no," he said. "They don't put the colonel's meat in cans. Those big-ass ships bring 'em in like passengers. And, according to the colonel, these aren't tomato pickers. These are journeymen who can do complicated shit. People who can run a lathe, do CAD-CAM, X-ray techs, or guys who can operate a big Caterpillar tractor."

"They come up in the ships from down south?"

"Right. The crews are all in on it—they're getting paid off, too. The ships feed 'em and maybe even work 'em. They go in a can just before the ship lands."

"And then?"

"Then those cans go out there, into the stacks. The ones with people in 'em go on the bottom of a stack, every time, real convenient-like. Then the colonel, he comes in with the boat, uses some of us to help him move them out."

"Help how?"

He shrugged. "I take a crew of those derelicts in, stir up some shit. You saw those people. They get desperate for their next bottle, their next rock, I offer cash. I send them in under the wire. They go pretend to bust a box, along come the cops, there's a big deal, lights and sirens, all the while the colonel's moving his goods in a different part of the yard."

"Where does he take them?"

"Away," Beard said.

"Who's paying for all this?" Pardee asked.

"The companies who're gonna use 'em here in the States," he said. "Like the colonel keeps saying: This is a seaport. Skilled people are just another commodity."

"Where does he take them?" I asked again.

Beard looked over at me with a disappointed expression, as in, *He doesn't tell us and we don't ask.* "You really want to go in there, or did you find out what you came to find out?"

I looked over at Pardee. Busted.

"That's what I thought," Beard said. "Can we go back now? Lieutenant?"

I'd begun to wonder why he'd been so forthcoming about what was going on down here. The bearded guy was grinning at us now. Then he fingered a slim government ID card from a slit in his belt. His name was J. B. Houston.

"ICE," he said. "Immigration and Customs Enforcement. And you would be the retired sheriff's office lieutenant with the two German shepherds that the local Feebs are so fond of."

Pardee was shaking his head disgustedly. Houston looked around to make sure none of the tramps had followed us and then indicated the fence. "Let's go up there, and I'll show you something."

I'd been trying to think of something intelligent to say but had failed entirely, so we followed him up the hill, slipped under a loose skirt of chain-link, and walked out into the stack yard. We were at the most remote end of the yard and a good half mile away from the active pier and the unloading activity. I kept looking for video cameras on the light standards but didn't see any. Houston took us into the space between two rows of stacked containers and then knelt down on the concrete at the base of a stack.

"See this?" he said, pointing to what looked like the top of a soup can buried in the concrete. "See how all these cans are stacked exactly the same way? This is a reader. Each can has a transmitter tag, which identifies the container by number, source, and destination. Every stack has a reader, and every reader is networked to a control room at the head of the yard."

He stood up and pointed to the lowest container's double

doors, where there was a lead seal and what looked like a padlock on each of the three operating rods. Upon closer examination, I could see that the locks, too, were actually electronic devices of some kind.

"Break the seal and open any door out here, that smart-tag there tells on you and sets off a strobe light on the top of the nearest light pole. Unless of course, someone in the control room disables that reader at a specified time."

"Can someone open the box from the inside?"

"Actually, yes. After they had a couple of incidents of illegals suffocating in containers, they modified all the cans so that if you get locked in, you can pull the latch plates off from the inside and bust the doors. Still be an alarm, though."

"Seems pretty damned secure."

"It is."

"So all that stuff about you and Trask moving illegals out of here? That was all bullshit?"

"Nope," he said. Then he waited for us to get the picture.

"You're saying that's all being done under government supervision?" Pardee asked.

"Yep," Houston said.

"What the fuck?" I said.

"Well, here's the theory, as it was explained to us snuffies who work the port: Homeland Security decided that it would be better to *know* who was moving through this port in the way of aliens, especially skilled people, than to play cops and robbers and never know what or who they might have missed."

"That's a lot like saying the government is selling cocaine so that they'll have good statistics on the drug market."

"Well," Houston countered, "you seeing any big progress on the control of illegal immigration into this country? You seeing bills getting through Congress?"

We all knew the answer to that.

"You're not seeing that," he continued, "because the major corporations who own the politicians don't want effective immigration control. Same deal for national ID cards. Why in the hell are we stuck with a Social Security card for identification that ties in with every aspect of our personal finances? Stupid—or intentional?"

"I hear you," I said, not wanting to get into it with yet another politically frustrated citizen.

"I can't prove all that, of course, but there would have to be some pretty high-priced top cover for this kind of program, don't you think?"

I thought back to what Ari had said about foreigners at the power plant, and wondered if that was just another manifestation of what was going on there. This was the second eye-opener I'd collided with here in beautiful downtown Wilmington, North Carolina. The first had been a military-operated civilian detention center. Houston must have read my mind.

"There's a war on, Lieutenant," he said. "J. Q. Public seems to forget that. And there are *two* fronts: one overseas, where regular soldiers are learning about street fighting from the jihadis. Then a second one here on our so-called borders, where the umpteenth guy in one of these shipments through here or any of the other ports might be a legitimate CAD-CAM wizard. Or he might be the final member of a cell that's been building for five years, the one guy who can actually wire up the satchel nuke. By becoming part of the pipeline, we get a look."

"And they only have to get lucky once," I said. "We have to be lucky every damned time."

He nodded.

"So what happened the other night, when that container erupted with stowaways?"

"Somebody fucked up," he said promptly. "It's a *government* program, remember?"

I smiled. "Why are you telling *us* this?" I asked.

"Two reasons," he said, again looking around. "One, word's out among the working cops here on the waterfront that you won't take go-away for an answer. I figured you might as well know what you're poking your nose into."

"And two?"

"Two: I want something. What's happened to Trask? Jungle drums are saying nobody can raise him."

"Your boss checked with the Bureau?" Pardee asked, giving me a warning look over Houston's head.

"Bureau doesn't share for shit. They're not part of Homeland Security, as I'm sure you guys remember."

I thought about it for a moment. Why not tell him? Why wouldn't the Bureau want that information to get loose? I told him what little we knew, or at least surmised, and he whistled in surprise.

"But there's no positive ID?"

"Nope, and there may not ever be one. The fella who runs the marina where Trask keeps his boat told me he goes off into the night all the time, so maybe that's what he's done, and it's somebody else who went dunking for neutrons."

"But you don't think so?"

I shook my head, remembering the shape of the body and that boot knife. "I think it's Trask. His boss at Helios thinks it's Trask."

"He's got a hidey-hole somewhere back in the jumble," Houston said, "but he's not there. I checked."

A pair of headlights surprised us, coming around the adjacent stack. I hadn't heard a vehicle, and neither had the dogs. Then I saw why: It was an electric golf cart that rolled up to where we were standing. The two men inside acknowledged Houston and then gave us a pointed once-over. The driver seemed to be especially interested in the dogs. They weren't in uniform, per se, but they had the look of federal officers.

"They're cool," Houston told them. "Tell Hanson I've got word on the colonel. I'll be on the air at the regular time."

The driver nodded, and they went humming away into the night without having said a word. At least they had recognized Houston, scruffy clothes, long hair, and all. He looked at his watch. "We need to get back," he said.

"You out there in that jungle all by yourself?"

"No, I've always got one backup. The kid with the face metal? They rotate people through the homeless network once a month or so. The real derelicts are clueless."

We started back for the fence. "Any of those people ever cotton to who you really are?" Pardee asked.

"Occasionally," Houston said, lifting the chain-link so we could get through. "But then I tell the colonel. He takes 'em somewhere in that steel jungle over there, and they don't come back."

"He's killing people?"

"No, I don't think so. There was one guy, a real whack-job, way off his meds, heard voices all the time. He started going on about spies, narcs, other wild shit, and aiming some of it at me because I kind of control the campfire. The colonel showed up one night, took him off for a little talk. We saw the guy again, maybe three days later, at the fire. Dude couldn't speak a coherent word."

"A suddenly mute schizophrenic—that would be a relief."

"Scared-out-of-his-squirming-gourd mute," Houston said. "Sat there, shaking like a leaf, and babbling about monsters and snakes out there in the container jungle. Freaked the rest of 'em out. Hell, it freaked *me* out. He wandered off after a coupl'a days, never saw his ass again. After that, somebody acts out, all I have to do is mention that I'm seeing the colonel that night, and all the regulars get big-eyed. Nobody fucks with me."

"How long you been under?" I asked, as we re-entered the container tunnel.

"Going on two years," he said.

"Damn! Hope you're not married."

"Not anymore," he said. "But, looking on the bright side, there's a ton of overtime."

It was after midnight by the time we got back to the beach house. We sat out on the front porch having a beer and some leathery leftover pizza, kicking around the next steps. I still wanted to focus on Allie: I needed to develop a detailed timeline of her visit to Wilmington. She'd made that single report back to the office the day after beginning her surveillance of the dallying lawyers. Got the goods, will be back tomorrow. But what was that personal business she'd gone to do? Who'd seen her? Who'd she talked to? How'd she end up at that convenience store? She hadn't filed a report, and I actually hadn't seen her videotape, which I now remembered I'd promised to share with the Bureau people. It might be in her car—maybe get ahold of that, see what it showed.

Tony amplified that idea. See how many miles she'd burned up on the trip. My people always set their odometers when they go out on assignment so they can log and then later write off the business mileage on their personal vehicles. See if there was any paperwork, bridge tolls, ferry tickets, hotel parking stubs, anything to indicate she'd left Wilmington. I said I'd call Bernie Price, find out what they'd done with her vehicle, which they'd supposedly recovered from the gas island at that convenience store.

"In other words, we need to do some scut work," Tony observed.

"It's what we do," I said. "It's usually what pays off, too. Any better ideas?"

No one had a better idea, so we went in. It was late, but I wasn't ready for sleep yet. I got a jacket out of the closet, poured a glass of Scotch, and went back out to the front porch with the shepherds. It was cold and damp enough for fog, but there was just enough of a sea breeze coming in from the estuary to keep the fog at bay. All the neighboring houses were dark. Channel buoy lights blinked here and there out there in the light chop on the river, and a large container ship slid soundlessly across my view, bound for the Atlantic and away.

A Southport cop car came along on a slow roll through the neighborhood. It went past our rental, stopped, and then backed up. The shepherds got up to watch from the top of the steps. A fifty-something uniformed cop with an Irish face, a prominent belly, and sergeant's stripes got out and put his cap on. He then walked casually up the front walk. He stepped up to the porch, patted each dog on the head, and asked if he could have a word. I pointed to one of the wicker rockers, and he sank into it with the sigh of a man who does not like to spend time on his feet.

"Sergeant Lloyd J. McMichaels, at your service, sir," he said pleasantly. "And aren't those lovely shepherds."

"They are indeed, Sergeant," I said. "Can I offer you a coffee or something?"

He eyed the Scotch briefly, smiled, and said thank you, no, on duty and all that. I then asked how I could help him.

"You would be the retired Lieutenant of Police Cameron Richter, would you not, sir?"

I nodded.

"And your two associates, also retired police officers, from up in the Triad of North Carolina?"

"Correct again, Sergeant. We're actually all retired from the sheriff's office in Manceford County. I formed a private investigations company when I got out, and several of my cohorts joined me when their time was up."

"Lovely, lovely," he said, nodding. "Sounds like an ideal setup, it does—cops working with other cops. It must save a lot of bother, not having to work for or with civilians."

"That was the point," I said. "We wanted to be around people who knew how to act, as it were." The shepherds were back to lying down again, obviously comfortable with a uniformed policeman on the front porch. They always reacted well to confident people.

"Would you be so kind as to share with me your reasons for being here in our little village?"

"Absolutely," I said. "And I apologize for not stopping by the House and making my manners. I actually didn't think you'd care."

He gave me a droll look over the bridge of his spectacles.

I explained who we were working for and a little bit about the case, focusing mostly on Allie's death by radiation poisoning. He nodded when I was done.

"It was the presence of all those fierce-looking G-men in town which provoked my interest," he said. "Southport is a touristy place, of course, although at this time of year, not many of them, to be sure. So seeing federal officers lurking about our streets, without so much as a squeak from the Wilmington office, by the by, piqued our attention."

"I guess we all forgot our manners," I said. "But this doesn't involve Southport, as best I can tell. Helios is where the action is."

"Ah, Helios," he said. "The land of the captive suns. Does this action perhaps include a homicide, as I'm being told?"

"Are you being told?"

"Actually, no, not officially. But you know how locals are, Lieutenant. People do like to gossip."

The EMS guys, for instance, I thought. I told him what had happened at the moonpool, and that the current thinking was that it might be Carl Trask who had drowned in the moonpool. Surprisingly, that produced another skeptical look.

I told him the Bureau special agent in charge was named Caswell, and then asked McMichaels if he knew Colonel Trask personally. He did. The colonel had made his manners some time ago when he took the physical security job at Helios. He'd called on all the local police departments and sheriff's offices within twenty miles of Helios, and he was a prominent member of the multi-county nuclear accident response organization, as was Dr. Quartermain. Then the sergeant asked why we thought the body in the moonpool might be the good colonel. I told him, explaining the problem of making the physical identification. He grimaced, thought about that for a moment, and then asked when, exactly, all this had happened. I told him.

"That's very odd, then," he said. "Because I think you may be mistaken. In fact, I'm sure you're mistaken. I saw Colonel Trask down at the Southport marina earlier this evening—he was refueling a rather large cabin cruiser, on which I believe he lives. Named the *Keeper,* is it?"

He was smiling now at my obvious surprise, and then he reached into his trousers pocket and produced a small envelope. "He even asked me to deliver this little love note to you; that's how very sure I am that the good colonel is alive and well. Drop by the House sometime; we always have a pot of coffee going."

He heaved himself out of the rocker and then paused at

the top of the steps. "Dr. Quartermain," he said. "An odd choice for the job he holds over there."

"Because . . . what?" I was hoping McMichaels wasn't some kind of closet racist.

"The word around town is that the good doctor has a bit of a gambling problem," he said. "Of the compulsive persuasion, or so I'm told."

"This something you know?"

"Indeed not. Just what I've been told by people who fancy the occasional game of cards."

"Does the company know?"

He eyed me over those antique-looking spectacles. "Probably not," he said. "Good night to you, sir."

I opened the envelope after he left. Inside was a single sheet of paper with a series of numbers handwritten across the top. If Trask was trying for a secret code, he'd succeeded—I couldn't make any sense of the numbers. The bigger news, of course, was that Trask was not the corpus delicti in dry layup at the plant. I looked at my watch—almost one o'clock. I decided to let my news wait until morning. There was no grieving widow, and, as best I knew, no clear and present danger to the plant.

The gossip about Ari Quartermain was interesting, if true, but I couldn't see any connection between that and Allie Gardner. My brain swirled with all sorts of possibilities and mysteries, but I elected to shut down and get some much-needed sleep.

In the morning I briefed Pardee and Tony on our late-night visitor. Tony examined the note, then passed it to Pardee.

"Why would he send you a note?" Pardee asked.

"I don't know—to let me know he's alive? Maybe he's heard all the rumors."

"Or to set up a meet?" Pardee said. Tony asked for the note back and took a pencil to the numbers.

"Right," he said. "The first set of numbers is very likely a latitude and longitude position; the second one is a date-time group, probably in Greenwich time—there's a *Z* at the end of it. So: place and time." He looked at his watch, which was festooned with time-zone dials. "Tonight, in fact, at 11:00 P.M."

"Good headwork," I said. "Can you tell where?"

"I'll need the GPS set on the boat, or at least a chart of the area. But these numbers look local—maybe in the Cape Fear estuary, or just off Carolina Beach, in the Atlantic. Did you tell him we have a boat?"

"He knows, and this makes sense, of sorts—a rendezvous at sea ought to be fairly private."

"Unless one of the alphabets planted some devices," Pardee said.

"Would they work out at sea?"

"They could record, but probably not transmit. But they could have placed a satellite tag, and if they did, they'll know someone's moving that boat around."

"Shouldn't we tell Dr. Quartermain?" Tony asked.

I hesitated. I felt ninety-percent sure that Ari Quartermain was not a bad guy, but the local police sergeant had sowed a seed or two of doubt. "Let's lay eyes on Trask; that way our information will be firsthand," I said. "Then we can tell Ari. In the meantime, let's confirm the rendezvous point, and then we'll start working backwards on Allie's timeline."

Tony went down to the marina to pull a chart so he could verify that the numbers did translate into a rendezvous position. Pardee and I called Ari's office and asked his new secretary to see if those visitor log copies were available for us to pick up. My plan was to get those and then go into Wilmington and talk to Bernie about getting a look at her vehicle, or the report of their search, assuming they'd done one. I called our H&S offices back in Triboro to get the videotape Allie had taken of the legal lovebirds.

"What videotape?" Horace asked. "She never returned, remember?"

I knew that, I thought. Back to Bernie Price. I was more tired than I realized.

As it turned out, Bernie couldn't help us, either. The feds had taken everything—the car, the contents, Allie's backpack and briefcase, everything—and since the front seat of her car had registered on a Geiger counter, the Wilmington police impound was just as happy to see Allie's radioactive ride go away.

Reluctantly, I called Creeps and explained what I needed. I harped on the fact that we were honoring our agreement: This was about Allie Gardner and not events at Helios. He told me he'd see what our Bureau could do.

For the moment, we were stymied. I called the marina over in Carolina Beach to see if the *Keeper* was present for duty. It was not, and Cap'n Pete had no information as to where the colonel had gone off to this time, as usual. He wouldn't have told me if he knew, I suspected.

Another blank wall. We were batting a thousand this morning.

I decided to go for a run. When I got back, Pardee had news. Creeps had arranged access to Allie's car, which was being held at the Customs and Border Protection office in Wilmington. They had, surprisingly, not yet put a forensics team on the car, so if we wanted to do so, the Wilmington resident agent would send an agent to be present. Any physical evidence would, of course, have to remain in federal control.

We stopped by the Helios admin center to pick up the visitor log copies and then went on to Wilmington. The Customs and Border Protection office was located on Medical Center Drive in a low, brick building that looked a lot like the local FBI resident agent's office. There was a fenced parking compound behind the building containing some boats and various vehicles with the CBP logo on the doors. We went up to the front doors and confronted a video camera. There were no actual signs on the building indicating it was a government building, but the roof was littered with radio antennas, and the flags of both the United States and the Coast Guard fluttered out front. The doors clicked, and we began processing through security.

The agent sent over to assist us in our enquiries was none other than the lovely Samantha Young, ex-administrative-assistant at Quartermain's office. She was dressed in a neatly tailored pantsuit, which did nothing to disguise her splendid physical assets. Even the CBP guys were impressed, which probably explained why we had four male agents helping us sign in.

"Hi, there, Ms. Judas," I said.

"Ouch," she said with a smile. "Nothing personal, you understand."

"Just business, I know," I said. "But it got personal once I went inside that Marine Corps rest home."

"Whatever that is," she said with a face chock-full of feigned innocence.

I rolled my eyes, and then we all trooped out to the impound yard. Allie's car was parked by itself alongside the chain-link fence.

"What specifically are we looking for?" Samantha asked.

"We don't know," I replied. "Anything that might tell us where she went while she was down here in Wilmington. Receipts, fast-food wrappers, her briefcase, a prescription for radioactive pills. Like that."

In the event, we found most of the above, including the videocassette onto which she'd downloaded her camcorder tape. Allie had kept a plastic grocery bag slung between the two front seats for trash, and we pulled out the usual collection of fast-food debris and two gas receipts. We copied down the dates, times, and addresses from those and the one Wendy's receipt I'd found glued to the floor carpet by a sticky French fry. Her purse, which had been jammed under the front seat, had the usual female stuff. Samantha held on to the videocassette while we poked around under the seats, in the trunk, and in the glove box. Pardee went through her luggage, which consisted of a backpack and a briefcase, and which he said contained nothing of direct interest.

We went back into the CBP offices, and someone rustled up a cassette player. Allie had done the tape professionally, with voiceovers on time, place, and the names of the subjects involved. There wasn't that much actual run-time video, but it was clear what the two lovebirds were there for, or at least clear enough for any suspicious wife and *her* lawyer. Pardee had taken one thing from Allie's briefcase: her hotel receipt from the Hilton. Nothing on the bill except room, meal charges, and lots of taxes. No phone charges. More blank walls.

We left everything with Samantha and went back out to my Suburban. As we drove away I speculated on the lack of any phone calls on her hotel bill.

"Nobody uses hotel phones anymore," Pardee said. "Especially when you have one of these." He produced what I assumed was Allie's cell phone, which he'd apparently palmed from the briefcase when Samantha wasn't looking.

"Hoo-aah," I said. "They'll git you for that."

"They have access to the central office records; we don't, not without some help. But this thing ought to have a call log, don't you think?"

He switched the phone on while I drove and accessed the call log. "Aha," he said.

"Aha, what?"

"I think I recognize a number, or at least an exchange. Hang on a minute."

He told the phone to recall the number and then waited. Then he said, "Sorry, wrong number," and switched off.

"That was the Helios general information number," he announced. "For some unknown reason, Allie called the power plant."

Aha, indeed, I thought. Now we had a tie, however indirect, between Helios and one of the unexplained radiation incidents. I maneuvered the Suburban through a very complicated cloverleaf to get up onto the Cape Fear River Memorial Bridge.

"Does it show the duration of the call?" I asked, in case Allie had simply dialed a wrong number as Pardee had pretended to do.

"Nope," he replied. "Just the call and the date, which was, lemme see, the day before she died."

"Call 'em back and ask for Quartermain."

A moment later, he was speaking to Quartermain's secretary. Pardee raised his eyebrows at me, and I told him to see if Ari could meet us in a half hour for a quick private conversation. She put him on hold, and then came back on to tell him that Dr. Quartermain could meet us in an hour and named a restaurant in Southport. I nodded, and Pardee told her we'd be there.

The restaurant turned out to be a New York–style deli, which opened for breakfast and lunch only, down on the main drag leading to the municipal beach. It was noisy and surprisingly full of people when Ari came in, saw us at a corner table, and excused his way through the counter line to join us. I'd decided to go ahead and tell him what we'd found out about Carl Trask.

"Can't stay," he announced, checking his watch.

"That good a day, is it?" I asked.

He rolled his eyes. "We are *infested* with agencies whose names are all abbreviated," he said. "A million questions, no answers. What you got?"

"A live Carl Trask?" I said.

He leaned back in his chair, visibly surprised. "Really," he said. "Maybe I'd better get a sandwich after all."

Pardee volunteered to stand in line and order for all three of us while I debriefed my visit from the local constabulary and the news that Allie had made a call to the power plant the day before she died.

That really threw him. "She did? Do you know who she called?"

I shook my head. "All we know is that her cell phone called your central number at Helios. Does your switchboard record calls coming in?"

"No," he said. "Unless it's a threat or a crank call; then the operator can hit a capture-record button, but otherwise, no, calls are just calls. And if that's not Carl Trask in the cask, who the fuck is it?"

"Slow down, Ari," I said. "We have one guy, admittedly a senior cop, telling us he's pretty sure he saw Trask at the Southport marina. Pretty sure doesn't hack it. Until one of us sees him, we don't actually *know* anything." Then I told him about the note and our plan to rendezvous with Trask to find out what the hell he was doing.

"Besides being AWOL from Helios?" Ari said. "We've temporarily suspended his access and clearances. If he's running some kind of security test, the only place he can get into right now is the public admin building, where his current security clearance level is zero."

"We have indications that Trask is part of a Homeland Security undercover operation at the container port," I said. "I don't want to go into detail about that just now, but it might explain some of his strange comings and goings. So: We'll meet, we'll talk, and then maybe we'll know more."

"That may well be," Ari said, "but as far as I'm concerned, he's got a job to do at Helios, and we have a major physical security breach investigation going on right now. That's where he's supposed to be, not out there playing cowboys and Indians with his black-ops pals. You want a new job?"

"Been there, done that. Look, until we actually confirm all this, I'd like you to *not* share this news with the Bureau."

He nodded. "Okay; we're not exactly best friends right now, anyway. Those guys are probing everything that's not nailed down, even stuff that has no bearing on the floater in the moonpool."

"That's what they do," I said. "Especially when it's new ground for them. They learn, then they dig, and learn some more. It's their strength."

"Well, right now, all their digging is upsetting my engineers. If this shit keeps up, our chief engineer is going to recommend a safety shutdown, and the NRC does not want that to happen."

"Why not?"

"Because they'd have to explain why to the secretary of energy *and* the rest of the power industry."

"So?"

He laughed. "*So?* If someone asks the right questions, that could lead to a system-wide shutdown. Think nationwide rolling blackouts."

"But you said the plant, the power-generation side, anyway, wasn't affected by the moonpool. So why a system-wide shutdown?"

"Because the technical and physical security systems are totally integrated; they're the same system for the whole plant. If it failed at Helios, it could fail at any of the BWR plants. That would technically make all the plants, by definition, no longer safe to operate. Those are NRC rules, so they'd be squatting on their own petard, to mangle the metaphor. I need Trask back, and yesterday would be nice."

"You're thinking the same thing that I am, then?" I said. "Trask had to be a part of getting that guy in, whoever he is?"

He ran his fingers over his shining bald head. "There are no indications that the security system failed in the physical or electronic sense. Ergo, yes, someone with access and clearance had to be involved."

"Trask, or a helper?"

"That's my problem: If we can't find out how the floater got in there, then the default assumption has to be that the system failed."

"And they're interviewing everybody? That Russian, for instance, and her people, the operating engineers?"

"Oh, hell, yes, three times a day. We're going to be sitting down with lie detectors shortly. The company's sending down a battalion of lawyers, which made the Bureau really happy."

Pardee showed up with sandwiches and iced tea. I could see that Ari wasn't really hungry, but he ate anyway. We chewed through lunch in silence, and then he looked at his watch again. I told him we'd get back to him first thing, either late tonight or in the morning, when we had something. He thanked us for lunch and then pushed back his chair.

"If it's him, you tell that crazy bastard to get back in," he said. "I don't care what or who else he's screwing around with—we need him back at Helios, now."

At eleven that night, Tony and I arrived at the designated rendezvous point, which was a point just to seaward of where the Cape Fear River poured out into the Atlantic. The night was dark and cold, with a steady fifteen-knot breeze kicking up some small whitecaps around us. Tony had noted that the rendezvous time would coincide with slack water following an ebb tide, which would minimize the current coming across the bar. Otherwise, we'd have had a tough time staying in the lat-long position designated in the note. To the north the lights of Kure Beach twinkled over the dunes; to our west were Southport and the Oak Island pilots' station. The actual rendezvous position was nearly alongside the so-called sea buoy, the first buoy that a ship entering the Cape Fear estuary encountered. The buoys had all looked small from a distance, but this thing was big, some fifteen feet high. It was festooned with barnacles, radar reflectors, bird manure, the blinking light, and a crowd of sleeping pelicans.

Tony kept checking the radar for any contacts, especially one of those huge container ships. There were some big blobs on the scope up near the container port, but they were most likely tied up to the pier. The layout of the river entrance and the shorelines of the estuary stood out in sharp green lines on the radarscope display. The boat had been bouncing around quite a bit when we stopped, so Tony put us on a two-mile racetrack pattern, which kept the motion to a minimum as we idled around, waiting for Trask. I'd left Pardee back at the house so we'd have a base of communications ashore, and I'd briefed Tony on the way out to the rendezvous. He'd had some questions.

"If Trask is working undercover for Homeland Security, how come the Bureau doesn't know that? I mean, aren't they supposed to be talking to each other these days?"

"That's the theory," I said, "but, remember, out of all those alphabets, the FBI is the one that is not inside the Homeland Security mantle. My guess is they both hold back from each other."

He turned the wheel to go back downwind and looked again into the radarscope cone. "But why would they do that? Wasn't that the point of those so-called intel fusion centers?

So everybody knew what everybody else was doing? So they could stop stepping on each other's toes?"

"It's a Washington thing," I said. "I think it's about budget money. The agency with the biggest budget has the most power. You bare your bureaucratic soul to an outfit that competes for budget money with you, you make yourself vulnerable. We played those games back in the sheriff's office, remember? Major Crimes versus Patrol, Patrol versus Community Relations? Same deal, bigger honeypot."

"We've got a contact," he announced, pointing down into the radarscope cone. I looked. There was a tiny green blip down in the direction of Oak Island. Tony turned on the leaders function, which put a green line on the blip. The length of the line represented the contact's speed, and the direction of the line indicated its course. This one was coming our way.

"It could be a pilot boat," I said.

"Then we'd expect a contact to seaward—an inbound ship." He flipped the range scale out to twenty-five miles, but there was nothing coming from seaward. He dropped the scale back down to ten miles, and the contact continued to close us. Whoever it was, he was coming out of the estuary.

Tony made sure the VHF radio was tuned to channel 16, which was the standard channel for ship-to-ship comms in restricted waters. Trask probably wasn't going to initiate voice communications, in case the Coast Guard had been alerted to watch for his boat. I still wondered if a Bureau team had put an RFID tracer on the boat. If they thought Trask was dead, though, why would they care about his boat? Even if they did know that Trask had been working undercover for the government, the boat's whereabouts still shouldn't matter.

"He's coming right for us," Tony said. "Or at least for that buoy."

"Our nav lights are on, right?" I asked.

He nodded and picked up binoculars to search the night ahead of us. The flashing light from the sea buoy wasn't helping with our night vision. The seas were confused, and I guessed that the tide had turned. When the sea began to flow back into the estuary, it collided with the outbound river current, creating a crazy patchwork of waves and whorls in the water. Tony was having to work to keep the boat on course as the currents opposed each other over the bar.

I checked my cell phone and found coverage. I called Pardee back at the house.

"We've got a contact headed our way," I said. "We'll call again after we have our meeting, or in one hour, whichever is sooner."

"And if you don't?" he asked. "Where are you?"

"We're loitering about something called the sea buoy," I said. "Where the seaward end of the channel into the Cape Fear River begins."

"Roger that," he said. "One hour, and then I call the Coast Guard."

I agreed and hung up.

"Five miles and closing," Tony said. "We're right in the main shipping channel. Want to go meet him?"

The water around the sea buoy was getting rougher and rougher. "Might be a little flatter inside," I said. I wasn't getting seasick so much as having trouble staying upright as our small boat bounced and pitched in the confused chop. I was glad I hadn't brought the shepherds.

Tony kicked it up a few knots, and we pointed into the estuary. When the sea buoy was a half mile or so behind us, channel 16 suddenly came to life.

"Hold your position," a voice said. No call signs, no identification numbers or names, just a voice. It sounded like Trask, but I couldn't be absolutely sure.

"Roger," Tony replied, also leaving out any identifying information. It was totally incorrect procedure, but it worked, and anyone listening would be clueless as to who was talking or why. Tony slowed and tried to find a stable course, but the water was still pretty rough. The current seemed to be pushing us into the estuary, although it was hard to tell in the dark.

"Two miles," Tony said, staring out into the night. He kept checking the radar to see where the other boat should be. I kept looking for lights but didn't see any.

"Shouldn't we be able to see his running lights?" I asked. "That's a big boat."

"You'd think so," he said. "Unless he's turned them off. That thing had radar, didn't it?"

"Yes."

Tony switched the range scale down to five miles, and the blip became larger, halfway in from the edge of the screen. The electronic leader pointed right at the center of our scope, where the rising chop had created a bloom of green sea return on the display.

Tony kept looking out with the binoculars, while I switched the range scale down to two miles. The contact was still visible, but it was getting perilously close to the edge of the blob from the sea return, which now covered the inner one-third of the display. At some point, the radar would become useless. That point was just about now.

"Cam," Tony said.

I looked up to see Tony staring ahead, no longer using his binoculars. I tried to get my eyes to work, night-blind from having been staring down into that radar screen. I was about to ask, "What?" when I saw the bows of what looked like the *Keeper* dead ahead, close, very close, and pushing up a huge wave. Tony reached for the controls, but a moment later, she crashed into us and I was spinning underwater in a coil of noise, roiling seawater, shattering fiberglass, and the thrum of two large propellers pulsing the water right in front of my face.

We both popped to the surface at the same time. Our boat was gone except for what looked like the front one-third, which was upside down and bobbing around in a debris field of fiberglass bits, flotation foam, and gasoline. Tony was gagging on a mouthful of gasoline and saltwater; I wasn't yet in the fuel slick, but the stink was strong. I paddled backward away from the smell and looked for the *Keeper,* but there was no sign of her, just a muffled rumble of engines disappearing. Then a small wave broke over me from behind, and when I went under, I realized that my clothes were really heavy. It took me several seconds to get my head above water again, and even though I was a strong swimmer, I felt a moment of panic in that black water. That cold, black water.

"You hurt, boss?" Tony called from somewhere in the darkness. I tried to spot him, but the dark out there was absolute, except for the regular pulsing of the sea buoy light.

The sea buoy.

If we could get up on that thing, we might not freeze to death quite so quickly.

"I'm okay, I think," I shouted back. "How about you?"

"Got a cut on my arm, but I don't think anything's busted," he called back.

"Tell it not to bleed," I called. I didn't have to tell him why. "Where are you?"

"Over here," I called, raising my right arm, which promptly caused me to submerge under the next wave.

"I'm hanging on to the bow," he shouted. He sounded farther away, which wasn't a good sign. "Here. Over here."

I tried to pop up out of the water, but my clothes weighed me down. I did, however, catch a glimpse of something white over to my right, so I began swimming in that direction. The seas were rising and smacking me from every direction, but I knew I had to get going before hypothermia worked its deadly spell on my shivering body.

Five minutes of thrashing brought me up next to the floating bow section. Tony was holding on with his left arm to a big crack in the fiberglass, and I thought I could see black rivulets running down his hand. He reached out with his right and pulled me alongside. I was more tired than I should have been, but the weight of my clothes had been a real surprise. The gasoline smell was gone now.

"Why's this part still afloat?" I asked.

"Unsinkable, remember?" he said. "It'll float until it gets waterlogged."

"How long's that?"

"We'll be dead of hypothermia long before that happens," he said with a crazy grin. Leave it to Tony to feel this was just another adventure.

"Try for that buoy?" I asked.

"What buoy?"

I looked around and realized I could no longer see the flashes of light.

"It's anchored," Tony said. "We're not. Tide's coming in, so we're drifting away from that thing." He spat out some water and rubbed the gash on his arm. "I think we're fucked."

"Well, at least we know who the bad guy is," I said, and then realized that, no, we really didn't. I couldn't *prove* that it had been Trask driving that boat. I tried to get my bearings, but the waves were just high enough to block our view. I was getting really tired now, and my arms and legs were beginning to numb up a little. My running shoes felt like a couple of bricks. I remembered seeing one of those time-versus-temperature life-expectancy tables for people adrift in cold water, and quickly put it out of my mind.

"Whoa," Tony said, looking over my shoulder. "I think that's a ship."

I turned around, wiped the saltwater out of my eyes, and looked where he was looking. At first I didn't see anything, then I did: two white lights, one over the other. It looked to be a long, long way away, though, up in the direction of the container port.

"She's coming right at us," Tony said. "Those are the masthead and range lights. I can't see running lights."

"Too far," I gulped, bouncing in the water to see over the hump of the shattered bow section. My fingers were like ice.

"Or she's really big and not far off," Tony said. "Oh, fuck!"

He was right and I was wrong. She was really, really big and she was right here. We could hear the crashing of the bow wave and feel the engine vibrations thumping through the water. It had to be one of those giant container ships, which looked big enough alongside the pier. When you get face-to-face with one in the water and can count rivets, big doesn't begin to describe it. With our own radar at short range, we'd missed it.

Then we were lifting out of the water as the pressure swell from the bulbous bow thrust us aside like two fleas and deposited us and our bow fragment right alongside the towering black steel wall of her port side, which hissed past us in the darkness. I thought about yelling for help, but it would have been like hollering up at an iceberg, with about as much effect. I wanted to swim away from those massive steel plates, vividly mindful of some very big propellers that were coming our way, but neither of us could really move. Our tiny wreck bounced along the side of the ship, spinning gently each time we bumped up against the sliding hull, and it was all we could do to hang on. Twice we were hit in the face by hot water coming from overboard discharges.

Finally the slope of the moving steel mountain changed to an overhang as her stern came up on us. We both instinctively looked up into the white light of her stern light, above which we saw a lone face looking down into the wake. And directly at us.

We saw the man's head snap up and his slanted eyes go wide when he spotted us, but then we disappeared out of the stern light as the monster spat us out into her broad, smooth wake. The wash from her propellers coiled the water like a field of hissing snakes. Then we heard a wonderful sound: the deep, booming groan of her ship's whistle. Three blasts, which Tony said meant she was backing down. With any luck at all, we were now unfucked, and just in time, too. The remains of the wake were dissipating, and we could see glinting, finny figures darting through the disturbed water, hunting for delicacies stirred up by the giant ship's passage. Out on the margins of all the activity were a couple of really big fins, moving slowly, biding their time. Through chattering teeth, I prayed they were porpoises.

Forty-five freezing minutes later, we were huddled in the ship's motorboat under two soggy blankets each, as the coxswain maneuvered under the boat falls dangling down from the darkness above. I've been cold before, but never like this. My bones felt like rubber, and I wanted desperately to sleep. None of the boat crew spoke a word of English, but they were expert seamen, and they'd been directed back to our position in the dark by someone who knew what he was doing, too.

Once on board we stumbled across acres and acres of steel deck to the massive superstructure amidships. They indicated we needed to climb the interior stairways, but I simply couldn't do it, and Tony slid down to the deck and hung his head on his chest. When they saw the blood leaking down his wrist, there was more excited radio chatter. Apparently the damned ship was so big they used radios to communicate inside as well as outside. A few minutes later, a medical team arrived and we were carried on stretchers to the ship's sick bay. They stripped off our wet clothes and rolled us up into yet more blankets, which produced about twenty minutes' worth of chattering teeth. A cup of hot tea, loaded with sugar, helped a lot, while the medical attendant worked on Tony's forearm. Then a ruddy-faced, bearded Englishman stuck his head into the sick bay and welcomed us aboard his ship.

"Right, then," he said approvingly. "We've got one of your Coast Guard helicopters en route. Drink up, we'll get you some dry coveralls, and then we'll see how well the pilot does with our landing spot." He looked slyly over at the medical guy doing his thing with Tony's arm, whipped out a flask, and dropped a wee dram of something wonderful into my tea.

"Thank you," I croaked. "For everything."

"You're most welcome. Made for an excellent drill before we got out to sea. You were lucky in more than one respect: This was the after-lookout's very first watch, so he was actually doing his job. Normally, the chances of your being seen down there were those famous twins."

I knew those twins: Slim and None. "I'd like to express my appreciation to him, then, if I may."

He whipped out a business card. "Send me a check. His name is Hassam Selim. I'll see that he gets it."

I thanked him again, and then we were rounded up for the approaching helicopter ride.

Once at the Wilmington Coast Guard station, we had to endure an interview about what had happened and fill out a dozen or so forms. On the ride over from the ship, I'd thought about how much to reveal. I decided to mostly tell the truth, under the theory that, if questioned again, it would be easier to remember. The young Coast Guard lieutenant listened to my story about going out to sea to meet the *Keeper* and getting run over instead. He frowned when I was finished, and then asked if we would mind hanging around for a few minutes.

I put a landline call in to Pardee at the beach house and told him what had happened. He said he'd drive up right away. I asked him to notify the marina and to tell them there'd be a Coast Guard incident report to follow. He confirmed that we had purchased full replacement insurance on the boat, so the marina ought not to be too excited. He asked if we should call Quartermain, but I told him to hold off. Then the lieutenant came back into the conference room, accompanied this time by an older officer wearing the stripes of a lieutenant commander. He introduced himself as the station's operations officer. He had one question: Did we think this was an accident or an intentional crash? I looked at Tony and then told the ops boss that it had to have been intentional. We'd exchanged radio calls, he'd told us to maintain our position, indicating he knew where we were, and we'd watched him come straight toward us on the radar. He'd arrived at the intercept point going full bore, plus, he had to have known he'd hit something, and yet he'd kept on going.

The lieutenant commander nodded and then said that he'd have to report this up his chain of command and that there would be law enforcement people, not to mention the marine insurance company, who would probably have further questions. I told him we were working for the Helios power plant and living temporarily in Southport. We'd be available to talk to anyone who needed more information—but for now, we had a ride coming, we were both beat to shit, and could we please just go home?

* * *

Ari Quartermain hung his gleaming black head in his hands and groaned out loud. It was nearly eleven the next morning, and all three of us were sitting in his office, which was not a happy place just then. Neither of us had physically laid eyes on the man driving that boat.

"So that still might be Trask in the lead-lined cookie jar," he said. "And now someone wants you dead?"

"Sums it up pretty well," I said. "How's your week going?"

He glared at me from between splayed fingers. That good.

"The Bureau know all this?"

"They were our next stop," I said. "I think I ought to tell Creeps before the Coast Guard does. He likes to know shit before anyone else. My cell's shot. Can I use a phone?"

He pointed to an extension phone on his conference table. I put it on speaker, got out Caswell's card, and called the RA's office. I asked for Special Agent Caswell. Not available. I told them we might have located Carl Trask of the Helios power plant. Hold, please. A minute of hissing from the speakerphone. Transferring.

"Mr. Richter," intoned my favorite voice from my favorite Bureau.

"Special Agent," I said. "We have developments."

"I'm all ears," he said, and then laughed at his own joke. He wasn't laughing when I'd finished, though, so I tried a little sucking up. "I'm letting you know in advance of the Coast Guard report, which should be hitting the wires this morning."

"Not so far in advance that your Bureau knew about it before you ventured to sea," he said.

"You're always telling me not to bother you with rumors, Special Agent," I said.

"Mmm-hnnh," he said. His confidence in me was overwhelming. Tony was rolling his eyes.

"And I must point out," I said, "I still can't prove that was Trask driving. All I saw last night was a big bow wave. The voice on the radio sounded like Trask, but . . ."

"Yes. But."

"Right," I said and stopped there, waiting to see what he'd do.

"Tell me, Mr. Richter," he said. "Did you find anything in your Ms. Gardner's vehicle that assisted you in your inquiries?"

I looked at Pardee, who shook his head. "Not really," I said. "Agent Young has everything we laid hands on, and frankly, we're still stumped."

"Special Agent Young says she thought she saw a cell phone in the briefcase, but it's not there now."

"Beats me," I said. "If you find it, I'd sure like to see the call log."

"Mmm-hnnh."

"Well, that's the news from the waterfront. Thought you ought to know."

"What are your intentions now, Mr. Richter?"

"We're going to keep working the Allie mystery."

"And your job with Dr. Quartermain?"

"Well, that's languishing in the Overtaken By Events box with this apparent homicide at the moonpool," I said. "Dr. Quartermain tells us he has all the help he can stand right now."

"Is he there right now?"

"Yes, I am," Ari called from across the office. "Any progress, Special Agent?"

"You will be the second person to know, Dr. Quartermain," Creeps said. "Mr. Richter? Keep in touch, will you?"

"Absolutely," I said. "You know me—I keep my Bureau informed as best I can." Tony and Pardee struggled not to laugh out loud.

"Mmm-hnnh."

Then the connection was broken. I made sure by punching off the speaker's power button. I'd been nearly undone one time by a speakerphone I thought was off. I looked over at Ari.

"If that's *not* Carl Trask's body in that container," I said, "then you've got to get an ID of some kind."

"NRC nuclear medicine people are working on that," he said. "We're trying to find something in the physical security office which might have Trask's DNA on it—coffee cup, a jacket with a hair or two, gloves, you know. If we can do that, they think they can get a core sample from the body."

"A core sample." I had visions of the major's horse syringe on the end of a long broomstick.

"He won't feel a thing," he said with a shrug. "The bigger problem, for us, is the unauthorized access issue. I explained that to you, I think."

I nodded. "Pardee here is a computer science expert," I said. "If you'd care to walk him through your access system, maybe he could give you a fresh viewpoint. Tony and I have to go back to Southport to meet with the marina's insurance agent."

"Appreciate any help I can get," he said to Pardee.

"Remember the redhead we brought with us that morning at your house?" I asked.

"Indeed."

"She's both a computer expert and someone who's apparently well versed in penetrating federal security systems. I think the feds have her right now. Why don't you suggest to Special Agent Caswell that they put her on the problem, too."

"She's back in custody?" he asked.

"Well, we think so," I said, ducking a detailed answer. "If he gives you a categorical no, I'd be interested to know why not."

"Okay," he said. "I'll pull that string for you."

At that moment, his secretary knocked on the door to tell him that Dr. Petrowska and her assistant were waiting to see him. That was my cue to get gone.

I told Ari that once we got out from under the boat mess, maybe we could take a look at the people who could have gained access to the moonpool, other than Trask. I suggested a records search, not interviews, something we could do away from the limelight.

"I'll see if I can arrange that," he said. "The NRC reliability program people are doing that, of course, and the Bureau types are looking over their shoulders."

"I understand, and we don't want to tread on any toes. Can't hurt. I think."

He barked a laugh. "What could possibly go wrong, as you are so fond of saying."

As we went out, La Petrowska gave me an annoyed look.

"Just what we need," she snapped. "More unqualified interference."

"Seems like what you do need is some qualified American management up at the moonpool," I said. "Isn't all that stuff supposed to stay *in* the pool?"

Her eyes blazed and I thought she was going to take a swing at me. The man with her grabbed her forearm and pointed her into Ari's office. I recognized him as the guy I'd seen on the ferryboat, coming back from Carolina Beach. He turned around as I left and gave me a perplexed look, as if he were surprised to see me there. What the hell was that about, I wondered. I asked the secretary what his name was, and she said it was Dr. Thomason, and he was a Ph.D., but that was all she knew.

Tony and I had lunch at the deli and, on the way out, ran into Sergeant McMichaels. He stopped to talk.

"Heard you had an excellent adventure last night," he said.

"Word does get around," I said. "We're lucky to be standing here."

"There was a river pilot on board the container ship," he explained. "They all live around here. And it was deliberate?"

"We think so."

"And it was Brother Trask at the helm of the other boat?"

"That's who set up the rendezvous point, which was the point of all the number strings in the note you brought me. He arrived going at full speed, drove over the top of us, and kept going."

"So if I happen to see him again, he is, what do the federals call them—a person of interest?"

"If I see him before you do, he'll be ER-bound."

"Tsk-tsk, Lieutenant," he said with a grin. "That would be vigilante talk. We'll have none of that in our happy little metropolis."

"I'll take him out into the county," I said. "Then I'll beat the shit out of him. The Bureau's been cut in on what happened, by the way."

His expression became serious. "I am hearing some truly strange stories coming out of the Helios power plant," he said. "You would not be involved in any of those goings-on, would you?"

"Tangentially, but our focus is something else. Our Bureau has invited us to butt out of the other matter, as it were, and we're obliging."

"Our Bureau, indeed," he said. "Oh, there's something else."

We took a few steps away from the busy entrance to the deli for some privacy. "There's an impious young lad in this town who has been, as they say, talking trash in your direction."

"Ah, that would be Billy," I replied.

"Yes, it would. Billy Summers. Previously employed by the good colonel at Helios, and now back on the dole and unhappy with that situation."

"Which he thinks I caused."

"He does, indeed. Working himself up to doing something about that, apparently."

"He have the moxie for it?" Tony asked.

McMichaels shrugged. "He's like a fear-biter dog. You never quite know what Billy Summers will do. It sounds like all talk, but then he can strike out. He is known to us, and we don't much care for the lad, truth be told."

"I appreciate the heads-up," I said. "Unless he's the kind to take a rifle shot through a lighted window, I think we can handle Billy."

"He was once accused of taking liberties with an underage child. Never proved, but he's very, very sensitive about that. If it ever comes to fisticuffs, mention of that will perhaps cloud his judgment."

It was my turn to grin. This was very useful information if I ever had to duke it out with Billy. If you could get your opponent to lose his temper, the fight became yours to lose. "I'll remember that," I said. "Say something like 'short-eyes.' "

"That would probably do it," he said. "And, Lieutenant: If you're going to indulge in any more adventures, a word in advance to me would be greatly appreciated."

"Will do, Sergeant," I said. "Hopefully we're done with adventures. At least in Southport. Where in Boston did you come from?"

"Chelsea," he said. "Got tired of all those taxes."

We met with the insurance agent and the marina owner. The agent was wriggling hard to get out of paying the bill, but that full-value-replacement-cost clause was fairly self-explanatory. They wanted to see the results of the police investigation before writing a check, and there was nothing we could do about that. I asked if we could get another boat. The marina owner said sure; the insurance agent said absolutely not. For the moment, we were in a boat-free zone.

But not idle. I had the beginnings of an idea about where Trask might be hiding out, assuming he was still in the area. The problem was, Trask's whereabouts did not relate, as best I knew, to what had happened to Allie. The man had tried to kill us, so we had a score to settle, but surely the Bureau was searching hard for Carl Trask, and didn't need us interfering with that, either. Tony suggested I call Creeps and tell him my idea, but I decided to just lie low for the moment. We went back into town to get new cell phones, and then to the beach house to check messages and look at those Helios visitor logs again.

In the event, Tony had to go back to Triboro to close up two cases that were overdue. Pardee was helping Ari over at the plant, which meant I'd have at least one guy in the area as backup. I told Tony to call me once he got his stuff squared away; I wanted him to run down a couple of things in Triboro relating to Allie's background. Then I took the mutts out on the beach for a leisurely run. When I got back, I checked the portable computer for messages, but there were none. We hadn't activated the house phone, so I was a bit surprised when it rang as I was getting out of the shower. No one I knew had this number; for that matter, I didn't even know what the house number was.

I picked up, trying not to drip too much on the carpet. A familiar voice was on the line.

"Sorry we missed you the other night, Lieutenant," Trask said. "In a manner of speaking, of course."

"Actually, you didn't miss at all," I said. "You just failed to follow through."

"Yeah, well, I was never all that good at completed staff work," he said.

"I thought we were going to talk."

"Well."

"Who's that in the moonpool, wearing your boots? Inquiring minds want desperately to know."

"Nobody important," he said. "I suppose you want to know why you went swimming in the ocean."

"I figured we were starting to get in the way of something imminent," I said. "Feel free to elaborate, of course."

"You're close. Tell you what: If you promise to back out, I'll promise to leave you alone. How's that sound?"

"Sounds like: Dream on, Trask. I think I know where you're holed up, and I'm never going to leave you alone."

He laughed. "You knock yourself out, then, Lieutenant, but you better bring some competent help."

"Count on it," I said, and then I had an idea. "Did you say 'sorry *we* missed you'?"

There was just the slightest hesitation in his reply. "I might have," he said.

"So who's we? Not perchance that moonpool engineer, Petrowska's number two? Dr. Thomason?"

"Hoo-aah," he said.

"I'll take that as a yes," I said. "Now: Why shouldn't I call Creeps Caswell and fill him in on this conversation? You're out there somewhere in the weeds like the snake you are, but

Thomason, he's right there at Helios. And I'll bet he'll stand up under competent questioning for, what, a good fifteen seconds?"

"You would be wrong about that, because, one, he's a lot tougher than he looks, and two, you still want to know what happened to your ace employee, Ms. Allison Gardner, don't you? I can answer that for you, but not if you go running to tell teacher. Let's talk. How's tonight work for you?"

"Tonight's just dandy," I said. "But I'm not coming to talk."

"Oh, hell, Lieutenant, we can talk and *then* we can rumble. I might even tell you what the fuck we're up to, and why. You seem like the kind of guy who might appreciate it, even. Either way, whoever comes out on top can talk all he wants to, or not, as the case might be, right?"

"I believe I know what you're up to, although I think that's no longer possible, what with all the attention you've brought to Helios. So: How's about the container junkyard, sometime after sundown?"

"Hah!" he said. "That was a pretty good guess."

"The word among the ICE people is that you have a spiderhole over there," I said. I wanted him to know we'd been there and that we were known to the operatives at the container port. He ignored me.

"And you'll bring the shepherds?" he asked.

"You betchum, Red Rider."

"Won't that be interesting," he said.

We exchanged cell numbers, and then I hung up. I went to find Creeps's number. I knew Trask had been talking about one of those *High Noon* moments, just the two of us *mano a mano,* alone in the middle of the street, itchy fingers dangling over holstered Colts. Conceptually, I was fine with that notion. Practically speaking, I wanted three Bucars' worth of heavily armed special agents lurking in the shadows on my side, plus a wire, plus a silenced helicopter with an operable death ray overhead. I sincerely doubted that Trask knew the first thing about Allie Gardner's death. What he really wanted was me in the open long enough for a clean

.30-06 head shot, followed by a quiet splash in the Cape Fear River at max tidal current. The quip about the dogs was just more BS.

Special Agent Caswell was not available, and would I like to leave a message? I asked them to have him call me before 6:00 P.M. Subject? Apprehension of Carl Trask. Spell Trask. I did. We'll be sure to pass that on.

Then I called Pardee, who said he was up to his eyeballs in the inner workings and hidden mechanisms of the station's security access system.

"Getting anywhere?" I asked.

"Anywhere I want to," he said. "That's the problem."

"How so?"

"Somebody's rigged the system to grant universal and unreported access to the right card. We're assuming it was Trask's card, which, of course, is missing."

"Didn't Ari suspend his access?"

"He thinks he has," Pardee said. "I'm not so sure. I think Trask has some pretty competent help."

I briefed him on my phone call from said Colonel Trask.

"Wow," he said. "You tell the Bureau?"

"I did leave a message with Creeps's office. As for Ari, you can tell him we think Trask is not only alive and well, but that he's aiming some kind of shit at Helios. I'll need you for this little op this evening."

"Got it; the head NRC data-dink is a little miffed that I found some things they couldn't."

"Try something for me while you're still in place: Get Dr. Thomason's access card, see if it has magic it's not supposed to."

"Who's he?"

"That Russian's deputy dog, in the moonpool building."

"Will do. See you shortly."

At ten that evening, Pardee, the shepherds, and I climbed through the tattered chain-link fence on the landward side of the container junkyard. No longer having a boat, we'd driven across into Wilmington and parked in an industrial area behind an abandoned elementary school. I'd sandwiched the Suburban between two semitrailers that looked as if they'd grown roots into the trash-littered concrete.

We'd ended up with two choices on the timing of our get-together with Trask. We could go early, find a decent tactical position out there in the junkyard, and wait for Trask, or we could go much later, making Trask do the waiting, while ceding to him a good ambush position. Pardee had suggested a third option: Don't go at all. Ask the Bureau to scour the junkyard at the appointed time and see what they came up with.

The problem was that my Bureau had never called back. Creeps either didn't get the message, or did and failed to care. Or he'd been told to stay out of it by *his* adult supervision. Unknowns abounded. I'd been about to chide Pardee for his lack of interest in a good fight, but then remembered the tension we'd experienced the last time he and Tony backed out.

We'd also talked about calling the port security people, but, as Pardee pointed out, we had no standing with them, and their domain probably did not extend to the junkyard. If we ran into the undercover ICE agent, he'd know who we were, but otherwise we were as unauthorized as Trask. My objective was to lay eyes and possibly a tire iron on Carl Trask, and find out if his little comment about Allie Gardner was real or just an enticement. We had new cell phones with all the appropriate numbers programmed into speed dial, guns, dogs, and a personal invitation. All we had to do now was find him, and hopefully not from the focal point of his kill zone.

We had a map, of sorts. Pardee had gone online to one of those satellite photography Web sites and bought a direct overhead picture of the entire container port area, zoomed close enough to make out individual features of the container junkyard. He'd printed out two copies, and we'd traced a route that should take us through the campfire area. From there we'd do an expanding square search. The plan was for the shepherds and me to go in and for Pardee to follow about five minutes behind in case I stepped in something.

If we didn't encounter Trask, we'd join forces at the gap in the fence, look for a place to hole up out there, and then I'd see if I could flush him out. It wasn't a very complicated plan, but then it wasn't a very complicated mission. In my experience you could plan all day, but, as the military guys say, no plan survives first contact with the enemy, so you might as well keep it simple.

We set our cell phones on vibrate, and I went through the fence and down a steep embankment into the jumble of wrecked containers. The night was clear and not all that cold for a change. There was plenty of light looming into the sky from the main container yard, but the junkyard was not lighted at all. I had to pick my way carefully through the shadowy pile while not showing any light of my own. After a few clumsy minutes of this, I found a piece of steel pipe I could use as a walking stick, which made things easier. I was wearing SWAT cammies and a tactical belt with holster, one spare clip, a small first aid pouch, and a military survival knife.

Our overhead photography showed that the area where we'd run into the derelicts was about two hundred yards in from the warehouse side of the junkyard. Beyond that was the creek inlet where we'd anchored when we still had a boat. I'd explained the mission to the shepherds, who'd been vitally interested for a good five seconds. Still, now they seemed to understand that we were walking into Injun country. Frick walked ahead of me, picking her footing carefully and stopping to sniff the ground frequently. I could only imagine how strong the scent quilt must be to that supersensitive nose. Frack walked behind me, stepping where I did, as if he suspected there were land mines in here.

I slowed it down, placing each step tentatively on the litter underfoot before putting my weight on it. Trask knew we couldn't come by water this time, so our way in would have to be through the container yard itself or the warehouse blocks on the landward side. That three-container tunnel was just too good a place for an ambush, which was why we'd come in from the Wilmington side. I leaned against the rusting sides of a fractured container and tried to think of what I would do if I were Trask. Would he simply want to finish the job, or did he really want to talk a little? Was he expecting just me or all three of us? Or was he out on his boat somewhere, having a Scotch and laughing at the thought of us poking around in the junkyard? If he was in here somewhere, had he ever wired his private concrete jungle for sound and night vision lights? The farther in I went, the better Pardee's option three sounded.

I had stopped in a sort of canyon of discarded shipping containers. I'd been keeping to the left side of the passage through all the containers because it seemed darker on that side, as well as less cluttered with debris. There was a strong smell of diesel oil in the air now, but I couldn't tell if I was standing in a puddle of it or it was just the rusting steel barrels oozing into the night air. It was nearly complete darkness where I was standing, but I could see a dim light flickering around the edges of the ten-foot-high steel boxes ahead.

Flickering?

Had I reached the hobo campfire already? It seemed too soon, but it was easy to become disoriented here in the darkness amid the jumble of industrial trash, wrecked containers, and other debris. The dogs had their ears up and appeared to be listening to something ahead of us. I tried to listen, too, but heard nothing but the low hum of the city behind me and the whine of semi tires out on Shipyard Boulevard. If that was the campfire area, the way to it was straight ahead on what was obviously a well-used path.

Too well used. It felt wrong.

So I retraced my steps until I came to the edge of a container, which I could feel more than see, and turned right to work my way around to a different approach. I'd be off the route Pardee and I had agreed upon, but I should have time to get to the margins of the campfire area before he came along behind me. Ten quietly crunching steps into almost total darkness and I bumped into the steel walls of another container that was blocking the way.

I was in a box canyon, literally. There were steel walls rising ten feet over my head in three directions.

There was a crack between the corners of the two boxes, through which I could now definitely make out the glow of a small fire reflecting off a two-high stack of ruined containers. I could see a few hunched shapes of the homeless guys silhouetted against the fire. I looked over my shoulder and saw that the shepherds were waiting for me back where I'd made the wrong turn. Lot of help there, I thought.

Then they both looked over their shoulders and disappeared.

I blinked and looked again. No dogs.

Keeping my back to one of the containers, I slid my way back to the entrance of my little detour, all by feel. I still had the steel pipe, but I laid this down in order to extract my .45 and a high-intensity penlight from my coat pocket.

When I got back to the entrance to my dead end, there were still no shepherds. What in the hell had they gone after? Hopefully not a rat. The wolf genes in any German shepherd might not be able to resist a fleeing rat. Discipline would eventually intrude, but the reflexive reaction would be a snapping lunge. I should have put them on a down, but that would have involved speaking the command in the darkness.

I waited by the edge of the container. I could feel sharp edges of ripped metal digging into my coat. How long had I been stopped? Would Pardee come around the corner in a minute? I tried to visualize our planned route in. I'd diverted into the dead end, but now I was back at the edge of the way we'd planned. Maybe the thing to do was to wait for Pardee before approaching those huddled figures out by the fire.

Except my scouts had gone missing. I felt like Lee at Gettysburg.

I waited and listened some more. The air had gotten colder the deeper I'd gone into the tangle. I was hoping for any sound I could recognize that might tell me where they'd run off to. It wasn't like them to leave me in the dark like this.

There was a solid wall of containers on the other side of the rough path. Firelight illuminated the very top edges. I stared at the containers, trying to make out what was different, and then figured it out. These were intact. Rusty, spray-painted with all sorts of hip-hop tags, dented and scratched, but otherwise intact. The three straight lift rods on the backs indicated working double doors. Three in a row, end on to the path, and sitting fairly upright, unlike the majority of the containers, which sprawled at all angles in the darkness. Everything around them was wrecked, but these three containers were definitely not wrecked. I decided to wait some more, hoping that Pardee would come creeping down the alley between the other containers. I had an increasingly urgent sense that I badly needed my backup, or what was left of it. Where were the damned dogs?

After another two minutes of just standing there, I got out my cell phone and keyed Pardee's number.

It wasn't Pardee who answered. It was Trask.

"Hi there, Lieutenant," he said. "How can I help you?"

"Let me talk to him," I said.

"Afraid he's somewhat indisposed just now, Lieutenant. Not harmed, mind you, but not available for phone-cons. Sleeping. In your Suburban."

"Sleeping."

"Yup. A little whiff of ether and down he went. It's a lot more efficient than whacking somebody on the back of the head. You never know what will happen then. Ready to palaver?"

"I suppose I am," I said, looking around again. I had the sense that he could see me.

"Right in front of you are three containers," he said, confirming my worst suspicions. "The middle door is the one you want. Watch your step."

He broke the connection. *Well, shit,* I thought. *We did agree to meet him in his jungle, not ours. We should have figured a way to come by boat.* I put my .45 away and slipped across the open space between my detour and the middle container. There were no locks on the operating handles, so I undid the latches and shoved the two halves open.

I flipped on my penlight. The container was empty, just a blank cube of space that smelled faintly of some kind of exotic animal dung. I tried to remember where I'd smelled that before. The deck of the container was about a foot above the ground level outside, so I stepped up and into the container, keeping an eye on those doors. If there was someone waiting outside to lock me in, I thought I'd have a shot at keeping one of the door halves open long enough to deal with him.

I stood there and searched the interior with the penlight again. I thought I heard a faint whimpering sound—the shepherds? I saw what looked like a big floor seam halfway down the container. Maybe there was a trapdoor of some kind? I took one more step in that direction and felt the floor sag under my feet. In the next instant, before I could step back, the half that I was standing on dropped down to a forty-five-degree angle and I went sliding down the plywood floor into serious darkness. The moment I hit bottom, the floor panel snapped back up behind me with a loud bang.

I'd managed to hold on to the penlight, which I quickly shone around into the darkness. Instantly two fuzzy shepherd faces pushed into view and then into my own face. While I was fending off an incipient love-in, lights came on in the ceiling. One of the dogs knocked the tiny light out of my hand, but I no longer needed it. The lights were bright enough to make me blink.

I found myself sitting on a dirt floor in an underground chamber. Actually, I realized, it was another container, submerged ninety percent under the surface level of the junkyard. For that matter, this might be the true surface level of the junkyard, depending on how old the place was. The walls and ceiling were made of what looked like aluminum or light steel; the only thing missing was a plywood floor. The air was dry and musty, but the ground smelled of damp. There were four small lights embedded in the ceiling, and an even smaller hole, maybe two inches square, at one end of the container, high up on the wall. It looked like there was a glass cover on that aperture. High on one side wall was a black circle about a foot and a half in diameter, which I assumed was an air hole. That was not a good sign.

My cell phone began to vibrate.

"Lieutenant," Trask said, when I opened it. "Glad you could drop by."

"How'd you get the dogs down here?" I asked.

"Dragged a rat on a string in front of them and into the double doors," he said. "Which were open when you made your little detour there, in case you didn't notice, and I don't think you did."

"Got me there," I said. I told the dogs to sit. I was trying to be really stern with them, but I was very glad to see them back. They sat, but they weren't happy.

"I've got you here, actually," he said, "and we're going to have some fun, presently. But first: I'm curious. What is it you think we're going to do at Helios?"

"I think you're going to create some kind of fake terrorist incident. That wake-up call you were ranting about. Something to do with moonpool water."

"You're close," he said. "Perhaps wrong about the fake aspects."

"So why knock us off?" I asked, examining the space again. I didn't like the sound of that have-some-fun comment, and I wanted out of here. Obviously I'd need to pull that plywood ramp back down, but I couldn't see a seam anymore.

"Because you're getting in the damned way," he said. "I don't have time for any more of your interference. We have a plan, and a window of opportunity, which is upon us, so to speak. I need you out of the way, which is where you are."

"You keep saying 'we.' "

"Some like-minded people in the nuclear power industry," he said.

"What did you do to my partner out there?"

"Put him to sleep," he said. "Temporarily, I hope. He's going to be medium useless when he does wake up, though."

"I told the Bureau you're alive and kicking," I said, "and where I was going tonight."

He laughed. "Nice try," he said, "but the Bureau is shortly going to be much too busy to worry about you."

"Going to turn some more of your aliens loose in the container yard?"

"My aliens?"

"We ran into an ICE guy the last time we came over here. He told us he's undercover over here in the junkyard, and that you're part of an alien immigration surveillance program."

"My, my, how some people do run their mouths," he said. "But I'm not worried about the Bureau. Their only interest in me right now is that I'm *not* their vic in the moonpool. Where's the little Italian wise-ass?"

"Out there somewhere," I said.

"Or back in Triboro," he countered. "That's what my sources tell me, anyway. Back home doing some homework. Something to do with the Helios visitor logs. You don't have any idea why your Ms. Gardner overran her sell-by date down here, do you?"

"You said you were going to enlighten me."

"I did say that, didn't I. But I don't know—you're a pretty resourceful fella. You might yet get out of that hole you're in. As long as you don't manage that in the next twenty-four hours or so, I won't care, of course."

I wondered if that meant tonight was the big night. "So give me a hint," I said.

"Okay, I will: What was her maiden name?"

"Beats the shit out of me," I said. "I guess I just assumed Gardner was her maiden name, after two divorces."

"Therein lies the tale, Lieutenant. Now: I have things to do, people to see. Some spectacular incidents to precipitate. That .45 loaded?"

"Of course."

"And you still have that baby penlight you were flashing around all over the place outside?"

I did, even if the single AA battery was running down. I

realized then that it had stayed on when I dropped it. The tiny spot of white light was now yellow.

"Okay," he said. "If it were me, I wouldn't go shooting that hand-cannon of yours down there. Steel walls over hard-packed earth, sides and floor. What goes around will almost certainly come back around, if you follow me."

"Why would I be shooting?" I asked.

"Because something's coming for dinner," he said.

The phone connection switched off. I put the thing in my pocket, retrieved and switched off the penlight, and then walked around the confines of the chamber. I tapped the side walls, and, although they seemed to be made of metal, there was obviously hard-packed earth behind them. They felt like brick walls. He was right about the .45—there'd be ricochets forever. The dogs just sat there watching me, panting a little, and waiting for orders. I wished I had some for them, but this looked like a modern version of an oubliette. Then the shepherds both looked up at that black hole high up on the left side.

A soft sound, like grain coming down a silo chute, began to fill the air, and then an enormous snake head came into view, its black tongue flickering urgently. The triangular head was pale white and the size of a partially flattened regulation-size football. The snake looked around, saw me, and then saw the shepherds, who were raising hackles and backing up. Locking on to the dogs, the snake continued to emerge from the hole. The body was proportionally smaller than it should have been right behind that enormous head, but then began to swell as the thing reached the floor and began to spread across it.

I backed up right along with the dogs. Time began to slow down as more and more snake kept coming, the body getting thicker and thicker before finally slimming down to a vigorously switching tail, itself the size of a full-grown rattler. The cell phone began to vibrate in my pocket.

"Isn't she a beauty?" Trask said when I picked up. "Albino Burmese python."

"Beauty's in the eye of the beholder," I said, pulling out

the .45. Ricochets be damned, I wasn't going to let that thing get a whole lot closer.

"Yeah, I get that," he said. "She's almost six meters, and did I mention that she's hungry? She just loves a good dog for dinner."

The snake wasn't coiling, which surprised me. It lay full-length-out on the floor of the container in a big serpentine arc, that flat bone-white head maybe ten feet away, watching all three of us. At the moment, its six meters looked like six miles. Wearing two German shepherds, I backed against the front wall of the container, and aimed the SIG at the thickest part of the snake's body. I recognized the smell now as the scent I'd picked up on the boat. Jungle smell, something rotting and hideously primitive. The tongue never stopped.

"She'll go for the dogs, not you," he said. "Unless you interfere, of course. But it'll be a fairer fight than if you were, say, doing this in the swamp. See the tail? Nothing for her to hold on to down there. They need to anchor that tail to really throw coils."

"I'm going to shoot this fucker, starting right now," I said.

"Only if you can see her, Lieutenant," he said. And then the overhead lights all went out. Almost immediately I heard that flowing-grain sound. I dropped the cell phone and nearly fired, but realized in time that that would be pointless. The penlight. Where was that goddamned penlight?

Both dogs began to growl deep in their chests as I fished for it in my pockets.

More sliding sounds, and that primordial stink was getting more pronounced.

My fingers closed in on the plastic light, and I popped it out of my shirt pocket. Tactical instinct took over as I held the light in my left hand, way out to one side, and pointed the SIG into the darkness. I switched it on.

No snake.

The light seemed a tiny bit brighter than it had been; maybe the battery had rested, or maybe it was just because the darkness was damned near absolute.

Where was the snake?

I scanned the floor of the container in an arc right in front of us, then sensed something looming to my right.

To my right, and up, not on the floor. I could feel the shepherds pressing harder against my legs.

I swept the light over there and found myself looking into that white snake face, which was no more than three feet away. The snake had lifted its forebody on its coils like a cobra, which still left about a half mile of snake on the floor behind it. Without thinking, I fired a round at that face.

The noise was terrific, a painful bang that hurt my ears and startled me into almost dropping the SIG. I felt the snap of the bullet as it smashed into the steel wall right behind my head, after clearly missing the snake altogether and then ricocheting around the container. Then something leathery and heavy whacked the side of my head as the snake finally struck, missing my face but ending up with its neck alongside mine for a single horrifying instant before it withdrew.

I lunged to the left before it could strike again and tripped over one of the dogs. We all ended up on the floor in a heap of scrambling legs. I still had the penlight but didn't stop to relocate the snake. I yelled at the dogs to come and bolted for the other end of the container, flying blind along one slippery side until I came up against the back corner of the can. The dogs were still with me, trying hard to get behind me in the corner.

I pointed the tiny light out into the darkness of the container and listened. Then I realized I was providing a target and quickly shut it off. I didn't know if a python could see well in the conventional sense or if, like a pit viper, it tracked by infrared. Either way, I didn't want to help it find us.

I heard the sliding sound again. It was a huge snake, probably a couple of hundred pounds, and it was making no effort to be quiet. I pointed the SIG out into the darkness and tried to control my breathing, subconsciously aware that breathing was what the snake intended to attack. One of the shepherds growled and then barked. I again held the light out to one side and flicked it on. The snake was right in front of us, head low and flat above the floor, shifting sideways. Two huge coils of its trunklike body were rising behind it as it prepared to throw a hundred pounds or so of hungry muscle at one of us.

I fired again, twice this time, aiming at the body. I hit it once, and possibly both times. The coils collapsed on the floor with a sodden thump, but this time that head came up, way up, rising almost to the top of the container as the beast arched in response to the trauma to its body. I rolled to the right, keeping the light on the snake, the dogs tumbling with me. We collided with the other side and then scrambled all the way down to the door end. The penlight could no longer reach across the container, so I shut it off.

We listened.

I tried to tamp down my own heavy breathing. The shepherds were better at that than I was and didn't make a sound, although I could feel their hearts going a hundred miles an hour. Like mine.

I knew I hadn't killed the thing. Primitive animals, Trask had called them. Like a dinosaur—hit it in the ass and it took a few minutes for the impact to register all the way up in the brain. But then, look out.

Sliding sounds again . . . and then a chilling, prolonged hiss, followed by the reek of primordial ooze that seemed to hang over this reptile. I had no sense of where that hiss had come from, other than it wasn't behind me. I looked up and thought I saw a small red square at the top of my line of vision. Then I remembered there had been what looked like a glass window up there. Was Trask watching, using night vision gear? Watching, and possibly even filming? Like Hitler when he had his rebellious generals hung on meat hooks in the basement of the supreme court building in Berlin?

That thought pissed me off. I raised the SIG and took careful aim at that dim red square and fired one round. When I can shoot carefully, I'm going to hit what I aim at, and this time no bullet came spanging back at me from the other end of the container.

Then the snake hit. I felt a hammer blow on my raised forearm, a sharp pain as several dozen backward-curving teeth sank into my arm, and then I was being buried under the satin coils of an infuriated python. I distantly heard the dogs get into it, with lots of savage growling and snapping, but I was too busy to wonder what they might be accomplishing. I crumpled into as round a ball as I could and switched the gun from my right hand to my left just before the snake pulled hard and took my forearm straight out away from my body. Before I could react or retract it, it had pushed a coil completely over me and now had a partial grip on my chest, a grip that instantly tightened.

But my left hand was still free.

And the snake's head was not free, attached as it was to my right arm. I knew there was only one way to end this.

I turned sideways, to my right. Instantly the snake increased the pressure and I felt my ribs starting to compress. I couldn't see anything, but actually didn't want to. I pressed the muzzle of the .45 against the snake's head and fired.

The first thing that happened was that the damned thing gripped even tighter. I could exhale, but I could not inhale. The gun was still pressed against something. Just before I fired again, I realized it was pressed against my arm. The area where the teeth were embedded had gone numb, but I moved the barrel slightly, found what I prayed was the head, and fired again.

This time I felt a lance of pain—the bullet must have grazed or even penetrated my own arm. Then the snake really constricted. I saw a red cloud coming toward me through the darkness, and I went out. The last thing I heard was another one of those hideous hisses and the roar of the shepherds as they attacked the snake in total darkness.

I could breathe.

I couldn't move, couldn't see, but I could breathe. I could hear.

The shepherds were whimpering and tugging at my legs, but I was wrapped in what felt like a ton of slippery muscle meat.

Slippery. Contrary to popular opinion, snakes aren't slippery, so I'd done some damage with those two body shots.

And the fact that I could breathe meant that I'd done some real damage with the head shots. Now the problem was to get out from under before the damned thing stiffened up and pinned me here forever.

I backed the dogs off and started to wriggle my way out from under a mile or so of dead coil. At one point the head flopped down into my hands. It was a satisfyingly soggy mess. I fished out the penlight. I had to see.

Bad idea.

The top of the snake's head was ruptured; the bottom was gone, with the lower jaw unhinged and gaping open large enough to accommodate a soccer ball. Its eyes looked no different dead than alive. I felt the coils moving slightly. My bowels constricted.

Was it dead, or just getting its second wind?

Then I examined the head and realized it had to be dead. *Had* to be.

Primitive creature. The head was dead, but the snake's body hadn't got the memo yet.

Frick stuck her face into mine. *You coming, or are we going to eat it?*

I slipped out from under the mess in one quick move and took a deep breath, which hurt like hell. All my ribs felt like they'd been cracked, and even my innards felt like they'd been repacked inside.

The penlight was failing fast, but I still took one more look back at the huge snake, just to make damned sure it hadn't revived. It was still there, leaking copious amounts of nasty fluids onto the container floor, its massive coils still moving. I turned off the light. The darkness was almost comforting, now that I knew there wasn't a Pleistocene worm monster coming for me. My right arm was starting to hurt. I was glad I hadn't wasted any flashlight on the wound. Besides, we had bigger troubles than that right now.

I checked the SIG. The slide was locked back. I extracted the spare mag from my belt and fed my friend. Then I realized I could see. Sort of, anyway. I looked up. The little red square up high at the other end was now a little white square.

Had Trask been watching our wrestling match down here in the box? I hoped he had, because that soft white light meant that night vision equipment was no longer running. With any luck, I'd parked one in his eye and he was no longer running, either, but that was probably too much to hope for. Right now we had to get out of here.

The small viewing aperture put just enough light along the ceiling for me to finally see the crack. The front third of the upper container's floor had dropped down to form the ramp. When my weight had come off, it had rotated on spring hinges back up into position, which meant there had to be a latch. The problem was that the ceiling was almost nine feet high. I couldn't reach it, and thus I couldn't use my knife to probe the crack and find that latch.

I looked around for the shepherds, and found them cautiously sniffing the snake's almost inert body. My ribs hurt just looking at that thing, and I still hadn't pulled back my shirtsleeve to see how big a mess I had there. I needed to get something antibiotic on it pretty soon, though, or the snake would have lost the battle and won the war.

The SIG. I could reach the ceiling with the SIG.

Now the question became: Was it a center latch or a side latch? I'd walked right down the middle of the container and hadn't detected any sagging or lack of support under my feet. I voted for center latch.

"Cover your ears, mutts," I said. I lay down on the floor, holding the gun up with both hands. I fired directly up into the crack on what I hoped was the centerline of the container. Once again, the noise was really startling. I missed the crack by about an inch the first time, steadied my grip, hit it with the second round, and then bracketed that with the next two rounds. The dogs were cowering in one corner, and the space was filling up with gunsmoke. There was a ragged hole of shattered plywood in the middle of the ceiling, and my face was covered with bits of wood. I rubbed the debris off my face and felt a scrape of metal on my cheek. The latch?

I rolled to my feet and got out my utility knife. My right

forearm was beginning to throb now, and my ears were ringing. Fortunately I still had that tiny square of white light, or I'd never have been able to find the crack, much less the latch. I held up my right hand and, yes, there were tiny bits of metal on my hand. I examined the crack, but it hadn't opened or changed shape. Center latch *and* side latches? Or maybe it just needed some weight.

I squatted up and down on my haunches a couple of times to limber up my thigh muscles. Then, pointing the knife straight up, I thrust my whole body, right arm rigidly extended, up at the ceiling as hard as I could. I jammed the serrated point of the knife into the plywood and held on as I fell back down to the floor. I felt burning lines of pain running up and down my right arm.

The plywood held and the knife came back down with me, showering me with more wood bits.

I tried again, with the same results, except this time I felt the plywood move just a little. I rested for a minute, and then took another stab at it, moving the aim point to one side of where I thought the latch should be. Definite movement, but apparently there was enough of the latch still there to hold the ramp. I got out the SIG again and used up two more rounds in the center of the hole already there. It was getting hard to breathe with all the smoke.

I rested again for a minute or so and talked to the dogs. Their sensitive ears wouldn't work for a week after this. Neither would mine, probably. I was really thirsty and beginning to wonder if we were ever going to get out of here. I kept hoping Pardee had recovered and was probing the boxes outside looking for the source of all the gunfire. Unfortunately, I was eight feet or more below ground level. If the upper box doors were closed, he could be right outside and unable to hear anything.

I stared up at the mess on the ceiling. If I'd learned anything in my life, it was that persistence was everything if you were in a jam. Maybe if I could use the knife to pry the seam down and get a hand in there, I might be able to hang, dead weight this time, and pull the whole thing down with just my body weight. The thought of jamming my unprotected fingers into the splintered hole up there made me wince, but I had to try something. The air was filling with CO_2 and there was no air supply that I could see except for the snake hole. The shepherds were lying down and panting heavily.

I put away the SIG, stretched my thigh muscles again, and tried my previous trick of jamming the knife. This time the center of the plywood panel bellied out a little, but it didn't come down before the knife pulled out again. So I took a deep breath, moved forward a few inches, and jumped again, jabbing at the crack with the knife in my right hand while grabbing for a fingerhold with my left. It would have worked except for the fact that my left arm, injured in a tussle with a mountain lion a few years back, let me down, literally. So I switched hands—the knife in my left hand and my right hand going for the gold.

It hurt. Splinters under the fingernails always do. But I managed to get four fingers jammed into that crack tight enough that I could hang there, extract the knife, and then jam it into the crack and turn it sideways.

Now I had two handholds. The one on the left hurt my upper arm, but the one on the right made my fingers feel like they were on fire. I began to bounce, trying to set up a rhythmic pull on that panel, and finally, with a loud tearing noise, down it came. It happened so unexpectedly that I forgot to hold on, and back it went, slapping into the ceiling with a mocking crack as I tumbled down onto the floor. My snakebite reminded me that it was still there.

I yelled in frustration, but then noticed that the whole panel was drooping an inch or so below the ceiling above. No more latch, so its own weight was working for me this time. One more straight-arm knife jump and I was able to pull it down to face level and, this time, hold on to the damned thing. The air became instantly fresher. I stared up into perfect darkness, though. No lighted aperture in the upper container. Who cared.

Using the knife in a series of sticks, I pulled myself up the ramp and to the base of the exterior doors. The dogs tried to follow but couldn't gain any traction. I told them to hang on and went looking for those latch plates Houston of the ICE had told me about. I had to do it all by feel, and then remembered the penlight. It still had a tiny spark of power left, and this allowed me to find the safety release lever. I pulled that, and the sockets for the locking lugs came off.

I pushed on the door in front of me. The bottom moved; the top did not. Persistence, I reminded myself. Almost there. A few more minutes of humping and thumping and I found and released the top latches. Now: Were they locked from the outside or just shut? Time to find out.

This time when I pushed, and to my vast relief, the door opened, and I rolled out onto the dirt of the junkyard path. I looked around for bad guys, but it was just me in the semi-darkness. The fresh air felt wonderful, but the shepherds became frantic when I rolled out of sight, so I went back to the container doorway to reassure them—and found that the ramp, with my weight gone, had come back up, leaving them in their subterranean prison. They were audibly not pleased with that result.

It took another fifteen minutes of wedging and hauling to get them out of there, and their frantic efforts to "help" had just the opposite effect. I swore at them, and they undoubtedly returned the favor, but finally all three of us were outside the dreaded snake pit and gratefully breathing in the smells of rotting junkyard debris, diesel oil, rust, and ancient grease. It smelled wonderful.

Now to find Pardee. And that bastard Trask.

Ari Quartermain joined me in the ER at a little past one in the morning. He looked like he hadn't been to bed in a couple of days, and that gray tinge I usually associated with cardiology patients was back in his face. I was sporting a bandage the full length of my right forearm and several new injection puncture wounds from an enthusiastic if not very competent male nurse.

The ER docs had been visibly disturbed when they saw the scale of the teeth marks on my forearm. It was obvious to anyone who looked at them that I'd been bitten by at least an alligator, except for the fact that the individual tooth marks were much too small, and far too numerous. The .45 had laid down a quarter-inch-deep gouge right through the middle of the bite area, but none of the docs had picked up on the fact that it was a bullet wound. That, in turn, meant no police report was necessary. For the moment, anyway; one of the docs had mentioned he was studying to be a tropical medicine specialist and wanted to talk to me later. I mumbled some promises I didn't intend to keep and then closed my eyes and gritted my teeth as he tended to the wound with some kind of liquid fire.

Pardee, on the other hand, was in trouble. Center stage, ICU trouble. Whatever Trask had gassed him with was still in control. The docs said that he smelled like ether, and that in the hands of a non-anesthesiologist, ether could be highly toxic and there was a chance of brain damage, or worse, if he didn't come out of it in the next few days.

I'd put a call in to Bernie Price and asked him if he could bird-dog Pardee's police report for us. I preferred to have someone who knew both of us working with the admissions staff, who had all sorts of interesting questions about how Pardee came to inhale ether.

"You're sure this was Trask's doing?" Ari asked.

"Once again, I never saw him, but it sure sounded like him, and we had prior indication that he was doing stuff over there in the container port."

"Stuff."

"You don't actually want to know," I told him, "but he was allegedly working with the government, so it's not a criminal enterprise. How's Helios?"

"You don't actually want to know," he parroted back to me with a wry grin. "The DNA comparison didn't work, probably because of all the radiation exposure. The coroner's office is freaking out because the body is not decomposing. Remember all that news about irradiating meat to prevent spoilage? Apparently it works."

"Lovely," I said. "Look: Whatever Trask is planning, he has inside help, and it may be as soon as tonight."

He looked at his watch. "Tonight is over," he said wearily. "It's tomorrow already. Who's the inside help, and what is the it?"

"I like the Russian's deputy, that Dr. Thomason, but I don't have any firm evidence. Is he competent to create some kind of incident?"

"Oh, yes, indeed," Ari said, "but it would have to be the moonpool. He doesn't usually work the reactor side, although technically he's licensed to do so. If he showed up over there in the middle of the night, everyone in the control center would wonder why."

"What's the worst thing that could happen to the moonpool?"

"Empty the pool," he said promptly. "Remember, it's mostly aboveground. Empty the pool, and the spent fuel stack could catch fire from the heat of decay."

"Would that be contained?"

"To start with," he said, "but if we got significant hydrogen generation *and* no remedial action was taken, you could get a gas explosion. Blow the containment building apart, and the Three Mile Island incident would look like an amusing Halloween prank."

"But there would be remedial action, right? You have automatic systems to deal with loss of the water?"

"Certainly, but you said you thought Trask had inside help. If it's Thomason, or someone with Thomason's qualifications, he could disable all of those systems, and he could probably do so in a way that would keep the control room from knowing it until it was too late. Hell, I could do that."

That wasn't what I wanted to hear. "What's your opinion of Thomason?"

"He's a good engineer. Ex-Navy nuke, like a lot of them are. Personality-free zone. Gets along with Petrowska, which takes some doing. Doesn't socialize much within the plant. Don't know his politics."

"Could he have some hidden agenda?"

Ari rubbed his cheeks with both hands while he considered that question. "I suppose he could," he said, "but I've never heard him ranting and raving, not, for instance, like Carl Trask."

"I still think you should alert your security people," I said.

He sighed and nodded. "And what, specifically, do I tell them?"

I had a momentary vision of Trask turning a couple of cobras loose in the control room. My arm twinged. "You have stages of threat alert over there, don't you? Like the airports? Raise the alert level immediately. You don't have to explain why. Lock the fucking place down for a few days until we can pull the string on Thomason and actually apprehend Trask."

"We've already got the FBI and the NRC crawling up our asses," he said. "I guess we could throw some more shit in the game."

"Ari, look: Your plant may be under attack. Two unexplained radiological releases. A dead body in the moonpool. Your physical security director is missing and presumed whacko. I get ambushed in the container port by a guy who has pre-staged facilities—in the junkyard. My partner is a gorp upstairs, courtesy of the same guy who turned a python loose on me. Pretend you're sitting in front of a congressional committee afterward while a senator recites all that and then asks why nothing was done."

He put his shiny bald head in his hands and thought about it. "Coming offline unscheduled is a *really* big deal," he said between his fingers. "I can lock the place down, as you put it, but if they're after the moonpool, that wouldn't affect the reactor side."

"Suppose the moonpool is a diversion?" I said. "Is the NRC looking at the reactor side? The Bureau? Anybody? Or is everybody focused on the moonpool?"

He looked at me from between splayed fingers. "Fu-u-u-u-ck," he said.

Then he got out his cell phone. Ignoring all the signs

about using cell phones in the hospital, he placed a call. He identified himself, but didn't give his phone number, and then made them call him back. Then he asked for the supervisory engineer in the primary control room.

"Hal, this is Ari Quartermain. This is an emergency communication. I have made an official determination that the reactor system is temporarily unsafe. I direct that you inform the grid operator that Helios is going offline. Once the generator hall comes off the grid, then I direct that you execute a deliberate reactor scram. I am ready to give you the authentication code word."

He listened for a moment, looking over at me with a grave expression.

"That's right. Make the appropriate log entries." A pause. "Yes, of course I will take full responsibility, but do it now. There is an inside security threat to the RCS."

He listened some more. "No, do not wait. Tell the grid operations center they have five minutes to adjust the load. If they protest, tell them you're going to scram in six minutes. They can handle it. They won't want to, but they can. Let me know when you're ready for the code word."

He listened, then put his hand over the phone. "He has to get a safe open," he told me. "Two-man rule and all that."

"Can he object, or go over your head?" I asked.

Ari shook his head. "He's a nuke. This is a certified emergency procedure. My phone has a unique caller ID symbol that confirms it's me. There are two code words, actually, one for duress, and one which means he has to do what I say." He turned back to the phone.

"I am ready to proceed," he said. He waited, and then said, "No," and then spoke a single word. He waited. "Yes," he said. "I'll inform the director."

He hung up and looked over at me. "Now the real fun begins," he said. "And this time, Mr. Private Investigator, you're going to get to play."

A weary-looking nurse in blue scrubs came into the waiting area, frowned at Ari's cell phone, and then called my name. Her name tag had an ICU logo.

"Your friend, Mr. Bell, is semiconscious," she said. "That's the good news. The bad news is that there's no one home."

I digested that announcement for a moment. "Will he recover?" I asked.

"We don't know, Mr. Richter. When I say he's semiconscious, I mean he's responsive to stimuli. His hand flinches if we probe a finger with a needle. We hope that Mr. Bell is still down there somewhere. For now, I'd suggest you go home until we contact you. Make sure Admitting has your contact numbers. Is Mr. Bell married?"

"Yes, to a trial attorney, up in Triboro."

"Terrific," she said. "Give that information to Admitting as well, please. She should come down here."

I did as she had asked, and called Alicia, Pardee's wife, myself, to tell her what had happened. She said she'd be down first thing in the morning after she'd set up care for the kids.

I stopped by the pharmacy to fill some scrips of my own. "I need a shower and some sleep," I told Ari. "People in there were keeping their distance."

"Yeah, you're a bit funky this evening."

"You should smell the snake," I said.

"I believe I do."

"But we're not done yet, are we."

"Nope. We have to go see the Man."

"We."

"Don't make me say it."

We drove in separate vehicles directly to the admin building. I left the mutts in the Suburban and followed Ari into the building. The plant director and two other worried-looking managers were waiting for Ari. Behind the admin building, the huge green buildings of Helios looked just the same. The only thing missing was the subdued roar of the condenser cooling-water tailrace. Since the generators weren't running, they weren't pulling lebenty thousand gallons of cooling water a minute in from the river anymore. Otherwise you couldn't tell.

I'd been doing a slow burn ever since leaving the hospital. I made a mental note to stop worrying about gathering evidence of whatever outrages Trask and his henchman were contemplating. If I found him before the Bureau did, there wasn't going to be any need for evidence. I'd rousted Tony to tell him what had happened, and he'd immediately said he'd be back in the morning. Mindful of the oblique hint Trask had given me, I asked him to stay in Triboro and to pull the string hard on Allie Gardner's family background. I wanted him to get to her personnel file from the sheriff's office. He thought he could con someone into helping him out.

Then I asked him to contact Pardee's wife and offer whatever help she needed, including a charter plane ticket if she wanted to fly down. If mystery-man Trask, with all his security toys, exotic pets, and fanatical ideas, had turned Pardee Bell into a vegetable with a handkerchief of diesel starter fluid, I intended to return the favor. Alicia was the kind of woman who would want to help with that.

The plant director was a tall, spare man in his early forties who looked to be of Scandinavian descent. Ari introduced him as Dr. Johannsen, and his demeanor was all business. He was obviously unaware of who I was or what I'd been doing down there, so Ari filled him in. Then I told an abbreviated story of the night's events and why I'd recommended they shut down the plant.

"You did not actually see Colonel Trask during all this?" Johannsen asked.

"I did not," I said. "Nor did I see him the night we got run over out in the Cape Fear River."

He raised his hands, palms up, as if asking the obvious question.

"It's what you don't know, Dr. Johannsen," I said. It had been a really long night. "Consider everything that's happened in the past week or so. The death by radiation poisoning of one of my associates, an unidentified body in your spent fuel storage pool, your physical security director's gone missing, oh, and did I forget to mention the radiation incident over in the container port?"

"Only one of those incidents connects directly to Helios," he said. "Admittedly, Colonel Trask's whereabouts are something of a mystery, but he's done unusual things like this before. I could make the reverse argument: Most of this has happened since *you* showed up."

The look on my face must have concerned him, because he immediately tried to make amends. "Look, Mr. Richter, I'm not accusing you of anything. It's just that shutting down the plant the way it was done tonight is going to cause industry and public comment. The nuclear industry lives under a magnifying glass. Everyone will assume we had a reactor problem. What do we tell them?"

"The truth?" I said. "That way it at least looks like you care as much about the security of your operation here as you do about your image."

I saw Ari look away. The director stared at me for a moment and then settled his face into a polite mask. "All right, Mr. Richter. I think you're really tired after your, um, experiences tonight. We'll excuse you now. Dr. Quartermain and I need to talk privately. Thank you for your services."

That sounded like a great idea to me, so I left. Once in the Suburban, I put my head back on the headrest and told the shepherds that I needed them to eat someone. They seemed amenable. All I had to do was come up with the name.

I had to assume the plant's technical people were on high alert by now, which should make it a whole lot harder for anyone inside or out to pull some shit. On the walk out to the hospital parking lot, I'd asked Ari what "scram" meant. He said it was slang for shutting a reactor down quickly by inserting all the control rods, thereby killing off the chain reaction. A scram was something the reactor usually did to itself if it detected a safety problem. Of course, even if the reactors were no longer critical, there was still plenty of heat and radiation present for duty, so it wasn't as if they were cold and dark, and therefore not dangerous. And there'd be intense NRC interest in why it had happened. I told him it was a good thing they were already here, then. He had not been amused. It was obviously time for me to get some sleep and then to regroup.

Tony called at about 10:00 A.M. from Triboro. He reported that Pardee's wife was in touch with the hospital and en route by car, and that he'd have his hands on Allie's archived personnel file sometime today. He wanted to know if he should still come down to the Wilmington area. I told him to get the file and then come down; I also asked him to bring some tactical equipment from our collection.

"We going colonel-hunting?" he asked.

"Something like that."

He said he'd be down by late afternoon.

The next phone call was from Ari Quartermain. His voice was strained and he sounded as if he hadn't slept all night.

"We've finally heard from Trask," he announced.

"Good deal," I said. "Now we know it wasn't him in the moonpool. The question is: Where is he?"

"On his boat, or so he says," Ari replied. "Says he's uncovered a security problem that turned out to be much bigger than he thought it was originally. Says he'll come in tonight after getting some sleep. I told him we were shut down, and why."

"The 'why' being my suggestion?"

"Yep. He said as long as we kept you and your people away from the plant, there was no need to be shut down. He said you are part of the problem."

"I'll bet he did—I tumbled to him and whatever shit he's got planned."

Ari sighed. "Well, I briefed the director. He knows Trask, and he doesn't know you. He said we'd stay offline until Trask shows up and explains all this shit. In the meantime . . ."

"In the meantime, you want me to stay the hell away from Helios, right?"

"Pretty please?" he said.

"I can do that," I said. "But I'm going to file a police report charging Trask with the assault on Pardee Bell. When he's done with whatever fanciful tale he's going to spin for you guys, the Wilmington cops are going to want a word with him. And the Coast Guard wants to examine that boat."

"Funny you should use those words," Ari said. "Fanciful tale. That's how the director characterized your story from last night. Who else should I be watching?"

"Watch the moonpool engineering crew," I said. "My measure of Trask is that he won't give up. Your shutting the plant down may have complicated that, but at least everyone's alerted, right?"

"They certainly are," Ari said. "Anna Petrowska is somewhat skeptical, as you might imagine. She told the director that she thought you were delusional."

"She would, if she's part of Trask's plan."

"Cam, what's her motive? What's anyone's motive to fuck around with the moonpool, for that matter?"

"I don't know, Ari, and I can't help you anymore. But here's a suggestion: Fill in Petrowska's timeline for the past three or four days. Account for her every waking moment, because the tie-in might be between her and the guy in the moonpool, not Trask. Especially now that you are pretty sure it's not Trask in your lead-lined cask."

Ari didn't say anything for a few seconds. Then he told me to keep in touch, and that he'd let me know when they actually sat down with Trask. I was being dismissed, and possibly so was the threat to Helios.

"Ari?" I said.

"Yes, Cam?"

"Remember what happened the third time the kid cried wolf."

I hung up. I recalled what Sergeant McMichaels had said about Ari. If the technical security officer at a nuclear plant had a loan shark on his tail, would he take money to let a terrorist cell in the back door? I didn't want to think about that. I made one more call.

"Federal Bureau of Investigation, Wilmington resident agent's office," the voice recited.

I identified myself and told the robot I needed to speak to Special Agent Caswell. As usual, he was not available, and could they take a message. Standard routine. I was tempted to tell them there was a bomb in the office, but I didn't. Tony would have.

"Tell him I called, and that I have information on the upcoming meltdown at the Helios power plant."

"Say again?"

"You heard me," I said, "and you're taping, I presume." I gave him my number and hung up.

Creeps called back in five minutes. "You unsettled our desk operator," he said.

"Did you know Carl Trask contacted Helios this morning?"

A moment of silence. "No," he said finally. "I was not informed of that. Who told you?"

I thought I heard a change in the background noise of the phone, although on a cell phone it was difficult to tell. Other people picking up muted extensions? "I need ten minutes of your time, especially if the upper management at Helios is no longer keeping my Bureau in the loop."

"Clock is running, Lieutenant."

Along with the tape, I thought. Fair enough. And he'd called me lieutenant, not mister. That meant he thought I might be useful, at least for a few minutes or so. I took them from the initial call from Trask all the way through my dismissal from the director's office last night. Ironically, Creeps asked the same question the director had.

"No," I said. "I never actually saw him. But I'm pretty damned sure it's Trask, and the people he called this morning think it's him, too."

"Very well," Creeps said. "Then this should be fairly straightforward. I will inform my counterpart at the NRC that we will be present at Helios for this meeting."

"You might want to watch for that boat, too," I said. "Whatever he's got in mind, it involves the boat."

"This is something you *know*?"

"It's how he gets around," I said. "You see that boat parked at the power plant this evening, I'd recommend staying upwind."

"You seriously think he's going to create some kind of nuclear incident at Helios, Lieutenant?"

"Yes, I do," I said, "and since all the attention has been focused on the moonpool, I'd say watch the reactors. They're shut down right now, and that might have changed the security equation."

"The body in the moonpool was a diversion?"

"Have you or any of your people ever been over to the reactor side of the plant?" I asked. They had not. Neither had I. Nobody was looking in that direction. If Trask had orchestrated all these previous incidents, he was certainly capable of an even bigger diversion. Creeps said he'd think about it, and then asked the one question for which I had no answer: What if nothing happens?

"Then I'm going after him for the boat collision and for what he's done to Pardee Bell," I said.

"Evidence, Lieutenant," he prompted. "You have no evidence."

"I will once I can get my hands on that boat," I said. "There's also his little fun parlor over in the container junkyard."

"I assume you haven't turned the television on, then," he said. "The container junkyard went up in flames last night. Major fire, attributed to homeless vagrants who were known to nest there on cold nights."

Shit, I thought. I should have expected that. "So what's that tell you, Special Agent?"

"In an evidentiary sense? Nothing. But we'll see what develops when Mr. Trask makes his appearance."

"Hopefully not a mushroom cloud," I said. "You've got my number."

"Indeed we do, Lieutenant," he said. "Have a nice day."

I said something impolite, but they'd already hung up. The shepherds were sitting in the kitchen, looking at me expectantly. Important business needed immediate attention: They hadn't been fed yet.

* * *

At four thirty that afternoon I pulled the Suburban into an overgrown driveway some fifteen miles upriver from the Helios power plant. According to my map, the Jellico River, a tributary of the larger Cape Fear River, was a quarter mile beyond the dense stand of white pines I was facing. The sun was slanting westward on a cool, clear day. There was a breeze whispering through the tops of the pine trees, and I could smell the earthy scents of river bottomland. The forecast had predicted high forties for this night, and the temps were on their way down.

It had eventually occurred to me that an eighteen-foot-long Burmese python probably did not live on Trask's boat, which meant that he had to have a base of operations on land somewhere. I'd run into Sergeant McMichaels at the deli at noon, and we'd had a sandwich together. I told him enough about what had happened to my arm to inspire some assistance at the county seat. I needed to know if Trask owned property somewhere nearby. He thought Trask lived exclusively on that boat he kept over at Carolina Beach. I pushed a little, wondering if there were any county records that could tell me more. I said I needed to get up with Trask, to find out once and for all if it had been him piloting the boat that ran over ours out in the river.

Apparently, McMichaels had gone back to the office and done some checking, because he called me back a few hours later with an address of some riverfront property that could belong to Carl Trask. He dutifully lectured me about not seeking revenge or otherwise indulging in illegal acts, and I'd solemnly sworn never to do such a thing. With that necessary formality out of the way, he'd said the property was recorded as an abandoned nursery and landscaping complex on the Jellico River, which had been bought for investment purposes by a privately owned company called CCT Enterprises. The attorney of record, when queried about a fictional tax matter, had come up with Trask's name and cell phone number as the principal point of contact for CCT. And was any of that information helpful at all?

I told him it was very helpful indeed and that I owed him one, if not more than one. He told me to save it for any occasion wherein the Helios power plant might pose a threat to humanity in the Southport community. I had to hand it to him: McMichaels kept himself very much in the loop when it came to matters involving Helios. His interest might have had something to do with all those concentric circles drawn on all the maps I'd seen of Hanover County, centered on the nuclear power plant. I asked him if there were known loan sharks in Brunswick County. None that he knew of, he said.

I pulled off the two-lane and drove down a narrow, weedy driveway through a stand of spindly pines until I came to a chain-link fence. It was nearly ten feet high, which was surprising for private property, and it stretched back into the trees. It wasn't a new fence, but it did look intact. There was a single slide-back gate, which was securely padlocked, and signs warning people to stay out. The signs were badly rusted, as was a larger sign indicating that this was, or had been, the location of the Ashlands Nursery, wholesale only. There were power poles leading into the property, and the overhead wiring appeared to be functional. The entrance drive bent around to the left inside the gate, and I couldn't see anything beyond that bend because of the pines. My cell phone stirred in my pocket. It was Tony, who wanted to know my twenty. I told him.

"I'm just crossing the Cape Fear River Bridge now," he said. "Gimme a data point for my GPS and I'll join up with you."

I gave him the address McMichaels had given me, and Tony said he'd be here in about twenty minutes, if Igor wasn't lying. Igor was the name Tony gave every electronic device he owned. I told him I was facing a seriously padlocked gate. He said he had a cure for that in his trunk.

I got the shepherds out, and we went for a little recon walkabout. I was looking for video cameras or other signs of electronic Igors that Trask might have put out there, if this was, in fact, his place. I checked the fabric of the chain-link fence for tiny sensor wires and scanned all the logical places for cameras in high places trained on the gate area. I examined the nearest outside telephone poles for taps, but there was nothing coming down the sides of the poles except spike holes and some tendrils of dead poison ivy. The sand around the gate did not look like it had been disturbed for years, and the dogs weren't especially interested in any aspect of the gate area.

Tony showed up right on his timeline, for which he gave his GPS unit an affectionate little pat as he got out of his SUV. He greeted the shepherds and then went to the back of his vehicle and produced what we cops used to call a master key, which was a large bolt cutter with three-foot-long insulated handles. The business end resembled that of a snapping turtle. Ignoring the kryptonite padlock, he quickly cut through the chain. I waited for alarms to sound or Dobermans to appear, but nothing happened. I then got Tony to hand-over-hand the gate and fence to see if he could see any signs of alarms. He went over everything I had inspected, but then got down on his hands and knees and fished in the sand for magnetic plates under the gate. To my chagrin, he found two, one under the locking end of the sliding gate, the other under the stationary part. There were wire conduits leading from the gate in the direction of that curving drive.

"Knew you were useful," I said, examining the shiny little boxes. They were the size of a packet of cancer sticks, and much newer looking than the rest of the gate apparatus.

"The good news is that they use the gate steel as the test probe," he said. "As long as there's ferrous metal above the plates, we can go ahead and open the gate."

He put the bolt cutters down on top of the detector nearest the locking point, and slid the gate open wide enough for all of us to go through. We started down the road. I kept the shepherds in front of us but not free-ranging. The light was beginning to fade here among all the trees, but the smell of the river was growing stronger. The driveway, which bore no sign of tire tracks, turned to the left and then back to the right in a wide S-turn, and then the band of pine trees ended. Ahead was a large, U-shaped greenhouse, with the two arms of the U pointing in our direction. We stopped at the edge of the trees, stepped back into them to maintain a little cover, and studied the layout.

There were three World War II–vintage Quonset huts on one side of the greenhouse, but they had obviously been derelict for many years. On the other side was a perfectly flat but weed-infested area where potted plants had probably been stored under plastic. The pipe frames for the plastic were broken down and rusting away. Beyond the greenhouse there was a battered-looking single-wide trailer home, and beyond that, a coil of the Jellico River was visible through some swamp grass. The nose of the single-wide had fallen off its blocks, which meant that it was unlikely that it was habitable.

"Everything's a wreck except the greenhouse," Tony said quietly.

I'd noticed that, too. No broken panes of glass or vines climbing the structure, and there was a battery of what looked like solar panels erected along the south side, all tilted to maximize insolation. The pipes serving the panels were insulated in heavy black foam rubber, and that was also intact.

"Nice, isolated place to grow a cash crop of weed," I said. "The nearest farmhouse has to be a mile or so from here."

"A little obvious to the DEA air patrols," he said. "My guess is orchids or something along those lines. The power lines terminate there, not at the trailer."

I'd missed that fact, a reminder of why it was always better to have a partner along. "What news on Pardee?" I asked, as we continued to scan our surroundings.

"Alicia made it down there about one," he said. "No change, either way, better or worse, which they say is good news. They're telling her it could be a few more days before he surfaces."

"Where is she staying?"

"Hilton."

A gaggle of ducks blasted off from somewhere to our right and bulleted across the greenhouse area. The breeze coming off the river was turning colder. The glass panels of the center section of the greenhouse appeared to be opaque, either from some paint or possibly condensation on the glass. I wondered if the whole thing was heated, or just that long center section. We were running out of daylight.

"I think we need to get around this and check the riverbank for a pier."

"And a boat, maybe?"

"Hopefully," I said. "And if it's there, we'll need some long guns."

"No problem," he said, and we began to move sideways, staying inside the tree line so as not to be perfectly obvious. The shepherds patrolled ahead of us, noses down, but not alarming at anything. We walked silently across a thick bed of pine needles. Once we got around the nursery area, we could see larger, hardwood trees draped along the riverbank. The mobile home looked even more forlorn from this angle, but there was a path leading down from the trailer to the bank. The remains of a rotting pier, its decking planks twisted sideways, stuck out into the river.

No boat. Plus, the water under the pier didn't even look deep enough to accommodate the *Keeper.*

"Okay," I said. "Now we have to check out that greenhouse."

"Let's not and say we did," Tony said. "I've just figured out what's in there."

I told him we needed to make sure. As we started back, I noticed a five-hundred-gallon propane tank on the back side of the greenhouse. That side faced west, and the windows were even more opaque.

To our surprise we found the back door, near the fuel tank, unlocked. Surprised until we read the little sign on the door's window: THERE IS NO POINT TO LOCKING THE DOORS IN A GLASS BUILDING, it read. BUT IF YOU COME IN HERE, THE CHANCES ARE VERY GOOD THAT YOU'LL NEVER COME OUT ALIVE. It was signed THE KEEPER.

That's all it said. No threats about trespassers being prosecuted or anything else. Seemed clear to me, and more than clear to Tony, who once again suggested we just spot this little expedition and get the flock out of there. I was tempted, but if this was Trask's snake house, I had plans for it.

I put the shepherds on a long down not far from the door. I opened the door and we stepped through, guns in hand, to face a wave of warm, humid air. I found a small power panel just inside the door and threw the breakers that were not on; the third and fourth ones turned on lights throughout the greenhouse, although they were very low-wattage lights. There was a round knob on one side of the power panel box, which began to make a noise when I turned the lights on.

The space right inside the door resembled an interior screen porch, with a very fine metal mesh. There was a large water heater with three pumps clustered at its feet, from which ran insulated water manifolds that spread out through the building, or at least into the right wing where we'd come in. There were stainless steel tables and painted metal cabinets along one wall, three refrigerators or freezers, and a glass-fronted cabinet with vials of different things inside, probably antivenin compounds.

"Fuck me," Tony said, pointing behind the heater. There we could see a separately screened annex, where there were five cages full of rats, and not the pretty white lab rats I was used to seeing in captivity. These were gray and brown Norway rats, some of them big enough to be worrisome and not at all afraid of us. They squirmed and squeaked when the lights came on, as if they knew what the presence of humans meant. There were wooden handles with metal snare loops hanging on each cage, and hand access plates on each door.

Outside the screened-in area, which was perhaps twenty feet square, there was a jungle. Literally a jungle, with huge green plants, vines, some flowers, tropical bushes, low-growing trees, and even thick, wet-looking grass. Then we realized that it wasn't an open jungle, but rather a series of screened-in cages, some small, some big enough for a horse. We could see the heating pipes running through the grass areas. Both of us stared pretty hard at those pipes to see if any of them were moving. There was one long black plastic pipe, perhaps ten inches in diameter, which ran the entire length of the screened area on one side and protruded into the jungle part.

There was a three-foot-wide gravel path bordered by four-by-six posts lying horizontally, to which the cages' front screens attached. Three stainless steel kitchen tables on wheels were parked along the pathway. Some of the riotous vegetation had poked through the screens and overhung the path. The large black pipe ended three feet into the jungle in a blank cap. Some kind of heat exchanger? The whole place smelled like greenhouses always do, moist, composted earth, wet vegetation, and high humidity, but with another smell overlaying it all. I recognized that smell.

"Now what?" Tony said, clearly implying that we'd seen all we had to.

"I'm going to check this place out," I said. "You can wait here, stand guard if you'd rather."

"No fucking way, boss," Tony said.

"You want to go first?"

"Hell, no."

"Because usually, with snakes, it's the first guy pisses 'em off, and the second guy who gets bit."

"I'll go first."

We went in single file, stepping carefully, although logic said that the handler, or was it the keeper, had to have one totally safe route through his reptilian kingdom. I'd seen some snake-handling sticks hung on the wall back by the utility room, but didn't want my hands encumbered by anything but my trusty SIG. I told Tony to fish out his flashlight in case the lights went out.

"Why would the lights go out?" he asked.

"Because the alarm we *didn't* see summons the owner?"

"Another good reason to get the fuck out of here," he pointed out.

The cages were on either side, filled with greenery that I didn't recognize. There were water feeders like the one I'd seen on the boat in all the cages, and sometimes rock piles or artificial burrows. Each cage had two stainless steel padlocks on its door. And, yes, there were snakes.

Most of them were smallish, compared to the Burmese monster. Some looked plain enough; others were dramatically patterned, with pronounced, flattened triangular heads sporting muscular, protruding venom glands on either side. All of them that we could see were tracking us with flickering tongues and glittering eyes, and I realized that the lights coming on probably meant feeding time to this crew. One thick bastard, which I recognized as a Gabon viper, coiled aggressively as we walked by. I saw Tony's finger slip down onto the trigger of his Glock, and then realized I'd done the same thing.

About half the cages were empty, or else the inhabitants were enjoying a postprandial coma in one of those artificial burrows. I wasn't about to open any doors to find out, nor did we have keys. We turned the corner into the base of the U-shaped complex, and came upon some really large cages and some equally large snakes: pythons, anacondas, and some other constrictors I didn't recognize from my days as a *National Geographic* subscriber. Some ignored us, some watched. I wondered if Trask threw the rats in dead or alive. I'd read somewhere that snakes could live for months after ingesting one good meal.

The final wing had a set of double doors made of clear Plexiglas, which created an airlock. When we stepped through the second door, we encountered a much drier heat. Gone was the jungle. This wing was more like a desert, and the cages were filled with sand, rocks, the ubiquitous water feeders, some deadwood from the beach, and not much else. The temperature gauges read eighty degrees, but it seemed hotter. Even the lights were different, although still not very strong. They'd been greenish in the other section; in here they were more like orange. Strangely, all these cages appeared to be empty, unless the whole crowd was down in their holes.

"*Now* can we boogie?" Tony said.

I was about to say yes when we both noticed that there was no exit door. We'd have to go back the way we'd come.

"What makes a man want to associate with reptiles, and especially snakes?" I asked the air.

Then the lights all went off.

We froze and listened. I hadn't heard any sounds from the outside except the offshore night wind starting up. I hadn't felt any pressure changes in the air indicating a door had opened to the outside. The dogs hadn't barked or set up a fuss outside. We both flicked our flashlights on at the same time. I pointed to the way we'd come, and we started back, keeping the lights down on the gravel just to make sure we hadn't missed a hissing something.

The airlock was still empty. We paused to listen with our flashlights off. Nothing seemed to move around us. I told Tony to keep his light off so as to lessen the target, and I pushed through the Plexiglas door. We were back in the jungle. I thought I could hear water gurgling through the heating pipes, and it seemed warmer than it had been the first time. A faint glow of lingering daylight came through the glass panes. It was difficult not to just bolt down the path, but one didn't go running in the dark in a snake house. I felt some vines brushing my face as we moved across the base of the complex and finally into the entrance wing. All we needed was some jungle birds making alien sounds off in the trees.

We stopped on the other side of the airlock door to listen. We could hear sounds out there in the dark, faint rustles and scrapes, but nothing that sounded human. That wasn't necessarily comforting. Was Trask here? Had there been an alarm we'd missed? He could just as easily have a house nearby where he parked the boat—we hadn't looked. The heated water continued to gurgle, and a metal pipe joint somewhere clanked in protest. I could hear a low hum, which had to be the water pumps. So it hadn't been a power failure. Had someone opened the breakers down there?

We listened some more. As our eyes adjusted to the gloom, we could see the ribbon of gravel path stretching out in front of us. All we had to do was start walking. Get to the screened-in utility room and keep right on going. Two hundred feet and we were out of there.

You can get in, but you won't get out, the little sign said. I nudged Tony, and we started walking, me in front this time, him right behind me. I could hear his breathing and then realized I could hear my own as well. I tried to ignore any movement in the cages as we passed them. Metal screens. Two locks. No problem, no matter what was in those cages. I formed a mental image of that thick viper with its murderous head and made sure I was in the exact center of the path

One hundred feet. The humming sound was getting louder.

Something hissed and struck hard against the screen to my right, and I damned near jumped out of my skin. Tony snapped his light on, and we saw a six-foot-long green snake disentangling ivory fangs from the screen, twisting its head to get them loose. Those fangs looked as long as toothpicks.

Tony turned his light off, and we kept moving. It was really hard now not to break into a full run. My mouth was dry and my heart was thumping in my chest. Steel screens. Double locks. No way they could get out.

Fifty feet.

More activity in the cages now. Snakes expecting dinner and now the lights had gone off? With no chow? Small sounds. Leaves moving. Scales against sand. Prolonged dragging sounds. One long exhalation.

Thirty feet to the door, which we could barely see now that we were closer. I focused on the door, trying hard to ignore the angry reptiles on either side, as I recited the mantra: Steel screens. Two locks. No way.

Fifteen feet. No way—and then something black rose up in the visual frame of the utility room door.

Tony collided with me when I stopped short, and we both switched on our lights. Directly in front of us was a dark green snake about ten, maybe twelve miles long. Okay, feet. The front five feet of him were vertical, weaving slowly back and forth as if he were range-finding. I thought it might be a cobra, but there was no hood. I moved my flashlight out away from my side, and Tony did likewise, going in the opposite direction. The snake's head stopped when the lights moved, and the base of the vertical part began to bow out toward us. It gave a low hiss and opened its mouth, which was jet black. Then I saw the end of that black pipe, which was no longer capped.

You can get in, but you won't get out. And here's why.

The snake continued its hypnotically slow approach, its head just barely weaving now, its hiss more like a prolonged exhalation. Its top half didn't seem to move at all, but that bottom half was definitely advancing. The snake wasn't afraid, just getting ready to take care of business. It opened its mouth again in a menacing gape.

I married the flashlight with the barrel of my SIG in a two-handed grip.

"On three," I said.

"Yup," Tony said, and we pointed our guns. I aimed for the juncture between the head and the body, and gave Tony a second to do likewise. The snake kept coming, rising higher on its back half now.

"Three," I said, and we both fired. A pane of glass shattered somewhere along the line of fire, but the snake's head disappeared in a red bloom. Its body collapsed on the path into a writhing knot of reflexive coils.

We both shone our lights all around us just to make sure he hadn't brought a brother into the weeds. Fucking Trask. He'd kept a sentinel in that pipe with some kind of automatic opening device. The whole greenhouse had only the one door in, one door out, and a black mamba for a doorkeeper.

We stepped around the still-moving mess on the path and reached the utility room. We did another sweep of the floor and the tables with the flashlights, just to make sure. The stink of gunpowder was strong in here, and the rat cages had all gone still. I looked at the breaker box. The breakers were still on, but that circular device wasn't making noises any more. Then I realized what it was: a light timer.

You can get in, but you won't get out. I wondered how many teenagers had not come home in these parts after accepting a beer-driven dare.

The shepherds were waiting anxiously outside the door after hearing the gunfire. I was glad I hadn't taken them inside. The air outside was much colder, headed for the low forties. It felt really good to be outside. I told Tony what my solution to the snake house was. He agreed. We propped the back door open, and Tony went around front to break a bunch of glass panes to improve air circulation in the hothouse. Then we went looking for the main breaker.

It took us ten minutes to trace the underground riser from the last telephone pole, but finally we found it, a big metal box with a lead-seal wire in the middle of the base section. A glass meter looked back at us from above the box. I ripped off the seal and opened the box. A spider jumped out into the darkness when I lifted the lid. I reached in and threw the D-handle. The dials on the meter stopped moving. The humming noise inside the utility room ran down to silence.

"There," I said. "See how they like North Carolina in November with no heat."

"If Trask comes back, all he'd have to do is turn that back on," Tony pointed out. "Let's go get that master key and cut the propane service line."

I called in the dogs, and together we made a sweep of the grounds around the greenhouse just to make sure no one was lurking. A fragment of moon was rising, throwing a thin wedge of white light across the river. If there were any boats out there, they weren't showing lights.

The shepherds seemed to be glad to move around. So was I. Tony retrieved the bolt cutters and went back to disable the propane tank. The fuel was a liquid in the tank, but would evaporate into the night air once he opened that line. He was back in five minutes, giving me a thumbs-up sign and displaying a two-inch-long piece of copper tubing. We walked back out to our vehicles, alert but increasingly grateful to get away from that place.

"Let's go find a bar and make some calls," I said, loading up the dogs. "In that order."

"Amen to that," Tony said.

* * *

We went back to Southport and stopped at Harry's because he and I had already reached an understanding about the shepherds. Having two of them with us at our corner table only seemed to reinforce said understanding. The first Scotch made me feel better; the second made it down to my throbbing arm. The pills had nothing to do with it. I reached Alicia by phone at the hospital; she reported that Pardee's vital signs were slowly but surely rising from whatever depths he'd been exploring for the past eight hours. The docs were now contemplating stabilizing him into a medically induced coma to allow his lungs more time to recover.

I asked if they were treating her all right, although that bordered on being a frivolous question. Alicia Barter-Bell was a litigator who specialized in suing hospitals and doctors when they mistreated black people in Triboro. I'm no admirer of the tort bar, but after hearing some of her stories, I had to admit that the occasional shark attack was probably good for the hospitals' QA program. Apparently, they were being treated very well indeed. She wanted to know if we'd caught up with Trask. I told her we were working on it, glad she couldn't see the Scotch. She asked that, if we did catch him, we save a part of him for her. I was afraid to ask which part she wanted saved.

I rubbed my tired eyes, which made my arm hurt again. I probably should not have been mixing single malt with antibiotics and the residue of a really spiffy tetanus shot, but I didn't care. Tony kept quiet, waiting for me to decide what we were going to do next, if anything. The bar wasn't very full, and the few regulars present were all watching the TV along with the bartender.

My cell phone went off. It was Ari.

"Where are you?" he asked, almost too quickly. I told him.

"Aw, shit," he said. "Someone's here."

"Where's here?"

"I'm at home. The Bureau people are still at the plant. Everybody's waiting for Trask. But I think someone's—"

Sudden silence.

"Ari?"

Then the connection was broken. I hit the received call log, dialed back. Four rings, then voice mail.

Not good. I told Tony, who suggested we call Sergeant McMichaels, ask him to go see. Great idea.

McMichaels had gone home, but they promised to call him. He called me back three minutes later, and I told him what had happened. He said he'd send a car over there, but wanted to know what was going on. I suggested we meet face-to-face. He gave us directions to Ari's house on the river. We threw money on the table and went over there in our two vehicles.

By the time we arrived, there were two cruisers there, both at the front gates, which they hadn't managed to open. Sergeant McMichaels was standing outside one of them and came over when we showed up. It was cold enough that his breath was showing in the early night air. Snakes hopefully were expiring upriver by the dozens.

"I've got people inside," he said. "You wouldn't want to be asking me how."

"And?"

"No one there," he said. "One window broken in the back kitchen door, said door unlocked and ajar. Lights on, a TV dinner in the microwave, but no signs of violence. They found this cell phone, but nothing else indicating trouble."

"Can I keep that?" I asked.

He looked at it for a second and then, obviously perplexed, handed it over.

"Anyone check the pier?" I asked before he could ask me any more questions.

"The pier?" he said. "Oh. You think this is the good colonel? Come by boat?"

"The not-so-good colonel, Sergeant," I said. The three uniformed cops were listening, so I suggested he and I take a little walk. I filled him in.

"A greenhouse full of snakes?" he exclaimed. "I'd heard that was his nickname, but I had no idea. But why would he take Dr. Quartermain?"

"I think he's going to the power plant. He needs Ari to penetrate the vital area security systems. It takes two people to get through the important doors, and his own cards have been disabled. He's going to do something, but I don't know what."

McMichaels stared out into the dark river. "Do something at Helios," he said quietly. "Do I need to trigger the area incident alert system?"

"I think we need to call the Bureau, tell them Quartermain's missing."

"Wonderful idea," he said. "I'll get someone to go have a look down at the boathouse."

I had the RA's office number on my cell phone, which I expected to get me a duty officer. Worse. It got me voice mail. I left a message that there were indications Dr. Quartermain had been kidnapped and that I urgently needed to speak with Special Agent Caswell.

We saw a cop climbing over the wall near the gate and went back to see what he had, which was not much. The landing float was wet, but there was a light chop out in the river, so waves could have done that. I wondered if Trask could have come alongside that float with a boat that big and still managed to tie it up by himself. It was possible, or maybe he had some help.

My cell went off. It was Creeps.

"Lieutenant," he said amiably. "Quartermain kidnapped?"

I told him where I was and why.

"Oh, I think not, Lieutenant," Creeps said. "I think we're going to have to start calling you Lieutenant Bum-dope. I just got off the phone with Dr. Quartermain five minutes ago. He's heard from Trask. We're meeting at the container port in just under an hour."

"The container port?"

"There's an echo on this line," he said. "Yes, the container port. Trask is arriving by boat, Dr. Quartermain by car, I presume. If he was under duress, he certainly didn't sound like it. Homeland Security will be there, along with the usual federal suspects. Is there evidence of a struggle at Dr. Quartermain's house?"

"Um, no, or not that the local police have found."

"Oh, dear, you've gone and upset the local police? Is there a boss present?"

I said yes and gave the cell to McMichaels, who identified himself and then listened. I told Tony what Creeps had told me. Tony threw up his hands and shook his head. McMichaels thanked Creeps, closed the phone, and gave it back to me.

"Well," he said, looking a bit embarrassed. "No harm, no foul, I suppose."

I didn't believe it. Not that Creeps was lying, but that Ari was on his way anywhere voluntarily. To prove that, though, I had to get to the plant, and there was no way the gate people were going to let us in. If I had a boat . . . but I didn't have a boat, and it wasn't likely the marina would rent me another one. McMichaels was rounding up his people.

"There's no way Trask can just drive up into that canal," I said to Tony. "We know they have that whole area under surveillance."

"It's his people who have it under surveillance," Tony pointed out unhelpfully.

"How else could he get in there?"

"Get in where?" McMichaels said as he rejoined us..

I explained my problem. The sergeant gave me a patient look, as in, *Why are we still talking about this—you heard the Bureau.*

"People like to fish around power plants," I said. "Something about the warm water. Is there another way to get close to the plant by boat, besides that intake canal from the Cape Fear River?"

"Certainly," he said. "The tailrace canal. That's where the warm water is, by the way. Not on the intake side."

I wanted to execute a Polish salute. Of course that's where the warm water was. That's where those two enormous jets came out of the condensers below the generator hall.

"Can you lead us there?"

"I can, but of course I'd be wanting to know why."

"Well, we're not going to swim up the tailrace and break into the power plant, if that's what you're thinking."

"Oh, I know that, Lieutenant. You haven't seen the tailrace when the plant is running." He paused for a moment. "You get something into your head, you don't let go, do you?"

"Not when I think I'm right, and especially when I hope I'm wrong."

He thought about that. "If it were anything but Helios," he said, "I'd be firmly requesting you to exit the jurisdiction. But."

"But you know the government's first instinct is to cover itself when they suspect someone's made a big mistake."

"Indeed I do," he said. "Okay, I'll take you. Let me get these boys on their way. Although getting in via the tailrace is just not possible."

What I knew that the sergeant didn't was that the plant wasn't running. The tailrace would be quiet as a millpond.

McMichaels led us down a narrow dirt road that seemed to be going absolutely nowhere until we popped out on the banks of a broad creek. The perfectly straight banks indicated that it was man-made. No current was visible, just a strip of dark water perhaps eighty feet wide. We got out of our vehicles and walked to the bank. To our right, the only light was the occasional sweep of a lighthouse that had to be several miles away. To our left, above the trees, was the loom of the power plant's lights, although the buildings themselves were not visible.

"I think I need to take these dogs for a walk, Sergeant," I told McMichaels.

"I understand perfectly, Lieutenant," he said with a grin. "By the by, I was just thinking that perhaps this would be a good juncture for me to resume my domestic duties back at home, from which I was so rudely summoned."

"This would be a great time to be at home, Sergeant," I said. "But may I please have your phone number?"

His grin vanished. "Look, boyo," he said. "If you discover that some evil bastard has or is about to let the fire genie out of that handsome power plant over there, you call me at once. I kid thee not. We all love our power plant, but we have few illusions about what could happen should all those smart boys manage to muddle things up, eh?"

"I promise," I said. "I think what Trask has in mind is a scare, not a disaster. He keeps talking about a wake-up call."

"Nine-eleven was called a wake-up call, Lieutenant. If the scary colonel has truly gone mad, he may no longer be able to tell the difference."

Tony and I got our gear, locked the cars, and set out with the dogs a few minutes later. We had entered McMichaels's phone number into our respective cell phones. Tony's battery was fresh; mine was showing faded green bars on the battery icon. We'd put on our tactical vests. Tony carried a shotgun in addition to his Glock. I stuck with my SIG and sent the shepherds out ahead. There was a cleared walkway along the tailrace canal, like a towpath. I had Tony stay about thirty yards behind me in case we walked into something unexpected. The sliver of moon did little to illuminate the woods, but as we got closer to the power plant, all those perimeter lights made the moon superfluous.

Then we got a surprise. We saw the *Keeper,* or a boat very similar to it, sitting out in the middle of the tailrace.

We simultaneously faded left into the woods, and I waited for Tony to catch up to me. The shepherds came hustling back when they realized I was no longer following them.

"That our boy?" he said.

"Looks like it, but I don't see any lights or hear a generator."

We watched the darkened boat for a few minutes. Trask could be hunkered down on board and sweeping the canal banks with a night vision scope for all we knew. Or he could have anchored the boat, turned everything off, and gone ashore in that rubber dinghy. In which case, we should be able to find the dinghy.

"Let's assume," I said.

"Oh, goody," Tony said.

"Let's assume he went ashore, took Ari with him to gain access to the vital area. There should be a rubber dinghy hidden somewhere along here."

"Or," Tony said, "he's over there on that boat with a thirty-aught, waiting for assumers."

"That thought crossed my mind," I said. "Okay, look: I'll go see if I can find the dinghy. You take a position in the woods here and cover the boat with the shotgun. If someone starts shooting, you keep their heads down while I . . ."

"Yeah," he said with a grin. "While you go see the Baby Jesus."

"He didn't come here tonight to get me," I said, perhaps with more conviction than I felt. "He's suckered all the authorities over to the container port for a meeting that's not going to happen, and by the time they tumble, something bad will go down in that plant. We need to move."

"Roger that." He then settled down behind a tree stump and unlimbered the shotgun. It was a long shot for a scattergun, but the noise might distract a shooter long enough for me to get to cover. Or at least fall down and die gracefully. I would have really preferred that Trask wait a night; my arm hurt, and I needed some downtime.

Frick found the dinghy. It wasn't hidden along the riverbank. Instead, it was partially deflated and hanging in a tree just high enough that a passing human wouldn't see it. Suspicions confirmed: Trask was ashore *and* ahead of us.

I signaled Tony, and we put on some speed going up the path. We were taking a chance that Trask was lying in wait ahead, but I didn't think he was. The controlling factor for Trask was how long the alphabets would wait before they realized they'd been had and came hotfooting back to the plant.

Frack tripped the trigger wire. He'd gotten ahead of his partner and gave a little yipe when a hank of piano wire snapped back at his leg. As he bent to bite at it, a green tree branch festooned with barbed wire came whipping across the path like an angry cobra right about face level on a walking human. Fortunately for us, we were both twenty feet back when it let go, but even from that distance, we could hear the barbs whistling. We stopped short. Frack, blissfully unaware of his near-miss, had untangled the tripwire and continued on to catch up with Frick, who'd dutifully plunged on up the path. Trees moved all the time; this one hadn't bothered her. It sure bothered me, and it reminded both of us that we were pursuing a guy onto his home turf. He probably hadn't assembled that little nasty an hour ago.

"We need to get off this path," Tony said, examining the still-quivering branch.

"That'll slow us down," I said, looking into the dark woods to our left.

"Not like a face full of barbed wire would," he said.

"Point taken," I said. We moved to our left and started pushing our way through the bushes. Fortunately, it was November, or we'd have gotten nowhere fast. I summoned the shepherds with a low whistle and then sent them ahead again, having been reminded once more of the value of four-legged scouts. Even in the woods, the lights of Helios were getting brighter.

After about twenty minutes, we ran up against the perimeter fence, which was a modern chain-link affair, twelve feet high at least, and topped with three strands of barbed wire slanting out toward anyone approaching. Red and white signs every fifty feet warned prospective intruders to go away or face large fines and many lawyers. On the other side was open ground, with the main generator hall almost a half mile inside the wire. To our right was the tailrace, which was also fenced across the water. A line of orange buoys stretched across the canal fifty feet downstream of the fence, and heavy-duty sodium vapor lights provided illumination of the water area for two tower-mounted TV cameras.

Just below the concrete generator hall, two enormous nozzles from the condenser outlets pointed in our direction. They looked like bus-sized caves, and the tailrace canal opened into a hundred-yard-wide, concrete-banked channel right below the nozzles. The silhouettes of the green buildings containing the reactors and the moonpool blocked out the night sky behind the generator hall.

The shepherds ran up to the fence and into the lighted area, so I called them back to where we stood in the relative shadow.

"Now what?" Tony asked, frowning at the fence line, the lights, and the cameras.

"Trask has had all the time in the world to make his plans," I said. "He knows every foot of this perimeter, and he'd know how to put a hole in that fence without getting caught. We just have to find it."

"Can the shepherds do that?" he asked.

"If we had a Trask scent article they could," I said. Then I realized I had something just as good. Ari's cell phone.

I gave the shepherds a good sniff of the cell phone in its leather case, told them to find it, and they began casting for scent. As always, it was fun to watch those exquisitely sensitive noses searching for mere molecules in the grass. Frick suddenly stopped at the side of the towpath, circled once, and then trotted toward the intersection of the concrete channel banks and the perimeter fence. The channel's bank was a terraced structure, looking like a set of concrete bleachers parallel to the tailrace. The dogs were halfway down the bank between the top edge of the concrete and the placid canal water.

Frack caught the scent, and they both went slower, tails wagging, noses down, zigzagging across the ground, back and forth along the base of the fence. Just outside the cone of illumination from the left-hand light tower, they stopped and began worrying the bottom of the chain-link. As I was about to recall them, Frick went under, followed by Frack, and then they ran up into the plant area along the concrete rim of the bank.

"There's our hole," I said. We emerged from cover and trotted over to the end of the concrete bank. I was hoping like hell that the cameras weren't being closely monitored now that the plant was shut down. If they were, we'd be met by a couple of Broncos loaded with SWAT types in about three minutes. As if confirming my fears, as we bent down to find the three-cornered tear in the fence, a noisy Klaxon horn sounded off on one of the light towers on the other side. It went on continuously, sounding like the dive alarm on a World War II submarine.

Tony looked at me, and I motioned for him to go ahead. We were this close, and I wasn't going to stop now, even if the guard force had been alerted. There had to be places to hide in the industrial area. The shepherds were waiting about a hundred feet up the concrete ledge. The Klaxon was beginning to hurt my ears as we struggled with the stiff wire and some of the canal bottom debris tangled into the fence. Tony went first and got under with a lot of grunting and puffing. I could almost feel the light from those towers giving us a sunburn, and my ears were unconsciously listening for the sound of braking vehicles and slamming doors. As I started under the fence, what I heard instead was a low rumble, which got louder and louder as I pushed my legs and then my stomach under the wire. I heard Tony say "Holy shit," which was when I realized what the rumbling noise was. Those two enormous jets were firing up.

Helios was going back online.

My chest got stuck, and Tony had to get down on his knees to pull on the wire. Trask was slim and wiry, like Tony. Ari would have had to fight to get under, but I was bigger than all three of them, and it was touch and go. Motivation became everything when I saw the tsunami coming down the channel. My vest was the problem, and I was rolling and twisting under the wire to get it unstuck as a churning, foaming wave of river water washed past the fence. Behind it the tailrace channel began to fill up in earnest, the terraced levels of concrete disappearing in sequence as the main condenser circulating pumps got down to business. I could feel and smell the cool spray wafting up to my level as I finally got the damned vest free and rolled out from under the chain-link. Whirling red strobe lights mounted up on the light towers threw psychedelic patterns on the concrete.

I stood up to behold the sight of those two giant plumes of water lifting out of the nozzles to crash into the channel almost a hundred yards below the generator hall.

"Gotta get higher," Tony shouted over the din of the thundering water, and I could immediately see why: The channel was swelling fast, and the water was already climbing the next terrace level below ours. I looked for the shepherds, but couldn't see them in the cloud of mist that was growing above the impact zone from the nozzles.

I looked up. The terraces were about five feet high, and the concrete was getting wet from all the spray. There was nothing to hang on to for a pull-up, and neither of us could jump five feet.

Tony pointed at my shoulders, and I understood at once. I got down on my hands and knees and braced myself. I could feel the rising water lapping at my boots. Tony stepped up on my back and then hoisted himself up to the next terrace. Then he pulled me up. We repeated the procedure twice more before we were on the top of the channel walls. Fine for us, but where the hell were the dogs? Then I realized we were standing out in full view of the cameras, and we started running toward the nozzles, if only to get away from those light towers. The noise from the jets sounded like a pair of 747s turning up on the takeoff ramp as we got closer to the generator hall. I wondered who'd decided to put the plant back online.

We made it to a stack of what looked like giant concrete barrels sitting next to the perimeter road. There were two rows of them, and they were fifteen feet high and easily eight feet in diameter. We ducked down between the two rows while I scanned the tailrace area for the dogs. I had this terrible feeling they'd been swept down the channel and were now pinned against the water fence. What I saw instead was headlights coming around the corner of the six-story generator hall.

Regular patrol? Or the response team?

We couldn't hear anything over the roar of those tailrace nozzles. All we could do was watch the headlights. The vehicle was coming directly toward us on the perimeter road, so we put one of the barrels between us and the lights and waited to see what they would do. As I clung to the smooth concrete sides, I saw the radiation triangles painted on them and realized these must be the storage casks Ari had talked about.

The security vehicle, a Bronco with a light rack on top, passed the casks and kept going on the perimeter road. Regular patrol. I looked over at Tony, who mouthed the words "Now what?" over the thunder of the nozzles. I was worried sick about the shepherds, but if Trask and his hostage were somewhere ahead of us and inside the plant, then that was the priority. The next big trick was going to be getting into the plant itself. Trask solved our problem when he and Billy the Kid stepped out of the darkness and pressed guns into our necks.

Billy relieved us of our weapons and phones as we stood spread-eagled against the concrete sides of a cask. He was thorough enough to check for ankle guns and boot knives. I had a knife, and Tony had one of each. He took our cell phones and smashed all of them, mine, Ari's, and Tony's, against the wall of a cask while Trask stood cover. Then we marched in single file, Billy ahead, the two of us, and Trask behind, toward the second Bronco, which we'd apparently missed while concentrating on the first one. Billy opened the right rear door and pointed. Tony got in first, then me. We joined a frightened-looking Ari Quartermain in the backseat. Billy stood outside, pointing his weapon at us, while Trask got into the driver's seat. Then Billy got in, sitting sideways to keep us covered. He was doing his strong-arm trick, holding the weapon high at an unnatural angle, but covering all three of us just fine. Once he closed his door, we could hear again.

"Welcome to my game, Lieutenant," Trask said. "I was almost hoping you'd find your way in."

"We found your way in," I said. "The rest wasn't all that hard until the waterworks started."

"Yes, isn't that something? I wish I could claim credit for the timing, but I was very impressed with your resourcefulness. First the snake, now this."

"You were watching?"

"I've been busy, Lieutenant," he said. He looked tired but determined. "I've reworked those two tailrace cameras to send two signals, one to the security control room, one to a portable monitor. When you showed up in the woods, I diverted the real picture until you were through. Yes, I was watching."

"Sir?" Billy said, without taking his eyes or that gun off us. "The time?"

"I know, Billy, I know," Trask said, glancing at his watch. "So what would you do with our two interlopers here?"

"Pop 'em and drop 'em in the rotor," Billy said promptly. He looked really eager to take care of that matter personally for his favorite colonel.

Trask looked at me. "Know what a rotor is, Lieutenant?"

"As in mechanical?"

"As in hydraulic. There's one at the base of every waterfall. The water comes straight down and then it rolls, under the surface, in a permanent horizontal vortex. That's why people who go over a waterfall often never come back. They get trapped in the rotor, where they roll around for a year or so until they, how shall I put this—return to the biosphere. There's a beauty of a rotor at the end of that tailrace out there, and if they happen to turn off the jets, the underwater section of the fence keeps things, um, confined."

Ari hadn't moved or said anything since we'd joined him in the backseat. His hands were folded in his lap, and then I noticed that his wrists were bound together with a white electrical cable tie. He was gray-faced, staring straight ahead like a condemned man.

"Well, hell, Colonel," I said. "If we're going into the disposal, you can at least tell us what this is all about, can't you?"

"Just dying of curiosity, are you, Lieutenant?" Trask said.

"It would appear so," I said.

"Billy, I think you have the right idea, and I'm even going to let you do the honors." He turned back to me while he started the vehicle. "You see, Lieutenant, I can use Dr. Quartermain here, but I don't need you—I just needed film of your intrusion. At the appropriate time, I'll inject that back into the surveillance system, which hopefully will pulse the reaction team to come out here and run around in circles while we're in there, doing our thing. Neat, hunh?"

"Sounds like a good diversion," I said. Neither Tony nor I had been cuffed, and I knew Tony wasn't going to just sit there and eat a round or six. Billy was watching both of us like a hawk, though, and he looked entirely ready to shred the both of us and the backseat. "But diversion for what, exactly?"

"The moonpool, Lieutenant. The moonpool. I'm going to show this decadent society what the future will look like once we cut and run over there in the Middle East. Give them a little taste of real twenty-first-century terrorism."

"You're going to drain it? Cause some kind of meltdown?"

"No, Lieutenant. That's much too messy. Why spoil a perfectly good atomic power plant? No, this has to do with a vulnerability they haven't thought about. That's why Dr. Quartermain there is looking so glum."

He put the Bronco in drive and turned back out onto the perimeter road.

"You have some more inside help, don't you?" I asked.

"In a manner of speaking, Lieutenant. I have somebody by the balls, and, as usual, when you have people by the balls, their hearts and minds tend to follow. The best part is, he won't know what he's done until it's much too late. But Dr. Quartermain here—he knows. Why don't you tell them, Ari?"

Trask turned the Bronco off the perimeter road and began a slow descent toward the tailrace. Any camera would see a security vehicle resuming its patrol. The booming of the water jets grew louder, even inside the vehicle.

"The water supply for the moonpool isn't river water," Ari recited. "It's municipal water. The pool loses water due to evaporation, so there's a connection between the pool's refill system and the municipal water system. He's going to reverse it."

Holy shit, I thought. "Municipal as in the county water supply?"

"Better than that, Lieutenant," Trask said patiently. "Municipal as in county *and* city water. Wilmington City, to be precise. The county produces more water than it needs, so they share. You remember what happened to your Ms. Gardner, don't you? Expand the scale just a bit and you'll get the picture."

I was impressed, all right, but, at the same time, I didn't think it would work. Trask must have read my thoughts.

"I can see you're skeptical," he said. He turned the vehicle to the right onto a side road, leading us away from the tailrace. The regular patrol, driving a random pattern, like they were supposed to. I shrugged, and the muzzle of Billy's weapon rose and fell with my shoulders. No genius there, but the boy certainly could focus.

"Well," I said, "I thought the idea was a wake-up call, not mass murder."

"I don't expect the hot stuff to actually get to people's water taps, Lieutenant. I just need to force it back along the mains to a water tower or three. Then I call the appropriate people and tell them the city water supply is radioactive. They laugh, say, sure, Snake, that's a good one. I invite them to test, even provide the equipment. I call the media, let them know where the tests will be done. Then the fun will begin. Of course, they'll want to know where it came from."

"From Helios."

He kept driving away from the tailrace, and now I wasn't sure why, except that each streetlight on the perimeter road clearly illuminated the Bronco for any watching cameras.

"Yes, from Helios," he agreed. "Not as the result of any Communist plot, either. Just a horrible mistake, an operational accident."

"Until they investigate."

"Exactly so," he said. "The investigation. *That* will be the wake-up call. And if they try to cover it up, well, there'll be leaks of a different kind."

"But where are the thirty-something Islamic males scrambling the gates and yelling *Allahu Akbar*?"

He grinned, and for the first time that lunatic gleam in his eyes was fully uninhibited. He suddenly reminded me of Mad Moira.

"No, Lieutenant," he said. "No whirling dervishes. Worse—much worse. An *American.* The scariest kind of terrorist—an American sympathizer. A computer expert. A genu-wine feminazi, who blames America first for all the evils in the world and who will happily help the poor, oppressed Islamic hordes defeat the Great Satan."

"Fucking Mad Moira," Tony said softly.

"Bingo."

"Moira's here? In the plant?"

"Hell, no, Moira's on the Web, where she lives like the subversive little spider she is. Only I've given her some codes and software. She's going to get us in while keeping the cavalry out at just the right moment."

"She's okay with this deal of poisoning the city of Wilmington?"

Trask laughed again. "She might not actually know the full extent of what she's going to be helping me with," he said. Billy snickered.

"She'll point at you when she figures out what you've done," I said.

"If she's still alive, right, Billy?"

Billy's grin grew. He was apparently warming to his new line of work. It occurred to me that perhaps Mad Moira might have an agenda of her own in Trask's little plot. The major had said she'd been using me. Was she using Trask, too? And how had Trask gotten her away from that angry major of Marines?

Trask glanced at his watch again and casually swung the Bronco around. Now I knew why Ari Quartermain looked like a condemned man. He was one. If Trask was going to kill his helper, he'd surely kill any additional witnesses. Like us. I needed to keep him talking.

"So who was the body in the moonpool?"

"One of those derelicts from over there in the container

junkyard. Easy to come by with a bottle of Ripple and a C-note."

He certainly knew where to look; I wondered if anyone else had ever gone downstairs to face a snake.

"Why'd you put the knife on his boot?" I asked.

"Shit in the game, Lieutenant," he said with a laugh. "Just throwing a little more shit in the game. That's my specialty: confusion to the enemy. If I have no specific objective other than chaos, it's pretty hard for the cops to figure out what I'm up to." He glanced back in my direction. "That's how the real bad guys see it, too," he said. "That's why you hear so much about 'no credible and specific threats.' "

We were now pointed back toward that boiling tailrace. I kept looking out the windows for the shepherds, but all I saw was those open fields between the perimeter fence and the protected area of the plant buildings. The roar of those high, arching plumes grew as we neared the part of the channel where all that water thundered down into the canal. An enormous cloud of mist boiled up out of the channel now, and that maelstrom seemed to be our destination. Once there, Trask's vehicle would be obscured from the cameras.

Keeping one hand on the wheel, Trask flipped open a cell phone, punched a speed key, and waited. Billy was bumping around in the front seat as Trask drove the Bronco over increasingly rough ground. That big cloud of spray and mist was now only about fifty yards away. I felt Tony tense up beside me, and tried to figure out what we could do, and when. Or even if, because Billy's hold on that gun was rock solid, its muzzle pointed right between us and carefully held back out of our reach. Trask spoke into the phone.

"About five minutes," he said. "Remember: stage one, then stage two. Once I give the go for one, two happens on the timeline, right? I won't call again."

He listened and nodded his head. Then, unwittingly, he gave us our chance. With his attention divided, he steered the Bronco into a hole, causing it to veer down and hard left. He swore, dropped the phone, and twisted the wheel, but not before Billy was thrown off balance and into Trask's right shoulder. The stubby muzzle of the submachine gun came over the back of the front seat for just an instant.

Tony moved with the speed of a snake. He grabbed the muzzle of Billy's gun and pushed it toward Trask with his left hand while punching Billy in the eye with one knuckle extended and some adrenaline-powered intensity. Billy yelled but did not let go of the gun. I jacked open the right rear door and bailed out. As I went, my ears were assaulted by the roar of the submachine gun as Billy reflexively pulled the trigger. I could hear glass shattering in the Bronco. The next moment Tony was rolling on the ground in front of me, and then we were both up and running for the tailrace.

"Peter Pan!" Tony yelled, recalling that wonderful comment by Tommy Lee Jones in the latest film issue of *The Fugitive*. We didn't bother to look back, but simply ran right off the edge of the concrete side and plunged into the channel, chased by fragments of dirt and cement as Billy or Trask did his best to ventilate us before we disappeared.

Disappear we did. The tailrace, which had been a calm, cold, and not very deep pond before the jets opened up, was now a surprisingly warm cauldron of Class 99 whitewater. We'd had to climb the terraces of the channel before. Now the channel was full right up to the top terrace. I went ass over teakettle several times as we were swept down toward that fence. I thought I heard the chatter of the submachine gun briefly between periscope observations, but that was now the least of my worries.

We'd gone in about fifty yards below the impact point of the twin plumes of water, which was good news and bad news. The good news was that we wouldn't be rolling around like bags of wet laundry in the rotor until the end of time. The bad news was that the tremendous current was carrying us into that reinforced chain-link fence spanning the final exit channel. I say "us" although I'd seen no sign of Tony since making that flying leap into the unknown.

I hit the fence upside down and with my back, and it was a good thing I'd taken a deep breath on the last tumble because damn near every bit of it was knocked right out of me. The force of the current pinned me against the heavy wire like a butterfly on a corkboard. I fought hard to get turned around and back to the surface. Then something dark and heavy thumped into the fence right alongside, which just for a second eased the pressure of the current on me as the wire rebounded. I scrambled, clambered, clawed, and kicked my way up the wire until the growing pressure in my ears told me I was going precisely the wrong way. Did I mention that it was really dark down there?

I reversed course as best I could, my lungs burning now, and my injured right arm becoming less useful by the moment. Without light, I couldn't be sure if I was going up or sideways, but the noise of all that turbulence seemed to be getting louder, and then my head popped into cold air, even as the current pressed my cheek into the chain-link. Realizing that the current had me pinned, I stopped struggling and concentrated on breathing again, which made for a nice change. The hank of chain-link wire pressing against my right cheek actually felt reassuring.

I looked around for Tony, but couldn't see him. There was light up here on the surface, bright enough to obscure the plant, whose lights were still blocked by the cloud of condensation and flying spray upstream. I scanned the banks for Trask and his ace helper, but didn't see anyone. He'd said five minutes, presumably to Moira, who I assumed was standing by to inject her own version of shit into the game remotely via the Internet. The federal host was probably not yet aware that they were in a deadly game.

Hopefully Trask had decided to cut his losses and get his plan under way. I tried to move sideways, toward the bank, but that current had me nailed to the fence. A moment later, Tony surfaced next to me like a Polaris missile and then went right back under as he, too, was smacked into the fence and held. I reached down into the black water and hauled on his shirt, managing to get his head above water, but just barely.

He hung there like a dead man, and for a horrible second I

wondered if I was holding a corpse, but then he coughed, threw up, went back down, and came up again spewing water everywhere. He grabbed on to the wire, saw me, and grinned. He mouthed the words "Hi, Wendy," and I snorted out a desperate-sounding laugh.

It took us twenty minutes to claw our way across the bulging fence wire and onto the concrete side of the channel, where we flopped like a couple of belly-hooked catfish. *Cue the shepherds,* I thought. This was when they were supposed to appear out of the darkness and lick my face. That didn't happen, though, and I couldn't avoid a pretty bad feeling. They were probably either trapped in the rotor or pinned down on the bottom of the channel, right below where we were recovering. Fuck.

"Who we gonna call?" Tony asked from his supine position on the wet concrete.

"Fresh out of cell phones," I said. "Did Ari get hit?"

"He might have," Tony said, propping himself up on one arm. "I had it pointed out the window, but Billy was shooting up the whole backseat, so . . ."

Then I remembered what Trask had said, about planting the video of our coming through the fence to distract the guard force. They'd be coming right here, and very soon, if that five-minutes business was accurate. Tony realized the same thing.

"We gotta move," Tony said. "We have to stop this thing."

"Or," I said, "we wait right here for the guards to find us, tell 'em what's going down, and let *them* get in there and stop those assholes." I didn't say what was really on my mind: *Then I can go look for my dogs.*

"You think they'd take us seriously?" he asked. "Their boss is going to fuck with the moonpool? This from the two intruders they just saw on the cameras breaking into the protected area?"

"He's supposed to be meeting with the feds across the river," I argued. "Why isn't he there instead of being in the spent fuel building?"

"Because the guards don't know that, and besides, he's

Trask and they never know where he's going to pop up. Plus, he'll have Quartermain with him to make it look legit."

"How the fuck do we get in there?"

"By evading the same guards he's distracting. Hell, we'll kick the damn doors down if we have to."

"Then what?" I persisted. "There are at least three doors to get through, all keyed to plant security." Trask had help. We had nothing.

I think Tony understood my real hesitation to go after Trask, but before he could respond, I looked over his shoulder at the blue strobe lights flickering through that big cloud of condensation. He saw where I was looking, swore, and then we were up and running down the perimeter fence, away from the tailrace channel.

C'mon, mutts, I thought: *This is when you come running out of the darkness.* But they didn't, and I wondered if I'd ever see them again.

The ground sloped up from the tailrace for about a hundred yards, and then it fell off again. We made it to that low crest just about the time the security vehicles emerged from the spray cloud. If Trask had been telling the truth, they'd have seen us coming through his hole in the fence on their cameras, so that's where they'd go first. Our problem, besides being soaking wet, unarmed, and very definitely unwanted, was that we didn't know what other cameras might be reporting right now as we ran toward the industrial area surrounding the plant. Tony pointed toward some large steel tanks, and we zigged right to get in among them.

The three big buildings were right in front of us, with perhaps a hundred yards or so of open ground to cover before we could get to the middle one, home to the moonpool. There were light towers everywhere and absolutely no way for us to get close to the main buildings if anyone was watching for us. The lone, thin smokestack was blowing air and steam beyond the generator hall, and subdued red strobe lights pulsing along some of the buildings indicated that the reactors were running and that the plant was online. I was starting to shiver in the night air, even though my clothes had begun to dry out.

"Just run for it?" Tony said. He was staring across the open ground at some small outbuildings that were close to the moonpool building's main entrance.

"Maybe walk for it, like we belonged here," I said.

It was worth a shot, because time was ticking away and we couldn't just stand out here in the dark for very much longer. We couldn't see what was going on down at the tail-race, but the security people wouldn't stay there forever, either. And Trask was already inside.

We stood up and started walking toward those small buildings. I hoped that we would look like two shift workers headed toward the building. We didn't have hard hats, there were no ID badges dangling from our necks, and this wasn't the time for shift change. All we could do was hope that no one in the security control room was reaching for the zoom controls.

It was a tense hundred-yard stroll, but we made it to the small buildings. We stopped in front of one of them. We were on a concrete sidewalk. Beside us the straight steel walls of the spent fuel storage building rose into the night. The even taller reactor containment buildings flanked us on either side, some two hundred yards apart. Steam pipes and other utility lines snaked overhead. The sign on the building in front of us said that it contained spill kits, decon suits, and firefighting equipment. Unfortunately, it was locked, or we might have been able to put on some suits and at least look like we belonged there.

At that moment, a man came out of the moonpool building carrying three clipboards. He was in his late fifties, wore glasses under his white hard hat, and had a sizable paunch. He was listening to a cell phone as he came out of the building and didn't see the two of us standing there until he was almost upon us. Then he did, and he stopped dead in his tracks. Tony coldcocked him and then grabbed him before he fell backward onto the concrete.

I snatched up the cell phone and heard a woman's voice saying, "Tommy? Tommy? What was that?"

I switched the call off and then dialed 911. An operator came on immediately and asked what was my emergency.

"This is a police emergency call," I announced in my most authoritative tone of voice. Tony was dragging the inert worker into the space between the buildings and removing his ID tags. "I am Lieutenant Richter of the Manceford County Sheriff's Office, and I need to contact Sergeant McMichaels in Southport concerning an emergency situation at the Helios power plant."

I think it was that last bit that did it, because she didn't say a word, and a moment later I was patched through to the Southport police station dispatcher, who said he was looking for McMichaels as we spoke. Another minute, and McMichaels himself came on the line.

"Sergeant McMichaels," he said. "Who is this again?" He sounded sleepy. I woke him right up.

"Cameron Richter, Sergeant," I said. "Listen hard: Trask is inside the spent fuel storage building at Helios. He has Dr. Quartermain hostage. He intends to release radioactive water into the municipal water supply. County and Wilmington. Shut it all down, Sergeant—it's starting right now."

I hung up before he could ask any more questions. Tony had the fat man's badge chain in one hand and was swiping the green one through the reader at the door marked SPENT FUEL STORAGE. The LED went from red to green and we were inside, although nowhere near the moonpool. That was the good news. The bad news was that we were facing a steel desk in the anteroom, behind which were sitting two very surprised-looking security guards.

Tony and I both had the same idea, and we simply did it: We ran at the desk, grabbed the front edge, and turned it over on the two guards, who still hadn't begun to move. It was a heavy desk, and, unlike such desks in police station anterooms, it wasn't bolted down. It went up and over, spilling logs, telephones, coffee cups, radio chargers, and newspapers all over the place. The two guards went over backward in their chairs, and then the leading edge of the desk came down on their chests and shoulders, pinning them to the floor. The upside-down chairs kept the desk pointed at a slant, so we were able to reach down and retrieve guns, cell phones, cuffs, and Mace cans, and then jerk their shoulder-radio wires out of the belt-mounted base units. Then we snatched the upset chairs out and buried the two guys under the full expanse of the desk with only their lower legs showing. They struggled until Tony stood on the desk, at which point I yelled at them to shut up and listen.

"Off," I heard one of them squeak. I hadn't gotten a good look at them during our surprise attack, but these guys were inside desk cops and definitely not the twenty-something, ex-military types like the tough boys in the reaction force. Tony told them to be still and then stepped off the desk so they could breathe. Both of us checked our newly acquired weapons, Glock nines, to see if they were ready to work. They were.

"Listen to me," I said. "We're not here to damage anything. Your Colonel Trask has gone nuts, and he's in here and he's going to melt down the moonpool."

"Bullshit," said the second guard, who sounded like he was regaining his composure. "You're the retired cop with the dogs. He said you two were loose in the perimeter and that *you're* gonna try to break in and sabotage the storage system. That it might be real or it might be an intrusion drill. There's a dozen SWAT guys on their way here right fucking now. Either way, you guys're toast."

More confusion from Clever Carl. "Is Dr. Quartermain with him?" I asked.

Neither responded. Tony stepped back up onto the desk, and they both said yes.

"Billy said he shot your dogs, by the way," one of them offered, with just a hint of a sneer in his voice. Tony looked over at me to see how I was going to react to this bit of news. For an instant I wanted to shoot them both, but then got control of myself. Then I saw what looked like spots of blood on the floor leading to the access stairway.

"Is Quartermain hurt?" I asked. Silence again. Tony started jumping up and down on the bottom of the desk, and they both yelled for him to stop. They said Quartermain had a bloody necktie wrapped around his head, and that all three were topside at the moonpool.

"That bloody necktie's because your friend Billy, who shoots dogs, tried to kill us in Trask's Bronco and got Quartermain instead. That sound like a security exercise to you, asshole?"

More silence. Tony pointed at the access door to the stairway. The card reader was dark. There was no little red LED glowing next to it. Had Moira managed to turn them all off?

"When's the last time you heard from Control?" I asked the inert forms under the desk.

No answer. I knew there had to be some kind of duress or other emergency signal that these guys could send to Control in an emergency. Every site security system had one. Had one of them managed to mash the button as we attacked? I didn't think so, but it might be a passive system: Call in every *x* minutes or we'll come running if you don't.

I tried to think it through while Tony bent down, cuffed the guards' legs together, and then extended the second set of cuffs to wrap it around one of the steel desk's legs. It had taken a card reader to get into the anteroom, but it looked like the interior access system had been disabled. Wouldn't that fact alone alert the main control room? Then again, if Moira, with Trask's help, had been able to jimmy the video surveillance system, perhaps she'd also been able to replicate the everything's-okay signal from this anteroom back to Control. They might not know anything was going on, other than the video images of intruders down by the tailrace.

The real question in my mind was this: Was Trask's moonpool story more bullshit? Another diversion? Was he going to do something here or over in one of the reactor buildings?

The guards weren't going to tell us anything more than

they had to unless we hurt them, and I wasn't willing to do that, not yet, anyway.

Billy shot the dogs? When the hell did he get a chance to do that? More bullshit? Billy trying to psych me out if we managed to get this far? The little black spots on the glistening linoleum led to the access door; Trask had either been in a real hurry or he'd gotten really careless. Maybe it was the timeline—he had to move because Moira was going to initiate stage two, whatever that was. The desk phone, lying on its side with the handset on the floor, began to make that off-the-hook noise.

"Watch 'em," I said to Tony while retrieving the phone. I had this awful feeling we needed to get topside, but I wanted to get some cavalry moving if that was at all possible. I put the handset back on the base, waited a second, and then picked it up. I heard a strange dial tone—typical of a Centrex system. I dialed 9. Nothing happened.

"How do you get an outside line?" I asked.

No answer.

"Take your knife," I said to Tony, "and stab that foot right there." Tony just blinked. He didn't have a knife, but the guards didn't know that.

"Dial 8-1," the older man said in a muffled tone. His face was probably pressed sideways against the floor, but I suspected he was up for only so much heroics just now. I dialed 8-1. There was a click, and I heard a normal dial tone. I hit 9-1-1.

"What is your emergency?"

"Armed intrusion at Helios," I shouted. "Physical security has been compromised. We need help over here—they're trying to breach the reactors. Tell the FBI—quick!"

Then I pressed the switch hook down, detached the handset, and crunched it under my foot. I pointed to the access door, and Tony nodded.

"You wait here and watch these two," I said in a loud voice while we both went to the door. "They start some shit, you finish it, okay?"

"Got it," Tony said in the same stage tone, giving the desk a kick and racking the slide on his Glock.

"And Sergeant?" I said. "Deadly force is authorized."

"Yes, sir," Tony replied dutifully.

The term "deadly force is authorized" was something both guards, even civilian rent-a-cops, would recognize. It might give us a few more minutes before they figured it out. Tony tried the door handle. The door opened. We went through and softly shut the door. A video camera looked right at us as we stepped through the door—but, once again, no red light. Mad Moira was good, really good.

The spent fuel storage building was built like a two-layered Chinese box, a building within a building. The inner box was the moonpool, surrounded by its really thick concrete walls. It was four and a half stories from top to bottom. The outer box contained the support systems for the moonpool on three levels: ground floor, mezzanine, and top floor. The bottom level was concerned with access and maintenance spaces, surrounding the inner box on four sides. The mezzanine contained pumping and handling machinery, and the top level gave access to the surface of the moonpool and the control room. One main stairwell gave access to all three levels via separately locked vestibules, supervised by access card readers and video surveillance systems. There were four flights of steel stairs between each two levels. We were standing on the bottom, looking up, when all the fluorescent lights went out.

The first thing that happened was that the emergency battery-powered lights came on, providing at least some illumination in the concrete stairwell. I tried the door marked EQUIPMENT ROOM NO. 7, but it was locked. Tony tried to pry open the door back into the guards' anteroom without making any noise, but it, too, was locked. We had our borrowed guns out now, and we each put an ear to the anteroom door to see if we could hear the guards moving around in there, but it was all quiet on that front.

"Up?" Tony whispered.

"Can't dance," I muttered, so we started up the steel stairs. We could see between the flights all the way to the top of the stairwell, but the higher we looked, the darker it got. Four flights later we arrived at the mezzanine level. There was one door that led into the moonpool's section, marked TRANSFER & HANDLING MACHINERY, and three unmarked doors leading out into the exterior ring of the building. The three exterior doors were locked; the machinery room was not.

This door opened out into the landing area. We looked inside, but saw nothing but large pumps, switchboards, a maze of piping, and what looked like the top section of an elevator hoisting cable assembly. We couldn't figure out how all this tied into the pool's access, although I caught a glimpse of a wall ladder leading up to the next level all the way at the back. The emergency lights didn't reveal how high it went.

"Next level's the pool deck and control rooms," I said. "There's another security force anteroom up there."

"So why didn't they react to the ruckus down below?" Tony asked while he made sure no one was lurking behind the big pumps.

I patted the wall, which Ari had said was ten feet thick. If the slabs between floors were anywhere near that thick, no sounds would penetrate. Large radiation warning triangles were painted all along the back wall of the pump room.

"Let's see where that ladder goes," I said and worked my way through all the machinery to the back wall. The emergency lights barely shone back here, and the ceiling of the room, some fifteen or even eighteen feet above us, was dark. Tony went to one of the emergency lights and took it down off its mounting so he could point it upward. At the top of the ladder we saw a steel scuttle hatch, complete with a circular operating ring on the underside.

"Emergency escape hatch?" Tony said.

"From here or from the moonpool?" I wondered. Since we hadn't seen any control consoles in here, all of this machinery was probably remotely operated, which meant that this was an unmanned space. So the hatch had to be a way out for someone on the moonpool deck itself. The big question now was where it came out—in a separate airlock, or right out in the open?

Then from down the stairwell we heard the bang of the door being opened back against the wall and voices. The guards had figured out they were alone and had finally summoned some backup. Tony closed the machinery room door and looked for some way to wedge it shut. There was nothing in the room that would help us.

"Up the ladder," I said. "Gimme that light."

Tony started up while I broke the light's bulb and lens and put it back on the wall. There were two other lights still going in the room, but they didn't illuminate the top of the ladder. I started up as the noise from the stairwell grew louder. Several guards were out there, but they were being really careful because they knew we had the anteroom guards' weapons. A gunfight in a concrete and steel stairwell is a scary thing, as I knew from personal experience. If the shooter didn't get you, the ricochets might.

Tony climbed as high as he could and then swung to one side of the ladder so I could get as high as he was. We hung there, listening to the people out in the stairwell.

"They come in here, see us, point weapons, we give it up, right?" Tony asked quietly.

I nodded. I wasn't going to shoot it out with cops who were just doing their duty, even if they were rent-a-cops. While we waited, Tony tried the operating ring. It was really stiff, but it did move, and he began to turn it counterclockwise. There were steel lugs embedded in the rim of the hatch, and we could see them begin to retract as he turned the wheel, degree by degree, slowly in case the hatch was visible to someone up above us. I tried to remember the layout of the pool deck, and whether or not there'd been a round, steel escape hatch in the floor anywhere.

The door below us banged open, and a voice yelled for us to throw down our weapons and come out with our hands in sight. There was still only emergency lighting out in the stairwell, so there was no blaze of light when they opened the door. Tony kept working the wheel in tiny increments, stopping every time one of the lugs made a noise. I watched as one of the cops stuck his head through the door behind his gun and then jerked it back. A moment later, three cops swept into the room below us and made a quick search of all the machinery. No one had a flashlight, thank God.

"Clear," one of them announced, and a voice outside swore. They withdrew from the machinery room as a discussion ensued out in the stairwell. One of them said that we had to be up on the pool level, but another argued that there was no way we could have gained access because all the vital area readers were locked up. More back-and-forth like that as they tried to decide what to do, and it was clear that they did not fancy climbing the next four flights of stairs with two armed bad guys up there. Tony nudged me—the hatch was unlocked.

He pressed his forehead up into the dome of the hatch and signaled for me to push up on the operating ring. He looked like a submarine skipper raising the periscope to take a look. A thin line of white light appeared around the rim of the hatch, and I wished those cops had closed the machinery room door when they withdrew. Anyone looking in right now would see us, and they were still all standing around down there arguing about what to do next. Tony dropped the hatch quietly back into place.

"Control room, I think," he whispered. "I could see chair legs, consoles, a trashcan, and a coffeepot."

"People?"

"Not where I could see 'em," he said, "but there's a chair damn near on top of the hatch. All the lights are on up there."

This all made sense: If there was some kind of problem out there on the moonpool deck, the technicians would run for the safety of the control room, which had glass walls and sealing doors. From there they could go out via one of the security doors. If things really got out of hand, like a fire in the stairwell, they still had a way out—down the escape hatch. There was probably a second hatch embedded in the floor of the pump machinery room that we hadn't seen.

It sounded like they'd made some sort of decision down there, because it got quiet again. We had two choices: go back down the ladder and see if we could escape behind them, or go up into the control room. I could see that Tony had come to the same conclusion and was waiting for me.

"We came here to stop Trask," I said. "Whatever he's going to do has to happen up there. I say we go on."

Tony turned around and began to lift the hatch. There shouldn't be anyone up there at the control level at this hour of the night, except possibly Trask and Ari Quartermain—and his mysterious inside man, I reminded myself, he of the hearts and minds.

White light spilled down into the pump room as Tony fully raised the hatch, which he pushed until we heard a lock-back latch snap into place. Then he went through the hatch, up into the control room, and out of sight. I followed when I saw his hand wave me up.

The control room ran the full width of the moonpool's open deck level. There were several consoles and instrument banks, and a rank of locking file cabinets all along the back wall. A window wall overlooked the surface of the moonpool, but we were crawling on the floor on our hands and knees. We needed to get a look out into the deck area, but not at the expense of being discovered.

There was one door from the control room out to the catwalks on the sides of the pool. It had a glass window in the top half, which was covered with notices taped to the glass. I pointed at it, and Tony understood. We crawled over to the door, and he slowly rose up to peek through the glass beneath the pieces of paper. He dropped back down immediately and raised two fingers.

"Quartermain and one other guy," he whispered. We could hear sounds from outside the access door, but they were indistinct because of the airlock. "They're lying on the bridge leading out over the pool."

"Trask?"

"No see'um."

"Are they alive?"

He shrugged. "No blood, but they're not moving. And: I can't see any water."

"That's because it's all going somewhere else right now," a voice said from behind us. My heart sank. It was Trask, standing head and shoulders out of the hatch on the same ladder we'd come up, pointing Tony's shotgun at us. He'd been hiding down in the pump room all along.

He waved the muzzle of the shotgun in a clear signal for us to shed our own weapons, which we did. Then he stepped up off the ladder and told us to get up. As we stood up, he picked up our weapons, stepped to the door leading out to the moonpool deck, and pitched them into the water.

"I was right behind you, the whole time," he said. "There's another escape trunk from the ground floor to the mezzanine level. And I am *so* glad you made it. I actually thought you might. You look a bit damp, though."

"You kill those guys out there?" I asked, indicating the two motionless forms on the bridge.

"Not exactly," he said. "The radiation might, once the water gets below a certain level."

"You are one sick puppy, Colonel," I said. "Where's Billy the Kid?"

"Busy, Lieutenant, busy." He laid the shotgun into the crook of his arm while flipping open a cell phone and hitting the speed dial. I was surprised that the phone would work in here with all the shielding; they must have an inside repeater antenna somewhere.

"How's the feed?" he asked, then listened. He was watching us, but not focused on us, and I felt Tony change his position fractionally. The two muzzles of the shotgun lifted an equal fraction, and I heard Tony exhale. No chance of rushing that thing.

"Okay," he said. "Another ten minutes and you can take it down." He closed the phone and went to the door to listen. Then he nodded, as if very satisfied with himself.

"Those guys can't figure out what to do," he said. "I've

killed the card readers, and Moira made the physical locks shut down. And I'll bet their radios just stopped working."

If your cell phone works, I thought, *then one of them is going to figure that out, too.* I hoped.

"I love it," he said, easing himself into a chair at one of the consoles. "I'm using their own machinery to do this. They have tanks under this building where they can dump the water. If the level drops unexpectedly, makeup water from the city system comes on automatically to restore the level. That gave me the pump I needed. Then all we had to do was defeat some check-valves."

"What's a check-valve?"

"A valve that allows the water to go only in one direction. Pressure on one side of the valve pushes open a flap. Pressure on the other side seats the flap against a steel ring so no fluid can go the other way. We just removed the flaps."

"We?"

He pointed at the two forms lying facedown on the bridge. "Dr. Thomason did the valve work; Dr. Quartermain got us in here. And the lovely Miss Moira is feeding the video and instrumentation system an enormous crock of digitized bullshit."

"Control doesn't know the water level is dropping?"

"Control knows there's something going on because of all those rent-a-cops outside. But radiation-wise, Control is seeing exactly what I want them to see. They think they're dealing with a break-in. You tell those guards why you were here?"

I nodded.

"Well, they'll have reported that. More confusion in Control. When she switches the instrumentation systems back to normal, they'll have a level-one radiation emergency in this building, and they'll forget all about the intruders."

"Why?"

"Because all those guards out there are going to leave the building as fast as their shiny black combat boots can carry them. Then Control will override the automatic refill plumbing and push huge amounts of water into the pool, with even bigger pumps. Only it won't stay in the pool—it's all going downtown, at least until they discover the problem."

I wondered if McMichaels had taken my warning seriously; I sure hoped so. Then a chilling thought hit me: If the water department turned off their pumps, there'd be zero resistance to the slug of radioactive water Trask was going to send back up the system.

Trask looked at his watch again. "Wondering how this is all going to come out, Lieutenant?" he asked.

"You bet," I said. Tony was clenching and unclenching his fists, but that shotgun wasn't moving. I thought the reflection of blue light from the moonpool was getting brighter.

"Mass confusion," he said. "Terror in the streets. And somehow, it's going to be all your fault."

"Hunh?"

"Well, look at it this way: I belong in here, as do Drs. Quartermain and Thomason. We work here. We have access. You don't. You climbed a fence. You assaulted guards. You broke in here. It was only my extreme vigilance that kept you from doing bad shit." He was laughing now, sounding crazier than a loon.

"Oka-a-y," I said. "I follow all that. But why would we want to do bad shit to a nuclear power plant? Are we supposed to be agents of a foreign power? Do we make money out of this? Where's our motive, Colonel?"

"Ah, motive," he said. "Yes, what was your motive? Well, remember why Dr. Quartermain hired you? Remember all that Red Team stuff? You were simply doing your jobs, and you succeeded beyond Quartermain's wildest expectations. Things simply got out of hand, that's all. You know, like most of the government's 'good ideas'? Occupying Iraq, for instance? Most of government's good ideas usually do turn to shit."

"So you're going to what—kill all of us?" I asked. "You'll be the last guy standing, so you get to tell the tale?"

"Oh, hell, no," he said, staring at Tony. "Not unless your twitchy buddy there makes me do it. Calm down, you." Then he turned back to me. "No, actually, I need you alive and intact. I need a couple of guilty bastards in cuffs when the mother of all investigations gets going. I've got a story, you'll have a story, Control will have a story, hell, even Mad Moira, if she gets caught, she'll have a story. Talk about a federal goat-grab."

There was a rumbling noise below our feet. Trask blinked and then said, "Whoops."

"What the fuck was that?" Tony said.

"Baby is having gas pains, I do believe," Trask said. "A bit early, but better late than never. Now, you two: Get your asses out there on the pool deck."

"And if we don't?" I said, with more bravado than I really felt.

"If you don't, I'll pull these triggers. Then, of course, I'll have to change my story, but, hey, I can do that. You can just bleed out. Move your interfering asses. Now."

We moved our interfering asses to the door and went through. Outside the control room there was a distinct smell of ozone and something else, something metallic. To my very great dismay, the water level in the moonpool had shrunk by about a quarter, and the formerly indistinct fuel bundles were no longer indistinct at all. Trask waved at us through the glass door, then threw a switch, which plunged the entire area into darkness. We heard the hatch cover clank shut as he went below. The only light now was that glow from the spent fuel assemblies, and it seemed to be a lot stronger. As we watched, another giant gas bubble rose from the bottom of the pool and lazily floated to the surface, where it popped right under the inert forms on the bridge.

I finally recognized the other smell—I remembered it from high school chemistry, one of those experiments where we made hydrogen. It was more of an acidic sensation on the palate than a real smell, but I recognized it. The pile of spent fuel at the bottom was beginning to outgas. Next would come the fire to end all fires.

* * *

We went out onto the bridge across the pool and pulled the two unconscious men back to the pool deck. Both of them smelled of the same ether that Trask had used to put Pardee Bell under, but neither seemed to be so profoundly drugged as Pardee had been. I thought I heard noises from behind the airlock into the control room, so I went back in there. I tried the escape hatch, but it wouldn't budge now. I went into the airlock and banged on the exterior door. Someone outside immediately yelled for me to open the door and come out, hands up, et cetera, et cetera.

"I can't open the goddamned door, you idiot," I yelled back. "There's no handle, and the card readers are dead."

That led to some consultation outside.

"Hey?" I said to the steel door.

"What?"

"Your buddy Carl Trask has turned on the pumps to drain the moonpool. The water's at about sixty percent, and there's hydrogen coming up."

This produced a couple of oh-my-Gods outside and lots more consultation.

"Can you shut the drain pumps down?" my interlocutor called.

"Negative, the consoles are all locked up. You need to get someone on the pumps themselves before you get a goddamned meltdown."

More excited conversation outside, and then the sound of feet on stairs. *Oh, shit,* I thought. *Trask was right. They're bailing out.*

I checked the consoles again to see if I could find anything that might kill power to all the pumping systems, but I couldn't understand the control instrumentation. The consoles appeared to be locked up in some kind of hold mode, with none of the knobs or switches doing anything when moved. Tony called from inside the pool deck area. I ran back out to find Ari sitting up and looking around like a drunk.

"He's conscious but not all there," Tony said, holding on to Quartermain's shoulder to keep him upright. Ari's face was splotchy, and his eyes were coming in and out of focus.

There was a bright red welt running centerline from his forehead to the back of his skull. I knelt down on the concrete beside him.

"Ari?" I said. "The moonpool's losing cooling water. What do we do?"

"Run," he croaked.

Tony snorted. Great advice.

I repeated the problem, and this time Ari seemed to focus a little better. "Water," he mumbled. I thought he wanted water, but then realized he was looking over my shoulder, so I turned around and saw the fire hose folded up on a rack. There was the water we needed.

Tony got up and started pulling the hose off the rack while I held on to Ari, who was still very wobbly. Thomason was unconscious next to him. Tony threw the entire length of the hose into the pool and then opened up the red valve wheel. The hose made crackling noises as firemain pressure came on, and then the end of the hose popped out of the pool like an angry snake and began blasting a jet of water all over the place. Tony frantically cranked back down on the valve while I tried to capture the hose without getting bashed in the face. I then jammed the head of it into the bridge decking, and he turned it back on. This time the stream of water blasted straight down into the pool, creating a maelstrom of bubbles, and lots more of that metallic smell.

"Out," Ari said weakly. "Radiation. Control room. Now."

I helped him to his feet, but his legs gave out, so we ended up dragging him by his armpits and legs back into the control room. My injured arm gave way halfway there. Tony moved to go back out for Thomason.

"No," Ari said, pointing at the radiation meters above the door. Both were visibly moving into the red zone. "Too late. Don't go out there. Need suits."

Somewhere outside the control room, perhaps even outside the building, a large, deep-throated siren started up. I found one instrument that appeared to display water depth in the moonpool. It read thirty-one feet. I watched it for a moment to see if the fire hose was going to help. The needle didn't move.

Either it was locked up, or the fire hose was just holding its own against the pumps. Two more instruments began to flash red lights; both were radiation meters. My ears popped as an automatic pressurization system came on in the control room. The big siren outside had gone to a steady wail, and I wondered if the surrounding population knew what that meant.

"We can't just leave that guy out there," Tony said.

"Must," Ari said promptly. "That gas is radioactive. Atmosphere out there much too hot. Gotta get out of here."

Better said than done, I thought, as I tried that hatch wheel again. Trask must have wedged something in there.

"Fire axe," Tony said, pointing to the other end of the room. There was another hose reel down there, this one for CO_2, and right next to it was an old-fashioned fire axe. There was also a glass-fronted locker with what looked like firemen's oxygen breathing apparatus hanging inside. The windows of the control room were beginning to fog up outside from all the heat and humidity being stirred up by that stream of water blasting down into the moonpool. I looked at the depth gauge again: just under thirty-one feet. Baby was losing ground.

"Should we mask up?" I asked Ari, but he had drifted away again, his head lolling on his chin while he mumbled something incomprehensible.

We examined the main door, which indeed had no handles—but it did have hinges.

"I'll get the masks," I told Tony. "You've got two good arms: Take the axe to those hinges, see if you can get 'em off."

Ari rolled over to the floor like a sinking ship while I went into the cabinet and pulled out four masks. They were attached to canisters, which were either oxygen generators or an air-mixture chemical, I couldn't tell which. Tony was hacking away with the fire axe at the middle hinge with some effect. There were more red lights on the control panel, and I noticed one that was labeled STACK TEMP. Its needle was red-lined, and the indicated temperature was certainly high enough to boil water, which was probably why the windows were now totally obscured.

Tony had the middle hinge destroyed and was hacking away at the bottom one. The top one would be tough, as there was no room to get a proper swing at it. I donned one mask and adjusted the straps. Then I put another one on Ari. His eyes came back into focus and looked at me with a glare of apprehension. When I saw his cheeks puff out, I ripped the mask off and pointed his face into a trashcan as the ether displayed one of its more disgusting side effects. He puked his guts out for over a minute. I pulled the tab on my canister, and the air was suddenly much better. Then there was a serious bang from the door, and Tony stepped back away from it as a second bang hit the structure. Someone was hammering on it from the other side, and the bottom half of the door was slanting open from the top hinge.

"Here," I yelled at Tony, pitching him a mask. As cops we were familiar with firefighting gear, and he knew how to don and activate the mask. The hammering on the main door continued, and we could see light from under the door.

"Gimme that axe," I said.

Tony passed it over and asked what I was going to do.

"You stay here, handle the cavalry. I'm going after Trask."

"Thanks a heap," he said. "And what do I tell all those happy campers out there?"

"Tell 'em the moonpool's boiling," I said, standing back and taking a semi-mighty swing at the hatch handle. "Oh, and tell 'em Thomason's still out there."

I hit the hatch handle again, and this time I heard something metallic clanging down the ladder underneath. I tried the handle, and it rotated. I opened the hatch and snapped it back. The hole underneath revealed that the lights were still out, but I didn't fear an ambush. Trask had done what he'd come to do: create pandemonium at the plant, and soon out in the civilian population if that big siren meant what I thought it did. His water-poisoning scheme might not work from an engineering point of view, but that had never been his objective. Breach plant security from the inside and cause a major radiation emergency in the moonpool. Create mass confusion, alarm the whole countryside with reports of radiation in the drinking water and a possible meltdown at the plant, and generate months' worth of investigations and horrific publicity.

I went down the ladder, awkwardly because of the breathing mask, and pulled the hatch shut just as the main control room door came crashing down in a flood of white light and several figures in moonsuits came piling into the control room, all talking at once. I was relieved to see no one pointing guns. This was the technical staff.

I slipped down the ladder to the mezzanine level, went to the closed door, and listened. There was more activity out in the stairwell, but it still sounded more like technicians than cops. The emergency lighting was still on in the pump machinery room, even though the stairwell lights had been turned back on. I took down one of the lights and searched for the escape trunk, which I found at the back corner of the room. The hatch was open and waiting.

I turned around to go down and then hesitated. Trask would have been in a hurry, but would he have left the hatch open like this? I knelt down, shone the light beam down the ladder, and tried to see what was in the room below. The ladder went straight down at least fifteen feet onto a concrete floor.

The ladder.

I felt the top rung and tested the ladder's strength. The top fixtures came right out of their sockets, and the whole thing began to lean backward into the room below. I had to pull hard just to hold on to it.

Nice try, Colonel, I thought. If I'd jumped onto that thing in a hurry, I'd have gone over backward onto the concrete and whatever else down there. I wedged the top of the ladder frame against the top sockets and went to look for some substitute pins. The best I could come up with was some pieces of electrical wire until I remembered the ladder coming down into the mezzanine room. It had pins securing the bottom fixtures. I removed these and set them into the next ladder, clambered aboard, and went down as fast as I could, my feet hitting every other rung. I was glad for the mask, because the oxygen-enriched atmosphere was giving me a real energy boost, which I sorely needed.

At the bottom I shone the emergency light around the darkened room, which had no battery-operated lights of its own. This room was much smaller than the equipment and machinery rooms above, and held nothing other than four steel clothes lockers. Three were locked; one was not. I opened that one and found four bags of dry cleaning hanging in clear plastic. Each bag contained a uniform, the same ones worn by all the contract cops. One looked big enough, so I went to the door, listened, and heard two men arguing out in the security anteroom about the best way to get more fire hoses up to the moonpool.

I shucked my wet clothes and put on the largest uniform, which fit well enough. I rolled my clothes into a wet ball and stuffed them behind the lockers. There was one well-used blue ball cap on top of the lockers marked with the word SECURITY. I retied my boots and went to the door.

What I needed now was to get out of this building and acquire a weapon on the way out. I tried the door handle from my side, twisting it in slow motion. It seemed to be working. I released it back to the neutral position and tried to think. One guy out there sounded like he was on a phone while the other was feeding him information. If I stepped out of here with the mask on, they'd assume I was one of them, at least for a moment. Then I heard a crowd of people come into the anteroom and lots of voices. The voices sounded muffled—were they in masks? I cracked the door and discovered an entire crew of suited-up technicians, all wearing masks similar to mine, and all carrying various pieces of handheld test equipment. Now was the moment.

I stepped through the door, behind most of the people crowding the anteroom. The two security guards, who were not wearing masks, were overwhelmed checking everyone in. I walked as casually as I could over to the front door and stepped out into the night air. Unfortunately, there was another security guard out there, incredibly, given all the alarms, smoking a cigarette, and he was one of the original two guards we'd chained up under the desk. He was wearing a Colt M4 strapped over his right shoulder now, and he blinked when I stepped out. I saw recognition flare into his eyes, so I didn't hesitate—I stepped into him, punched him once in his overlarge gut, and then put him out with a medium-strength rabbit to the base of his neck. I let him down easily onto the concrete steps, dragged him around to some bushes by the door, took off the breathing rig, and very happily relieved him of that lovely Colt and the spare clip of ammo.

Then I began trotting down the walk toward the tailrace, suddenly very aware of that big-voiced siren blaring into the night air, telling the citizens of Brunswick County that there was trouble, big trouble, right here in River City. The good news was that I didn't see anything, vaporous or otherwise, spewing out of the spent fuel storage building, even though there were now big red strobe lights going on all four corners. I hoped that calling it a containment building wasn't just a PR expression.

I crossed the perimeter road and headed out into the open space between the industrial area and the perimeter fences. I went through the cask storage area, stepping into the shadows to look behind me for any signs of security forces. More vehicles were pulling up to the moonpool building, but the only blue strobes I saw were all the way out around the main gates to Helios. I wondered if they were inside or outside the perimeter.

And where was fucking Trask? He'd talked as if he was going to stick around for the inevitable fun and games once the problem with the moonpool was contained. If that was so, there'd be an awful lot of loose ends. Me, to start with, and then Tony, Ari Quartermain, Pardee, and Thomason, assuming he survived his radiation bath. He'd acted like he was going to stand up and testify against everyone. I wondered when the adults at Helios would begin to see what they were dealing with.

I finally made it down to the fence itself, near the tailrace. The whole time the siren had been going, the two big jets of cooling water had never stopped. I remembered what Ari had said: The moonpool was separate. It had nothing to do with the reactors, and Helios was firmly on the grid. I kept looking for the shepherds, hoping against hope that I'd see two bounding, sharp-eared friends coming to join me in the next adventure, but there was no sign of them anywhere. I tried not to think of that insidious rotor at the base of the cooling jets' impact area. I squeezed away images of my two loyal companions rolling around in that for eternity.

Where was Trask? Running to his boat? Had Billy moved the boat around to the inlet canal for easier access? Not possible—that would take too long. So where was Billy? *He's busy,* Trask had said. Busy doing what?

Behind me I sensed lights. When I turned to look, I saw two security vehicles coming full tilt in my direction. Okay, someone in the control room had pulsed the system about one of their people down at the tailrace. *What people? We don't have anyone down at the tailrace. It's them.*

I hit that hole in the fence and struggled to get through. It was easier without my vest. Once through, I ran as fast as I could as the two vehicles came screeching to a halt inside the fence. I was into the trees before they had a chance to climb out and position their weapons. Just in case, I hit the deck as soon as I was out of sight, and a good thing, too, because some eager beaver cut loose with a burst, which showered bits of trees all over me. I was tempted to shoot back, but these were still just security guys doing their jobs. I crawled diagonally through the weeds until I was pretty sure they'd lost interest. Hopefully they hadn't brought any dogs, and would now be asking Control if they had authority to go outside the fence.

I trotted through the woods, which were getting darker the farther I got from all the lights at Helios. I swerved to my left to regain the towpath along the canal, swatting branches out of my face, and unlimbering that Colt as I went. After five minutes, I stopped to regain my breath and check out the gun. It was an M4 6920, a law enforcement model, and a beauty of an assault weapon. I made sure it was ready to work, and then resumed my advance through the woods to where we'd left Trask's boat. I wondered if it was smart to be running out here in the open area of the path. About the time I thought maybe I should divert back into the woods, Billy the Kid stood up in the path, pointed some kind of short-shoulder weapon at me, and told me to stop right there. One of his eyes was swollen shut, but the other one radiated true rage.

If that guard hadn't said something about Billy shooting my dogs, I might have reacted properly and stopped in my tracks. Instead I looked at him and then said, "Hi there, short-eyes, fucked any little boys lately?" As his one working eye widened, I screamed to further distract him and then ran full tilt into him, the butt of the Colt held at face level. I stabbed the stock into his forehead before he could even think about pulling his own trigger, and then, as he staggered backward, a waterfall of blood blinding him, I kicked him in the crotch. Hard. Fourth-down punt hard.

He gave a mortal grunt of pain and pitched forward to his knees with a gagging sound, and then I struck down with the butt of the Colt and put his evil young ass firmly on the ground. It was all I could do not to shoot him. Instead, I took some deep breaths, and then I delivered four precise kicks to the so-called charley-horse points on his arms and legs. That would ensure limb paralysis when and if he came to.

I took his weapon and pitched it into the canal.

Trask, I reminded myself. *Find Trask. You can't know what this is really all about until you take Trask.*

I started trotting down the towpath, into increasing darkness, now that Billy had been neutralized.

Big mistake. What had Trask said when I asked him where Billy was?

Busy.

I hit the tripwire at full tilt and went flying, legs ensnared in something wiry and my body arcing through the air until I was hanging upside down from a tree limb above the towpath. As I twirled in the air, I looked around frantically to see who'd come to gloat.

Nobody came. I could see the lights of Helios from over the treetops, but the ground spinning below remained dark and silent.

I unlimbered the M4, got it into shooting position, even though I was upside down. *Come on out, sumbitches, and see what happens*. But nobody came out of the woods to declare victory.

Okay, I thought. *Engage brain and get your ass down.*

It was harder than getting under that fence. The blood was pooling into my head, and my brain resisted doing anything useful.

I took another look around, still saw no one in the dark woods, and started bending myself into a U-shape. I finally got ahold of the wire, which had been thoughtfully greased for my climbing enjoyment. Busy Billy, indeed. But where was Trask? Watching from the woods? I didn't think so. And the fact that Billy was lurking on the trail leading back to the boat told me that the boat might still be there.

Get down, get to the boat, and wait for Mr. Trask.

Sounded like a plan to me.

A wire noose had my right foot in a tight vise. I was bent double, holding on to my right foot, since the wire was slipperier than owl shit. I couldn't climb the wire.

Swing. Swing until you can grab the branch, I thought.

And that's what I did—I induced a broad swing, doubled up in the shape of a climber's carabiner, until I could reach out and grab the branch from which the wire was suspended. After that, I could release the noose, and then use the noose to swing myself back down and drop to the ground.

My arm hurt, and now my ankle hurt. My pride hurt. I was no closer to Trask. That big siren was still wailing at Helios, and I had a fleeting vision of Tony facing off with the cast of thousands dealing with the moonpool. I think I was the one better off.

I tried to remember where Trask's boat had been anchored, how far down the outlet canal. I decided to walk, not run, and this time stay inside the woods line instead of on the path. I became more careful of what else might be waiting for me. Trask had thought ahead of me all the way here, and it probably wasn't over.

Twenty minutes later, I caught a glimpse of the *Keeper,* still anchored out in the outlet canal. There was a bow wave visible at her stem as the current from the condenser jets pushed downstream toward the Cape Fear estuary. I'd forgotten to check to see if that partially deflated dinghy was still in its tree.

No matter. There was the boat. Still no lights. Still no signs of life, and no Trask. Okay, then: What's the plan? Billy wasn't going to be able to come out and play anytime soon, so: Swim out there? Or play AT&T, and reach out and touch someone?

I settled down on the dark bank of the canal. It was cold now. That was good. Evil reptiles were still dying upcountry. I unslung the M4, leaned against a tree trunk, and waited. The siren was not as loud down here in the woods. Surely they'd found a way to refill that pool by now. So why was the siren still going?

It was late and I was one cold, weary bastard.

What in the world had Trask been thinking? That he was going to get away with this? Cause chaos at a nuclear power plant and then casually stroll into work the next day, see what was shaking? Hi, guys, I need to make a statement?

Technically, it didn't make sense to me, even if I was technically ignorant when it came to nuke power plants. On the other hand, he'd rolled a terroristic bowling ball into a clutch of bureaucratic tenpins: the NRC bureaucrats, who loved nuclear power but had to live a split-personality life in their regulatory personae; the power company, providing the only source of totally nonpolluting electricity, except when something went wrong; the FBI, suspicious of everybody, painfully aware of past failures in intelligence and counterterrorism, and now seeing wild-eyed, virgin-obsessed ragheads under every truck; Homeland Security, at war with the terrorists, the flying public, *and* the FBI; and don't forget the benighted local cops—state, county, city—trying hard to live right while the federal host maneuvered all around them, often creating as much chaos as they were untangling.

Trask may have had it right. Don't execute an actual terrorist plot. Ignite a bureaucratic calamity. Make it seem as real and scary as possible. These days, in a complacent country, the perception of terror would be indistinguishable from the real deal, at least until the pregnant lady in the headscarf walked into the day-care center and pulled the wire hidden under her burkah.

I looked out at that boat. For some reason, I was convinced that he was there. He was probably sitting on that comfortable screened deck, having a drink, and smiling in the dark. His Billy Boy was taking care of business out there in the woods. His primary antagonists were in custody at the plant, trying to explain to a bunch of outraged nukes what they were doing there. The locals were cowering in their houses as the plant siren proclaimed that there was an invisible Destroyer abroad in the countryside. As he figured it, all he had to do was wait until daylight, and then appear back at the plant and add to the confusion.

I settled into what shooters called the sitting position, even though I did not have a marksman's sling. The *Keeper* was perfectly aligned with the center of the outlet canal, broadside to me, its anchor line taut in the tailrace current. I aimed the M4 at the waterline of that lovely old boat, took a deep breath, and opened single fire. The noise was shocking, even one round at a time. If there were any fishermen out there in the dark, there'd be some frantic pulling of engine cords going on about now.

The M4 shoots what looks like a small round, 5.56 mm, but that little bitty bullet has a great big powder case behind it and travels at the speed of heat, squared. I started at the bow and worked my way back to the stern, stitching a dotted line of holes right at the waterline, inch by inch, until the magazine was empty. The sudden silence was dramatic. On the outside, the holes would be tiny punctures, but inside, they were probably the diameter of a coffee cup.

Then I scrunched back into the woods, reloaded, and waited. The *Keeper* didn't do anything, at first. I wondered if Billy had come to yet. If he had, he was probably praying for unconsciousness to return right about now. I actually thought about going back there and doing it all again. That kick would have gone eighty yards, easy. I looked back at the boat.

She hadn't moved from her anchored position out in the canal, but I could see her deck now, barely tilting toward me. I moved behind a stout tree just in case Trask decided to get one of his guns and rake the bank. But there wasn't any movement out there. No emergency lights, no sudden starting up of engines or bilge pumps. Nothing, just more and more deck coming into view as she began to heel over.

I missed my shepherds. They should be out there in the woods now, making sure no one was creeping in on me. It was quiet enough for me to hear pretty well, but still, not like they could.

Quiet?

I realized that big siren had gone off the air. Good. They must have their moonpool problem under control. Or the last guy leaving the plant had turned it off as he ran for his life out the door. I couldn't detect any wind, which was probably a good thing.

Keeper was really listing now, and I thought I heard some stuff inside falling over. Her port side railings were in the current, the stanchions lifting tiny individual bow waves of their own. The anchor line was also at a much flatter angle as she settled. One hole in a boat can be dealt with; thirty holes cannot. The water finally reached the rear hatchway, and a minute later, she went completely over with a lot of creaking noises and a couple of big vents of air from inside the hull. She flopped upside down for a few seconds, and then she went out of sight, leaving only a long trail of bubbles in the current.

Current.

The plant was still running, or there wouldn't be any current.

I relaxed just a bit, not that I'd really been afraid of some big radiation release. Much. Still, there was always a chance that the moonpool had not been the main event. Trask might even be up there in the plant, pretending to help, ordering his security forces around while Moira went after the main reactor control systems and I sat out here in the cold darkness, thinking I was doing something worthwhile. Maybe it was time to just get up, find my vehicle, and go home. Tomorrow would be a very interesting day, to say the least.

But I didn't do that. If Trask *had* been on the boat, he was now out there in that black water, maybe holding on to a cushion from the main cabin. My guess was that he would deliberately drift downstream until clear of the shooter on the bank, and then come ashore for a little one-on-one. Or, being smart in his crazy way, he'd go to the other side and simply walk away

I was sitting behind a tree twenty feet or so from where I'd done the shooting. I decided that I needed to move downstream, in the direction of the current. Movement was dangerous, though; an old Ranger like Trask would get to the bank and then cling there like a crocodile, listening hard. If he was coming this would be a battle of sound, because it was pitch-dark out there now as even the ambient starlight was gone. But I still needed to move, because otherwise, if he came to my side of the canal, he could get behind me. That was not a happy thought.

I rolled slowly to my right, holding the M4 out in front of me, and began the tortuous process of inchworming my way through all the litter on the forest floor, one elbow forward, the corresponding hip forward, then the other elbow, and so on. Foot by foot, I crawled in the downstream direction, parallel to the canal banks, orienting myself as much by smell and sound as sight. That was a strong current out there. If Trask had gone into the water about the time she began to keel over, he'd have been swept a hundred feet or more downstream before he could achieve either one of the banks.

If he was even out there.

He was out there. I sensed it, and I wanted it.

I almost collided with a large white pine tree, from the

smell of it. Its fragrant, heavy branches swept out over the ground in all directions, and I'd crawled under them without even knowing it. I was tempted to stop right there; it was good cover. The blanket of pine needles under the tree would deaden any sounds I made, and besides, I was really tired.

I got close to the trunk, conscious of a zillion tiny insects moving around in all those pine needles. Even in the cold, the chiggers would be waking up about now, the mother of all blood meals right on top of them. My cheek touched the trunk and was rewarded with a dollop of pine sap.

Sap running? In November?

I turned my face full on to the trunk, brought my left wrist up, pointed my watch at the trunk, and flicked on the tiny light. There was a very fresh gash on the trunk, which was weeping sap. I quickly covered the light just before it winked out, and then began to roll over onto my back, a degree at a time, while trying to get the M4's barrel pointed in the up direction.

"That you down there, Lieutenant?" Trask called from somewhere way up in the canopy.

"You bet, Colonel," I said. Did he still have that shotgun? "Sorry about the boat."

"Not as sorry as you're going to be," he said. His voice was muffled by all those pine branches, so I had no idea of precisely where he was. I considered just emptying a clip straight up, but the tree was much too dense, and I only had the one clip left.

"Billy's not busy anymore," I said. "In case you were waiting for some reinforcements."

"He dead?"

"No, just wishing he was. One of the guards told me he shot my dogs."

"You bring an extra mag for that Colt?" he asked.

"Two, actually," I said.

"Bullshit," he said. "We only issue one in the weapon and one on the side."

"Tell me, Colonel," I said, while I tried to think about position. It was comforting to be next to the trunk, but I was completely blind, and, in fact, a shotgun blast straight down the trunk had a better chance of getting a hit than I did through all those branches. I started to move. "What was all this really about?"

"My contribution to the war effort, like I told you before," he said. He was speaking amiably enough, but there was strain in his voice. He knew this was endgame.

"Won't work, you know," I said, gaining another few inches of distance from the trunk. It was hard, moving on my back while keeping that weapon pointed up in the direction of potential business. Pine needles were dropping into my eyes as I moved, and that wasn't helping.

"That siren said otherwise," he said. Was he moving, too? Could he hear any changes in the location of my voice? How high was he?

"No, I didn't mean that you didn't scare 'em," I said, "but they'll never admit it."

"They'll have to," he said. "I spun up too many different agencies before we hit the pool itself. They'll tell on each other just to cover their asses, and that's how it'll come out."

"I don't think so," I said. I was about one-third of the way from the trunk to where the branches began to thin out. "That's one of the benefits of all this new coordination and cooperation. And it's the one situation where bureaucracies always cooperate: to cover their collective asses."

"Where you trying to go, Lieutenant?" he asked. "You move out there in the open, me and Mr. Greener here will have your ass."

"We got each other, then, Colonel," I said, but I stopped moving. "As I remember, the branches thin out up there in the air."

"Depends on which tree I'm in, smart-ass."

Now, that hadn't occurred to me. Pine trees came in groves, didn't they. He could well be up another tree. Except for that gash in the tree trunk. Keep him talking, see if you can locate him.

"Tell me something else, then, Colonel: What'd you have on Thomason?"

"He murdered his sister," Trask said. "I found out."

"How'd he do that?" I asked. Should I come all the way out from under those big branches, or perhaps change sector? He'd get a shot if I was in the open, unless, of course, it was a dense grove and there was no open.

"With a bottle of water," Trask said.

What did he just say? I felt my brain blink.

I heard him bark a short laugh. "That get your attention, Lieutenant?"

It certainly had. "Allie Gardner?"

"The one and only," he said. "I correlated a key card swipe with a radiation hit on a hall monitor. Had him cold, so to speak."

Then I finally made the connection. Allie's unmarried sister's name was Thomason. If she had never been married, then that was Allie's maiden name. I remembered that visitor log entry: Thomason visiting Thomason.

"Why'd he do that?"

"It involves family money, Lieutenant. That's all he'd tell me. I got the impression he took her share. I didn't push any further, because I needed him, not his back story. How 'bout it: You ready to rumble?"

"What, you coming down to join me?" I asked, tightening my grip on the Colt and anchoring the butt. God, I wished the shepherds were here. Even now, a piece of my brain heard them coming through the woods at high speed to rescue my ass one more time. But they weren't.

Then Trask made his move, and it was impressive. Turned out, he *was* in my tree. Our tree, I guess. He was all the way at the top, and he did what you can only do in a big pine tree: He jumped away from the trunk, arms and legs out like a spider, fell through the first tier of branches, and grabbed one. As it bent under his weight, it slowed him down just a little, and then he let go and dropped through the next tier, and so on, each time braking his descent just enough to be able to drop damn near right on top of me in a hail of needles and broken branches. I heard him coming all the way down, and it didn't do me one bit of good. I didn't even have time to fire the Colt, because my weary brain just wasn't working fast enough to understand what he was doing before there he was in a whoosh of air, pine needles, and a black mass of shadow, his angry face twisted into a murderous rictus and his hands reaching for my throat.

The Colt saved me, after all.

I'd had it pointed straight up the whole time, the stock wedged on the ground, my finger near, but not on, the trigger. Trask landed right on it and drove the barrel and even some of the action through his solar plexus and right out his back. My left hand, trapped under his body, felt a sudden warm flood. Trask screamed.

There we lay for a moment, in a truly grotesque embrace. Trask didn't make a sound except for one ghastly inhale, and then he sagged against me, insane eyes wide open, the fingers of both of his hands curling and uncurling, as if he still wanted to choke the life out of me. My sight line was directly over his shoulder, and I could see the muzzle of the Colt tenting the back of his shirt, even as a really big blood vessel emptied itself all over my left side.

I wanted to roll out from under him, but I was suddenly exhausted, so I just lay there and let him bleed. He was still breathing, sort of, and then I realized he was actually looking at me. His eyes were a hundred years old.

"What the fuck were you thinking?" I said. "With all of this?"

"Duty," he gasped. "Duty to warn."

"I'm sorry, man, but all they're gonna think is that you were just nuts."

"No," he wheezed. "You don't understand." He was going fast, but determined to tell me something. "Moira came to me."

My brain, even befuddled as it was, did a double take. "This wasn't *your* idea?"

"No," he said, whispering now as his life drained out of him. "Listen. Important. Moonpool. Diversion."

He coughed some blood, which must have hurt like hell. I saw the muzzle of the Colt throbbing under the shirt with what was left of his heartbeat. One of his hands suddenly tightened on my neck, but he was trying to get my attention, not hurt me. "The reactors," he said. "She wants the reactors."

His eyes rolled back in his head and he went limp.

I rolled free with a shudder and wiped off my hands in the pine needles.

The moonpool was a diversion after all? Obviously Trask had given Moira access to the plant's security computers. Was he telling me she might have access to the main reactor control system as well?

I tried to remember what Ari had said about that—same system, or were they split? Now that the moonpool was stabilized, they'd stand down from the emergency—and then she'd strike.

I looked over at that canal; the current was still running, and I thought I could smell diesel fuel now. Would the Helios people be expecting a second attack? I remembered the utter confusion at that university in Virginia, when they thought the shooting in the dorm was the main event and stopped looking.

I saw something moving through the upper branches of the trees. It looked like a blue ghost. I closed my eyes, took a deep breath, and looked again. Then it penetrated: blue strobe lights from a police car, reflecting off the tree trunks. Then there were headlights pointing down the towpath. I waited until the lights were shining right over my head and raised one bloody arm. The cop car dipped to a stop and two sets of doors clunked open. I kept the arm in the air until I knew they could see me, or rather us. I heard one of them say, "Holy shit," and then there was lots of excited radio conversation.

"Goddamn, bud—what the hell happened here?" one of them asked, approaching warily with his weapon in hand but held down by his leg. Trask lay facedown on the ground, the barrel of the M4 still pinning him.

I didn't know if they were county or Southport, but I told him to contact Sergeant McMichaels at Southport and tell him they'd found Trask and Richter. Then I lay back in the needles to rest as they played flashlights around the scene. They obviously thought I was wounded, based on the fact that my entire left side was glistening with all that blood, and I wasn't going to clarify that right now because they'd put their weapons away. Then I remembered Billy.

"There's another one out there," I said. "Back along the towpath, not too far from the perimeter fence at Helios. He'll need a meat wagon."

"What happened to him?"

"He shot my shepherds."

"He hurt bad?" the cop asked, radio microphone in hand.

"Not bad enough," I said.

Once the reports went in to their dispatcher, I asked them to get a message to the FBI in Wilmington.

"Report the same names," I said. "Trask and Richter. Then tell them there may be a second attack, on the reactors this time."

The cop's eyes went wide. "Second attack?" he said. "Whole county's going apeshit right now. Some shit about radiation in the water supply—you saying this was deliberate?"

I nodded and told him to ask for Special Agent Caswell at the Wilmington RA, and to make sure they knew this was a no-shitter.

"How do you know all this, mister?"

I pointed at the corpse of Carl Trask lying next to me. "This is the guy who did it," I said. "But it's not over. They *must* shut that plant down."

I could see he was hesitating.

"Okay, look," I said. "You got a cell phone I can use?"

He looked at his partner, who nodded. Then he passed me his cell. He was a county deputy, as revealed by his shoulder patch. I used my right hand so as not to get blood on it.

I called 911. The operator came on, but instead of the standard what-is-your-emergency, she simply stated that the system was in overload and that they could not take any reports right now. I asked her to patch me through to the central control room at the Helios power plant and said that this was a radiation emergency. She said they already had one of those. She sounded pretty frazzled, and I could just imagine what the 911 center looked like tonight.

"Listen, operator," I said, "right now you've got a possible radiation problem in the water system. Unless you want to see the sun rise in the west tonight, patch me through, please."

She had to think about that for a second or two, but then my meaning penetrated. "Right," she said. "Patching."

While I waited, I tried to think of what to say that would get their undivided attention. A man finally answered the call, identified himself as the Helios control center duty engineer, and asked if I could please hold.

"No!" I shouted, startling the two deputies. "This is Lieutenant Richter. One of the people who attacked the moonpool tonight has hacked into your reactor control system."

"What?" he said. "Hold on." He sounded tired and harassed, but then he put his hand over the mouthpiece and called out to someone. Then I heard a woman's voice say, "Give me that." I thought I recognized that voice. Sure enough, my favorite Russian came on the line.

"Who is this, please?"

I told her. She started yelling at me about making infantile crank calls when responsible engineers were dealing with a genuine emergency. I knew she was going to hang up in a second, so I broke into her tirade.

"Shut your mouth, you stupid, arrogant bitch," I yelled. "She's got your whole system—your reactor controls and probably all your safeguard systems."

"What? *What?!* What are you saying to me?"

I was having trouble concentrating. "Is your RCS responding to you?" I asked.

A split-second hesitation. "I am not permitted—"

"Trask gave her the codes. You have an expert hacker riding your system. If you have a manual mode, now's the time, comrade. Remember Chernobyl." I was trying desperately to remember the word Ari had used. Run. Fall.

No, scram.

"Scram those reactors, before she shuts down your control room."

In the background I heard someone yell that Unit One was ramping to full power, uncommanded. She hung up on me. I lay back in the pine needles, suddenly conscious of the two deputies gaping at me.

"Which way is the wind coming from right now?" I asked one of them. It took him a few seconds to realize I'd just asked him a question.

"Uh, why?" he said.

"Guess," I said, as a second set of blue lights began to show through the trees, followed by the wail of an approaching ambulance.

I let them transport me to the ER along with what was left of Carl Trask. I figured that federal agents of some variety would be along soon enough. Once the ER people cleaned me up and realized I wasn't really injured, I was sent back out to the waiting room while they dealt with the loaded and chambered assault rifle sticking out of Trask's back.

It was zero dark thirty, and I was done. I didn't want to play twenty questions with anyone, so I asked the front desk to call me a taxi, let myself out the front door, and had the guy take me to the beach house in Southport. I wanted to take a long, hot shower, but, of course, there was no water pressure. *I knew that,* I told myself. I had a Scotch instead, and then had an idea. This was a beach house.

I went outside and walked across the street, onto the beach, and right into the water. What was I thinking: That water was cold as ice, but it did the job. I stood out there up to my neck, occasionally dousing my face, and grateful for the lack of any real surf. When some submerged *thing* bumped my right leg, I decided enough was enough. I went back inside the house, stripped down in the kitchen, had another Scotch, and fell into the bed. My hands and face still smelled of pine pitch. It was better than snake.

Buroids were on deck bright and early the next morning. There was some heavy-duty cop-knocking on the front door, and then they waltzed right in. When they got upstairs and found me sitting up in bed, one agent told me to get up and get dressed while the other notified someone via radio that the subject had been apprehended.

Not having had any coffee, the subject was still trying to restore color vision and coherent thought. I asked them if they had a warrant for my arrest. This produced some awkward hemming and hawing, and then verbal foot-shuffling. I told them to leave my ass alone or I'd smear them with pine pitch and get ticks in their Bucar. I also mentioned that I was probably still somewhat radioactive. That made them both back up a few steps.

"Tell Creeps I'll meet with him down at the deli on Main Street," I said.

"Why not right here?" one of them asked, not bothering to pretend not to know who Creeps was.

"Because there's no coffee and there's no food. I'll be there in an hour."

"Sir, we've been ordered to bring you in to the RA's office."

I started to make inhalation noises. I held my nose, took a deep breath through my mouth, and let it out slowly. "I inhaled twenty million curies of moonpool radiation last night," I said, still holding my nose. "I'm going to sneeze. Then I'm probably going to die, and so are you."

They vanished.

Once they left, I prayed that the water was back on. It was, and I finally was able to delouse in style. If the water was still radioactive, it might actually get the pine pitch off, but I kept my mouth shut just in case. Once out of the shower I had a thought and called Mary Ellen again, this time at her office phone number.

"I miss you," I said. "Even if you are getting married."

"Tell me the truth," she said. "Are you up to your mendacious ass in deep camel dung? Are there bad guys looking for you? Are there good guys mad at you? Have you killed anyone in the past twenty-four hours?"

"Um."

"Unh-hunh."

"And that's why I'm calling. I need a spot of information.

You ever heard of a woman named Moira Maxwell? She's an—"

"Mad Moira? Of course I've heard of her. Everyone here has."

"What's she famous for?"

She told me to hang on a second. I heard her dismissing a student. Then she was back.

"Moira Maxwell is the resident campus Bolshevik," she said. "The UNC system is a liberal, left-leaning establishment, to say the least, but Moira Maxwell is a one-off. She makes even the professional liberals squirm. Wa-ay out there."

"All talk, or is she capable of being a doer?"

Mary Ellen had to think about that. "She's a modern revolutionary, which means she lurks on the Web instead of in dingy Parisian garrets."

"A virtual Bolshie."

"Well, by that I mean she doesn't burn underwear down in the campus Union, or picket the dean's office and chant the "Internationale." Please God you're not mixed up with that nutcase?"

"Better that you don't know," I said. "Not romantic, if that's what you're asking."

She laughed. "Got that right, Mr. Investigator. Reportedly, Mad Moira doesn't keep *boy*friends."

She did in that detention center, I wanted to say, but held my peace. "It's possible she's involved in the same matter I'm looking into," I said. "I guess what I really wanted to know is whether she has the courage of her convictions, or if the Red Square stuff is all about getting attention."

"She's called Mad Moira by the faculty people who know her," Mary Ellen said.

"Mad as in nuts, or mad as in angry?"

"Both," she said. She hesitated. "These are the calls that scare me, Cam."

"I understand," I said. "Stick with your plan, lovely lady. I'm probably not going to change."

"Nor should you," she said. "Doing this stuff, well, that's just you."

But not you, I thought sadly. "I'm still going to miss you, even when you're Mrs. Professor."

"Yes," she said. "Me, too. Good-bye, Cam. Please, keep safe."

"Absolutely," I said. "I mean, what could possibly go wrong?"

I thought I heard a small laugh, but then she was gone.

Creeps and Missed-it Mary came through the deli's doors like Batman and Robin, stopping most of the subdued conversations among the locals, who had been discussing last night's atomic panic. They were both dressed up in metallic-looking Bureau suits, and they appeared very official indeed. They saw me and walked over to my table, while the locals adjusted their places as if they anticipated gunplay or some other drama. I'd stuffed two, count 'em, *two* apricot Danish down my gullet, along with enough coffee to restore both stereo vision and sequential sentences. I told them the Danish were terrific, and suggested they get themselves some coffee and then we could talk.

"Your Bureau is incredibly busy this morning, Mr. Richter," Creeps said, slipping off his sunglasses. He looked a little ragged around the edges. Missed-it nodded emphatically. Very busy, yes, sir, you're certainly right about that.

"You have breakfast yet, Special Agents?"

Mary looked over at Creeps. He said no, and then Mary said no.

"The earth will no doubt continue to rotate if you do, so: I say again—why don't you guys go get some coffee and Danish, come back to the table, and we'll talk like civilized people often do."

They stared at me for a moment and then, amazingly, did what I suggested.

Once they were seated, I asked them if everything was reasonably secure out at Helios. Creeps said yes; they'd isolated the moonpool, and the engineers had taken the reactors into local control and shut them both down before there were any further excursions.

"Excursions?" I asked.

"Nuke-speak," Creeps said. "When the power levels in the reactor rise or fall out of ordered limits."

"Or, in other words, when the engineers no longer have control of the reactors."

"Just so." He looked around nervously to see if the civilians were listening. They were, raptly.

"And that actually happened?"

"I believe so, yes. Fortunately, the, um, individual who penetrated the control network did not know what she was doing. The danger was that she had the network, and the engineers in the control room did not."

"Did radioactive water get into the county water system?"

Creeps was lifting his coffee cup to his mouth when I asked that question. He stopped. I admired his self-control in not looking down into the cup. Then he went ahead and took a sip. Missed-it was looking at her cup as if she had seen a roach operating at periscope depth, but when Creeps took a sip, she dutifully did, too. They're big on loyalty in our Bureau.

"It got out of the plant and all the way to the first water tower, about two miles away. The system is engineered to recognize back-pressure in the lines, and the primary supply valves shut themselves. When the back-pressure continued to build up, relief valves lifted and the water was diverted out onto the grounds of the water tower."

"Lovely," I said. "They'll never have to cut that grass again."

"Well, that's preferable to decontaminating the entire county and possibly the municipal water system," he said. "Dr. Quartermain was able to tell the response team how to shut down the moonpool's internal pumps. Now then: Would you care to recite your evening's activities?"

I did. They just listened, not taking notes, which told me I'd be asked to go through this all again downtown with some office scribes. When I was finished, I became suddenly aware that the entire café had gone silent. Apparently, everyone, including the cooks and the waitstaff, had been listening to my tale of horrors from the night before. Creeps looked around the room as if realizing for the first time that the great unwashed public was now privy to Bureau secrets. He cleared his throat and suggested that we reconvene in the Wilmington office.

"Can do," I said, "but first I need to check on Tony Martinelli and Pardee Bell. Can you guys spare me a couple of hours, and then I'll come over?"

That seemed to work for them, and they left. Missed-it had her notebook out as she went through the door, writing furiously as Creeps dictated something to her.

"That was you, called in the warning last night?" an older man sitting nearby asked. The pair of pagers on his belt and a small radio on the table suggested he was an EMT. He had the look of a man who needed more sleep.

"Yep, that was me," I said. "I'm sorry for all the uproar that must have caused, but I figured better safe than sorry. Did that big siren mean what I thought it did?"

Several heads were nodding. "Everybody goes inside and stays inside," another man recited. "Close all the windows. Bring in the pets. Turn on the weather radios and wait for instructions. Don't go outside until that siren stops."

"Don't forget the last part," someone said.

"Oh, yeah," the older guy said. "If the siren goes steady, then go into an interior room, sit down on the floor, put your head between your knees, and—"

"Kiss your ass good-bye!" the rest of the crowd shouted in unison.

"Well, y'all dodged a bullet last night," I said. "The first thing that happened was a diversion. The real attack was on the reactor control systems. But they got some warning, too."

It was clear I could have told my tale several times over, but I decided it was time to go. When I tried to pay my bill, however, the pastry guy said it was on the house. I thanked him and went outside. Out of habit, I was still looking around for the mutts, but now there was just some local traffic out on Main pushing along under another clear, cool November day on the Carolina coast. I looked for my Suburban and then realized it was still parked over in the woods next to the outlet canal. I guess I knew that; I was more worn out than I'd known. I started walking.

When I got back to the house, I found Sergeant McMichaels sitting on the front porch, watching a dozen seagulls harass some beachcombers across the street. His police cruiser was parked out front. He might have been asleep when I started up the walkway; he looked like he could use it, too. There was a plastic bottle of drinking water sitting on the porch table next to him, and my Suburban was parked in front of his cruiser.

I thanked him for retrieving my ride, and then got to tell my story again, this time answering some of the questions I'd ducked out on in the deli. Then he told me his side of it, of receiving my warning and trying to verify it through the Helios control center, only to be told by some very unhappy woman that their instrumentation showed no problems at the moonpool.

"Then it was that I had to make something of a judgment call," he said. "You've seen those concentric rings on all the maps? There is a city- and county-wide alert system and also preplanned evacuation routes in place, all because of Helios. One call can put both systems in motion."

"You made that call?"

"I did," he said. "It's the one time you don't have to say anything twice. The threat of radiation concentrates the mind wonderfully, you know. Of course, the county managers all wanted to know my source, and my source's credibility."

"That must have been the hard part," I said.

He smiled. "Not that hard," he said. "Everyone admired those German shepherds of yours. It's a small enough town, when it comes right down to it. We may love our power plant, but many of us work there, too, and it frightens us sometimes."

"Hostages to the dragon."

He nodded at the bottle of water. "That's hot," he said. "We had no real sampling equipment, so I dumped out the good water, took a sample off the water tower manifold nearest the plant. The EMTs brought a dosimeter around. Pegged right off the scale, it did."

"Then you shouldn't be driving around with that," I said.

"It was a lab meter," he replied. "You'd have to drink it to hurt yourself. Or so the Helios people told us."

"But they wouldn't take it with them, would they," I said.

He frowned. "No, they would not, actually."

"Just like Allie Gardner," I said. "You were closer to real catastrophe than you knew, I think. I don't believe Trask ever intended to do widespread harm. His ally, that left-wing nutcase, was way ahead of him."

"And this is the same left-wing nutcase whom you helped to escape from the alleged DHS detention center?" he asked slyly.

"Other way around, Sergeant," I said. "She made it possible for *me* to get out of there. She had the magic card that got us out of our rooms and into the basement."

"And what is her problem with this great country?"

I told him what Mary Ellen had told me. "To hear her side of it, we're becoming Nazi Germany. She, of course, is nothing more than a civic activist exercising her First Amendment rights. Mainly with a computer. Think Freedom of Information Act on digital steroids. But when they came to the boat for her, I wondered if there wasn't more to it."

"And, of course, it was Trask and his some of his service buddies who took her, not DHS."

I nodded. "Had to be, although one of them was the Marine major who ran the 'alleged' detention center. He did warn me, actually, about Mad Moira. I'd assumed she was working for Trask. It appears I had that backwards. That's what I get for making assumptions."

"Surely you know the old saying."

"By heart. Look: I need to find out where Tony Martinelli is and how my other investigator, Pardee Bell, is doing over at County."

"I can help with part of that," he said. "Mr. Martinelli, I've been told, ended up at New Hanover County Hospital for twenty-four hours of observation, ostensibly for radiation exposure. Apparently, he didn't care for it very much and checked himself out. My spies tell me he's at the Hilton in Wilmington. Your Mr. Bell I don't know about."

"Ari Quartermain?"

"Ah," he said. "Not so good, there. He suffered a heart attack as a result of his exertions. He's been transported to Duke, upstate. Touch and go there, I'm told."

"I'm not too surprised; he was under serious stress even before Trask grabbed him. How about that Dr. Thomason?"

McMichaels shook his head. "In the woods. Deep in the woods. Not glowing, but close."

"There's a loose end there," I said. "Dr. Thomason was connected to the case that brought me down here in the first place. My associate, Allie Gardner? Trask told me that Thomason killed her with a bottle of radioactive water. Trask found out somehow and blackmailed Thomason into helping him."

"Did he now," McMichaels said, taking out a notebook.

I told him about my strange conversation with Allie's sister, and the fact that the Helios logs had revealed a Thomason visiting a Thomason. He said he'd inform the Wilmington police. I told him to talk to Detective Bernie Price in homicide.

"And the plant?" I asked. "How far did she get?"

"My niece's husband, Bobby, works on the reactor side," he said. "The hacker didn't have a clue as to how the RCS worked, but was able to enter commands. They were in the process of shutting both reactors down when your warning came in. Once they understood the problem, they used a manual system and scrammed them both, and that was that."

"But if it had been a knowledgeable hacker . . ."

"Oh, yes. Bobby said that a knowledgeable intruder with that kind of access would have crept into the system instead of barging in. They could have made it very much worse, and left the control people with dangerously limited options."

"I meant to ask Ari this: Why in the world is there even a way in for a hacker? Why would the reactor control system ever be exposed to the Web?"

"Ah, that. Yes. I asked the same question. Bobby told me

that PrimEnergy decided about two years ago to network their plants here in North Carolina. They maintain a sort of super control room at their headquarters. They want to be able to see a problem developing in case the local control room misses it."

"And they used the Web?"

"No, no, they have an encrypted network. *That's* what Trask gave the hacker."

"They catch up with her?"

"Not yet, but there are lots of agencies looking. Listen, I have to ask: What happened to Billy Summers?"

"He shot my dogs."

McMichaels paged backward through his notebook for a second. "They had to do some very unpleasant surgery on young Billy," he said. "A double amputation, I'm told. Something to do with orchids. And he is temporarily unable to move his arms or legs."

"He shot my dogs," I said again.

"Right," McMichaels said, closing the notebook. "I'm very sorry about that. The whole town will be sorry to hear it." He paused. "Do you *know* that he did that? That they're dead? Should people be on the lookout, perhaps?"

"I never found them," I said, "and they failed to find me. They may still be trapped in that tailrace from the condenser jets. But, yes, I'd appreciate people being on the lookout."

"The tailrace," he said. "We took a teenager out of that rotor once; he'd been missing a year. An unlovely memory. I am very sorry."

"Thanks," I said. I looked at my watch. "Now I have to go see Creeps Caswell and do this all formally. Will you let me know what you find out on the Thomason matter? That was why I came down here in the first place."

"You might ask your friends at the RA; they supposedly interviewed Thomason before he went into isolation."

I thanked him for all his help, and he left. As I went back into the house, I noticed he'd left behind his bottle of glowworm juice. I made a note to remind him to come back and get it later. I'd had well enough of radioactive water. Then I decided to bring it into the kitchen—no point in someone snitching it and then getting the ultimate bellyache from hell.

Since Billy had destroyed our cells, I used the house phone to call the Hilton and leave a message for Tony. He met me an hour later at County, where we found Alicia in much better spirits. Pardee was significantly improved, and they were planning to surface him tomorrow morning. We made some casual inquiries at the desk about Dr. Thomason, but nobody seemed to know his status, or else they just wouldn't talk to us. Tony reluctantly agreed to accompany me for my debrief at the resident agency building.

On the way over, he told me about the exciting finish to the moonpool flap, and how Ari had saved his ass by telling the irate technicians that he, Tony, was one of the good guys. After that, he said, they went to work getting their dragon-shit covered back up with lots and lots of water. That had even helped the county water problem, because they sucked a lot of the contaminated stuff back into the moonpool when they restarted the pumps.

The rest of my day was spent talking to the FBI. Sometimes they really like to talk. I was more than ready to get out of there that evening and get back to Southport and my dwindling supply of Scotch. Tony said he'd met someone interesting at the Hilton and asked if I'd mind if he stayed in town. Fine by me. I thought I might just go "home" and sulk, maybe even get wasted, something I hadn't done in a long time. I also thought briefly about going over to County on the way back to visit young Billy Summers. Maybe squeeze an IV tube or three. But if McMichaels was right, and they'd amputated what I thought they'd amputated, that was good enough. For the moment, anyway. I could probably find him again if I wanted to.

I grabbed a greaseburger on the way into Southport and then went to the beach house. I was disappointed to find Buroids waiting. They warned me that subject Moira Maxwell was thought to be still in the Wilmington area, and said they would like to stake out my pad on the possibility that she might try to contact me.

"Why on earth would she do that?" I asked.

The young agent looked at me patiently. Then I understood. "My Bureau didn't tell you why to stake out my house," I said. "Just to effing do it, right?"

They both nodded, happy to not have to explain something they probably didn't understand anyway. I asked them if they wanted to come in the house or just hang around within visual range. They chose the latter, and one of them gave me his pager in case something happened.

I went back inside, and they disappeared up the street. I wasn't too worried about Mad Moira. I might have foiled her big show, but she had plenty of spleen left for her native land, and I assumed she'd know not to get within a mile of me or my people.

Another assumption shot to hell. When I turned on the lights in the kitchen, there she was, my favorite redheaded harpy complete with a nasty-looking, nickel-plated handgun and her computer bags. She'd cut her lovely red hair down to a skullcap that only a lesbian could love, and she appeared to be dressed for travel. Through the back window I could see Tony's vehicle.

"Hey, cellmate," she said. "Why don't you just relax and sit down for a minute."

"You know there's Bureau in the neighborhood, don't you?" I said, sitting down, and regretting that the kitchen could not be seen from the street. How in the hell did she get Tony's car?

"Oh, them," she said, waving her hand dismissively. "I have some friends taking care of that problem."

"You have friends?" I asked.

She slid into a chair opposite me and gave me that fire-eyed grin. "Believe it or not, Lieutenant. Not only friends but like-minded citizens who are more than willing to help me on my little crusade. We're not done, not by a long shot."

"What are you doing here, Moira? You're not mad at me, are you?"

She barked a laugh. "Do you think?" she said. "But actually, this"—she waved the purse gun—"this is for my protection. I just wanted to tell you face-to-face that we'll never stop until America regains its freedom and the rest of the world is safe from our grievously aggressive government and our runaway military-industrial complex. We intend to show them that the people are the real weapons of mass destruction when it comes to tyranny."

I almost said *blah-blah-blah.* I hadn't heard this bullshit since watching some of those sixties movies, but it was coming from the same quarter it usually did: arrogantly overeducated people who'd never been out there on life's front lines. I said nothing, and just waited. I wondered if there was any way I could activate that pager in my pocket without her noticing.

"You don't believe me?" she asked, frustrated at my silence.

"Don't you think, Moira," I said, "that creating incidents of terror will only strengthen the government's resolve? Make it grab even more authority? If Trask was right, and the country's become dangerously complacent, what you guys tried was exactly the wrong thing to do, wasn't it?"

She shook her head. "What we'll create is doubt—doubt about the government's ability to protect the masses of citizens in this country who already feel powerless. Doubt about the moral underpinning of this so-called war on terror. Doubt about who the bad guys really are: them or maybe us. And from doubt springs true revolution."

I'd finally had it, even if she did have a gun. "Oh, c'mon, Moira," I said. "Masses and classes? That bullshit went out with Karl Marx caps and granny glasses. Communism is dead, or hadn't you heard?"

"Don't tell Comrade Putin that," she replied. "Or better, visit Russia and see for yourself. I have."

"The Russians can't help themselves," I said. "They *like* their tyrants. You, on the other hand, sound like a one-woman propaganda machine. What other Americans are going for revolution? None."

"You think?" she said. "Have you asked yourself *why* Carl Trask told your boys where you were? It wasn't to get you out, big guy—it was to get *me* out. That's why you changed rooms. Our thing is a lot bigger than you know."

"You're telling me the major was part of this?"

"No, but he's devoted to Carl Trask and his ideas about the decay in this country."

"You and the military guys are on different sides, Moira."

"They think so, and you think so. The difference is that my side is using them." She glanced at her watch and got up. "I've got a plane to catch." She pointed at our portable computer on the kitchen table. "You might want to get rid of that. That's the computer that actually hacked into Helios. It's a slave to the ones I have in here."

I blinked. I was impressed and said so. Then I asked her where she was going.

She laughed. "As if I would tell you?" she said. "Oh, let's see, then—how about, I don't know, Mexico?"

"Mexico."

"It doesn't matter where I go," she said, pointing at her computer bags. "As long as there's one or two of these around." She zipped up her jacket and headed for the back door. She saw the water bottle. "May I?" she said.

"Be my guest," I said, keeping my voice absolutely neutral. She grabbed the bottle, stuck it in her jacket pocket, and pushed open the back screen door.

"Moira?" I called. "If you actually do go down to Margaritaville?"

"Yes, dear?"

"Don't drink the water."

The next morning, Tony and I went back to the hospital to be there when Pardee surfaced. We were too late. Alicia was beaming at his bedside. Pardee had come out of it on his own and announced he was hungry, damned hungry. The doctors were very pleased and yet equally adamant that there would not be a party just yet. They asked us if we would mind very much just going away and coming back later. We slunk away to find some coffee in the hospital cafeteria. I told Tony about what had happened last night, and he looked at me with new respect. I told him that he'd eventually get his vehicle back if he'd just be patient, and that, no, I didn't intend to share the news of Moira's departure call with Creeps and company.

We had our coffee and then went down to see Bernie Price to close the loop on the Thomason case. He had been in touch with the reluctant sister, who was now on her way home to the U.S. to see about her brother, and possibly even her sister, Allie. She had told Bernie that there had been an inheritance from their parents, but Allie's revolt and subsequent enlistment with the sheriff's office had provoked their father to verbally disown her. When the second parent died several years later, the money had been much larger than they'd known, and the older brother, acting as executor, had divided it between himself and Allie's sister, even though the trust had specified a three-way split. Allie had apparently just found out, and had gone to Helios to confront Dr. Thomason. Whether she threatened to expose him wasn't known, but when I had made that call to the sister in Turkey, she had known that the chickens might be coming home to roost. I suspected Thomason had admitted to Allie what he'd done, and when she threatened to expose him, he poisoned her with moonpool water. The loving sister would probably never admit that, but Bernie said she was in for some pointed questioning.

Alicia took Tony back to Triboro when she went back for a day with the kids. The docs would not let Pardee go until he'd been observed operating normally for forty-eight hours. I drove back over to Southport. I decided to stay at the beach house as long as Pardee was still stuck in the hospital, even though Alicia said she'd be back down in a day or so. That evening, Sergeant McMichaels stopped by the house again. He had a rustic-looking individual with him. I thought he'd come for his bottle of radioactive water, but fortunately that wasn't the case. He introduced the other man as a local fisherman, who had some news for me.

"Think mebbe I got your dogs," the man said. "One German shepherd, one black wolf-lookin' one?"

My heart jumped. "Where?"

"My place," he said. "On the river. They wandered in yesterday mornin', I called the sergeant here. He'd had word out, you was lookin'."

"Are they hurt?"

The man shuffled his feet and looked warily at McMichaels. "You can tell him," the sergeant said.

"The black one? He's done lost him a back leg. Looks like somebody shot it off. Got him a hurt eye, too. Bad hurt, I reckon. The other one's okay, but she won't eat nothin' and she keeps makin' teeth at me."

That would be Frick, I thought. "Let's go," I said. *Frack's lost a leg?* The thought of that almost made me wish it wasn't them. Almost.

The man turned out to be an inshore fisherman. He ran a one-man-band operation and plied his trade in the Cape Fear estuary for the Wilmington restaurant markets. His riverside place was in a small community of riverbank places whose yards were cluttered with boat gear, junked cars, wobbly-looking piers and boats, and weathered mobile homes. He took us out back to a makeshift dog kennel, where I heard a familiar bark.

Hallelujah. It was them. Frick was thin and a bit tattered, but she perked right up the moment she saw me coming across the backyard. I heard a couple of other cars pulling up out front but concentrated on greeting Frick and then examining Frack. I could tell immediately that his right eye was a total loss. His left rear leg was gone from the elbow down. The fisherman had put some kind of horrible goo on it that stank of fish, but I didn't see any swelling or other signs of infection. He couldn't stand up, but he was very glad to see me, and his tail worked just fine. I sat down in the pen between them and just talked to them, trying to keep a dry eye and not really succeeding as I watched Frack try to get closer to me. It was such a relief to see them alive, battered as they were.

"Y'all gonna put that one down?" the fisherman asked. McMichaels studied his shoes, as if already knowing the answer to that one.

"Hell, no," I said. "He's going to be like me—retired."

"Well," Sergeant McMichaels said, "there's one more thing. Lots of folks in town appreciated what you did. We talked about what happened to the shepherds. So, well, over there."

I looked through the pen wire to see a dozen or so locals standing by the corner of the fisherman's trailer. I recognized some faces from the Southport diner.

"Seems that some of the folks in town wanted to do something, pay you back," McMichaels said, pointing to my dogs with his chin. "Your partners here getting hurt and all. We got together. We have something for you. Some*one,* actually."

He signaled to the small crowd by the trailer, and a man came around the corner with a very large sable shepherd on a leash. No one spoke as he walked over to where I was sitting in the pen. Frick got up and stared, but the big dog ignored her and simply sat down and looked at me through the wire. I don't think I'd ever seen a shepherd with as much gravitas as this one. She turned out to be a female. Calm, amber eyes, erect ears, broad chest, and an aura of complete superiority.

"This here," the man said, "is Kitty. She's yours, you want her. Folks here were trying to think of some way of repaying you. I bred her, but she's yours, if you can use her."

"Kitty."

The man smiled. "My wife's idea of a joke, before we knew how big she was gonna get. Should Carol ever get herself into trouble, she wanted to be able to say, 'Here, Kitty, Kitty,' and have a big-ass ol' German shepherd come around the corner. The bigger she got, the funnier that got. What do you think?"

I got up, patted my two pals on the head, and went out to meet Kitty. I sat down on the ground in front of her, and she examined me gravely. I let her smell my hands and the big bandage on my right forearm. Frick gave a jealous woof.

Frack, on the other hand, put his head down between his paws. I think he knew that his replacement was on deck. I realized I'd have to work on that.

Kitty stood up, walked around me once, and went to the pen to touch noses with Frick, who wagged her tail, before coming back to me. She sat down again.

"Shake on it, Kitty," the man said.

Damned if she didn't put out a big old paw. The people over by the trailer started to applaud.

And me?

Well.

Read on for an excerpt from the next book
by P. T. Deutermann

NIGHTWALKERS

Coming soon in hardcover from
St. Martin's Press

They came out of the darkness, riding lean, hungry horses. The engineer put down his unlit pipe and reached for the shotgun in the cab, but then relaxed. The riders were Reb cavalry, not goddamned bluecoats. He could tell by their slouch hats, the mish-mash of uniforms and weapons, and those big CS buckles gleaming in the engine's headlight. The officer who appeared to be in charge rode right up to the locomotive. The others slowed to a walk and spread out in a fan around the train's guard detail, who were lounging in the grass beside the tracks while the engine took on water. The riders were greeting the men with soft drawls and questions about what was going on up there in Richmond City.

The officer wore the insignia of a major, and he tipped his hat to the engineer with his left hand while holding the reins close down to the saddle with his right. He was wearing a dirty white duster that concealed the lower half of his body.

"Major Prentice Lambert, at your service, suh," he declared. He had a hard, hatchet-shaped face with black eyes and fierce eyebrows. "This the documents train?"

The engineer said yes, a little surprised that the major knew. There were only four cars behind the engine and its tender, three of them passenger cars stuffed to the windows with boxes of official records from the various government departments up in Richmond. The twenty-man guard detail rode in the fourth car, but they were all disembarked for a smoke break and calls of nature. The guards, who were an odd mixture of old men, teenagers, and even some walking wounded from the trenches at Petersburg, seemed relieved to see Confederate cavalry.

The major nodded, as if the engineer's answer was hugely significant. The engine puffed a shot of steam from the driver cylinder, spooking the major's horse sideways, but his rider held him firmly.

"Any more trains behind you?" the major asked, shifting his reins to his left hand as the horse danced around.

The engineer shook his head. "We heard ole Jeff Davis took one south two nights ago, but ain't nothin' comin' down thisaway that I know of. Jig's 'bout up in Richmond."

"All right, then," the major said, and raised the big Colt Dragoon he'd been holding down beside his saddle horn, pointed it at the engineer's belly, and fired.

The engineer sat down hard on the steel grate of the engine cab, the wind knocked clean out of him, and this awful, ripping feeling in his guts. He grasped his midsection with both hands and felt the blood streaming. He was dimly aware of more shooting now, as that arc of cavalrymen also opened fire, shooting down the stunned soldiers as they sat in the grass or leaned against trees, all their weapons still back on the train. He bent over to look down at his middle, lost his balance, tumbled off the engine steps onto the cinder bed, and then rolled into the grass. His knees stung where he'd hit the track bed, but then that pain faded, and he relaxed into the sweet feel of that long, cool grass against his cheek. His middle was going cold now, and his legs were buzzing with pins and needles.

He looked back up at the train, his vision shrinking into a red-hazed tunnel. He saw a single white face at the nearest window in the front car, a young face, no more than a kid, maybe fifteen, sixteen. One of the guards? He tasted salt in the back of his throat, and it was becoming really hard to get a breath of air.

Why hadn't that kid gotten off the train? What was he doing in there among all those boxes, while his comrades outside were being slaughtered like beeves?

One of the horsemen saw the kid's face and surged his horse forward, his black cap and ball pistol pointing at the window. The engineer heard the major's voice call out, No. Not him. Leave that one be.

The horseman reined up. "*That's* your spy? That *boy*?"

"Train was right here when it was supposed to be, weren't it?"

"Yeah, but you said now. No goddamned witnesses."

"There won't be," the major said, getting down off his horse. "But I need to know one more thing."

Then the engineer heard the other horseman swear. He realized he'd been spotted, eavesdropping on their conversation. He tried to crawl up the bank, trying to get under the locomotive, but his limbs had turned to rubber. He thought he heard the Major say, Oh, goddammit, and then a bolt of lightning exploded in his head and he was gone to see the Baby Jesus.